# Praise for *Cradles of the Reich*

"*The Handmaid's Tale* meets WWII in *Cradles of the Reich*, which explores the little-known history of Hitler's Lebensborn program and its goal of mass-breeding racially fit babies for the master race. Three German women are destined to collide at a Bavarian breeding home: a blond beauty desperately concealing her unborn child's Jewish heritage, a Nazi official's fanatical young mistress, and a nurse determined to keep her head down in the home's increasingly sinister program of forced adoptions, queasy eugenics, and racial cleansing. Jennifer Coburn's debut historical novel is adept, unforgettable, and brilliantly unsettling!"

—Kate Quinn, *New York Times* bestselling author of *The Rose Code*

"I loved *Cradles of the Reich*, Jennifer Coburn's fascinating and incredibly well-researched look at this little-known Nazi breeding program and three women whose lives intersect there. Don't miss this wonderful historical fiction debut!"

—Martha Hall Kelly, *New York Times* bestselling author of *Lilac Girls* and *Sunflower Sisters*

"In *Cradles of the Reich*, author Jennifer Coburn takes on the subject of Nazi Germany's Lebensborn program, a breeding scheme designed by the infamous Heinrich Himmler. Coburn's tale follows three women—one a conflicted nurse, one the pregnant girlfriend of a now-deported Jewish man, and one the fanatical mistress of a high-ranking Nazi officer—all of whom wind up in Heim Hochland, the same Lebensborn home for pregnant young women. As the story progresses, the overwhelming inhumanity of the program—babies whisked away for adoption by 'good German families' despite the mothers' protests, sex parties for officers, and even kidnappings of children in occupied countries—becomes clear, testing the mettle of the protagonists. Well-researched and sprinkled with fascinating details, Coburn's historical debut is an illuminating look at a little-known piece of the horrifying World War II–era Nazi puzzle. Don't miss Coburn's detailed author's note at the end!"

—Kristin Harmel, *New York Times* bestselling author of *The Forest of Vanishing Stars*

"Jennifer Coburn brings an untold story brilliantly to the page in this fast-paced, heart-wrenching, at times harrowing novel. With a resonant plot and complex, well-drawn characters, this book will stick with readers and leave them clamoring to know more."

—Michelle Gable, *New York Times* bestselling author of *A Paris Apartment* and *The Lipstick Bureau*

"*Cradles of the Reich* masterfully delves into the warped underbelly of the Nazi's Lebensborn program for racial engineering. With grace and a deft hand, Jennifer Coburn creates indelible female characters that leave us heart-torn. This book kept me breathless from chapter to chapter. I couldn't put it down until the final heroic page."

—Sarah McCoy, *New York Times* bestselling author of *Mustique Island*

"With this novel, Jennifer Coburn gives compelling and necessary literary voice to those impacted the most by Adolf Hitler's haunting and ironically dehumanizing scheme to generate racially pure infants. Skillfully researched and told with great care and insight, here is a World War II story whose lessons should not—must not—be forgotten."

—Susan Meissner, bestselling author of
*The Nature of Fragile Things*

"Coburn captures readers with the story of three brave women tangled in the web of the Nazi's Lebensborn program, part of Hitler's efforts to build a master race…a tale almost too unbelievable to be based in truth. Sensational!"

—Tracey Enerson Wood, international and *USA Today* bestselling author of *The War Nurse*

"The hopes and dreams of three women collide in this shocking story about a little-known Nazi breeding home in Bavaria. Jennifer Coburn has written a brave and highly original novel; fans of historical fiction will find it compelling—and indeed essential—reading."

—Kitty Zeldis, author of *Not Our Kind*

# Also by Jennifer Coburn

# CRADLES
## OF THE
# REICH

# CRADLES OF THE REICH

## A NOVEL

## JENNIFER COBURN

sourcebooks
landmark

Published by Sourcebooks Landmark, an imprint of Sourcebooks
P.O. Box 4410, Naperville, Illinois 60567-4410
(630) 961-3900
sourcebooks.com

The Library of Congress has cataloged the hardcover edition as follows:

Names: Coburn, Jennifer, author.
Title: Cradles of the Reich : a novel / Jennifer Coburn.
Description: Naperville, Illinois : Sourcebooks Landmark, [2022]
Identifiers: LCCN 2022011067 (print) | LCCN 2022011068 (ebook) |
   (hardcover) | (epub)
Subjects: LCSH: World War, 1939-1945--Women--Germany--Bavaria. | LCGFT:
   Historical fiction. | Novels.
Classification: LCC PS3603.O277 C73 2022  (print) | LCC PS3603.O277
   (ebook) | DDC 813/.6--dc23/eng/20220308
LC record available at https://lccn.loc.gov/2022011067
LC ebook record available at https://lccn.loc.gov/2022011068

Printed and bound in the United States of America.
VP 10 9 8 7 6 5 4 3 2 1

*For the children of the Lebensborn Society whose lives were stolen by the Third Reich*

This novel follows the *Chicago Manual of Style*, which capitalizes German nouns and italicizes foreign words. However, when the author uses German words that are commonly used by English speakers, used frequently in the text, or found in the Merriam-Webster Dictionary, they are neither italicized nor capitalized unless they would be formatted as such in English.

"In the cases of SS families who had the 'misfortune' not to be able to produce sufficient children of their own, it should become an 'accepted custom to take illegitimate or orphaned children of good blood and bring them up.'"

—Peter Longerich, quoting a 1936 memo by SS
Reichsführer Heinrich Himmler,
*Heinrich Himmler: A Life*

# 1

# *Gundi*

I F GUNDI SCHILLER THOUGHT SHE HAD FELT SICK THIS morning, it was nothing compared to the wave of nausea that hit her as she walked into Dr. Vogel's office for the results of her pregnancy test and found her mother perched on a chair, knitting needles clacking against each other.

Elsbeth looked up and smiled at her daughter, never dropping a stitch, the thick brown wool in her lap growing into a blanket. Though her mother's presence in the waiting room was an unwelcome intrusion, at the same time, there was nothing that made Gundi feel more safe than having her mother by her side. Since she began university two years ago, Gundi found that she had a tangle of conflicting feelings about her mother.

"Mutti, are you not well?" Gundi asked, hoping that this was all just an odd coincidence. Perhaps Elsbeth was here to see Dr. Vogel about her stiff shoulder. He was the family physician after all. Maybe Dr. Vogel had asked to see Gundi in person rather than reporting the test results over the phone because he wanted to discourage her from having premarital sex. He might want to wag his finger and warn her that next time, she might not be so lucky. *Please God, let this be the case.*

"I'm feeling wonderful, *Liebchen*," Gundi's mother said, her knitting needles finally stopping. Elsbeth's smile reminded Gundi of a buttered roll, sweet and filling. It didn't hurt that her mother's body was short and round. Elsbeth lifted her eyebrows. "The more important question is how are *you* feeling?"

*She knows.* Gundi's heart sped, and she felt prickles of cold sweat forming around the soft blond wisps of hair that fringed her forehead. *How did she find out?*

Gundi clung to the fraying possibility that maybe it was an innocent question. "I think my lunch disagreed with me. That's all," she returned with a thin smile.

A nurse with a slick bun resting on the nape of her neck opened the door leading to the exam rooms. "Gundi Schiller," she announced with a melodic voice that belied her severe appearance. When the nurse's gaze found Gundi, she gave her a look the girl had grown used to: instant approval. People seemed to know all they needed to when they took in Gundi's angelic face. Even her one imperfection, the sliver of a gap between her two front teeth, seemed disarmingly appealing. Gundi had enjoyed the attention when she first started to blossom into a woman, but now, by the age of twenty, she was starting to realize that her beauty didn't give her any actual power but rather the illusion of it. Fewer and fewer people seemed interested in what she had to say these days; they smiled and nodded as she spoke while creating their own version of who they wanted this beautiful girl to be.

Gundi silently begged God to confirm that she was not, in

fact, pregnant. But she was almost certainly carrying the child of a man she hadn't seen in two months. Gundi knew that Leo would have never left Germany without her, though. And yet where was he?

She closed her eyes for a moment, recalling his voice urging her to run off to Paris with him. They would never have to see another Nazi again. Their resistance work could be even more effective from a safe distance, Leo promised.

She should have listened. No one in the Edelweiss Pirates was anywhere to be found anymore. The only people she could rely on for information were likely in hiding or, worse, had been arrested.

"Fräulein Schiller, the doctor will see you now," said the nurse with some impatience.

Elsbeth rose from her chair and placed her hands on both of Gundi's cheeks, offering a gentle smile. "Dr. Vogel called me this morning. We have a plan."

Gundi's eyes welled with tears. These were the exact words she needed to hear, just not from her mother.

As they walked down the corridor, Elsbeth took two steps for each of Gundi's long strides. Mother and daughter entered Dr. Vogel's office, where there was a second white-coated man.

"Gundi, Frau Schiller, it is good to see you both," Dr. Vogel said, gesturing for Gundi to sit on the exam table and Elsbeth to take the stool in the corner. "I've asked Dr. Gregor Ebner to join us today."

Dr. Ebner was no larger than Dr. Vogel, but somehow he occupied more space. His round, owlish eyeglasses rested on the apples of his cheeks. As he jutted his chin, Dr. Ebner moved about the exam room, circling Gundi with icy appraisal, hands clasped behind his back.

Gundi recognized the black swastika pin on Dr. Ebner's lapel. The gold rim meant he was one of the early members of the National Socialist Party, a true believer. Many Germans jumped aboard Hitler's bandwagon after he became führer, but the men who had pledged their loyalty to a fringe National Socialist Party were a different breed.

Gundi turned her head from Dr. Ebner and focused instead on the wall clock over the door. It was twenty minutes after four. Sitting on the padded exam table, she imagined herself instead in a wooden chair at the front of the lecture hall at Humboldt University, where Professor Hirsch would be finishing his economics lecture and beginning to field questions from students. How she wished she were there, less than a kilometer away but a universe apart.

Dr. Vogel hadn't changed the décor of his office in the fifteen years Gundi had been in his care. The room was sparse—a full-size skeleton next to an eye chart on the white wall and a scale planted on the floor. Beside the exam table was a metal rolling cart holding cotton swabs, glass vials, and something that looked like the drawing compass she had used for geometry class in *Gymnasium*. Gundi rubbed her bare arms, feeling a chill.

She looked through the window and noticed that the *Kirschbaum* on the street outside was already blooming. Its tiny pink flowers were half-open, as if they were waking from a deep sleep.

"Well, I see you weren't exaggerating. What a beauty." Dr.

Ebner gave a short laugh, patting Dr. Vogel on the back. Finally, he turned to Elsbeth. "Dr. Vogel tells me you are a widow," he said, tilting his chin down in a manner that seemed rehearsed. Elsbeth nodded solemnly as Dr. Ebner continued. "It takes a strong woman to raise a child alone. I'm sorry you had to bear the burden by yourself."

Gundi saw her mother's tight smile and sensed her bristling internally. People often presumed that raising a child alone was a burden, but Gundi's mother always said life was simpler as the sole parent. Without Walter, there was less money, but there was also peace.

Dr. Vogel's voice brought Gundi back to the present. "Your test results came in this morning, and congratulations are in order, though the circumstances are not ideal, of course," he said, nodding as if to coax her agreement.

Gundi's fear landed with a thud in her heart. She was going to be a mother. Her missed periods, swollen breasts, and nausea had told her as much. The timing couldn't be worse. Germany was becoming more dangerous every day, and her child's father was missing. Yet Gundi couldn't help also feeling the slightest flicker of joy. She was going to have Leo's baby. In another world, at another time, Gundi would have run straight from the doctor's office into Leo's arms. The two would rush to marry and playfully bicker over names. She would tell him she knew it was a boy; Leo would insist they were having a girl. Gundi knew he would want to name his daughter Nadja, after his grandmother who had recently died. Gundi would agree easily because she was certain they would be naming the child after her grandfather Josef anyway.

Before Gundi could fully absorb the news, Dr. Ebner slipped a small envelope from his pocket. He opened it and slid out cards in various shades of flesh tones, from porcelain white to a rich vanilla cream. He glanced up at Gundi and laid out on a rolling cart three skin shades that most closely resembled hers. Placing the color swatches beside Gundi's cheek one by one, Dr. Ebner was silent until he offered a light huff of approval, signaling that he had found the perfect match for her pale skin.

"*Hellhäutig*. Number three," he snapped at Dr. Vogel beside him, signaling that his colleague should mark Gundi's chart accordingly. Gundi had first seen this kind of racial screening tool five years earlier, when Jewish students were still permitted to attend public schools, before the Nazis had deemed classrooms too crowded for children no longer considered German citizens. The Nazis were as obsessed with skin, hair, and eye coloring as they were the size and positioning of facial features.

Even before Jews were banned from public schools, some of Gundi's teachers had shown students how to quickly detect physical characteristics of the inferior *Untermenschen*. When Gundi was in *Mittelschule*, her teacher, Herr Richter, humiliated her classmate Samuel Braus by calling him to the front of the room for inspection. The teacher held a fistful of Sammy's thick brown curls and turned his head to the side so hard that his eyeglasses fell to the ground. Offering the other students a profile view of their Jewish classmate, Herr Richter pointed out that Sammy's nose looked like the number six. That was just one way to spot a Jew. As the teacher was pacing, he stepped on Sammy's spectacles. Everyone in the class heard the crunch. Herr Richter was no kinder to Gundi's friend Rose, whom he addressed only as "the Jewess in the back row." Gundi was often required to line up beside the object of her teacher's ridicule to serve as a counterpoint, an example of pure German beauty. As she stood at the front of the classroom, her cheeks reddened, but Herr Richter called it a healthy glow. Herr Richter also favored Gundi's best friend, Erich Meyer, a boy whose chiseled features and butterscotch hair made him look as if he'd been plucked straight off a Nazi propaganda poster.

Much like Gundi's schoolteacher, Dr. Ebner now peppered his inspection with praise. "The freckles are sweet. You love the sunshine, Gundi?" he asked, reaching into his white coat pocket for a card with a row of tiny blue, green, and hazel buttons fastened to the oak tag. Each color had a corresponding number. "I think Gundi's eye color is a five," he said to Dr. Vogel with professorial authority. Holding the iris color samples next to Gundi's right eye, Dr. Ebner squinted to double-check the match. "And I am correct," he said, lips curling with pride. "Such pretty blue eyes." Dr. Ebner was ebullient once again when he found a hair sample that exactly matched Gundi's sandy-blond locks.

Gundi turned to her mother, furrowing her brows to silently communicate her confusion and concern. But Elsbeth seemed relieved, letting out a sigh and nodding with Dr. Ebner's praise. Gundi perched herself at the edge of the exam table and looked around the room. *What is going on here?* She took a deep breath and regarded the skeleton in the corner. *Why is Dr. Vogel saying nothing? Why does Mutti seem so agreeable?*

Dr. Ebner lifted Gundi's chin and opened a pair of calipers to measure her skull, nose, and forehead, issuing grunts of approval after each measurement.

Turning to Elsbeth, Dr. Ebner asked if she had remembered to bring documentation of her family lineage. She reached into her bag for a thick folder and held it out for him with a hopeful smile.

Dr. Ebner set it down next to Gundi, who watched him leaf through not only her baptism papers, birth certificate, and medical records but similar documents for her parents and grandparents. She knit her brows when she saw the old-fashioned daguerreotype wedding portrait of her paternal grandparents. She hadn't seen them since her father's funeral. What did they have to do with her baby?

Looking up from Gundi's file, Dr. Ebner turned to Elsbeth planted in the corner. "Frau Schiller, I will need to examine the girl further. Please wait outside."

"Of course, Doctor," Elsbeth said, too quickly for Gundi's comfort.

When the door closed, Dr. Ebner turned to Gundi, raising his eyebrows as he scanned her from head to toe. "What are you waiting for? This is not a dental exam."

"I don't understand," she responded, her voice catching. How many times had she practiced sounding calm in the face of danger? *Apparently, not enough.* Gundi focused on the sound of the clock, inhaling deeply, trying to let her heart slow to the cadence of its steady ticking.

But Dr. Ebner's throaty laughter broke her concentration. "University girls," he scoffed with a shrug toward Dr. Vogel. "They know how to lie back and spread their legs like whores, but when a doctor needs to examine them, they suddenly don't understand."

Gundi's eyes darted toward Dr. Vogel, sure that he would object to such a crass characterization of her. But he only laughed awkwardly and looked down at the speckled oilcloth flooring. Dr. Vogel had known Gundi since she was a child, always encouraging her curious nature and answering her endless questions about why there were buds on her tongue and wax in her ears. Now this trusted family doctor slinked to the back of his own office, suddenly fascinated with a shelf lined with glass jars of cotton balls and swabs. Gundi clenched her teeth. How vile she found his weakness.

Could she just run? If she refused to be examined, would Dr. Ebner look more closely into her private life? How long would it take for him to discover that her boyfriend was Jewish? When would he find out about the anti-Nazi flyers Gundi and her friends had distributed or the resistance meetings they'd attended? Gundi couldn't afford to be impulsive, so she began unlacing the black shoes she'd bought when she first started university. The girl she had been then seemed like a different person than Gundi now, though not even two years had passed since Mutti had taken her shopping for smart outfits to wear to class. The two had been giddy with hope that day. Gundi had needed a fall jacket, but she certainly didn't need one with red lapels shaped like two halves of a heart. It wasn't the most sensible choice, but Elsbeth had said, "Everyone at university will know you as the girl with the beautiful heart."

Gundi's mother had not gone to university and had worked as a file clerk at the Reich Chancellery over the last decade, so the start of Gundi's university career was something they had both anticipated with equal excitement.

Now, as Dr. Ebner stood waiting, Gundi unbuttoned her linen skirt, and it fell to the floor. She knelt down to pick it up, embarrassed by her shaky hands, and folded it on the stool where her mother had been seated. The skirt was a favorite of hers: buttercup with peach pleats peeking out. As she unfastened her white short-sleeved blouse, Dr. Ebner watched her, leaning back against the wall, arms crossed. When she was down to her undergarments, Gundi mustered the courage to ask for a gown to cover up.

"That will not be necessary," Dr. Ebner said. "Come now. Off with the rest of it."

"I don't think—" Gundi began.

"No, you don't." Dr. Ebner chuckled. "Which is exactly how you got yourself into this situation."

Gundi felt the urge to stride across the room in her underwear and kick Dr. Ebner in the groin. Instead, she fell mute, the shame of her predicament beginning to sink in. She always thought of herself as smart, but clearly she hadn't been smart enough to avoid being an unmarried, pregnant woman locked in an office with a Nazi measuring her head. Exhaling deeply, Gundi resigned herself to endure the humiliation of the exam and leave as soon as possible.

Moments later, she stood naked before Dr. Ebner while he regarded her as if she were a sculpture in a museum, slowly examining her from many angles, scanning up and down. When he stopped in front of her, he met her eyes. She noted they were the same height, and he seemed to understand that too, straightening his spine and removing a comb from the top of Gundi's head in order to unwrap her braids. Dr. Ebner then used his fingers to loosen the plaits and sweep Gundi's hair behind her shoulders. "You, my dear, are perfection," he said. "I have been waiting for a girl with your features since we started the program four years ago."

"Program?" Gundi asked, projecting her voice in hopes that Dr. Vogel would turn his attention back to her. She boiled with rage, betrayed by the doctor she had trusted since she was five years old. *Help me, you pathetic* Feigling*!*

When Dr. Vogel finally turned around, Gundi thought he resembled a frightened animal, his eyes wide, his body tucked into a corner of the room, trying, it seemed, to disappear. He mumbled, "There is no need to be shy, Gundi. Dr. Ebner needs to make sure your baby is healthy." Gundi tried to catch his eye before Dr. Vogel turned his back to her again and recommenced moving instruments from one side of the shelf to the other.

Dr. Ebner pressed the front of himself against Gundi's naked backside, reaching his hands around to grasp her breasts. Her body tightened with revulsion as a volcano of acid began to rise from her stomach. Dr. Ebner squeezed her, speaking softly into Gundi's ear. "These will be good for the baby," he whispered as his erection pressed against her. Then, in a normal volume, he added, "Gundi, everything looks beautiful. You're a strong and healthy expectant mother." He patted the exam table. "Now, let's see how your baby is growing."

# 2

## *Hilde*

*Munich*

**B**EFORE SHE EVEN REACHED THE FRONT DOOR OF HER house, Hilde Kramer smelled the rich aroma of frying bacon and simmering red wine, and she knew it meant that Mama was making her signature hasenpfeffer. Hilde quietly opened the door and walked toward the kitchen threshold, knowing she would gain far more information by observing her mother than she ever could by asking questions. Johanna only served braised hare stew a few times a year, and it was never just to fulfill a craving. She was trying to impress someone, thought Hilde, likely the family of a marriageable young man.

When Hilde had left for *Gymnasium* that morning, her mother told her to make sure she was home in time to prepare herself for a very important supper guest. She was certain her mother had invited yet another friend who not so coincidentally had a son around Hilde's age. With graduation in just months, Hilde could see Johanna growing more anxious about her daughter's future.

Over the Christmas holiday, a steady flow of "old friends" stopped by the house with sons whose eyes widened at the sight of Hilde's broad shoulders and shot-putter's build. In the new year, Johanna had set her sights lower and dragged in a cast of misfits, one more ludicrous than the next. Hilde's least favorite was a boy who was shaped like an egg. "He had no neck!" Hilde protested. Johanna reminded Hilde that the young man was studying to be an engineer and that she should stop being so picky. February's offering was a university student who was nothing but neck—a long, slender one with brown moles splattered about. Hilde couldn't help wondering if this was her mother's idea of humor. *What, I thought you wanted someone with a neck!* Hilde didn't see what the big hurry was; she had just turned eighteen.

She remembered a time when the smell of hasenpfeffer had been a warm invitation to the comfort of her mother's kitchen. Now, it simply reeked of desperation.

*Where did Mama even find a hare, much less one plump enough to cook, this time of year? I guess it pays to be an officer's wife.*

Hilde watched Johanna shifting fluidly from the cupboards to the stove, reaching up to grab spices, then turning to slice shallots on the wooden block. The whole kitchen seemed to join her mother in the dance. A chandelier of cast-iron pots hung overhead as the largest of the set boiled on the stove, its lid quivering in response to the bubbling beneath.

In the dining room, the good dishes from the display cabinet now adorned the crocheted tablecloth. She hadn't seen their swirls of pink roses called into action for years now, not even for potential suitors. *This one must be very special,* Hilde thought. Freshly polished silver candlesticks held tall brown candles.

Finally sensing her daughter's presence, Johanna turned to

the doorway. "You're here," she stated. She was wearing a dress with ivory and mauve stripes and puffed sleeves that looked straight off the pages of *Modenschau*. She turned back to the stove. "Go upstairs and change into the outfit I laid out for you. Everything needs to be perfect tonight."

Hilde slowly made her way up the steps, each hand gripping a banister. She bit her bottom lip, knowing that when Johanna said *everything* needed to be perfect, what she really meant was that *Hilde* needed to be perfect. But even when Hilde did everything that was expected of her, she managed to disappoint her mother and remain invisible to her father. Her older brother, Kurt, was a carbon copy of their father in both looks and character. He was a serious young man who had joined the Wehrmacht the moment he was old enough. Now, at just nineteen, Kurt had already earned his first medal. Hilde's younger sister, Lisa, had been the spitting image of Johanna, which made her the favorite. Hilde took after neither of her parents and often felt as though the stork had dropped her down the wrong chimney.

Hilde didn't excel at anything that mattered. Just months earlier, Hilde had placed second in the Bund Deutscher Mädel's fencing tournament. BDM was the girls' division of the Hitlerjugend, so Hilde was certain her parents would be impressed. Her BDM troop leader, Jutta, regarded the silver medal as a great accomplishment. After all, twenty-five girls had competed, so even second place meant she was just a few parries and ripostes away from the top prize. But Johanna had taken the medallion from Hilde's outstretched hand and placed it onto the kitchen table with barely a glance. "Do you know what they

give a person who comes in second place in a *real* sword fight?"
Johanna asked. "A funeral."

Hilde's stomach churned at the memory. Or perhaps she
was just hungry. Why had she bothered to rush home? Her
mother didn't seem to want her around. Hilde would have paid
a heavy price for her late arrival for supper, but she couldn't
help thinking that she should have stayed lost a little longer
this afternoon.

---

How Hilde wished she hadn't ducked into an alley and run
when she saw one of her classmates, Rudolf Fritz, riding his
bicycle through the square. It had been a month since their
humiliating misunderstanding, but the sting was still fresh. She
had seen him at school, of course, but they had always been surrounded by friends. Once they were alone, though, Hilde knew
Rudolf would confront her. With her luck, her classmate would
offer an apology for the miscommunication. His pity would be
unbearable.

Rudolf hadn't meant to be cruel. He had just been so unclear
when he asked Hilde for advice on how to win a girl's affection.
When Rudolf realized that Hilde thought he was asking *her*
on a date—and that she had eagerly accepted—he stammered
his correction. It was her best friend at school, Margot, that
he liked. Thanks to Rudolf's bumbling mistake, Hilde had
become lost.

She had spent her entire life in Munich, so it seemed
impossible that she had never seen the narrow artery near the

Marienplatz. At least she thought she was near the Marienplatz. Hilde couldn't be sure anymore, as there was nothing in her line of vision that was remotely recognizable. Looking upward, Hilde couldn't even spot the zodiac clock tower, the defining landmark of the city center.

Hilde stopped for a moment in front of a hat shop window displaying its spring collection. She could imagine herself in the orange straw topper with a cap so shallow it looked like a plate balancing on the mannequin's head. Margot would probably die for the ultrawide gray hat, its rim upturned so high it could pass for a U-boat. And although Hilde knew her mother would never sport a turban, she couldn't help think the one in sky blue would look stunning on her.

On the corner where the alley met a wider street, Hilde spotted a newsstand with its valance of color magazines and stacks of newspapers from around Germany. A young mother bent down to hand her daughter a cookie frosted to look like a daisy. It could have only come from the bakery near the Rathaus. Hilde had her bearings again and turned the corner to continue home.

Narrowly escaping the nose of a blue tram emerging from the clock tower archway, Hilde took a moment to admire her city. She wondered if she would ever grow tired of Munich's bustling Marienplatz or the city's magical skyline, its delicate spires and fanciful turrets, the town hall with its façade that looked like church organ pipes.

Hilde turned toward home and strode efficiently, staring down at her green leather shoes. She had finally convinced her mother that she was adult enough to wear high heels. Hilde's pumps lifted her only five centimeters from the ground but had a sophisticated lacelike pattern of leather around the topline that could not be found on the shoes in the girls' section in the store. She loved the way they made her feel, though sometimes it was hard to tell what elevated her more: the heel or the concession from her mother.

As Hilde crossed Dienerstrasse, she watched people chatting with one another and saw them through the windows of cafés, sitting down for a bite. Everyone seemed to know their place in the world. They were salesgirls or shopkeepers, a young woman buying a brooch, a man shopping for a necktie. Could Hilde really be the only person who felt this unmoored? Quickening her pace, she asked herself what she *would* do when school ended. A few of the girls she knew would be attending Ludwig Maximilian University in the fall, but Hilde was thoroughly uninterested in four more years of geopolitics and race science. She was relieved that her parents weren't the type to push her toward university, but without a plan for the future, her lack of suitors was escalating the tension she felt at home.

It wasn't as though all German girls were marrying straight out of *Gymnasium*. Jutta had married an illustrator with the Ministry for Public Enlightenment and Propaganda a year earlier. Jutta was twenty-three by then but had never seemed anxious; she knew her pretty face would always net prospects. Hilde's father's offer to find her a secretarial job within the Reich sounded dull. A year of Land Service had some appeal, though Jutta had warned Hilde it wasn't all mountain hikes and stargazing. Other girls had returned saying that they rose with the sun to do heavy farmwork, complaining of sore shoulders and chapped hands. Hilde thought her host family would take one look at her sturdy form and strap a plow onto her back.

What she wanted most was something she couldn't admit to anyone—to be an actress. She always had her friends at BDM in stitches with her comedic impersonations. How she would love to be the next Gracie Allen or Zarah Leander. Hilde realized she didn't have a single person with whom she could share that dream, not even Jutta, who was so involved with her new family that she barely asked Hilde about herself anymore. Margot was too much of a gossip for Hilde to risk sharing anything of value. Hilde felt isolated, but she also knew that self-reliance like hers was an asset. She had friends in her life for fun and amusement, but Hilde didn't *need* any of them.

The last people she could talk to about her dreams were her parents, who now seemed singularly focused on people's *productive contributions* to Germany. Franz had never been a particularly affectionate father, so his exaggerated stoicism after becoming a Schutzstaffel officer six years earlier had not surprised Hilde, nor had it affected her much. Johanna, though, had once been the picture of content motherhood, sometimes even joining her children on the playground rings and poles. Once, Hilde even convinced Johanna to try the Rome wheel. Her mother shrieked with a combination of thrill and terror as Hilde and her friends rolled her nearly upside down in the wheel. There was something about seeing Johanna's bloomers on full display that made Hilde realize her mother was an imperfect person. She had never loved her more.

That was before Lisa fell ill last winter. These days, Johanna was concerned solely with utility, so much so that she only grew vegetables and herbs in her garden, explaining that flowers served no purpose. "It's foolish to waste fertile soil for something that won't be put to good use," Johanna had recently told Hilde as she pulled a bulb from her garlic bed.

⌐•⌐

Hilde turned the crystal knob on her bedroom door and reminded herself to relax her shoulders and release the breath she'd been holding. As her eyes found Lisa's bed, Hilde dug her fingernails into her palm, a habit that had become a ritual offering. Of course, Hilde knew there was no actual benefit in forcing herself to focus on Lisa's rag doll resting on her pillow or cutting into her own flesh. Still, it was a sting of pain that she could control, gathering it into one place, like sweeping a mess from the kitchen floor into a tidy pile.

On Hilde's bed was her uniform for the BDM Werk Glaube und Schönheit, Faith and Beauty Society, a branch of the Hitler Youth for older German girls. She tightened her black neckerchief against her crisp short-sleeved white shirt and tucked the hem into her skirt.

Hilde looked at herself in the full-length standing mirror. She pushed out her chest slightly and checked her profile, hoping curves had developed since she'd last checked. Of course this was unlikely, since her last inspection was that morning. Practically all the other girls in Hilde's class had figures like Coca-Cola bottles; hers looked like a can of evaporated milk. The unfairness of life was maddening.

Hilde decided not to wear her boxy brown jacket. She

looked masculine enough without adding the *Kletterweste* to the ensemble. Hilde remembered when Jutta had sported a similar jacket. She had looked as stylish as Marlene Dietrich in *Blonde Venus*.

*Stop!* Hilde scolded herself, trying instead to focus on the gifts she did possess. She smiled into the mirror, a closed-mouth grin that her mother had told her looked cheerful. She trotted down the staircase and joined her mother in the kitchen.

***

*"Guten Abend!"* Franz's deep voice rang through the front door. Another man was with him, one with the vocal resonance of someone her father's age. Hilde hoped she would soon hear the man's son. It was far too soon to be considering old men.

In the kitchen, Johanna smiled with nervous excitement and handed Hilde her wooden spoon. With the nod of her chin, she instructed her daughter to take over at the stove. Hilde knew to keep stirring to keep the meat from burning and gravy from bubbling over. Johanna ordered Hilde to place sour cream in a small porcelain bowl and take the dumplings out of the boiling water in exactly two minutes. "Tonight is very important for your father. We need you on your very best behavior," she instructed before heading toward the front of the house.

Three adult voices hailed Hitler before softening their tone. *"Guten Abend, die Herren,"* Johanna sang with a flutter. Hilde figured she must have misheard her father when he introduced Johanna to Obergruppenführer Werner Ziegler, Reichsführer Heinrich Himmler's right-hand man. But when her mother told their guest that it was an honor to have him in their home, it confirmed that Hilde had heard correctly.

*Why is Obergruppenführer Werner Ziegler in our home?*

Thanks to Hilde's keen eavesdropping, she knew that although her father was an SS officer, he wasn't particularly well regarded by the party. She'd heard her parents whispering behind closed doors that Franz had recently made a particularly costly mistake, placing his trust in an unreliable informant. No one suspected Franz of being disloyal, simply foolish, but that was only slightly better.

Hilde's father was not the sort of officer one would imagine deserving any attention from Werner Ziegler.

*Is he in trouble? Can I help Vati redeem himself?*

Hilde's thoughts were interrupted when Franz called out for her. Silently, she thanked Jutta for drilling German history and Reich principles into her since she first joined the BDM. Hilde had always preferred group calisthenics and mushroom hunting to her Nazi studies and domestic skills, but she was more than grateful now for the knowledge.

Rallying her confidence with a shake of her fists, Hilde stepped out of the kitchen to see the obergruppenführer standing in the foyer, handing his coat to Johanna to hang. Although he appeared much as he did in his pictures in the newspaper, she still had to blink a few times to reset her focus.

Herr Ziegler wasn't a handsome man, but his power was attractive to Hilde. He sported the same black uniform as Franz; both held their *Totenkopf* hats in their hands and wore swastika armbands around their jacket sleeves. They even wore the same style of eyeglasses and slicked-back hair, but it was clear that

Herr Ziegler was the more important of the two, though Franz was about five years older than his superior. Franz's deference to Herr Ziegler's authority made him smaller, weaker in Hilde's eyes. To her surprise, she took pleasure in this diminished view of her father.

Herr Ziegler's brows furrowed. "Your daughter looks different from the photo on your desk."

Hilde had gotten used to this routine: A person who had seen pictures of both Hilde and Lisa but had only registered the pretty one. People were always asking Franz about his daughter, seeming to forget that he had two. Only now they were right; there was only one.

"We..." Franz hesitated. "Our youngest was ill. Lisa didn't..." His eyes darted toward Johanna, gauging her reaction.

"Ah yes, of course," the obergruppenführer mumbled, remembering that the family had lost a child. "All Germany suffers when one of its children dies." Turning his head toward the kitchen, he asked, "What smells so good?"

Johanna swallowed down the casual condolence, shifting into what Hilde recognized as her performance mode. Hilde saw the muscles in Johanna's neck tense like tree roots, her voice trilling higher. "We have a feast befitting a guest of your esteem," she said.

At the table, Herr Ziegler addressed most of the dinner conversation toward Franz and Johanna, but Hilde kept herself involved by murmuring notes of agreement. Emboldened by Ziegler's occasional nods of approval, Hilde decided that the next time the obergruppenführer spoke, she would add to the discussion. What she had to say would only reflect well on her father. And why not speak? She was a grown woman now and had her own opinions to share.

Dabbing his napkin against his lips, Ziegler said, "I find there's nowhere more beautiful than Munich in the spring."

Before her parents could respond, Hilde chimed in that she found the sight of colorful blossoms and scent of cut grass hopeful, inspiring even. Sure, she was laying it on a bit thick, but the obergruppenführer seemed charmed by her youthful optimism, so she continued. "All my classmates say the Reich is giving our generation a fresh start, and what better reminder is there than nature's season of renewal?" Hilde smiled internally, wondering if her teacher, Frau Weber, would be proud or annoyed that she had borrowed her words.

Ziegler turned to Franz and gave a hearty guffaw. "Well put, Hilde."

Franz nodded and turned the conversation back to the expansion of the Beauty of Labor program, which he hoped to manage for the party. "I am an architect by training, so I know I can help make workplaces more efficient, safe, and beautiful for the *Volk*." His voice wavered, not matching his confident words. "I have ideas on how we could build on what we've done in the factories." Everyone at the table could sense what Franz wasn't saying. *I've learned my lesson and won't mess up again.*

"Herr Ziegler," said Hilde, sitting upright in her seat. "There's no one more committed to building the Reich than my father. If he says he's up for the job, you can count on him."

The obergruppenführer gave a smile that looked both impressed with Hilde and embarrassed for Franz. It was a weak man whose daughter had to do his bidding for him.

When Franz lowered his eyes, Hilde couldn't tell if the gesture was anger or shame. As mental snapshots of Franz's cold indifference to her over the years began flashing in Hilde's mind's eye, she realized she didn't care what he thought. "Obergruppenführer," Hilde said, holding out her hand for his plate. "Would you care for another serving of hasenpfeffer?"

# 3

## *Irma*

LIVING IN A WOMEN'S BOARDINGHOUSE, IRMA BINZ HAD grown accustomed to the sound of urgent knocking on her bedroom door. Whether it was a broken heart or a pan fire in the kitchen, the young women at Frau Haarmacher's house always ran to Irma for assistance. She resented the assumption that her age automatically gave her expertise in every area of life. What did she know? *Find a new love. Grab a garden hose.*

"Irma, I know you're in there!" Ava demanded while continuing to pound on the door. "It's an emergency! Please open! Charlotte hurt herself!"

Irma turned away, pointedly ignoring Ava's pleas. She held up a single shoe from two different pairs, deliberating between her tan shoes with grosgrain bows at the buckle and her black patent leather T-straps, eventually deciding that the lighter ones would look best with her new dress. She slipped her feet into the high heels while the knocking continued, more furious now.

It had been so peaceful when Irma first moved into Frau Haarmacher's house three years ago, after her mother had passed away. All four of the other residents had been old maids, awkwardly shy and mercifully quiet. To Irma's dismay, each of them had moved over the years, three to live with family in other parts of Germany and one to take a job as a governess in England. Those women had never tried to include Irma in their lives. But these peach-faced secretaries and new schoolteachers were constantly clustered together for Sunday afternoon picture shows or winter ice-skating at the pond. Irma wanted none of it.

She huffed, fishing her sole pair of earrings from a white porcelain bowl that, like everything else in the room, had been there when she moved in. As she fastened the black pearls onto her lobes, Irma scanned the room. The carved mahogany headboard and matching vanity had been in Frau Haarmacher's family for generations and were emblazoned with her family crest: an H with two crossed swords. The eggshell walls were as bare as they had been on Irma's first day at the boardinghouse. Back then, she had assured herself she would leave the day she found a husband, so there was no sense settling in. Irma understood that the moment she hung a picture, she would have officially given up on starting a new life. She'd been smart, she thought, checking her reflection in the mirror. *I will only have to carry one small suitcase to Eduard's home after we marry.*

"Irma! Charlotte cut herself. *Bad.*"

Irma sighed, then made her way toward the door and reached for the cold brass knob. She could not wait to leave this house of perpetual crisis. Patting her sweater pocket for the third time, Irma made sure her friend Marianne's letter was still there. It was more than just a note between old wartime pals: it was ammunition for the discussion she planned to have with Eduard this evening.

Breathless, Ava stood at the threshold of Irma's bedroom, looking like a bisque doll with her long brown waves and porcelain skin. "Thank goodness," she said, leaning against the doorframe. Charlotte's screams from downstairs filled the house like an air-raid siren. Ava opened her mouth, horrified by the sound. "Charlotte cut herself with the meat cleaver, and she's bleeding buckets. She needs stitches."

"Then take her to a doctor." Irma reached to close the door, already thinking of her dinner with Eduard. She had planned to surprise him by arriving at his house a half hour early, before his children showed up. After months of dallying, he had agreed to finally set a wedding date, and tonight Irma would hold him to it. There was no way Charlotte's clumsiness was going to delay her plans.

Irma hesitated for a moment. Ava's lips quivered with fear, but this was not Irma's problem, was it? Shifting the weight from her heel to her toe, Ava's fingers tapped the sides of her skirt. Just witnessing her housemate's anxiety exhausted Irma.

Ava pressed, her voice high with urgency. "Charlotte says you were a nurse in the Great War."

"I haven't practiced in more than twenty years, and I'm certainly not going to start by stitching up someone's finger," Irma snapped. "Wrap it up, apply pressure to stop the bleeding, and get the girl to a doctor."

Ava's forehead lined with worry. "Please, Irma, can't you go with her? She says you'll know what to do. She will be more comfortable with you there at the hospital with her."

With Ava's last plea, Irma lifted her hands in surrender and closed her eyes. "All right, fine. Wait for me in the kitchen, and I'll be downstairs in a moment."

Ava thanked Irma before running down the main staircase. When Ava was out of sight, Irma turned toward the back of the house to make her escape. Charlotte could figure out how to get a finger stitched without Irma's help. She reached the landing of the back staircase and removed her shoes, walking gingerly down the bare wooden steps and slipping out the servant's entrance. If she walked quickly, she could probably make it to Römerberg Square before anyone realized she'd left. Soon enough, she would be married to Eduard and finished with these frivolous girls.

*More comfortable! This generation is spoiled to think they deserve comfort. Live through a war. Lose your loved ones. Then come talk to me about how you need someone to hold your hand through a simple medical visit.* Irma slipped her feet back into her shoes and closed the door quietly behind her.

Rounding the narrow corner onto Braubachstrasse heading toward the Main River, Irma began to feel a twinge of regret before steeling herself again. Silently, she muttered, *It's Ava and Charlotte who should feel guilty for bothering me with this nonsense.*

<hr />

It had been more than two decades since Irma had seen the inside of a hospital, and she wanted to keep it that way. She had felt this way since the day she left her ward at Potsdam Military Hospital when the war ended. When she had packed her footlocker to return home to Frankfurt, Irma left behind her nurse's uniform, telling her supervisor, Marianne, that she wanted no reminder of the war. She soon realized it wasn't that simple.

Irma still regularly woke herself, gasping, in the middle of the nightmare she always had. It was about Karl, a soldier she'd cared for toward the end of the war, who had survived a lower leg amputation but died weeks later of a staph infection while Irma held his hand and he called her *Mami*. But in her dream, Karl was furious at Irma, blaming her for his death. He pulled her toward the hospital bed, which transformed into a murky lake. Soon, she was submerged, Karl's grip tight on her wrists as she fought her way to the surface. Irma always woke gulping for air.

Although she admitted this to no one, her night terrors once drove her to a psychiatrist, who advised her to imagine her wartime memories as articles of filthy and torn clothing she no longer needed. During their session, she was instructed to imagine picking the items off her messy bedroom floor and throwing them into a garbage pail. The exercise wasn't particularly helpful, because Irma kept thinking how wasteful it was to dispose of clothing that could be put to good use. At the very least, they could be used as cleaning rags. Young doctors were never particularly adept at seeing the world through the lenses of their older patients. Maybe this was true of young people in general, especially those lucky enough to have no real memory of the lean Weimar years.

———

When Irma reached Römerberg Square, she stopped at the Fountain of Justice for a moment and remembered the night

Helmut, her *Gymnasium* sweetheart, had proposed. She was so young, just nineteen years old. Now, Irma could barely fathom that she had once been filled with such naïve dreams. How arrogant she and Helmut had been, thinking that they could plan for a future in such an uncertain world, where the kaiser acted like a little boy constantly poking at a hornet's nest.

*Enough with nostalgia.* Irma shook herself back to the present. She hadn't been the only one who suffered. Wallowing in self-pity would do no one any good. Irma cast her eyes forward and began walking confidently toward her future.

As Irma continued her walk, she tried to focus her mind on pleasant thoughts. She loved crossing the Main River, its banks bursting with leafy poplar trees; nearby were hedges trimmed into perfect spheres. The evening light began softening the hues of the skyline, as if a thin layer of pink watercolor had been brushed across the entire city. The yeasty aroma of bread baked earlier that day layered itself with the earthy scent of oncoming rain.

When Irma arrived on Schulstrasse five minutes later, it was with renewed determination. Surely Marianne's letter would give Eduard the push he needed.

～･～

Marianne's note had arrived six days earlier, written on thick paper rimmed in blue cornflowers and folded within a cream linen envelope. It was the third time in a year that her old friend had extended an invitation to work for the Reich at a maternity home in Steinhöring, a village just outside Munich. When she first received the letter, Irma sat in her room, pressing her lips with irritation, wondering if her friend had forgotten that she wasn't able to bear children. In any case, Irma had told Marianne repeatedly that she would never step foot in a hospital of any kind again. She was sure her friend was not cruel, just terribly insensitive.

Irma had no intention of accepting the position but was grateful for the offer, because now she could show Eduard the letter and pretend she was tempted to accept the job. After all his delays in setting a wedding date, perhaps it would be best if she went, she would say with a look of rueful contemplation. Sometimes men just needed a little reminder that they might lose an opportunity if they did not seize it.

Irma practiced her smile and congratulated herself on her clever decision to wear the yellow sweater Eduard had bought for her two weeks earlier. A realization settled in, though. The souvenir of their date was bright and cheerful, yet their time together had not been.

---

Irma had been irked by how distracted Eduard seemed, his heavy-lidded eyes darting about, then lingering far too long on other couples visiting the Städel Museum. It had been his idea to visit the museum, telling Irma he wanted to see the new Arno Breker sculptures. Irma hadn't been to the museum in years and was eager to see the Ludwig Dettmann and Adolf Ziegler paintings that had recently replaced the degenerate art by Jews. Once there, however, all Eduard wanted to do was stand around the lobby and people watch.

She had always found Eduard's habit of rustling his hands in his pants pockets mildly irritating, but on this visit, she felt fury over the way he kept picking up and releasing coins. The jingling seemed to be a soundtrack to his indifference toward her. Eduard's voice had been hollow when he defended himself against Irma's reprimand, explaining that he thought he saw an old schoolmate. "Yes, that is him," Eduard confirmed, quickly excusing himself to greet a portly older gentleman with a wife far too young for him. They had spoken for a moment, then had shaken hands and parted with no introductions made. Irma would have to work on his social graces.

As if Eduard had read Irma's mind, he apologized, then offered his full attention. "I'm sorry. I should have introduced you, but I couldn't remember his wife's name," he said, palms upturned in a gesture that begged forgiveness. After a few hours in the museum, as they stepped outside into the early evening air, Eduard had taken note of Irma rubbing her upper arms and offered his jacket. Still smarting, Irma declined, but she noticed Eduard glancing into store windows until he finally spotted a yellow cardigan with stemmed orange marigolds embroidered on the bottom, as though they were in a garden against the backdrop of pure sunshine. Eduard had insisted on buying it as an apology for the incident at the museum and as a promise that he would always take care of her. He didn't actually say any of that, but Irma knew that was what he had meant.

Their arms threaded, the couple had walked down the Schaumainkai, past a row of Nazi posters freshly plastered onto the sides of buildings. There was Hitler, surrounded by three small children, holding a little girl with a baby-blue bow in her blond hair; a sweet-looking BDM girl holding out a collection can for the poor; a broad-chested German man standing protectively over his wife and young children. Some of the posters Irma had seen in the past were frightening: Jews with ghastly green faces and giant hooked noses. An old man in one of those funny hats and long beards smirking as he panhandled, sitting on sacks of gold. The most terrifying one was a Jew with pebble teeth dropping meat into a grinder that spewed out money.

Eduard had stopped to examine the posters, scanning the one of Hitler and the children. He waited until a carriage passed and the clopping of horse hooves quieted. Turning to Irma, he gestured to the images of the hopeful children. "What do you think of all this?"

She reached for Eduard's hand, calloused from gardening, and started walking again, not wanting to wait any longer than necessary to eat dinner. "It's nice to see people take pride in Germany again," she offered with a smile. "And you?"

Eduard looked behind him and lowered his voice. "The anti-Jewish laws keep getting more draconian. Do you have any concerns about the Jews now being forced to hand over all their jewelry and silverware?"

Irma's head turned quickly to Eduard. "Did the Jews have any concerns about profiteering and stabbing Germany in the back during the war?"

Pulling his hand away from Irma's, Eduard began jingling the coins in his pocket again. "I'll take that as a no."

Weissfrauenstrasse was festooned with a spiffy row of swastika banners. The shock of the red flags against a purple twilight sky was beautiful. A few minutes later, the couple arrived at the

Klosterhof, their favorite restaurant, the one where Eduard had proposed six months earlier.

The dining room was an illustration of modern German values—cozy and modest, clean and orderly. The couple followed the host, their steps cushioned by the floral carpet. Dark wood paneling covered the walls, and the round tables were clothed in white linen, surrounded by sturdy chairs.

Soon, however, Irma found herself smiling through gritted teeth at the half-eaten beef roulade on her plate as she pressed for a wedding date. They had decided three months earlier that they would wed at Saint Justin's Church in Frankfurt and honeymoon in Vienna. The only remaining question was when. Eduard's response was to move the potatoes and carrots across his dinner plate as if they were chess pieces. His deliberative nature had once been endearing to Irma. Now, it revealed weakness. But every man came with a list of improvements a new wife would have to make, so she wouldn't complain.

Reaching across the table for Irma's hands, Eduard had sighed, seeing her face pinched with frustration. "Please trust me when I tell you that I would love to marry you this evening if I could, but the timing is…" His words drifted off. "It's difficult right now."

◠•◠

Tonight, Irma had a plan to simplify matters. She would show Eduard her job offer before his children arrived for supper. They would have a half hour alone to talk, and she always found her discussions with Eduard went more smoothly when she caught him off guard. By the time Gerda and Heinz arrived, Irma would have a wedding date, and the evening meal would become a celebration.

Or, she thought, perhaps she should mention the letter at the dining table so Gerda and Heinz could chime in. Irma often lamented that her future stepchildren didn't really need a mother any longer, but there were also advantages to Eduard having children in their twenties. They were mature enough to understand that she wasn't trying to replace their mother, who had died from influenza when both of her children were still teens. She could have adult relationships with them, especially Gerda, who often pressed her father to stop dragging his feet and set a wedding date.

Irma had thirty minutes to pour Eduard a nice drink and get him in the right frame of mind. She knocked on Eduard's heavy wooden door several times, reminding herself to install a brass knocker when she lived here. A person could break a knuckle trying to gain the attention of those inside.

Rapping on the door once more, Irma decided to let herself in. In a short time, this would be her home anyway; there was no need for formality. "Hallo," she called, only to hear the clattering of what sounded like pots and pans in the kitchen. "Eduard, is that you?" Irma walked through the entrance and down the hall toward the living room, which adjoined the kitchen. "Eduard?" she called again.

Her hollers were unanswered, though a female voice lowered in volume. *Is Eduard listening to a radio show?* Irma then heard a woman's whispers and scampering feet. *Is Gerda here already?*

When Irma made it to the doorway of the kitchen, it took a moment for her brain to catch up with her eyes. Everything looked like it usually did on a Friday evening before dinner with Eduard and his children. The embroidered tablecloth was already laid out; the green glass lamp shone overhead. Then it registered. At the corner of the room, she saw the blur of a woman's back, her long brown braid lifting off her burlap coat as she went through the open cellar door.

# 4

## *Gundi*

*Berlin*

G UNDI RUSHED TO THE GARBAGE PAIL IN THE CORNER OF the doctor's office, dropping to her knees just in time to vomit. She crouched there as her stomach convulsed. A moment later, Dr. Vogel was by her side, offering her a white handkerchief, but he was too late with this flimsy assistance. Gundi flinched and raised her elbow, pushing away his hand.

Dr. Ebner faced her sternly. "Gundi, I must examine your baby if I am to tell how far along you are. Once I do that, we can see to it that you and your child receive proper care, but I cannot do this if you don't control yourself."

Gundi took a deep breath, remembering what her friend and fellow member of the Edelweiss Pirates Erich had instructed before he was conscripted last month to serve in the Wehrmacht in Austria. *Never be the first to fill the silence. Never let them know you're upset or afraid.*

She wondered how he was now. Gundi shuddered, thinking about Erich living among men he reviled, soldiers who would likely kill him if they knew the truth about who and what he was. She tried to chase away a memory of Erich being bullied on the playground when the two were in primary school together, when she and her friend Rose were the only ones who spared him constant taunting. He was so scrawny then and ran with arms that pumped awkwardly. But that was a long time ago. Erich would be fine as long as he remained quiet about his private life. Gundi closed her eyes in a moment of prayer before the Nazi doctor interrupted.

Dr. Ebner patted the examination table. "Come now, Gundi."

The examination lasted less than a minute, little more than Dr. Ebner inserting his finger inside her and commenting to Dr. Vogel about cervical thickening before pronouncing Gundi three months pregnant.

*Four months*, Gundi silently corrected. This was not merely guesswork. She remembered the night she got pregnant, after the Edelweiss Pirates' first gathering of the new year at one of their regular meeting spots, the cellar of Café Kranzler. It was the night when Gundi and Leo's friendship became something more.

⌐•⌐

Gundi had been a little tipsy that evening, not just from the New Year's wine and sweets but from knowing that her mother was in Hamburg visiting her sister until the following day. Falling snow glittered in the lamplight as Leo walked her through Kreuzberg to her apartment. As they reached the front door of Gundi's building, she tried to delay their parting by going over what had happened at the Edelweiss Pirates meeting that evening. Gundi told Leo things he already knew, having been with her the entire night. Yet he seemed grateful that her rambling added to their time together. It was easier for them to discuss what had already occurred instead of what they hoped would happen next.

"It was so nice to see everyone again," Gundi said, a sentiment she had already shared several times. The only thing keeping her from feeling completely humiliated was Leo's equally clumsy response.

"Very nice. They seem hopeful about the new year."

Gundi smiled and nodded. "Yes, I'm hopeful too. I... Are you... Do you feel hopeful?" She resisted the urge to roll her eyes at how dull she was being.

Snow frosted Leo's hair, giving Gundi a peek at what he would look like as an old man. The way he hunched his shoulders in the cold added to the effect. For a moment, Gundi considered telling Leo that he would be a handsome grandfather someday but stopped herself. She didn't want to reveal that she was imagining a future with him. Instead, she rubbed her mittened hands together and patted Leo's face. Any excuse to touch him.

Leo looked down shyly. "I should let you get—"

"Do you know who I really enjoyed meeting tonight?" she asked.

It wasn't a tough question, since there was only one new person at the gathering. And Gundi had already told Leo how much she admired Sophie, the Edelweiss Pirates' newest member. At least twice. Nonetheless, Gundi spoke animatedly about how bold Sophie was when she characterized Hitler's habitual lying as a mental illness. At the table, this had given

Leo a new idea for an anti-Nazi leaflet. He grabbed a napkin from the supply closet and began to sketch, Gundi watching the muscles in his forearms as his pencil tapped the paper. "Ours will picture the führer with electrodes on his head and a bite plate in his mouth," he said, raising his thick eyebrows. "And the headline will read Heil*en* Hitler." Heal Hitler.

Now, furtively studying the bas-relief of chariots above the front door of her apartment building, Gundi grasped for something—anything—to say.

Leo placed his hands in his pants pockets and straightened his arms. He looked down and moved his right foot against the sidewalk like a windshield wiper.

There was a long pause before Gundi mustered her courage and continued. "My mother is in Hamburg until tomorrow." She kept her head lowered for fear that her reddened face would give away her excitement and nerves. "Would you like to come upstairs for some hot cider?"

Leo nodded shyly, wet brown curls bouncing. "I'd like that very much." He smiled and blushed, taking her hand and following Gundi inside.

This walk home had been Gundi and Leo's first time alone together except for their awkward conversations when they met at university and Leo suspected that her loyalties were with the Nazis. In the five months they had been friends, their time together was spent either at Edelweiss Pirates meetings or at Leo's family dinner table.

Inside her kitchen, Gundi busied herself at the stove, warming the apple cider over a low flame. She wanted to keep her back toward Leo until she could wipe the ridiculous smile from her face, so she opened cupboards looking for spices she already knew were in the marked jars on the countertop. Deciding to splurge, she spooned a bit of sugar into the simmering saucepan, then feigned surprise when she spotted the cinnamon and cloves nearby. Gundi pinched the black stems, taking in the sweet woodsy scent, and dropped them into the warming cider. She then grated half a cinnamon stick and let the sweet snap blend into her brew. Soon, aromatic tendrils, reminiscent of a Christmas market, rose and filled the room. She closed her eyes and inhaled deeply, feeling like a child ready to ride her sleigh downhill.

"Should we sit on the love seat?" Gundi blurted. Her body was a mix of anxiety and joy. Her stomach fluttered.

"All right," Leo answered, albeit looking a bit confused by Gundi's tense delivery of such a benign suggestion.

Once they were situated, Gundi turned toward Leo and smiled. "This is nice." *God, just cut out my tongue right now if I can't control the idiocy coming out of my mouth.* She held her mug of cider in both palms and blew to cool it.

Leo set his down on the small oak table covered with a lace doily. "Gundi, I've been meaning to talk to you about something."

She shook her head, encouraging Leo to continue.

"I am very fond of you, and, well, I'm more than fond of you, actually." The clink of Gundi biting the mug interrupted Leo. "Are you all right?"

She was more than all right. Gundi had been waiting to hear these words from Leo since she first laid eyes on him months earlier, talking to Professor Hirsch outside the lecture hall. Her teeth against the porcelain was the combination of her smiling and reminding herself not to speak. Instead, she nodded for him to continue.

"I would love to kiss you right now, I mean, that's if you…" he said, reaching back for his cider and taking a sip. "I want to take you ice-skating and to a picture show and do a thousand things with you." Leo was saying everything Gundi wanted to hear, but his serious tone didn't match his words. "It's, well…I could get you in a lot of trouble. You know it's illegal for you to have a relationship with a Jew."

Gundi wondered for a moment if Leo was simply being polite and didn't actually like her romantically. Maybe he sensed that she had feelings for him and wanted to let her down gently. After all, they had already broken half a dozen Nazi laws in their work with the Edelweiss Pirates. Now he was a rule follower?

She had never experienced male rejection and was at a loss on how to respond. Gundi had always been in the position where she was trying to thwart male advances, not plead for men to kiss her. It was oddly exciting.

"Leo," Gundi whispered. "Please kiss me."

His face crumpled. "You have no idea how much I want to, Gundi. I've imagined kissing you every day since we met, and I… Oh, Gundi, there's so much trouble—"

Gundi interrupted him by leaning forward and hooking Leo's collar with her finger and pulling him closer. As thrilling as it was to taste the sweet apple on his lips, what inebriated her was the feel of his breath washing over her neck and wrapping itself around her. As Leo pulled back, a small fluttering gasp escaped, as though he was struggling to gain control of himself.

Gundi placed her hands on Leo's face, stubbled from several days without shaving, her palms melting into the hard jawline she'd yearned to touch for months. Running a thumb across Leo's bottom lip, she looked at him and knit her brow. "Is…is something wrong?"

Leo offered a rueful smile and shook his head slightly. "Not with you, Gundi," he said, returning his lips to hers. Her body seemed to magnetically pull itself toward his until she could feel every button, every seam of his clothing. Leo's hands gripped Gundi's waist and pulled her tighter into him until she was the one who sputtered a helpless breath.

---

Dr. Ebner was talking about Gundi's due date. "October," he said. "Wouldn't it be grand to have your baby on Reichsführer Himmler's birthday? He takes special interest in children who are born on October seventh."

Gundi turned her back on the doctors as she buttoned her skirt and tucked her blouse back in. It seemed absurd after Dr. Ebner's recent invasion of her body, but it was a sliver of dignity she could hold on to. And Gundi could pretend she hadn't heard Dr. Ebner's ludicrous comment. Of course it wouldn't be grand to give birth on Himmler's birthday.

Dr. Ebner placed her records on the exam table, pressed a stamp into a black ink pad, and marked the folder: *Lebensborn Society.*

*Lebensborn? Spring of life?*

Gundi hadn't even realized that her mother had returned

to the exam room, but there she was, standing beside Dr. Vogel, who was holding another stuffed folder.

Dr. Ebner reached for the new file and placed it beside Gundi's family history. It had a blue label on the tab and was marked in black ink in handwriting she had seen before but was unsure where.

She searched the faces of her mother and the doctors for explanation. She found none but heard Dr. Ebner tell the others that everything was in order in terms of Gundi's lineage and physical health. *She* qualified for the Reich maternity home. The final step was establishing the father's Aryan roots, Dr. Ebner said, tapping his finger on the new file.

Before Gundi could open her mouth to speak, Elsbeth gave an incredulous laugh. "Erich Meyer?! If ever there were a pure-blooded German, it's that boy."

*Erich?* Yes, of course people would assume her best friend was the father of her child. They had been inseparable since kindergarten. But in the last seven months, most of their time together had been spent working to undermine the Nazis. They often posed as a couple so they could make their way across Berlin without arousing suspicion. Gundi hadn't realized her mother had jumped to this conclusion without asking first.

Gundi swallowed hard, suddenly realizing that it was Erich's mother who had prepared his file. She now recognized the familiar handwriting as Frau Meyer's. Gundi had seen it when flipping through Erich's family scrapbook, laughing at his mother's clever captions. Now, Frau Meyer used her pen to document her son's genetic value to the National Socialist Party.

Had his parents written to Erich in Austria to tell him the news? How many people had known about Gundi's pregnancy before she did? Her body flushed with heat from both humiliation and rage. Knowing it was best to remain silent, Gundi didn't correct them. They could never know this baby was Leo's.

Gundi wished her mother hadn't sounded so gleeful about Erich's lineage. Yes, Erich had deep German roots, but it was disturbing that Elsbeth had so readily accepted the rallying cry of Aryan supremacy the Nazis espoused. When she was a child, Elsbeth's father had many Jewish colleagues at the hospital where he was a doctor. She had never objected to Gundi's friendship with Leo; she'd called him a sweet boy. Elsbeth had never seemed particularly anti-Semitic, but after working for the Reich Chancellery for so long, she seemed comfortable with the notion of Aryan supremacy. And after six years of Hitler pounding that drumbeat, Elsbeth was hardly alone in her thinking.

Dr. Ebner rested Erich's medical files on the exam table next to Gundi's folder, examining each page as closely as he had Gundi's body. She watched the doctor hold papers next to the lamplight, then try to smudge signatures with the finger that had just been inside her.

After what seemed an eternity, Dr. Ebner looked up, removed his eyeglasses, and offered his first genuine smile of the afternoon. "Good news, Gundi. You are going to a very special maternity home for German girls, where you will receive top-notch medical care." He added, "Not everyone has the pure lineage you do. Only forty out of every hundred girls are accepted. It is very exclusive."

*Forty percent is hardly exclusive. Five percent, ten percent, now that is highly selective, but forty percent is practically a coin flip.* She reminded herself that raising this point would not help her case. Gundi needed to muster every bit of graciousness she could manufacture and put as much distance between her and Dr. Ebner as possible.

"Dr. Ebner, Dr. Vogel, naturally I'm very honored to have been chosen, but I must decline." The room was perfectly still until Gundi made the mistake of filling in the silence. "Another girl can have my spot. Mutti will help me with the pregnancy while I complete my studies."

Gundi could see Dr. Ebner's jaw tighten as he set down the paperwork. "Do you think that is best for your mother?" he asked, recycling his earlier chin tilt of concern. "It is foolish to have your mother use her time and talent caring for a child that we are equipped to provide for."

A crease formed between Elsbeth's eyebrows. "Dr. Ebner says they offer university courses at the Lebensborn home, *Liebchen.*" Gundi realized that her mother was trying to do the right thing; she'd even asked about how Gundi would continue her studies.

Gundi shot a pleading look. *Don't make me go.* She felt relieved seeing her mother smooth the skirt of her dress, a gesture she knew meant that Elsbeth was about to assert herself. Anytime her mother spoke up, she smoothed her clothing or tucked back her hair first, as if to remind herself that she was still, in fact, a lady.

"I may have spoken too soon, Dr. Ebner," Elsbeth piped in. "We can raise Gundi's baby together." Sure, their neighbors would whisper, but they had grown used to that before Walter died. Elsbeth folded her hands in her lap and added, "Erich's family will help us until he returns home."

Noticing the grateful smile Gundi gave her mother, Dr. Ebner cleared his throat. "Gundi, do you know why we measured you?" She chilled at the memory of his hands on her breasts. "It turns out that you are a perfect specimen of German womanhood. Naturally, every pure-blooded, healthy German girl is desirable, but we have certain targets we are looking for in terms of height, weight, distance between the eyes. I could go on, but suffice it to say, we have dozens of traits we consider when measuring fitness." He paused and smiled at Gundi, clutching her file close to his chest. "In the four years the Lebensborn Society has been in existence, do you know how many girls have met one hundred percent of our criteria for genetic and aesthetic perfection?" Dr. Ebner paused again, turning to Dr. Vogel, then Elsbeth. "One. One girl—you, Gundi."

The silence was thick and uncomfortable. Did Dr. Ebner honestly expect her to be flattered? Did he not understand how disgusted and violated by him she felt? Couldn't he feel her rage?

After a long pause, Dr. Ebner smiled. With that, Gundi had her answer. He had no idea. Nor did he care.

Dr. Vogel cleared his throat and spoke up. "Gundi, surely you can see this is the wisest choice."

Gundi remembered when Leo told their group that if they were ever questioned by the Gestapo, they should be polite. The more they could convince the Nazis that they were loyal to the Reich, the more the police would loosen their grip. "Promise to return with a list of names," Leo had advised. "Say you'd be happy to help them. You just need an hour to get what they need. Then run."

Looking at Elsbeth, Gundi sighed deeply. "I hate to be away from Mutti, but I suppose we all have to do our part for the Fatherland." Placing her hands protectively over her belly, she turned toward Dr. Ebner. "I'll need to say goodbye to a few people before we leave in the morning."

"It's best if we go right away," Dr. Ebner told her.

"I should explain to my professors that I'm leaving Berlin for a few months," Gundi said. "Please, Dr. Ebner, I'll leave with you first thing in the morning."

"Very well," Dr. Ebner said, his mouth tight, his brows furrowed with irritation.

"Thank you," Gundi said, looking down and clasping her hands so no one would notice them shaking. She knew she could convince Elsbeth to go along with her plan. As long as Dr. Ebner didn't pay them a surprise visit that evening, Gundi and her mother had time to pack a valise and catch an evening train to Hamburg that night. By morning, when the doctor came to take her to the maternity home, Gundi and Elsbeth would be long gone.

# 5

## *Hilde*

**D**URING DINNER WITH HERR ZIEGLER, HILDE'S ENCYCLO-pedic knowledge of National Socialist history and current events continued to prove useful as she dropped facts like coins in a slot machine, hoping with each one to win the jackpot of Ziegler's approval. She owed Jutta a huge debt for drilling her BDM troop on everything from Hitler's Beer Hall Putsch to the party's protective Nuremberg Laws.

Herr Ziegler didn't seem to mind Hilde's eager, often forced, interjections. Hilde appeared confident, but as she watched Ziegler continue to eat his hasenpfeffer, she hid her hands under the table and nervously cut into the skin under her fingernails. She found that Herr Ziegler enjoyed regaling her family with stories from Reich events, so Hilde gave him another opening.

"The celebration of Herr Hitler's fiftieth birthday was mar-velous here, but it must have been thrilling to be right by the führer's side in Berlin during the festivities." She returned her father's icy stare with a smile that feigned obliviousness.

Johanna placed her hand on Franz's forearm and shot a look

of warning at Hilde. *I told you this is an important night for your father*, her mother's narrowing eyes seemed to say. Hilde hadn't forgotten that this evening was Franz's chance to prove himself ready to oversee the expansion of the Beauty of Labor program. She knew that turning the spotlight on herself would cost her father precious time to make his case. But Hilde had dreams of her own, and somewhere over the course of the evening—even she couldn't pinpoint when—she decided she was willing to let her desires eclipse those of her father.

Herr Ziegler sat back in his chair and recounted the events from Hitler's birthday celebration last week. Hilde nodded her head eagerly but was disappointed that the obergruppen-führer merely reported what had been in the newspaper and on the radio. She had seen the front-page photos in *Der Stürmer* showing fifty thousand Wehrmacht soldiers marching against the backdrop of the Brandenburg Gate with its columns draped with Hakenkreuz banners. Hilde already knew about the marching bands and cheering crowd.

Nonetheless, she smiled brightly at Herr Ziegler's account as though it weren't the third time she'd heard about Hitler receiv-ing enormous porcelain vases, a bronze bust in his likeness, and a personalized Volkswagen. Hilde lifted her eyebrows in delight as Ziegler spoke of young children presenting the führer with poetry and old women showing off their needlepoint designs of the eagle and swastika. Inside, Hilde sighed, let down. *Does he really think I haven't heard about this already?*

She wanted him to whisper something no one else knew about the führer's celebration, something just for Hilde. What did Eva Braun wear to the parties afterward? What secrets were shared? Who left with whom? Hilde silently chided herself for thinking the obergruppenführer would divulge such private details to someone like her, so she forced her lips to form a circle of surprised delight. "My goodness, Obergruppenführer, this is all so fascinating." Hilde continued in her most grown-up manner. "If you don't mind, Obergruppenführer, I am equally interested in the Reich's efforts to aid the mentally handicapped," she said, leaning a few inches toward him. "I read in *Neues Volk* that the party is looking at ways to make sure future generations aren't afflicted with defects." In truth, she had no real interest in the subject, but she wanted to make it clear that she kept up with Reich news, that she read its journal of racial purity.

Ziegler nodded with admiration.

Johanna shrugged, sheepishly jockeying for her husband. "Franz has always encouraged our Hilde to take pride in the Fatherland." Hilde's eyes darted toward Franz, whose Adam's apple was rising and falling quickly, which she knew meant that he was swallowing anger. Trying to interrupt the bond being forged between Hilde and Ziegler, Johanna interjected. "Franz always tells the children—"

"You read *Neues Volk*, Hilde?" Ziegler asked.

Hilde pointed her chin down and raised a brow coyly. "Obergruppenführer, I read *Frauen Warte*." She knew that he would be impressed to learn that she also read the journal for women her mother's age. Not that she wanted to seem like an old lady, of course, just insatiably curious about everything the Reich was publishing. She was a young woman of substance, not a silly girl who only cared about movie stars and pretty shoes.

"My generation is fortunate to live in an era of *real* news, rather than the Jew-controlled *Lügenpresse* yours had to endure."

"You have raised a lovely young lady, Frau Kramer." The obergruppenführer smiled at Franz. "And you should be proud of Kurt. I'm told he is one of our most dedicated young soldiers." Ziegler coughed into his napkin. "My condolences on your youngest."

Johanna quickly thanked the obergruppenführer, then looked down at her lap. Hilde lowered her head for a moment as well.

Hilde lifted her head and returned her gaze to the obergruppenführer. "Lisa is dearly missed, but I am so grateful that she was able to be part of our history making last November. She told me it was the most wonderful night of her life."

Franz opened his mouth to speak when Ziegler lifted a hand. "Ah yes, Kristallnacht. I am always eager to hear about young people's experience of the evening. Tell me, what inspired you to participate?"

Hilde squared her shoulders and turned to speak directly to the obergruppenführer, who was waiting intently. Johanna shifted in her seat.

Sitting straighter, Hilde said, "Kristallnacht..." She sighed heavily, shaking her head with nostalgic recollection. "Naturally, I was furious when Ernst vom Rath was murdered by that Jew in Paris. My friends and I decided that retribution was in order."

This wasn't entirely true. In fact, it wasn't even partially true but rather a lie that had evolved into an alternative reality. It wasn't until the morning after the first night of riots that Hilde had even heard of the German diplomat or his assassination.

And she hadn't so much decided to storm the streets of Munich as she had been summoned. No one ordered her per se, but when Jutta had pounded on the door late Wednesday night and told the Kramer women that all Germans were needed to defend the Fatherland, they knew they were expected to join her. If they refused or even hesitated, Jutta could report them for disloyalty to the Reich, years of friendship be damned. Plus, if Franz was doing his part in the SS and Kurt was setting up Reich head-quarters in the Sudetenland, the least the women could do was help Jutta here in Munich.

"Hurry!" Jutta had shouted at Hilde. Waving her arms at Johanna and Lisa, Jutta beckoned. "Come now. You two as well!" Jutta handed Johanna and Lisa rocks from the gray canvas satchel she had once used for her schoolbooks. The group raced toward Herzog-Max-Strasse but came to a halt at the sight of the melee in the streets. The first thing Hilde noticed was the acrid smell of smoke, then the blaze of a burning building illuminating the night sky. The only other time she had ever seen flames reach so high was on the final night of BDM camp when the girls built a giant bonfire. But that smelled like wood, not this nostril-singeing scent of chemicals. Her focus was soon shattered by the sounds of breaking glass and shrill screams.

Hilde's mind scrambled to piece together the scene. *Someone has set fire to a building? Why do we need rocks to help with that? Why are hundreds, maybe thousands, of people in the streets break-ing windows?*

Jutta pulled them toward the center of the action. It wasn't just any old building that was burning: it was the synagogue. Neighbors Hilde had known most of her life were rolling up their sleeves, winding their pitches, and hurling bricks toward the round, stained-glass windows of the Ohel Jakob Synagogue engulfed in flames. Each time glass broke, the crowd erupted into cheers, as if this were a sporting event. Hilde watched Jutta bend down to meet Lisa's eyes. She smiled and whispered, "This is all for you."

"For me?" Lisa cried, her face crumpled with fear. She was just ten years old; Lisa hadn't wanted to be a part of this in any way.

Jutta smoothed Lisa's hair and spoke softly. "You and your generation." When Lisa turned away and buried her face in Johanna's bosom, Jutta continued. "I know this seems frightening right now, but I promise you that a better world will come because of it."

As Johanna lifted her hand to stop Jutta from continuing, they all heard a thunderous crash. A few doors down, Hilde watched as a burgundy velvet love seat was pushed through a second-floor window of Hertz's tailor shop. It looked exactly like the one in Hilde's home, and for a split second, she thought it might be. As the love seat fell to the street below, a wooden leg cracked off and the body split in two, prompting another round of cheers. More glass shattered. A man appeared at a second-floor window across the street and released a stack of porcelain dishes onto the sidewalk below. Hilde turned her head in a dozen different directions, unable to focus on one spot for more than a moment before another explosion erupted.

"Jutta, what is all this?" Hilde asked. Lisa turned to listen, sticking the knuckle of her index finger in her mouth, a habit she had outgrown as a young child.

Jutta smiled while wiping the tears from her eyes, stinging

from the smoke. Sweeping a tendril of auburn hair away from her face, she started to respond but was distracted by four boys who looked like they were still in *Mittelschule*, dragging a stumbling, bearded old man onto the street, his wife and granddaughter chasing after them. "Please," the old woman shrieked. "He's done nothing!"

Hilde quickly realized that the old man was Herr Baum, the candy seller. Grabbing Jutta by the arm, Hilde tried to explain that Herr Baum was one of the good Jews. She remembered Herr Baum in his white shirt and black suspenders, digging a scoop into his barrel of gumdrops. He had always been kind to the children who visited his shop, giving them a bit of extra candy, telling them they were sweets to the sweet. She thought about her friend Hannah, whose family moved to Prague after the girls finished *Mittelschule*. They were Jewish but certainly didn't deserve this. She must have said this aloud because Jutta grabbed Hilde's face with fierce intensity and looked straight into her eyes. "That is exactly what they want you to think," she shouted over the crowd, now singing an anthem about Jewish blood running through the streets. "They get you to trust them, then they show their true nature. It's us or them, Hilde. *Us* or *them*."

The boys gathered around Herr Baum were children, with chubby, hairless faces. The tallest of the boys swung the old man onto the ground, then kicked his stomach. Hilde closed her eyes so she wouldn't have to see the horror, but she was so close she could hear the thud of his boot hitting the man's flesh and the pained grunt that followed. "The only good Jew is a dead Jew," the boy shouted. How she wished she could cover her ears without anyone noticing.

When Hilde opened her eyes, she saw Herr Baum's grand-daughter, dressed in a long nightgown with lace trim. She looked too young for even kindergarten. Noticing the child's soft, bare feet, Hilde turned away with shame. All the little girl could manage through her tears was "Opa!"

"Stop them!" Lisa whimpered to her mother just as another boy ran toward the scene with a brass cash register overhead and spiked it onto the man's skull.

Johanna pulled Lisa into her embrace and gasped at the sight. "Hilde, I'm taking her home," she called out. "This is too much for a child."

Hilde agreed; she too was horrified by the mayhem around her, the smashing of scrolls, the cascades of shattered glass from above, the old man's bloodied head. Some people in the crowd, mostly women, looked at Lisa and shook their heads sympa-thetically. *This is hard for such a young girl to watch.*

The following morning, when Hilde sat at the breakfast table, she spread blueberry jam on a sweet roll and read the newspaper. She learned that Kristallnacht was retribution for the brutal murder of a German diplomat by a Jewish teen. So Jutta had been right. Hilde reached for a slice of ham and con-tinued reading. It seemed that Herschel Grynszpan, upset by some perceived injustice, stormed into the German embassy in Paris and shot Ernst vom Rath five times.

*Of course we were going to hit back,* Hilde told herself. *If it is so terrible for the Jews in France or here in Germany, they should go back to where they came from.*

Yes, Kristallnacht had been unsettling for Lisa—she slept in Johanna's bed that night—but the Jews had brought this on themselves. Hilde rebuked herself for questioning Jutta. As her BDM leader, then as a friend, Jutta had never steered her wrong. And according to the radio reports, thousands of furious Germans were driven to the streets, all of them like Jutta, feeling that this retribution was just. They couldn't all be wrong.

It was true that Herr Baum had been kind to Hilde and Lisa, but maybe that *was* just an act. Maybe his motives were not what they seemed. Anyone could pretend to be generous. She thought about the times her grandfather had taken her fishing at Lake Waldschwaigsee. *I'll bet those fish thought whoever was offering them a juicy worm was a swell guy. Then they found themselves with hooks in their cheeks, flipping and flopping for dear life on the floor of a rowboat.*

≈•≈

Recounting the story for Herr Ziegler at dinner, though, Hilde cast herself as the leader, running house to house, summoning her neighbors to the streets. At the conclusion of this revised account, Hilde straightened her back and said, "Obergruppenführer, an attack on one German is an attack on all of us. It is never one Jew who fires a gun. It is the lot of them. Herschel Grynszpan said as much himself when he claimed he was acting in the name of twelve thousand Jews."

Hilde shuddered inwardly with embarrassment, realizing suddenly that she might have heard this line—this attack-on-us-all language—somewhere else. Perhaps it was even from the führer on a news broadcast on the *Volksempfänger.* But when he smiled, it became clear to Hilde that Herr Ziegler appreciated her perfect recitation of the party line.

"What a remarkable young lady you have," Herr Ziegler said again, lifting his wineglass.

Hilde let the praise float like a bubble through the air, knowing that, in a moment, it would burst. Her mother or father would make sure of that.

Herr Ziegler turned to Franz and asked about Hilde's plans after school. "Will she do Land Service?"

Feeling bold, Hilde decided to answer their guest directly. "My friend Jutta said her year on the farm was the most rewarding of her life, next to being a mother of course." Franz and Johanna were silent as they reluctantly let their daughter finish. "But I feel like I could be of far greater service to the Reich in an administrative position, perhaps someday even a leadership role in the Women's League, like Reichsfrauenführerin Scholtz-Klink."

The obergruppenführer cocked his head toward Hilde, amused. "What a coincidence that you mention her. She has an open secretarial position in the Frauenschaft," Herr Ziegler said with a bounce of satisfaction in his voice.

*A coincidence indeed*, Hilde thought as she smirked. *I most certainly didn't hear it from Jutta's husband last week.*

The obergruppenführer wagged his empty fork. "I will take Hilde to the inaugural Mutterkreuz awards ceremony, and she can meet Frau Scholtz-Klink and her staff," he said. "I trust you know what the awards ceremony is, Hilde?"

"Of course, I do, Obergruppenführer. Tell me, do you expect that most of the child-rich mothers will receive the iron cross medal for producing four healthy children, the silver for six, or the gold for eight?"

Herr Ziegler's gaze lingered on Hilde a moment too long. Jutta had once told her that when a man looks into your eyes for two seconds, he loves you like a little girl, but three seconds or more means he wants to *rumsen*. The thought warmed her body like a shot of apricot schnapps. Could a man like Herr Ziegler be interested in Hilde in that way? She smiled, feeling herself swell with excitement.

The obergruppenführer clapped his hands together and nodded toward Franz. "I'll send my driver for Hilde next Sunday afternoon."

Hilde leaned back into her chair. This, she thought, was the moment her real life was beginning. Her parents were angry, but that wasn't her fault. Their generation always said they were working toward a better Germany for the benefit of young people. Now it was time for them to step aside and let her reap those benefits.

# 6

## *Irma*

IRMA STOOD FROZEN FOR A MOMENT, TRYING TO THINK OF reasons a woman with long brown hair would be running from Eduard's kitchen into his basement. *She is a new house-keeper*, Irma rushed to explain to herself. *But why wouldn't Eduard simply introduce her?*

*Maybe Eduard is planning a surprise. Perhaps this woman is a cook from a local restaurant, and he is preparing a special dinner for me.* That explanation didn't ring true either. Eduard was too careful with his teacher's wages to have hired a cook to prepare a Friday night meal.

There was only one explanation. Eduard had been unfaithful to Irma. She had heard a version of this story a dozen times at the boardinghouse. Every few months, someone at the breakfast table whispered about her friend, poor So-and-So, who thought she was about to walk down the aisle only to discover that her intended was just stringing her along for sex.

Now it seemed Irma would lose her second chance at love in the most humiliating way. Not only was he having an affair, he was carrying on with a Jew.

"Irma," Eduard finally began. "What...what are you doing here?"

She stepped back and held her palms protectively over her chest. "What am I doing here?" Taking another step back, Irma almost bumped into the china cabinet. She crossed her arms. "Who was that woman, Eduard?"

"Irma, please," Eduard said, moving toward her slowly with his hands half raised. "Keep your voice down," he said, his eyes darting toward the window.

"Stop stalling and tell me *right now* who that woman is!"

Eduard lowered his voice to a whisper. "Listen to me, Irma. She's the mother of a student who needs help—"

She interrupted, snapping back, "Jews haven't been allowed to attend public schools in more than a year!" Her moment of pride in her prosecutorial skills was interrupted by a pinch of guilt over her casual acceptance of Germany's anti-Jewish laws. But perhaps the fears about the Jews were right. Here was a Jewess seducing a good German man, just as the Nazis had warned.

"A former student," Eduard corrected.

"Do you take me for a fool?" she returned. "It's illegal for you to have a Jew in your home, even if she was the mother of your former student. What does she want, help with a mathematics assignment?"

Eduard whispered his plea. "Irma, if we are going to be married, you must trust me."

*Men are so manipulative*, Irma boiled silently. *They try to make us think we are in the wrong when they're caught red-handed.* "Now I understand why it's taken you so long to set a wedding date. Have you promised to marry her too?"

Eduard's mouth went slack before he pressed his lips together to suppress a smile. *Is he amused? How dare he be entertained by my heartbreak!*

Eduard pushed his hair from his forehead, then held back another laugh. "I am sorry. It's just so ridiculous. She is twenty years my junior, and I swear to you that there is nothing unseemly going on."

"Of course you would say that!" Irma shouted, making her way toward the cellar door. "Who admits to keeping a secret lover?" With every step she took forward, Eduard walked back. Finally, he was pressed against the cellar door, and their faces were inches apart. How had she never noticed the hair sprouting from his nose? Or the full pouches under the old *Mistkerl*'s eyes? "Step aside. I'm going down to the basement."

"You're doing no such thing," Eduard returned firmly.

They stood stock-still, neither willing to give ground. Irma could hear the ticking of the cuckoo clock on the wall. She had always hated the sound of that stupid little bird announcing the hours, but now she noticed the steady tick of the pendulum swinging.

Irma lifted her chin, daring him to explain. "All right then, Eduard, what is her name, and why is she in your cellar?"

Looking uncomfortably at his shoes, Eduard shifted his weight from one side to the other. "I can't answer those questions, Irma."

"If you aren't doing anything wrong, you should give me details." Irma's lips puckered with accusation. When she released a sigh, she realized it was her last breath of hope. "This is your final chance, Eduard. Either tell me why she is here or I am walking out…forever."

They stood in silence, staring at one another. Eduard inhaled so deeply, it strained the buttons on his white shirt. He opened his mouth to speak several times but quickly decided against it with a shake of his head. "Would you please just trust me?"

"I'm leaving," Irma said, proud that her voice did not quiver as it typically did when she was angry. "Just tell me why, Eduard."

Neither said a word for twenty seconds. Irma knew because that damned clock would not relent. Eduard began to speak, then stopped himself, glancing back at the cellar door. *What did I ever see in this bumbling idiot?*

Finally, Eduard sighed. "Irma, I am terribly sorry, but you are right. I've fallen in love with someone else. I never meant to hurt you. It was something that happened unexpectedly."

Although this was exactly what Irma had suspected, the words speared her. It released in her a rage she hadn't felt in years. "You're in love with a *Jew*?" Irma shouted. "Haven't you been paying attention? You can't marry an *Untermensch*!"

He placed his hands in the pocket of his gray wool pants, but Irma could see his fingers fidgeting with a coin. "She is not Jewish," he told her, clenching his jaw.

*Is he angry with me now? The nerve of this man!*

"Please do not mistake me for a fool twice, Eduard. I know a Jew when I see one, and that woman is a Jew."

"Irma, please, she's not Jewish—"

Irma interrupted with a guttural yell, which was satisfying but not quite fulfilling. The release of her anger made her crave more, so she stormed toward his kitchen table, picked up a crystal wine goblet, and hurled it at Eduard, nearly hitting his head. Irma knew he was guilty because he didn't even try to dodge the glass as it flew toward him and shattered against the wall, raining shards onto the floor.

"I am sorry that I've hurt you," Eduard said, his voice cracking. "Irma, tell people it was you who ended our engagement."

"Of course I will tell them I ended things with you, because that is exactly what I am doing!" She stormed through the hallway and toward the foyer. When she opened the front door to leave, Eduard's daughter, Gerda, was on the other side, holding a loaf of bread and a bottle of wine.

"Irma!" she sang, reaching in for a hug. Then she saw the look on Irma's face. "What's wrong?" Gerda asked.

Irma hesitated for a moment, then with ragged breath, she replied, "I am sorry. I broke my engagement with your father. I…I've fallen in love with someone else." As she hurried away, Irma silently chided herself for using Eduard's transgression as her own. Surely the girl would know she was lying, especially since she had likely met her father's new lover.

Irma wasn't completely surprised that a man could deceive her. Of course Eduard wanted to keep two women for his pleasure. But Gerda had always seemed to have a special affection for Irma. They had an easy comfort with one another and loved discovering shared tastes in sailor-style dresses and horror films. Gerda was the only other person Irma had ever met who admitted that she thought *Vampyr* was a brilliant film and forgave Fritz Lang for the questionable messages in his work. *How could she be party to her father's boorishness?* The betrayal by Eduard's daughter stung as much as his.

The tree-lined street leading away from Eduard's house was no longer beautiful to Irma, now that it was blurred by her tears. She kept her head down as she walked, pretending to be fascinated by the way her feet clopped against the pavement. Irma didn't want to talk to anyone, nor let them see her tear-stained face. God forbid she ran into Frau Fuchs, the old *Tratschtante* who knew everything about everyone. It should have been she who was the party *Blockleiter* instead of her husband. He was the one who reported to the Gestapo, but Frau Fuchs was the eyes and ears of the neighborhood.

*Maybe she already knows about Eduard's other woman. Perhaps everyone does and I am the last fool to realize it. If they don't already know, it is only a matter of time before I am the object of everyone's gossip and pity.*

After she crossed the bridge, Irma sped her pace, grateful that it had not rained but not wanting to take her chances either. The sun was setting and the periwinkle sky dimming. A young mother pushing a baby buggy quickly passed Irma by. Walking through Römerberg Square, she noticed how claustrophobic she felt with a skyline of buildings crowded so closely together. She had once admired the half-timbered houses that set long, dark wooden planks against lighter backgrounds. Now the building façades looked like a well-armed battalion coming toward her. The cobblestones beneath her feet felt precariously uneven. Her mind flipped unbidden to Marianne's letter in her pocket, promising a new life far away from the inquiring eyes and flapping tongues of Frankfurt.

Maybe it was time for a fresh start at the maternity home in Steinhöring.

Irma considered what it would be like to spend her days with babies. During this tour of duty, her patients would be sweet and doughy. They would coo as she rocked them to sleep singing lullabies. Yes, they would cry too, but an infant could be pacified by a bottle or nap.

Babies didn't have secrets or hide people in their cellars. They didn't make promises they had no intention of keeping. Working at the Lebensborn home in Steinhöring would be nothing like the Potsdam hospital during the war. This time, Irma would be there for the beginning of life, not the end.

# 7

## *Gundi*

*Berlin*

WALKING HOME FROM DR. VOGEL'S OFFICE, GUNDI watched her mother chew her lip and mull over the suggestion that they leave Berlin for a few days.

"Let's take the train to Hamburg tonight and stay with Ulla for a few days," Elsbeth proposed, knowing that her sister was the sort of woman whose door was always open to family—no word needed to be sent ahead, and no questions would be asked. Elsbeth would simply tell her sister that she and Gundi needed refuge, and soon the two would be tucked into a cozy bed under a thick wool blanket. Touching her daughter's face, Elsbeth assured Gundi that the situation would smooth itself out. As they began their walk home, heels clacking against the pavement, Elsbeth dug in. "Once Dr. Ebner sees we've left, he'll realize that you are serious about not wanting to go to the Lebensborn home." They nodded their heads in agreement, though Gundi wasn't so sure. Still, she clung to the hope that Dr. Ebner might give up.

If there were so many girls clamoring to be part of this program, surely she couldn't be so special. Remembering how Dr.

Ebner had characterized her as perfect, she silently rebutted his point. *If you had checked my heart, you'd understand why I'm not at all qualified for your Nazi maternity home.*

⟍•⟋

As Gundi and Elsbeth packed their green leather valise, Elsbeth shrugged at the sight of her swimwear in the top drawer of her dresser. "We'll be back home long before it's warm enough for the lake," she said.

Sidling up next to her mother, Gundi opened drawers, her hands rustling about on a mission. Finally, she found what she was looking for. Nestled in the back of Elsbeth's lingerie drawer, she spotted a black velvet box containing her grandmother's dragonfly brooch. Its body was an elegant row of emeralds that sprouted two wings glittering with white, yellow, and red diamonds. Elsbeth had once shown Gundi the family heirloom in case she died unexpectedly. Holding up the small box, Gundi raised her eyebrows to ask permission to bring it. Her mother shook her head.

"*Liebchen*, let's not be dramatic. We are simply going to stay out of sight for a little while until everything returns to normal," Elsbeth offered, tenderly brushing a piece of Gundi's hair away from her eye. "Come now. Let's not miss our train."

As Elsbeth turned away, Gundi slipped the box into her pocket.

Gundi grabbed a dark-blue fedora before she and Elsbeth made their way out the front door. She owned hats with wider brims that would have cast a greater shadow on her face, but this one would blend into the crowd best. Insisting they take the tram to the train station, Gundi agreed with Elsbeth that a taxi would have been faster, but the fewer people they interacted with—the fewer conversations they were forced to have—the better.

Her head low, Gundi linked arms with Elsbeth and scurried into the massive tomb of Berlin's Stettiner Bahnhof and purchased their tickets. Before Gundi's eyes could adjust to the hazy light of the early evening sun pouring in through three tall, arched windows, she could only see the silhouettes of fellow travelers. Soon, she noticed half a dozen Nazi soldiers stationed along the periphery of the room, scanning passengers sitting on wooden benches. "Let's wait in the WC until it's time to go," Gundi suggested.

"Do you really think that's necessary, *Liebchen*?"

A soldier's eye stopped on Gundi. She reached for Elsbeth's elbow and coaxed her along. "Let's go, Mutti."

The two boarded the seven o'clock train to Hamburg and settled onto their red cushioned bench seat for the journey. Gundi dug through her satchel, pulling out her primer on political economy and pressing her thumb up the spine to keep it open. She was already a week ahead in her work for Professor Hirsch's class, but she wanted to review and take notes on a chapter she'd been struggling with. Scratching into the margins, Gundi asked: *Postwar reparations the sole cause of Germany's depression? Wasn't it partially due to the U.S. stock market crash?* She dared not write the question she really wanted to know, the one most of her friends were asking. *Was Hitler's promise to keep another war at bay realistic?*

The evening sun illuminated the countryside scrolling past them. Gundi leaned forward toward her mother, not noticing that the steady rumble of the train had lulled Elsbeth to sleep. She tapped her arm gently. Elsbeth's eyes fluttered open. "Do you think it's safe to let my professors know where I am?" Gundi asked.

With a groggy laugh, Elsbeth dismissed the notion. "You poor dear. I remember feeling anxious when I was pregnant with you. We're not fugitives, Gundi. You can tell your teachers whatever you'd like."

Was her mother willfully ignorant of the fact that Germany was growing increasingly dangerous? Or did Elsbeth not care because she believed that she and Gundi were immune from it?

Gundi looked out the window of the train and squeezed her folded hands tight, trying to hold back her tears. "Thank you, Mutti," she managed to say. The sun was setting, so she closed her eyes and imagined she was with Leo's family, preparing for Shabbat. She wasn't sure she believed in God anymore, but remembering Shabbat kept Gundi tethered to the Solomon family. She envisioned the faces of the family she had grown to love over the five months she had spent visiting their home. She remembered the smell of roasting chicken and pictured the glow of tiny candles. Silently, Gundi recited the now-familiar Hebrew words.

*Barukh atah Adonai Eloheinu, melekh ha'olam, asher kid'shanu b'mitzvotav v'tzivanu l'hadlik ner shel shabbat.*

The Solomons welcomed Gundi and Erich to their Shabbat dinner early in their friendship with Leo, and if the family had had any concerns about inviting two blond-haired, blue-eyed gentiles into their home, they never showed it. At the time, Gundi hadn't considered how remarkable their hospitality was. She had never considered herself a danger to anyone, and goodness knew Erich was as harmless as a butterfly, but the Solomons had no guarantee of that. How Gundi wished she could travel back in time and properly acknowledge the risk they took by trusting her. That first evening in September, Leo's mother, Rivka, opened the front door and spread her arms for hugs. "*Shabbat shalom, schöne Kinder.* Come inside where it's nice and toasty."

Leo's father, Yosef, rushed by, calling into the back hall-way, "Schel, get your nose out of that book and say hello to our guests." Turning to Gundi and Erich, he held out his arm in his younger son's direction. "The boy does nothing but read Sherlock Holmes and futz around with his oboe."

The sitting room centered around a hearth made from large, dark stones. Thick wooden beams sliced the white ceiling. Cherry wood bookshelves stuffed with worn leather and canvas-covered books stretched across the expanse of the walls, peeks of damask velvet flocking wallpaper adding a flourish. Perched on a table beside the pink-and-gold love seat was a dainty lamp with a shade made from small glass pieces that looked like leaves on a tree.

Gundi's favorite part of the evening was when they lit candles to usher in Shabbat. Rivka lit six, one for each person at the table. She moved her hands over the flames, circling them three times, before covering her eyes and reciting a blessing in Hebrew. The glow against the window turned the pane into a mirror, and when Gundi caught a quick glimpse of her reflection in the amber light, she saw herself in a different way. She saw a young woman who, at long last, felt she was exactly where she belonged.

At supper, Yosef regaled them with stories of fighting for Germany in the Great War. "*Ach*, how many times do we have to hear this?" Leo's twelve-year-old brother, Schel, teased his father. It amazed Gundi that Yosef still spoke with such pride about defending a country that now embraced hostile policies toward Jews. The Solomons weren't even legal citizens any longer, just barely tolerated guests of Germany.

The family had a delicious flavor. It went beyond the way they roasted chicken and seasoned cabbage. Their food, in fact, came in a variety of flavors. The braided bread was practically cake, and the red wine was sweeter than any *Eiswein* Gundi had ever tasted. She and Erich exchanged a look of surprise at their first sip, then forced down the treacly drink.

She loved the way the Solomons bantered, like four-wall handball, bouncing from politics to family stories to books to playful ribbing. But mostly Gundi enjoyed how the family made room for differing, often conflicting views. Yosef told Gundi that he was an atheist and shrugged when she questioned how one could be both a Jew and a nonbeliever. Gesturing toward the table illuminated by candles and covered in their prayers, Gundi asked, "Why do you observe Shabbat?"

He shrugged again. "It's important to Rivka."

Gundi marveled at the man's comfort with praying to a

God he didn't believe in. She had never known anyone who could allow thoughts to flow simultaneously in two different directions and sit with them as though it were perfectly normal.

Her own family wasn't particularly observant in their Christian faith, but they attended services on holidays. She didn't have a distaste for the church the way Erich did. Rather, she felt nothing at all. Gundi memorized the hymns she was told to memorize and stood and sat on cue, but the rituals had never resonated with her.

Rivka cleared her throat and shot her husband a look. *It's also important to me for you to zip your lips*, she seemed to say. "Leo tells us you're an art lover," Rivka said to Gundi.

*He mentioned me?*

She asked if Gundi had a chance to see the *Entartete Kunst* when it was in Berlin. This was a test, and Gundi knew it. What would it say about her that she had been to the Nazi's degenerate art show? At the time, like many of her friends, Gundi had gone to the exhibition out of curiosity, but now she knew better and was ashamed of her attendance. She looked to Erich for support. He nodded fractionally to encourage her.

"I did," Gundi said, thankful that her voice didn't quiver. "The thing I found truly fascinating was watching people revolted by the very same pieces they had fawned over at museums not too long ago."

Rivka smiled and looked at Leo.

Gundi continued. "Maybe they should have called it the Degeneration of Memory exhibition and featured a melting brain instead of Dalí's melting clock in *The Persistence of Memory*."

Rivka laughed with approval. "I like her," she said to Leo, then winked at Gundi. "I heard they had several paintings by my favorite, Max Ernst."

"You would have loved this show then. They made a big fuss over Dadaism being the downfall of Germany."

Rivka held her hand to her chest. "Goodness, I thought we Jews were responsible for that. I wish these Nazis would make up their minds."

Gundi laughed at the joke, but her overwhelming feeling was gratitude. The Solomons wanted to hear what she thought and how she viewed the world, a refreshing change from other parents who stuck to simple conversation about the weather or autumn fashions. She was ashamed to admit this, even to herself, but Elsbeth had become so invested in Gundi being the perfect daughter that it left little room for her to speak freely to her mother. She didn't risk being seen as the flawed person she really was. It wasn't as much for Gundi's sake as it was her mother's. Why should she cause Elsbeth any more hardship than she had already suffered at the hands of her treacherous father?

After dinner, Leo blushed with embarrassment as Rivka and Gundi sank into a love seat and looked at family pictures. Gundi's belly was full from their meal, but the scent of Rivka's rose perfume stirred a different kind of hunger in Gundi. As much as she loved Elsbeth, Gundi longed for a happily intertwined family like this. There was a shot of Leo, Schel, and four other boys on the shore at Arendsee as they'd stacked their bodies into a pyramid. Then there was Rivka and Yosef as newlyweds, looking over the rail of a cruise liner toward white Grecian villas perched on the hillside in the distance. Gundi wondered if Leo's parents had posed for the shot or if someone just happened upon them looking perfectly content. She smiled at the picture of Yosef and Rivka posing in front of Solomon's Books right after they first purchased it. Rivka held baby Leo in her arms as the couple posed by the large glass storefront window, lettering painted the same dark green as the wooden door and window frame.

Joining the women on the couch, Erich looked at Leo's baby picture and teased that he looked like a dumpling.

"We called him our little matzo ball—if matzo balls had a full head of curls," Rivka said. "He'll never go bald, this one. He was born with that mop, and he'll die an old man with all those curls. Just look at his father."

<hr />

Changing her position in her seat, Gundi continued looking out the train window to calm her roiling stomach. Placing a hand on her tiny belly, she hoped her baby could hear her thoughts. *All is well, little one. Mutti will keep you safe.*

When the train pulled into Hamburg Hauptbahnhof, the conductor did not open the doors. Instead, he instructed the passengers to remain in their seats and refrain from collecting their belongings until authorities made their way through each car. Gundi reached for her mother's hand and furrowed her brows. *They know about the leaflets the Edelweiss Pirates distributed. They know about everything,* she fretted silently.

Elsbeth laughed. "*Liebchen,* we are hardly who they are looking for," she said, patting Gundi's knee.

As Elsbeth returned her hand to her own lap, a Gestapo officer stopped in front of them, his eyes volleying between Gundi's face and the sheet of paper in his hands. "Gundi Schiller?"

She lifted her eyes to meet his, trying to remain calm before she answered that no, she wasn't Gundi Schiller, that he must have confused her with someone else.

But before she could respond, Elsbeth sighed and snapped, "Come now. Don't you have better things to do than bother a poor girl trying to visit her *Tante*?"

Gundi closed her eyes and clenched her jaw, reminding herself not to blame her mother. The Gestapo would have asked to see her identification, and the outcome would have been the same. Dr. Ebner was looking for her, and he had the full resources of the Nazi Party to track her down. *Could one girl really be this important to the Nazis? Or is Dr. Ebner just a man who enjoys flexing his muscle and lording his power over women?*

Another officer appeared before Gundi and Elsbeth and instructed the other passengers to disembark quickly and quietly. "*Frauen*, remain on board," the first Gestapo agent ordered, strumming his fingers over the pistol in his holster. Gundi's skin prickled with the realization that the men were armed; she and Elsbeth were powerless.

Elsbeth stood and placed a protective hand on Gundi's shoulder. "You have no right to stop her," she said, the confidence in her voice waning slightly. Still, she pressed on. "You can't do this."

Reaching for her mother's shaking hand, Gundi hoped that this was the moment Elsbeth finally woke up to the reality of life in the Reich. In addition to the flutter of fear in Gundi's stomach, she was also amazed at how quickly information was transmitted among the Nazis. How had they discovered that Elsbeth had a sister in Hamburg in just eight hours?

The exodus of passengers was swift, with jackets quickly tossed into the crooks of elbows, newspapers hastily stuffed under armpits. A young girl in a BDM uniform and double braids looked over her shoulder at Gundi with an expression of fear. It was only after the girl's mother tugged her daughter's arm to hurry her along that Gundi realized the child was probably not afraid *for* Gundi; she was afraid *of* her. In her world, the Nazis were the good guys. If they had stopped Gundi, she must have posed a danger.

"Sit down, Mutti," Gundi pleaded, immediately deciding that she would comply with whatever the Gestapo asked and beg her mother to go on to *Tante* Ulla's house without her. "I'm happy to speak with these gentlemen," she said, flashing her best smile at the men. Gundi knew she would have a decent chance of lying her way out of trouble, but Elsbeth could be rash when she felt threatened.

Gundi could hear the chatter of dozens of people outside on the platform. She cast a quick glance out the window, a momentary escape. She saw a stylish-looking older woman in a thin wool coat and a hat with an oblong pearl pin through it. The woman held the hand of a young boy, a grandson or nephew perhaps, wearing lederhosen and white knee socks. Beside them on the platform were full families clustering in reunion, small children on tiptoes for hugs, one little girl hopping as if she were on a pogo stick. A male passenger pointed to the train and spoke with a pinched expression of consternation. His wife held a gloved hand over her mouth and stretched her neck to peek through the cells of the train windows.

Gundi turned her attention back to what was before her. Looking like a blond eagle with his sharp features and unblinking eyes, the Gestapo officer continued. "You are wanted in Berlin by order of Dr. Gregor Ebner."

Reaching for her beaded handbag, Elsbeth announced that she was not leaving Gundi's side. "Please, Mutti, it will be fine," Gundi lied. "You go on. I'll talk to Dr. Ebner, and we'll reach an understanding." Gundi would remind the doctor that her father had a weak heart. He had been a drunk. Gundi's blood wasn't so pure after all. Perhaps Gundi could get out of this Lebensborn sentence. She turned to Elsbeth, who had removed her hat and straightened her favorite hairpin, a marcasite flower.

*Thank goodness she doesn't know the truth about the baby being Leo's.*

There was a time when she had no secrets from her mother. Gundi hadn't appreciated what a rare, fleeting gift it was to be fully known by someone. Now she had a vest of pockets filled with half-truths, lies, and omissions.

Gundi and Elsbeth never made it farther than the Hamburg train station. As they were escorted back to Berlin in a swastika-emblazoned Mercedes-Benz, Gundi gazed out the window at the countryside streaming by. Everything looked peaceful and quiet, but Gundi knew too well how quickly that façade could crumble.

On the first night of the Kristallnacht riots, she, Leo, and Erich had planned to assist Jewish shop owners by standing in front of their stores in solidarity. The three friends watched the scene unfold in disbelief at the sheer volume of human bodies in the streets. They had expected a dozen; there were thousands. Gundi and her friends sat crouched in an alleyway, hands quivering at the realization that there was nothing they could do.

At the sight of Fasanenstrasse Synagogue ablaze, Leo's shoulders sagged and his body rooted into the ground, motionless. Gundi turned to him, the reflection of flames flickering in his brown eyes, and knew he was lost in memories of his family at their temple, now being destroyed as he watched. She placed a hand gently on his forearm, snapping him out of his shock.

Fire trucks were on the scene, but instead of trying to extinguish the flames, they aimed their water hoses at the buildings flanking the temple to ensure that the fire did not spread. Gundi, Leo, and Erich exchanged a glance. *This is a state-sanctioned action.* "We need to get out of here," Leo whispered, grabbing Gundi's hand and taking off through a maze of alleys.

The patter of their feet against the pavement sounded like an old woman tut-tutting at their failure. Gundi would never admit to this aloud, but she had entertained heroic fantasies in which she would break into Hitler's Eagle's Nest while he slept, grab him by the hair, and slice off his head like Judith did to Holofernes. In Gundi's version, though, she would skip the seduction and go straight for the kill. She wanted to feel powerful, strong, and important. In reality, she did little more than disseminate anti-Nazi leaflets. *Did anyone even read them? Had they made any difference at all?*

Gundi's shame only intensified the next day, when she and her mother crossed paths with a neighbor, Herr Lambert, on Kurfürstendamm. Most Germans hurried past the damage, trying to avoid the eyes of the Jewish shop owners. They looked away from the sharply dressed older man in his Deutsches Heer uniform, decorated with medals from the Great War, as he swept away glass from his shattered store window. If anyone felt sympathy for the Jews or disapproval over the riots, they would be wise not to show it, especially with the Gestapo out on the streets in full force. Herr Lambert was the exception. He looked at Elsbeth and Gundi and shook his head as he surveyed the charred remains of wooden beams and shards of broken glass. "What a waste," he lamented.

Gundi felt her hope rekindled. Maybe there was some way out of this; maybe the sentiments of ordinary Germans would sway, and the Reich would fall. She smiled at Herr Lambert, checking to see if she was out of earshot of the Gestapo before she replied.

As she opened her mouth to respond, her neighbor finished his thought. "Silly, really. Why destroy property that will soon be yours?"

Gundi felt herself stumble, righting her balance just in time to see Elsbeth nod her head. She wanted to ask her mother whether she truly agreed with Herr Lambert or if she was merely guarding their safety. She started to pose the question but quickly choked back her words. Gundi wasn't sure she was ready for the answer.

~·~

Gundi and Elsbeth arrived back in Berlin just before midnight. After their long night of travel, Elsbeth needed rest. Gundi noticed that her mother appeared as if she had aged ten years overnight. There were heavy bags under her eyes, and the skin on her face hung loose. Gundi swore she spotted strands of gray in her mother's tousled hair that she hadn't seen that morning.

The front door of their house was ajar, but before they made their way inside, Dr. Ebner stepped out, shaking his head with great concern. "Frau Schiller, Fräulein, I have bad news," he said, slick with sympathy. Stepping back and opening the door for them, Dr. Ebner told Gundi and Elsbeth that bandits had invaded their home earlier that night. "I'm afraid it is quite a disaster inside." He held out his hand like a circus ringleader inviting guests into his tent.

As her eyes scanned the living room, Gundi heard her mother try to suppress a gasp. She, on the other hand, had to hold back the urge to scream. Fury coursed through her veins at the thought that this animal felt he was entitled to manhandle and destroy whatever he pleased.

The wreckage reminded Gundi of a photograph she had seen at school: the inside of a San Francisco house after the Great Earthquake of 1906. Everything had been torn from its place and cast onto the floor, so Gundi stepped gingerly over books, noticing that the Persian rug beneath was glittering with broken glass. Splintered planks of wood topped a pile of cracked porcelain plates. Her grandfather's piano lay facedown, like it couldn't bear the sight of its fallen comrades.

Gundi felt Dr. Ebner trailing in her wake as she went from

room to room to inspect. Tensing at the sound of the doctor's boots drumming the floor, Gundi didn't dare protest or even request privacy. Seeing their precious belongings tossed to the floor chilled Gundi almost as much as Dr. Ebner's hands on her had done earlier. He could do whatever he wanted, touch whatever he pleased, and there wasn't a thing Gundi could do to stop him.

At the same moment Gundi made the slightest whimper, she heard her mother shriek from her bedroom. Hurrying to her aid, Gundi saw Elsbeth kneeling on the floor, frantically searching through the pile of clothing that had been emptied from the dresser. "It's gone!"

*Oma's brooch!* Gundi tried to catch Elsbeth's eye, but her mother remained fixed on a pile of clothing haphazardly thrown onto the floor. She shook sweaters and checked pockets before sweeping her hand across the rug.

Gundi had heard of Nazis ransacking the homes of Germans they suspected were disloyal to the Reich, but never for a minor infraction like opting out of a program. This was clearly a threat, a way to let Gundi know that it was time for her to cooperate with the party. Dr. Ebner was either obsessed with Gundi or a power-hungry sadist. Crossing her arms over her belly, she realized that the two were not mutually exclusive.

"I'll go," Gundi whispered, defeated. She would have five months to figure out how to escape from the Lebensborn home, but her mother was in imminent danger. "I would be pleased to stay at your maternity home until my baby is born."

Dr. Ebner nodded his head. "I'll see to it that your home is restored to your mother's satisfaction."

Gundi looked at the valise she shared with her mother and realized she would need to separate her belongings.

"If you don't mind, Doctor, I'd like a moment alone to gather my things."

He pressed his lips together and cleared his throat as though he was about to scold a child. "In fact, I do mind, Gundi."

# 8

## *Gundi*

GUNDI LOOKED OUT FROM THE WINDOW OF THE BACK SEAT of the Mercedes-Benz that drove her on the final leg of her journey. The young driver had just passed Munich, so Gundi knew they were only forty kilometers from Steinhöring, where the maternity home was situated on a secluded estate. The car continued past the open fields and farmland dotted with cattle that stretched along the countryside.

A wooden road sign announced their arrival in the small town of Ebersberg, which had a Tudor-style pub called Das Frankengold. There was a grocer with a worn, mustard-colored awning. A mother in clunky black shoes inspected the fruit selection in the baskets outside as her three young children orbited her, chasing one another. Next door was a bakery and a cobbler that showed their allegiance to the Nazis with large flags. The car passed a white church with a clay roof and an onion-capped tower reaching toward the sky, the Mangfall mountain range a distant backdrop.

Soon the car began rumbling as it made its way onto a winding dirt road through the woods. When after ten minutes the car turned off the road and onto the gravel driveway of the Heim Hochland estate, Gundi noticed a large stone statue of a mother nursing her baby and gazing at him as he cupped her breast in his hand. The way the woman's fingertips caressed the child's earlobe was a gesture Gundi would normally find tender but, under the circumstances, felt unsettling.

The driver, a young man with round facial features and a chipped tooth, turned to look at Gundi in the back seat. "Welcome to Heim Hochland, Fräulein. I hope you enjoy your stay," he told her in a serious voice that reminded Gundi of a schoolboy playing soldier. Gundi's eyes traveled down to his Hakenkreuz armband, reminding her that this polite exchange couldn't make a Nazi into a gentleman. She needed to stay on guard.

The main house of the Heim Hochland estate was a sturdy four-story Bavarian Alpine vernacular, stark white with dark wooden balconies stretching across the top floors. Nazi banners flapped from the pointy rooftop and hung from windows: one with the traditional swastika, the other twin lightning bolts—the insignia of the SS—enwombed in a double circle. Two smaller houses for staff and servants stood off to the side, looking almost deferential.

As if on cue, two nurses emerged from the front door. Although they wore identical white uniforms and stiff caps, it was clear that the heavyset woman in her fifties was in charge. She walked briskly, waving to Gundi through the car window as her counterparts followed. "*Guten Tag*, Gundi. I am Sister Marianne," the nurse said, smiling, as Gundi stepped out onto the driveway. "This is Sister Dorothea," Sister Marianne said, introducing a nurse with icy blue eyes and thick brows. The nurse had a sharp nose and dull brown hair with streaks of silver that gave her a severe appearance.

The driver hurried toward the back of the car and unloaded Gundi's valise.

"We are so pleased you are joining us," Sister Dorothea offered stiffly, clasping her hands behind her back as she led Gundi inside.

Sister Marianne showed Gundi into the house, while Sister Dorothea excused herself. As Sister Marianne pointed out the common room on the left, Gundi couldn't help notice the entryway floor, an expansive black-and-white checkerboard pattern, split down the middle by a spiral staircase in its center. She walked forward with Sister Marianne, counting each black square she stepped on to calm herself. To her right was a long white hallway with what looked like a dozen or so closed doors, each with a number screwed onto it. Sister Marianne told her that the numbered doors were the bedrooms where half the girls who were expecting lived. The other half stayed on the west side of the house, just beyond the common room. Immediately past the bedrooms on the right was Sister Marianne's office. At the very end of the hall was the labor room, maternity ward, and nursery.

Gundi looked to her left and saw two young mothers-to-be sitting in the common room, listening to Lale Andersen crooning on the radio, one flipping through *Sonne ins Haus* magazine, the other embroidering a handkerchief with a hoop loom. A small marble-top table held a Tiffany lamp, its shade made of delicate stained-glass flowers.

Then Gundi eyed two glasses of milk and a plate of iced gingersnaps and hazelnut cookies and realized that, despite the sophisticated furnishings at Heim Hochland, its residents were

practically children. The girls looked no older than sixteen in
their matching mustard-colored dresses with Peter Pan collars.
A pregnant brunette nestled deep into her plush velvet chair
reading a magazine, whose cover featured a smartly dressed
young woman pushing a baby buggy.

Sister Marianne held a stiff smile as she watched Gundi
take in the scene. Rather than comment on the residents, Gundi
felt it safer to inquire about the lampshade.

"Is that an original Tiffany?"

Nodding, Sister Marianne added, "All our Lebensborn
Society homes are decorated by Reichsführer Himmler himself."

*Makes you wonder how important his job is if he has time for
decorating.*

"Herr Himmler has marvelous taste," Sister Marianne continued. "A real eye for fine pieces."

Sister Dorothea peeked her head down from the spiral staircase and, in a reedy voice, told Sister Marianne that there was
a small problem upstairs. Gundi suspected the issue was pressing. "Stay put, Gundi," Sister Marianne said, squeezing her hand
gently. "This will take only a moment."

Looking into the common room, Gundi caught a glimpse
of her reflection in the oversize mirror hanging beside the
fireplace mantle and felt her stomach turn. Her appearance
hadn't changed in any significant way since her appointment
with Drs. Vogel and Ebner the day before, though she did look
somewhat disheveled from the eight-hour journey. What was
unnerving about her reflection was how foreign everything
around her looked. She turned away, trying to focus instead
on smoothing her messy plaits, tucking loose hair up with

pins. *Who is that nurse passing behind me?* She twisted a chunk of hair. *How far back does that long hallway reach? How many expectant mothers live at Heim Hochland? This house is not newly built. Was it a resort before?*

Sister Marianne returned and set her hand on Gundi's back to coax her along toward the common room. Placing each foot in the center of the checker squares, Gundi smiled at the memory of playing hopscotch with Erich and her girlfriends in primary school. Their friend Rose always won, which was no wonder since she had been taking tap and ballet lessons since she could walk. The Kaufman family had left for America when both she and Rose were teens, right after the Nuremberg Laws were enacted, and Gundi hadn't heard from her since. The girls had promised to write letters, but Rose never sent a card with her new address. Gundi could understand Rose's desire for a fresh start, leaving all memories of Berlin behind. Still, she missed her friend. Closing her eyes for just a moment, Gundi tried to imagine what Rose looked like now, four years later. *Does she still dance? Maybe she moved to Hollywood and performed in pictures. Perhaps Rose is sitting next to Ginger Rogers by a swimming pool right this moment.*

A herd of slender teenage girls wearing white sleeveless tops with SS bolts and athletic shorts made their way down the spiral staircase, their feet thundering past Gundi. Most turned to check out their new housemate, one even waving sweetly.

"The girls who live upstairs are mothers in training," Sister Marianne explained. "It's time for their calisthenics."

Gundi followed Sister Marianne as she clipped efficiently

toward the far corner of the common room to a door that led to a long corridor with even more numbered doors. *How big is this place?*

Questions spilled across Gundi's mind like loose marbles on the sidewalk. *Why have I never heard of the Lebensborn Society before? How many ordinary Germans know about this hidden estate where there seem to be no rations on sugar and the milk is whole? And what in the world is a mother in training?*

She turned to Sister Marianne as they reached a door with a metal number 14. "This is your home for the next six months, Gundi. We know you will be very happy at Heim Hochland." Sister Marianne paused but then continued before Gundi could respond. "When you're further along, we'll arrange for you and Erich Meyer to marry. Or, if your plans change, your baby will be highly adoptable."

Gundi placed her hand on her belly as if to shield her baby from these threats. She felt the slightest flutter and wondered if it was fear or her baby's first kick. If only she could ask her mother. Instead, there was only this Nazi matron.

If Gundi couldn't escape from Heim Hochland, maybe she should marry Erich. It would certainly help him stave off SS officers' daughters. And it would keep her baby safe. At least she hoped it would. When she had flipped through the Solomon photo album with Rivka back in September, every single baby portrait had the same thick dark curls, sand-colored skin, and deep brown eyes. She prayed her coloring would be dominant, or else there would be no way Dr. Ebner or Sister Marianne would believe Erich was her baby's father. They had seen his photo in the file his mother had prepared. There was no chance

Gundi and Erich could produce a child who even remotely resembled a Solomon.

Sister Marianne set Gundi's valise on a small white stand in the corner of the modest room, decorated sparsely with a single bed, a white dresser, and a statuette of an angel set on a night table.

As much as Gundi viewed Sister Marianne as her captor, she also recognized that the woman was a wellspring of information, perhaps Gundi's only source. "Do you know where my mother will be staying while our house is restored?"

"I'm sure she's fine," Sister Marianne said, opening Gundi's bag and starting to transfer clothing into the dresser.

"I can unpack myself," Gundi said, trying to steady her voice. Sister Marianne said that her job was to assist Gundi in every way and continued opening the side compartments of her valise. Quickly, Gundi reached for her underwear, knowing that if she didn't grab them, Sister Marianne would get to them first. The whole process was intrusive enough without this beastly woman clawing at her intimate apparel. She was thankful that she had the good sense to keep her oma's diamond brooch in her skirt pocket.

"You'll probably receive a letter from your mother soon, but we only deliver mail once a week so our girls can focus on their health." Reaching her veiny hand toward Gundi's belly, then patting her tiny bump, Sister Marianne smiled. "It's good for your growing baby to have as little stimulation from the outside world as possible."

Gundi hadn't noticed the sheen of sweat on her body until it chilled her skin. Letters from her mother would hardly be a disruption to her peace of mind. As Gundi placed her brassiere in the top dresser drawer, she heard Sister Marianne tut disapprovingly. She turned to see Sister Marianne holding Gundi's favorite red school jacket, the one with the heart lapels. Marianne kept it at arm's length, her fingers pinched like clothespins. "This is certainly frivolous." Tossing Gundi's jacket onto the desk chair, Sister Marianne suggested, "Let's donate this to the ladies sewing blankets for our men in the Protectorate."

<hr />

On Gundi's first night, she and the other girls were required to attend a documentary film in the common room. Sister Marianne billed it as part of their continuing education. Really, it was Nazi propaganda they had already seen in school.

Gundi saw the familiar words appear on the screen: *Alles Leben ist Kampf.* All life is struggle. "Obviously, a comedy," Gundi muttered to Gisela, who sat beside her, two long braids framing her perfect Kewpie doll face.

"Oh no," Gisela replied. "It is a eugenics documentary." Her full pink lips sprang into a smile. "We get to watch a new one every week."

This film began with animals fighting for survival in the wild. Antelope charged at one another, battling to the death. The narrator explained that the strongest lived and passed along their superior genes to their offspring. The weak, sick, and injured perished. Most of the girls covered their eyes and made a show of their disgust as birds plucked at animal carcasses. Renate, a slim

blond from upstairs, made a point of seeming bored by the car-
nage, never once flinching. She looked as though she should be
holding a cocktail and complaining that life was so dull; she'd seen
it all.

Gundi had assumed that Gisela was taking copious notes
about the film. When she glanced at the pad of paper in Gisela's
lap, though, she realized that the girl was sketching the portrait
of Hitler that hung above the mantle. Hers, however, cast long,
dark shadows across half his face, deepening creases and dis-
torting shapes. It was an unexpectedly haunting character study
coming from such a sugarplum of a girl. Gundi wondered if
Gisela meant to capture the darkness of the führer's soul so
poignantly. Her question was answered when Gisela signed her
name in the right corner with a bubbly, swirling cursive and a
tiny heart dotting the *i* of her last name.

———

Gundi spent her first few nights at Heim Hochland creep-
ing out of her room, hunting for something—anything—that
would tell her more about this bizarre maternity home. *Are
there other Lebensborn homes? How many babies are born here?
How many have been adopted?* Perhaps there was some way to
use information about the workings of this secret society to
help undermine the Nazis.

She also wanted to find out what was going on in the world
outside Heim Hochland. The world was changing quickly. Even
a day without news was unmooring for Gundi. *Have Hitler
and Mussolini formed their alliance? Is Germany still honoring its*

*nonaggression pact with Poland? Would Sister Marianne even tell us if Hitler had declared war?* Gundi needed answers.

Padding down the long hallway, Gundi peeked into the dark kitchen. *Surely, there are no files or letters in the cupboards,* she thought as she continued to walk. Spotting a door to the cellar, Gundi reached for the knob before she heard the wind rustling leaves on the trees outside.

Finding the door to the backyard, Gundi put her hand on the knob and lifted straight up, raising the door slightly so that it pressed against the top of its hinges. This way, it would be less likely to squeak and alarm the others. Quietly, she opened the door and stepped into the yard, and the cool spring air felt like a balm against her flushed cheeks. Gundi scanned the dozens of windows at the back of the house to see if anyone's lamps were still lit, but at 2:00 a.m., the only light came from the full moon and an abundance of stars, far more than she had ever seen in Berlin. Gundi had never been more grateful for katydids, whose steady ticking she hoped would mask the sound of her rustling through the garbage cans. Thankfully, the bins were placed alongside a fence, so no one inside could see her as long as she remained on her knees.

The smell of damp grass was suddenly overpowered by that of rotting food after Gundi waded through a garbage bin filled with an ungodly mass of fruit pits and milk-soaked muesli. Finally, though, she found a newspaper. Shaking dry a copy of *Der Stürmer*, Gundi held the paper close to her face so she could read in the dim light. The headline read, JEWS ABANDON BUSINESSES ACROSS GERMANY. Gundi gritted her teeth. *Yes, they are abandoning them all right, just like one abandons a burning building.*

Another article reported that nine hundred Jews would set sail from Hamburg to Cuba on the SS *St. Louis* in May. "One step closer to a *Judenfreies* Fatherland," the reporter wrote. Gundi skimmed an article about an event honoring mothers of multiple German children. The story focused on the elderly women who would be receiving the first Mutterkreuz medals for bearing four or more healthy children. There was a small notice that enemies of the state were being sent to the Dachau labor camp to perform essential work for the Nazi Party. She dug further into the garbage can, searching for letters, loose papers, or telegrams, but found nothing that was of use.

Finally, as Gundi was just about to give up, she noticed a torn piece of paper about the size of a postage stamp. Heart racing, she scavenged for the rest of the paper but could only find about a quarter of the scraps. She sat down on the dew-coated grass, spreading the pieces out before her. Listening carefully for footsteps, she arranged and rearranged the torn paper bits until they formed an incomplete message:

*not to be able to produce*
*become an accepted custom to*
*of good blood and bring them*

She fought back hot, frustrated tears. This vague message could mean anything. Gundi buried her face in her hands, only to retch at the smell of spent tea leaves and old peach pits. As her stomach roiled, she began to cry. Finally, she had found something, but she couldn't make a bit of sense of it. *Not to be able to produce what? What would become an accepted custom? And bring good blood where?*

Good blood. How that expression chilled her when she thought about what it meant for Leo—and their baby.

Gundi felt the moist earth seep through her nightgown as she sat on the grass, looking at the paper. Her shoulders slumped. When would she ever be able to do something that actually mattered for the people she loved?

# 9

## *Hilde*

*Munich*
*May*

ON THE DRIVE TO THE MUTTERKREUZ AWARDS CEREMONY
for Munich mothers, Obergruppenführer Ziegler
explained to Hilde what a challenge it had been to organize the
inaugural celebrations. "It is my honor," he told her, loud enough
for his driver to hear. "Next year, we'll have far more time to
plan, so the events across Germany will be even more grand."

Herr Ziegler explained that the führer had come to him
in November with the idea of a Mother's Day celebration,
giving him just six months to coordinate events across the
Fatherland. Municipalities had to identify and screen racially
fit, child-rich German mothers, but it was tough because the
criteria for fitness were vague. Obviously, children who were
unable to walk or talk were unfit, but the less severe abnor-
malities were difficult to characterize definitively. What one
doctor classified as feebleminded might be considered useful
by another.

To ease pressure on municipalities, the party decided that,
for its first year, Mutterkreuz awards would be given only to

mothers who were sixty years or older. That made for a far more manageable pool of women to screen in such a short time.

Hilde took in the scent of the obergruppenführer's cologne. It was an intoxicating woodsy pine; it smelled to her like nature and power combined.

Darting his eyes between Hilde and his driver, Herr Ziegler lowered his voice to a whisper. "Can you keep a secret?" Hilde nodded, and he smiled. "We almost let one slip by." Herr Ziegler was finally sharing the kind of inner-circle information Hilde had longed for. Pinching his fingers, he told Hilde, "We came *this* close to giving a Mutterkreuz to a woman who was renting a room to a Jew."

Hilde remembered the laws that forbade Jews from entering German homes, even for a short visit. So of course, harboring a Jew was a big deal. Still, the mother had raised good German children. Couldn't the party pardon the transgression? Hilde felt sorry for the mother who would miss out on today's celebration and her Mutterkreuz medal. Plus, wouldn't everyone in her town wonder why she didn't receive one? How humiliating.

Hilde didn't dare reveal her sympathy for the woman, though. She felt that the obergruppenführer's approval of her grew in direct proportion to her agreement with him.

Setting his hand on her knee, Ziegler lowered his chin and peered over his spectacles. "Does that disturb you?"

Hilde knew the next words could set her life on a new path, so she formed the perfect ones and cleared her throat. "To think that a mother would endanger her children that way," she said, mouth scrunched with contempt.

"Her children are grown, Hilde. That is not the point,"

Ziegler returned with disappointment. Leaning back into his seat, he removed a handkerchief from his pocket and cleaned the lenses of his eyeglasses.

The act itself was innocuous, but Hilde felt the sting of rejection. *How stupid I am! Of course a sixty-year-old woman wouldn't have children living at home.*

Hilde looked down at her hands folded in her lap as her face grew hot with shame. Then she remembered what Jutta had told her: *A mother is a mother for the rest of her life.* Hilde smiled internally and lifted her head. "A good German mother will be visited by her grown children and her grandchildren. She is always a fierce protector of her family, so I can't imagine a mother being cavalier about their safety regardless of their age." Then, as if possessed by someone else entirely, she turned to Herr Ziegler, gave him a pat on the knee, and quipped, "So I stand by my point."

The obergruppenführer lifted his hands slightly in mock surrender and laughed. "Hilde Kramer," he said, letting her name sit for a moment. "I must say, you are one of a kind."

Bathing in Ziegler's attention, Hilde sat up a bit straighter and crossed her legs.

⌒⌒

Hilde had imagined the Mutterkreuz awards ceremony being hosted at a private estate in a polished hardwood ballroom dimly lit by a three-tiered chandelier. She had envisioned herself standing at the center of a cluster of elegant party guests, all charmed, delighted, and entertained by her musings on motherhood and family.

Instead, she found herself standing awkwardly at the periphery of a municipal hall amid a sea of old ladies who all seemed to have known one another for years. They were clad in frumpy dirndls and potato sack–inspired dresses, and Hilde abided by Herr Ziegler's request that she wear her drab brown BDM jacket and blue skirt. He had suggested that her modesty would allow the spotlight to shine on the mothers being honored. A shiver of excitement ran through her, thinking that the obergruppenführer had considered her a possible distraction.

The solo accordionist brought attention to the absence of sophistication in the room, playing too loudly through his repertoire of folk songs. Hilde wrapped her fingers around a glass of wine, feigning comfort, but clung to the edges of the room, engaging with no one. She had expected Herr Ziegler to be by her side all evening but quickly abandoned the notion when the obergruppenführer became absorbed into a small huddle of men in SS uniforms. At first glance, the officers looked identically suited: immaculately shined black boots, jackets with the crisp swastika armband, and boxy hats proudly bearing the SS *Totenkopf*. But there were subtle details that differentiated them. She could tell that more decoration indicated higher prestige, though she didn't quite know what each pin meant. What distinguished Herr Ziegler to her was the ever-so-slight swagger that came with power.

Hilde forced herself toward a cluster of Mutterkreuz award winners at the center of the room, all of whom had apparently borne the strongest, most brilliant sons to ever grace the Fatherland. She feigned fascination with the ramblings of a woman whose gray head bobbed as she recited a long list of her sons' accomplishments, starting with their school athletics and continuing to their professional pursuits. She was so, so blessed, the mother said smugly. Hilde wished she would be blessed with a quick end to the conversation, but she smiled and nodded intently.

In an instant, Hilde got her wish. Her eyes followed the turn of heads toward the entrance of the room, where none other than Gertrud Scholtz-Klink walked in, flanked by two women in their twenties. Scholtz-Klink led the German Women's League and strode into the room with a confidence—and an outfit—Hilde envied. Sporting her signature crown of double braids, Scholtz-Klink wore a navy-blue dress with an unusual collar: small white rectangular patches of cloth trimmed the neckline, looking almost like a mouthful of gapped teeth. Her features were sharp, serious, like a woman with a clear purpose.

Her assistants both wore matching uniforms, tailored khaki blazers and matching pencil skirts, and did their hair in the same style as the reichsfrauenführerin. The lithe one with flaxen hair noticed Hilde standing in the cluster of older women and approached with a knowing smile. "You're Hilde, aren't you?"

Hilde's expression betrayed her confusion.

"I'm Lotte," she said, leaning toward Hilde and lowering her voice. "Don't look so shocked that I could pick you out of *this* crowd." Lotte took Hilde by the hand and led her away, so they could speak privately. "Obergruppenführer Ziegler told us he was bringing you today. He said that we should hire you. That you're a real Hitler Girl. Is that right?"

*Herr Ziegler mentioned me? He said the Women's League*

*should hire me?* She willed herself to refrain from asking, afraid she would seem like a schoolgirl with a crush.

Lotte must have noticed Hilde's cheeks flush and mercifully changed the subject. "Have you spoken to many of the honorees?"

Hilde nodded her head. "Yes, yes, what an inspiration they are. To bear children for the führer, what an honor." Hilde hesitated. Both women knew that none of the mothers in the room had borne a single child *for* Hitler; he had only been führer for five years.

Hilde debated whether she should clarify this point. On one hand, it was just a thing to say; on the other, she didn't want to seem foolish, thinking that a sixty-year-old woman had conceived a child for Germany's brand-new führer. She reached into the pocket of her *Kletterweste* and slid her nail across the cut she had opened earlier.

"To be clear," Hilde began, suddenly feeling the same confidence she had in the car. "The mothers here today had the foresight to bear children for Hitler." Even that didn't quite make sense, but Lotte smiled politely.

Narrowing her eyes slightly, as though it would help her better assess the young woman, Lotte pressed. "Tell me, Hilde. Would you feel the same way if one of their babies were born defective?" It seemed like an odd question to ask out of the blue. Who would bring up something as unpleasant as defective babies at a social gathering? One thing Hilde knew about Nazis was that they did not engage in idle chatter. If Lotte was asking a question, there was a reason. Thankfully, Hilde knew the correct answer.

"If a child is born defective, then it is not a child for Hitler."

In a flash, an image appeared in Hilde's mind. It was of Ursula, a three-year-old girl who once lived next door to the Kramer family. The child squealed too loudly and could never quite wrap her arms firmly around Hilde's neck when she offered hugs, but the little girl was as sweet as could be; she had the disposition of a puppy. Hilde immediately regretted her callous reply, but the look of approval in Lotte's eyes muted her conscience. She continued. "I'm not without compassion for babies born with flaws, but it is important to consider what these children cost our country as a whole."

Lotte's silence demanded more, so Hilde continued. "Survival of the fittest is the natural order of life," she said, grateful that she had been paying attention in biology class that year. "If a baby bird was born with only one wing, the mother wouldn't make a new one by plucking feathers from her healthy babies. That would only make everyone weaker."

As Hilde drank in the attention, she let the image of Ursula slowly fade away. It was as though Hilde was a passenger in an automobile, looking out from the back window. She watched Ursula getting smaller and smaller, then disappearing entirely. In full focus was the woman standing before her with the double band of braids and steely blue eyes.

An officer tapped the microphone onstage, cutting through the women's chatter.

"Let's continue this discussion later," Lotte said quietly, touching Hilde's hand. "We're hiring another assistant in our office in Berlin. Herr Ziegler says you'd be perfect, so the reichsfrauenführerin asked me to talk to you," she said. "I think you'd make a nice addition to our staff."

Hilde wanted to hold on to her elation but knew that this job was just a pipe dream. "I'm a fast typist, but I've never..." Swallowing her disappointment, she continued. "I have no work experience." Why hadn't she accepted that summer job her father had offered so she could have something—*anything*—to make herself a viable candidate?

Lotte winked at Hilde. "The reichsfrauenführerin considers that an asset. It takes valuable time to help girls unlearn the bad work habits they've picked up in other offices." She smiled. "We prefer a blank slate. I'll ask her to make it official tonight."

Hilde stood still, stunned. "I'm thrilled," she said, unable to contain her excitement. "When do I start?" She was barely able to keep herself from jumping up and down in celebration. "Thank you, thank you so much," she repeated several times.

Hilde noticed the officer onstage asking people to find their seats, so she turned toward the back of the room before catching Lotte's quizzical look.

"Where are you going?" Lotte laughed. "You are a guest of Obergruppenführer Ziegler. We sit in front."

<hr />

Each of the two hundred honorees was awarded a blue-and-white enameled iron cross with a black swastika at its center. Inscribed *To the German Mother*, it hung from a blue-and-white ribbon. Hilde's heart drummed with excitement at the thought of the führer placing a medal around her neck someday. Herr Ziegler told Hilde that from now on when Hitlerjugend and

BDM youth saw a woman wearing a Mutterkreuz, they would be required to stop and salute as reverently as if they were greeting the führer himself. Now that was something.

An elderly mother of *seventeen* children received a diamond-encrusted gold medal and tearful applause. Hilde refrained from rolling her eyes. *There were easier ways to get diamonds.*

At the end of the night, Hilde had a chance to meet Reichsfrauenführerin Scholtz-Klink herself, who formally offered her the job in her Berlin office. "A smart, ambitious girl like you," Scholtz-Klink told Hilde, "could go far in the Reich."

As she left the hall, cheeks aching from hours of forced smiling, Hilde walked with the obergruppenführer through a tide of old women with chests puffed out to better display their new crosses. Hilde pitied them. These women were weary relics of a lesser Germany, while most of Hilde's years would be lived in a modern, progressive Germany, that of the Third Reich.

On the drive home, she kicked off her shoes, her feet blistered from an evening of standing in her mother's fanciest shoes. Herr Ziegler opened a bottle of champagne and offered a glass to Hilde. She took it and relaxed into her seat, watching him pour another for himself. "This has been the best day of my life," Hilde said before draining her glass.

Obergruppenführer Ziegler turned to Hilde, loosened his necktie, then began twisting his wedding band. Turning toward Hilde, he scanned her body and covered his mouth as a small burp escaped. His pine cologne had worn off, and now the scent of sausage and gas permeated the back seat. "Shall I have my driver take you home, or would you like to continue the celebration?"

Hilde had come too far to be distracted by superficial concerns like the smell of a hardworking man. She smiled demurely. "The night is young, Obergruppenführer Ziegler."

"Call me Werner."

# 10

## Irma

After Irma unpacked her bags, Marianne Keitel invited her old friend for tea in her office at Heim Hochland. Sitting at an imposing white desk trimmed with gold flourishes, Marianne looked like Saint Peter at the Pearly Gates. Even Marianne's white nurse's dress looked as though it could double as the gatekeeper's robe.

"You look well, Irma," Marianne said, placing her pen back in its holder. "I'm so pleased you decided to join us."

"Yes, well, thank you," Irma said, looking down, not quite ready to share the reason for her newfound interest in Marianne's invitation.

Marianne switched gears, sounding more like a resort hostess. "Heim Hochland is the party's premiere Lebensborn Society home. Reichsführer Himmler started the program four years ago, and today we have ten maternity homes throughout Germany with plans to expand to new territories soon."

Irma's eyes scanned the framed photographs on the wall, which formed a half circle around Marianne. Herr Hitler's official portrait was at the top, placed over Sister Marianne's head. Smaller photos descended on a curve, like a halo: Hitler receiving flowers from a young girl, a couple admiring a bundled baby, BDM girls in identical sleeveless sport tops standing in a row, Herr Himmler holding his daughter on his lap, the Goebbels family saluting Hitler at their Christmas dinner.

"I've never heard of the Lebensborn Society before," Irma said, taking inventory of the bejeweled enamel egg, Picard gold cups, and marble statuettes on the bookshelf beside Marianne. Although she knew it was irrational, Irma's heart sped with fear that she might break something. Every object in the room felt precious and important.

"Good," Marianne replied with a smile, pulling the chain of the frosted-glass desk lamp that looked like angel's trumpet flowers. "We like it that way, so your discretion is important." Marianne nodded her chin in the direction of Irma's notepad to indicate that her orientation would begin.

"The Lebensborn Society provides the very best maternity care for racially pure girls until their babies are born," Marianne said. "Most expectant mothers at Heim Hochland are unwed, but several are married or engaged to men who are serving in the Wehrmacht away from home."

Perhaps it was just seeing her friend in this new role, but Irma thought Marianne seemed more formal than she had remembered. Irma's eyes darted toward the window as she caught a glint of sunlight hitting a crystal vase shaped like the bulb of a rose, layers of petals opening to make room for water and stems.

Marianne must have noticed Irma taking in the setting. She raised the porcelain teacup on her desk and smiled. "You'll find that our circumstances are far more comfortable here than they were in Potsdam."

"I'll say," Irma replied. Though she had no objection to being surrounded by beautiful things, it was the mission of the Lebensborn Society that appealed to her. Delivering babies. Ushering in life. The only soldiers she would see at Heim Hochland were visitors celebrating impending fatherhood.

Marianne's voice interrupted Irma's thoughts. "Unwed mothers have two choices," she clipped. "They can marry the father, if he's willing, and raise the child. If not, our children are highly adoptable." Marianne refilled Irma's teacup. "We'll show you the nursery later. Two girls delivered babies last week, and they are extraordinary. You'll see the difference right away. Babies with good blood are healthier, stronger, and more alert."

Marianne explained that sometimes, when a child was the product of an extramarital tryst, the baby was adopted by the father and his wife. She lowered her voice and raised her palm to indicate that Irma should stop writing. "Herr Himmler asks that we regard all the girls with equal respect, but it is hard to fathom how depraved one has to be to seduce another woman's husband."

*Amen to that.*

Marianne whispered, "German wives are saints for taking in these babies and raising them as their own." Leaning in closer, she lowered her voice even further. "If any husband of mine had a baby with some *junge Hure*, I'd fix it so he would never be able to father another child with anyone."

Irma couldn't help giggle at her friend's fighting spirit, though she wondered if it might have been a hindrance to

Marianne ever marrying. Quickly, Irma changed the subject. "What do the girls' parents think of all this?"

Marianne waved a hand. "Most don't even know their daughters are pregnant. The party says the girls are doing Land Service or claims there's a training they need to attend, and they come here instead."

Shifting slightly in her seat, Irma wondered whether she was comfortable with what Marianne had explained. Lord knew she wanted to be. She had moved her life to Steinhöring on the promise that it would be better than what she had left behind in Frankfurt.

Irma had one last question. "Some of the girls out front earlier didn't look like they were pregnant. Are they recovering mothers or just very early on?"

Marianne's mouth tightened before she molded it into a smile. "Ah, yes," Marianne continued. "We have twenty-five apprentice mothers living upstairs on the second floor of the house. They're schooled in becoming good wives and mothers. The girls learn how to manage a home, raise children, and tend to their husbands. When a girl comes out of our apprenticeship program, she's considered a much more attractive candidate for marriage. It's a seal of approval for those in the know."

Irma nodded. "I wish I had the chance to come here when I was younger," she said lightly. "My mother was a terrible cook, and every time she darned our socks, they had thick seams on the bottom, so I went into my marriage with no skills."

"Yes," Marianne said, shifting her gaze toward a stack of papers on her desk. "We're making sure our girls will be the best generation of German wives and mothers yet." Marianne set her hands on the table and stood, an indication that their meeting had come to an end. "I know you'll be very gratified by the work we do here at Heim Hochland," she finished with a smile, then rang a small bell on her desk.

Moments later, an older nurse with a stony face appeared in the doorway. "Yes, Sister Marianne."

Marianne pointed toward Irma. "Sister Dorothea, this is Sister Irma. She will be joining us at Heim Hochland. Please show her to the nursery so she can have a look at our beautiful babies. Then introduce her to the girls."

<hr />

Irma woke at sunrise to the sound of birds nervously fluttering away from a small tree outside her window. Slowly regaining a sense of where she was, she realized that she was sitting straight up in bed, throat scratched from her own shriek that awakened her. Had anyone in the house heard her? She placed her hand on her chest to calm her racing heart, regretting that she had frightened the birds. At the same time, she couldn't take her eyes off them, envying the ease with which they flew off.

The night before, Irma had spent hours deliberating whether to stay at Heim Hochland before realizing that she had nothing to return to in Frankfurt. Frau Haarmacher had been eager to rent out her room at the boardinghouse. Two other secretaries at the Rheinhold Brothers' architecture office had thrown her a going-away party, complete with cake and champagne, and her job had been filled within days. She had always taken pride in her role in the building of a new Germany, but after she gave her notice, Irma soon realized that the Rheinholds thought of her as just another typist. With a shudder, Irma remembered how old and obsolete she had felt in the week she had spent training her replacement, watching her supervisor's eyes follow the bright young thing around the office. And, of course, there was the whole mortifying situation with Eduard. People would surely be buzzing about that. The girls in her boardinghouse would bask in Irma's failure. To be fair, Irma conceded, how could they not take some delight in her embarrassment after the way she had treated them?

Pulling back the gold brocade curtains, Irma watched the morning sky brighten in Steinhöring. She rested her chin on the windowsill and looked out to a large meadow with dewy grass that led to a pond in the distance. She smiled at the sight of colorful chaffinches digging into the soil for worms. She slumped back onto her feather pillow, pulled her quilt up to her chin, and resolved to make the best of her lot. She promised herself that she would focus only on what was positive about working at Heim Hochland. Like her room at Frau Haarmacher's house, Irma's walls were bare, but her window here was like a landscape painting that came to life like a picture show in Technicolor. This was a big improvement from her view of an alley and her neighbor's brick wall in Frankfurt. Heim Hochland furnished Irma's room with an oak armoire with an inlay of a bucolic village. She would have preferred something less frivolous, but it was large enough that she could fit all her belongings inside. She could close the doors and never have to look at clutter of any sort.

The best part of Heim Hochland, though, was that she was there to help bring new life into Germany while supporting selfless young mothers. There was honor and dignity in that.

After Irma's first week, she had to admit that Heim Hochland was growing on her. Her job was fairly simple: care for the eight pregnant girls who lived on the first floor. She would have to assist with childbirth eventually—from the looks of it, Hannah's delivery would be in about a month—but her other duties were relatively easy. Irma charted blood pressure daily. She monitored the girls' diets to ensure they were eating Herr Himmler's recommended daily portions of fruits and vegetables. And, most importantly, according to Marianne, Irma was to be a calming presence, there to answer questions and reassure the girls that their mission was noble and sacred. "The most contagious illness in a Lebensborn home is cold feet," Marianne had warned. "If you even suspect that one of the unwed girls is getting too attached to a baby, it's your job to step in as a caring friend, a *Tante*, and remind them that they must remain strong. Our adoption contract is binding, so it's best if we avoid any dramatic episodes."

Irma felt conflicted, but her concerns quickly evaporated. None of the unmarried pregnant girls seemed to have any misgivings about signing away their maternal rights. They had all agreed that their babies belonged to the Reich.

While Irma prided herself on her pragmatism, this system felt awfully transactional. Yet as she glanced toward the window, she recalled how happy the apprentice mothers looked fencing in the sunshine earlier that day. Despite the fact that their faces were shielded by screen masks, Irma saw their bright smiles.

She could hear their laughter and playful ribbing, even when a girl named Renate came on too aggressively. A blond girl had stepped back and lifted her mask to the top of her head. "You're not actually *trying* to kill us, Renate," the girl had said, pressing her free hand against the swastika emblem on her sport top. Irma smiled at the memory and told herself that the National Socialists might be onto something. The German birth rate had been declining for years, and this was a solution. If everyone understood the agreement, why *not* help girls who had gotten themselves into trouble? And why not also offer training for the next generation of German wives and mothers?

⚊•⚊

"Sister Marianne told me that Herr Himmler himself might adopt *my* baby," said sixteen-year-old Hannah, pouring herself a glass of water at the dinner table. If Marianne hadn't told Irma the ages of the girls, she would have pegged Hannah for a twelve-year-old, not just because she was so tiny, but her chubby face always bore the expression of a child in wonderment over soap bubbles or a giraffe at the zoo.

Mila, who appeared older than her seventeen years, large breasted and wide hipped, leaned in on her elbows. Sweeping a loose chestnut wave of hair back into her headband, she piped in, "Can you imagine the lives of luxury these children will live?" Others like Agnes and Edith seemed more focused on their duty to the Fatherland, militantly repeating what a privilege it was to have a baby for the führer. The other four, whom Sister Marianne privately referred to as her "good girls," were engaged to the fathers of their babies. When their *Schätze* were stationed close by or on leave from the Wehrmacht, they could visit and could marry the girls in Steinhöring. After childbirth, the young women had the option to stay at Heim Hochland or return home.

Irma first met nineteen-year-old Gisela as she approached the door to the back patio where the girl was sketching. Irma only saw her from behind, her hands stroking a brown pencil across paper in a small notebook. The girl drew a disturbing portrayal of skylarks, not in a tree but as the bark itself. There were dozens of birds toppled on one another, flattened against the cylinder of the trunk. Irma held her hands over her mouth so the girl wouldn't hear her repulsion at the sight. Focusing on the likeness of the birds—the girl clearly had talent—Irma decided to offer positive feedback. "I've always thought their wings looked like wood too."

When Gisela turned her head and looked up at Irma standing above her, the nurse couldn't catch herself quickly enough. She stepped back and almost lost her footing. Gisela had strikingly similar features to her beloved Helmut when they had first met at *Gymnasium* a lifetime ago. Everything from his wide face to his chin dimple, even the way his bright green eyes shot open with surprise, was mirrored in Gisela. Irma couldn't help wonder if this was what a daughter of theirs would have grown to look like. She found the resemblance unsettling at first. Within a few days, though, it was oddly comforting.

Gisela was a sweet but dull-witted teenager who had questions for Irma almost every day. *How badly did childbirth hurt? How quickly could she resume her relationship with her future husband, Otto? Was it true that sometimes girls pooped during delivery?*

Normally, Irma was irritated by rapid-fire questions, feeling like people were unloading their fears onto her. She imagined herself running from left to right trying to catch bricks being tossed her way. Internally, she shouted, *Give me a moment! Let me regain my balance!* But when the cherubic blond asked for help, it was as if she reached straight into Irma's heart and grabbed hold of it. Perhaps it was her likeness to Helmut, giving Irma a fleeting sense that she was living in a parallel universe where her husband had survived the war and her pregnancy had grown to term. She wondered if Helmut had ever even received her letter telling him she was expecting. *And now our little Gisela is to become a mother herself,* Irma imagined herself telling him. She tried on the words for size like a dress she admired in a shop window.

———

The slow pace at Heim Hochland afforded Irma the time for meditative walks around the estate each afternoon. Behind the main house was an expansive field with an endless supply of plump bilberries and vibrant wild mallow flowers that Irma picked for the cook to make into jams and bouquets. In exchange, she brought leftover baked goods for the birds. Ducks waddled fearlessly toward Irma as she sat on her knees in the grass. Geese seemed to demand larger pieces of bread as they honked at Irma, while a smattering of sparrows and finches flitted about skittishly between the larger birds, taking whatever crumbs they could grab quickly.

Beyond the lake, at the far end of a cluster of rapeseed

blossoms, was the entry to a forest that Irma began to think of as the edge of the earth. Heim Hochland was nestled away safely, protected from the world outside. Here, there were no riots in the streets. At the maternity home, no one spoke of the possibility of war.

As Irma walked back to the house, she looked into the round window in the door to the kitchen, her favorite place at Heim Hochland. Once, Irma passed by at the very moment a neat row of perfect oval loaves emerged from the oven. She quickly started making a habit of standing in the doorway of the kitchen so she could watch the cooks birth their master-pieces, from glazed breads to rich pastries to elaborate desserts. The buttery scent of the crust of a plum tart was a balm. She was nearly hypnotized by the sight of a thin line of sugar frosting drizzling across a fresh braid of marzipan stollen.

Irma also rose early to observe the choreography involved in putting together breakfast for nearly forty people. She saw the backs of two female cooks as they fluidly peeled and chopped the colorful array of fresh vegetables and fruits. Another kitchen worker moved her whole body back and forth as she stirred a vat of hot porridge on the stovetop. Meanwhile, a young woman stood on tiptoe and leaned toward the door of the prodigious oven to retrieve trays of fresh-baked berry *Brötchen*.

Irma found herself enjoying the babies in the nursery as well. Technically, it wasn't her responsibility to care for the newborns; Sister Dorothea was the head of infant care. But Irma had convinced Hannah and Gisela that the three of them should visit the little ones to help the girls feel more comfort-able with their upcoming deliveries. As long as she could frame it as a lesson for the expectant mothers, Irma—who also needed to learn diapering and swaddling—could practice without undermining anyone's confidence in her.

⌁

Settling into her role, Irma bounced a baby boy, Bernhard, in her arms, then handed him to Hannah once he had quieted. The girl held him awkwardly, at arm's length, as though he were a delicate glass ornament that might break if she breathed too hard. Gisela gently touched baby Bernhard's back and eased him closer toward her friend's chest. Irma turned in the direction of the three apprentice mothers gathered by the window, nowhere even close to the babies, and raised an accusing brow at the trio. "Fräulein," she said, clearly addressing the leader, Renate. "It would be wise to focus on learning to care for your future babies."

On other occasions, Irma heard their boppy music and dancing shoes upstairs. But when it came time to learn about motherhood, they dragged their feet. They knew how to put on a show when Marianne was in the nursery, though. Then they fussed over how soft and sweet the babies were, how their little toes looked like corn kernels on the cob. Once Marianne left, the girls started gossiping about the world outside: new music, picture shows, and dreamy boys.

"We're not even pregnant yet, Sister Irma," Ingrid said with a squeaky voice.

Renate placed a hand on her hip and replied with a world-weariness that came from having to explain the simplest truths over and over. "It's more important to attract a good husband. Then we'll have servants to take care of our babies."

Irma strode to the girls and fixed her stare on Renate. "The three of you are extremely fortunate to be here at Heim Hochland, and very little is asked of you in return. And I'm certain that Sister Marianne would be very disappointed to hear about the way you are shirking your responsibilities." The girls were visibly rattled. Even Renate cast her eyes down, emboldening Irma to press further. "What's more, Bernhard here has a soiled diaper, and I think that Renate needs to get herself to the changing station and take care of it." She wasn't quite sure what she would have done if they had dismissed her, but to Irma's great relief, the girls widened their eyes and nodded obediently.

Even Renate looked worried that she had angered Irma and hurried to her side. "All right, Sister Irma. We're sorry," she said.

Turning to include Hannah and Gisela, Irma spoke with growing confidence. "Girls, I want you to be strong, capable mothers. But that takes work, even when we don't feel like it." The pregnant young women seemed to be drinking in Irma's wise words. Irma smiled internally. She never had the chance to be a mother to her own child. But this was the next best thing.

# 11

## *Irma*

F OR TONIGHT'S PARTY, WE SERVE AS SOCIAL FACILITATORS,"
Marianne explained to Irma, fanning herself with a folded
sheet of paper. "Job number one is making sure the officers
enjoy their conversations with the girls." Marianne looked up
and gestured toward the pencil on her desk. *Take notes, dear.*

"If the officers look bored or indifferent, we very deli-
cately remove the young ladies and introduce them to officers who might enjoy their company. These girls don't have
the experience to realize when they've lost a man's interest,"
Marianne explained, tapping her finger on the desk. "We
hope they've mastered social skills and manners in their
coursework, but sometimes the chemistry just isn't there, so
we'll step in."

Tonight would be the largest garden party Heim Hochland
had hosted in the month Irma had been a nurse at the maternity home. Thirty-five officers would enjoy a meal and social-
ize with residents after their conference in Munich about
Germany's new communications regulations, and everything
needed to run smoothly. Better than smoothly. Perfectly.

Marianne folded her hands as she normally did, but today
she was rubbing her thumbs together nervously. "Irma, I am

asking as a friend," she said. "This evening has to be the most marvelous party the officers have ever attended."

"How could it possibly be anything less?" Irma asked. "Who wouldn't enjoy a night of socializing with pretty young women who admire them?"

Marianne let out a sniff of a laugh. "Anytime you have more than three girls in a room together, expect trouble of some sort. A houseful is a guarantee that something will go wrong." She explained to Irma that at the last party, one of the girls had stolen an officer's wristwatch. Irma knit her brows in confusion, so Marianne tried to fill in the story. "She wanted to try it on, and he must have forgotten to ask her to return it."

Irma was even more baffled. Why hadn't the officer simply asked for his watch when he realized the girl still had it, even if it was days later? And why would a young woman ask to try on a man's watch? The scenario seemed implausible at best.

Responding to Irma's crumpled facial expression, Marianne waved a hand dismissively. "I don't remember exactly what happened. Maybe he left it somewhere and it was gone when he went to retrieve it. You know how that goes."

No. Irma had absolutely no idea how that could happen. She couldn't think of a single time when she had taken off her wristwatch, or any piece of jewelry for that matter, at a social gathering.

Her thoughts were interrupted by Marianne's voice. "In any case, the only thing I want the officers talking about when they leave is the splendid time they had at Heim Hochland. A lot of women would be happy to work at a Lebensborn home, and Herr Himmler likes to keep me sharp by reminding me that other nursing posts aren't as luxurious."

Back in her room, Irma heard a light, almost inaudible knock on her door. It was three girls from upstairs: Renate, Ingrid, and Marie, wearing their sport uniforms. Two had their hair wrapped in towel turbans, and the other held a silver hairbrush. "Sorry to bother you, Sister Irma," said Ingrid, her slight frame making her look like a child. "Sister Dorothea was going to help us with our hair, but now she's nowhere to be found."

After a moment's hesitation, exchanging reluctant glances with one another, they began asking if she knew how to do popular hairstyles. Ingrid wanted a golden halo with big loops to frame her willowy features. Renate begged for thick celebrity waves, which reportedly had taken Jean Harlow's hairstylist two hours to set. And Marie, the sole brunette of the trio, wanted short finger waves that would accentuate her blunt bangs.

"We…we've been practicing our mothering skills too, Sister Irma," Ingrid added quickly. "It's just that tonight, we need to look pretty."

Irma agreed and began walking upstairs with the girls, surprised by how much she welcomed this invitation.

The excitement was as thick as the perfume that filled the second-story common room. Girls buzzed past one another holding dresses up to themselves for feedback. Giggling and chattering, they exchanged thoughts in shorthand. *Too sexy. Not sexy enough. Too French. Just right.*

Irma took in the posters on the walls extolling the virtues

of German motherhood. They were much like the ones she and Eduard had seen plastered to the sides of buildings in Berlin, but a new one caught her eye. Hanging between two vanity tables was a black-and-white poster with no image, just the Nazi slogan in bold print: *Blut und Boden*, blood and soil. It served as a reminder of what was most important: the German blood that ran through their veins and the fertile land the Reich needed to prosper.

As Ingrid sat under the dome of the dryer, flipping through a magazine, Irma instructed her to stay put. "Your hair is half dried. I'll start on Renate while you wait." She positioned her-self behind Renate at the vanity table and gently brushed out her long blond hair, holding it at the roots so she wouldn't feel the tug of the comb. Irma caught Renate's eye in the mirror and asked, "Do the girls from downstairs ever prepare for parties with you?"

Renate looked at the reflection of Irma behind her and scrunched her mouth in confusion. "Why would they come to the parties?"

Irma began to comb Renate's hair, creating sections and wrapping them in metal curlers. "Just because a woman is pregnant doesn't mean she can no longer hold a conversation."

Flying past the mirror was Marie, who hadn't missed a word of the exchange. "I'm next," she reminded her. "And, Sister Irma, that's not how it works. Officers visit with us to relax and enjoy themselves, not stare at a big fat belly."

Just as she was ready to correct the girls, Irma was inter-rupted by Renate, who reached into her dressing gown pocket and retrieved a velvet box. "Do you think this necklace is too big for me?" she asked, opening the case with a cameo silhouette choker hanging from twisted strands of pearls. Noticing Irma's eyes widen, Renate replied with a coy, satisfied smile. "A gift," she said.

The three erupted into laughter, an inside joke that left Irma feeling like the odd one out. Back in Frankfurt, she wanted nothing to do with the women at the boardinghouse. Now, the exclusion was an icy stab.

Ingrid caught Irma's hurt look and brought her into the fold. "That's the best part of these parties," she shared, checking her reflection in a hand mirror. "The officers bring all sorts of gifts for us. Last year, a girl got a mink coat!"

Irma's hands froze as she was rolling Renate's hair into a curler. *If the girls are being given fur coats and jewels, why would they risk their place at Heim Hochland by stealing an officer's watch?*

Making a smug little huff, Renate corrected her friend. "I for one don't think the presents are the best part of the parties. For me, it's the free sex." She winked at Ingrid and Marie, who quickly agreed that yes, the sex was the best part. They were modern young women, after all.

Ingrid leaned forward to grab her friend's brooch from the vanity table and purposely pricked her fingertip, pressing out droplets of blood to dab on her cheeks.

Renate smiled mischievously, her head now covered in rollers. "Sister Irma, you won't tell the führer that we make our own rouge here, will you?" Holding up her fingertip, offering it to Ingrid, Renate winked. "You know the saying. *Blut und Hoden.*"

Blood and *balls*. Working to maintain her composure at the crass joke, Irma forced a stiff smile.

The fact that the girls were defying the Nazi Party prohibition on makeup was the least of Irma's concerns. Marianne had lied to her. The upstairs girls weren't apprentice mothers; they were at Heim Hochland to have sex with Reich officers. She shuddered, realizing what this made her. More importantly, what was it doing to the girls?

# 12

## *Irma*

IRMA WOKE UP TO THE SOUND OF SISTER DOROTHEA knocking on her door. "Wake up, Irma," she said with urgency. "Hannah is in labor. Get to the birthing room as soon as you can."

Irma squinted in the darkness, trying to distinguish the hour and minute hands on her clock. Her eyes felt the sting of light when she turned on her lamp. It was 3:00 a.m., and she had a baby to deliver. Irma splashed a handful of cold water on her face and prayed she was up to the challenge.

This was it. Heart drumming inside her chest as she hurried to the labor room, Irma reminded herself that this was the most important part of her job: safely ushering babies into the world. If there was an emergency—a breech position or a wayward umbilical cord—the consequences could be dire. Irma had thoroughly reviewed the birthing manual Marianne gave her—and the two had run a series of practice drills—but this was the first actual labor of her Heim Hochland tenure.

There, Hannah lifted her head from her pillows and smiled at the sight of Irma, though her breathing was ragged and her face scrunched in pain. "Get me some cool rags," Marianne demanded of Irma as she entered the room.

Sister Dorothea stood at the foot of the bed, her eyes never leaving her patient. She patted Hannah's knees. "This baby will come much easier than the last."

*The last? This wasn't Hannah's first pregnancy?*

Hannah lifted her body so she was resting back on her elbows. "It still hurts," she squealed.

For a moment, Irma thought to offer her a stuffed bear as comfort, like she would a child sick with a stomachache. Instead she returned with a cool rag and placed it on Hannah's flushed cheeks.

"I know it does, dear," Marianne offered. "You are a strong girl, and you can handle this." Looking up toward Irma, she continued. "We're going to get ready to push."

The delicate girl gripped Irma's arm with unexpected strength. Irma reassured Hannah that all was well. "You're doing beautifully. Take some nice deep breaths with me, all right? Let's breathe in and—"

"*Mein Gott!*" Hannah cried, then let out a guttural howl. "It wasn't this bad before!"

Sister Marianne lifted her head from the foot of the bed and snapped, "Keep breathing with Sister Irma!"

Irma reached for Hannah's face and turned it toward her so the two locked eyes. "Look at me and only me, Hannah," Irma said in a voice as gentle as small waves lapping the shore of a lake. Hannah nodded, tears filling her eyes. "Now take a deep breath in, and let it fill your lungs before you let it out in short puffs like this," Irma said, imitating the exhalations. The birthing manual advised nurses to encourage mothers to regulate their breathing to help the body relax and let nature take its course.

Hannah's lips fluttered as she went through the exercise with Irma, but she pressed on. Just as Sister Dorothea had promised, Hannah's delivery was a fast one. The baby's tiny head emerged, topped with a swirl of pale downy hair. Soon, delicate shoulders pushed out of the birth canal, one by one, like a passenger shoving his way off a crowded tram. Marianne gently pulled the baby out.

"A boy!" Irma called out to Hannah, who smiled, exhausted but elated.

Marianne nodded her head toward the scissors on the instrument table, which Irma grabbed and brought to the delivery bed. "Go ahead," Marianne instructed, pointing at the tether between mother and child.

The metal ring handles pressed against Irma's fingers as she closed the blades. She had never thought about the texture of an umbilical cord before but soon felt resistance from the ropy blue flesh.

Sister Dorothea took the infant to the basin and invited Irma to join while Marianne congratulated Hannah. "What a strong girl you are," Marianne said, brushing back wisps of Hannah's hair, identical in color to that of her baby.

Irma and Dorothea rinsed the newborn with soapy water and stretched the baby's folded legs from the fetal position. The boy opened his eyes for a moment, then scrunched them shut again. Sister Dorothea wrapped him in a soft white towel and took him to the changing table to diaper and swaddle. As Sister Dorothea brought the baby to Hannah to supervise feeding, Marianne removed her hat and slumped in a chair by the bed. Her perfectly set gray hair was now dampened by sweat, and the top buttons of her dress were undone. At the sight of Irma, she straightened her posture. "Exhilarating, isn't it?"

"Yes. I only wish we could tell the babies that we prefer afternoon deliveries."

Marianne laughed. "Wouldn't that be nice?"

Irma jolted when she took note of the time. She could have sworn the delivery had lasted half an hour, but according to the clock on the wall, it had been three. Her heart rate was just starting to slow and fatigue beginning to set in. She was tired but felt more alive than she had been in a long time. Maybe ever.

Her reverie was interrupted by Marianne getting back to business. "Hannah will nurse the baby for two weeks before she returns home to her parents and finishes *Gymnasium*." Marianne paused and lowered her voice. "Provided she can keep her legs closed for the next two years," she whispered with a laugh. She stood and led Irma to her office. During the short walk, Marianne spoke softly, careful not to wake any of the pregnant girls along the east corridor. "Once Hannah leaves us, we'll host the baby's naming ceremony with his new family. It's part of your job to make sure this goes smoothly. Continue reminding Hannah how much we admire her selflessness and patriotism."

<hr>

Two nights later, just as she was heading to bed, Irma heard a faint knock on her bedroom door. Heim Hochland wasn't due for another baby for weeks, and none of the staff ever came by her room to say good night.

"Sister Irma, it's me," she heard a voice whisper. "Gisela."

She opened the door. "Is something wrong?"

"No. I'm sorry to frighten you," Gisela said with a sweet pout. "I can't sleep. I just wondered if I could stay with you tonight."

It had been more than twenty years since Irma had lost her baby, doubling over in the ward at Potsdam, just moments after she had watched a patient swallow down his pills. Until she had met Gisela, Irma forbade herself from thinking about what her child would have looked like if she had made it. Irma had never let herself imagine birthdays or mourn the first days of kindergarten and zoo visits that never happened. She had convinced herself that it was best to look forward, but as Irma's eyes trained on Gisela standing in her doorway, she realized it wasn't that simple. Her loss was compounded by guilt. Irma's doctor had warned her that her high blood pressure warranted bed rest in her third trimester of pregnancy. But she had been swept away by a combination of patriotic duty and youthful arrogance and convinced herself she was immune to harm. Her country needed her, but Irma hadn't stopped to think that her baby needed her more. It was as though her daughter understood Irma's choice and abandoned her with the knowledge that her mother would never care for her the way she deserved.

"Is that all right?" Gisela asked, returning Irma to the present.

"Yes, *Mädel*. Come on in."

*So this is what it would be like*, Irma allowed herself to think. *When your little one knocks on your door in tears saying she had a nightmare or needs Mutti to snuggle.*

Irma bargained. Just this once, she would let her mind drift into maternal fantasy. She pulled back the blankets from her bed and invited Gisela in. It wasn't as easy as she had hoped, Gisela shifting about to find a position that was comfortable but allowed her to stay physically connected to Irma. They lay on their backs and held hands for a few minutes before Gisela tossed her ankle over Irma's. After moving about the small bed, the two finally found a position that worked. Irma spooned Gisela and placed her hands on her rotund belly. When she felt how cold the girl's feet were, Irma placed them between her calves like a flatiron.

A half hour later, Irma could tell Gisela had not fallen asleep yet. The girl continued fidgeting, and her breathing hadn't relaxed. Irma realized that it wasn't merely Gisela's physical discomfort that was causing the restlessness. "What's troubling you, dear?"

Without hesitation, Gisela asked Irma if babies could remember their mothers. "I mean, I know my baby will have a new mother, but will he forget me completely? Will he even know I exist?"

The words wrapped themselves around Irma's throat. "I think..." She hesitated. "I think your baby's heart will always remember you."

"Thank you, Sister Irma," Gisela said, yawning. "That's what I think too."

Irma had serious misgivings about how these young women were being used, but her love for the girls was absolute. Marianne would argue that every young woman in the Lebensborn Society had volunteered to be there, but Irma knew better. For the past six years, these girls had heard that they should happily sacrifice anything in order to bring glory to the Reich. Could a sixteen-year-old girl really agree to have sexual relations with a fifty-year-old man? Part of Irma desperately wanted to pack her bag and leave this terrible place. The bigger part knew that she needed to stay for the girls.

Gisela soon drifted off to sleep, but Irma remained wide awake.

# 13

## *Hilde*

*Munich*

**H**ILDE WALKED THROUGH THE FRONT DOOR OF A LOCAL inn as Herr Ziegler held it open for her. She tried to emulate Jutta's fluid, feminine stride as she headed into the four-table dining room but quickly felt a hand on the small of her back. Turning around, she found Herr Ziegler nodding his chin toward the small stairwell to their left.

She forced a smile, disappointed that she would not be dining at one of the intimately lit tables covered with cozy plaid linens. Hilde wouldn't get to sit beneath the hazy glow of the hanging caged light bulbs, casually sharing a meal with one of Germany's most powerful men.

Noticing Hilde's eyes linger on the tables, Herr Ziegler gave her a slight tap on the bottom and winked. "We'll come downstairs later and order whatever you'd like to eat. I promise."

*That is fine*, Hilde told herself. *Better than fine, really. Something more important is happening.* Herr Ziegler wanted her undivided attention. And she was certain that he wanted to be intimate with her. Every boy who had overlooked Hilde over the years had been wrong. Dead wrong. A real man could see that Hilde Kramer was, in fact, desirable.

Before she met Herr Ziegler, Hilde had never considered having a relationship with an older man, much less one more than twice her age. Now, cementing Herr Ziegler's interest was all Hilde could think about. Really, it made perfect sense. Hilde had always been mature for her age, so of course boys would find her intimidating. Plus, Mama always said that the surest way to a man's heart was through his ego and that flattery was a woman's greatest feminine wile. What had eighteen-year-old boys done to earn her adulation? Was she supposed to compliment them on their classroom performance? The way they played marbles? No, Hilde needed a real man. Herr Ziegler's interest was more than vindication for past slights like her classmate Rudolf Fritz; being desired by him whet her appetite, and now she was ready for a gluttonous feast.

Ascending each of the wooden steps, a smile spread across her face. How special she was to have been chosen by the obergruppenführer.

She followed Herr Ziegler's footsteps as they walked down a hallway wallpapered with a jacquard floral print of ivory and rose. She stopped briefly to examine one of the framed portraits on the wall, a painting of a stern-looking soldier with an upturned mustache like the kaiser had once worn. Herr Ziegler placed his hand on Hilde's lower back, coaxing her along. *Really, who cares?* Hilde told herself. *I'm not here to learn about the history of the inn.* He turned the doorknob of an unlocked room and gestured for Hilde to go inside. She felt her heart drum in her chest.

Once inside, Ziegler announced plainly, "You need to bathe." His words sounded official, as though it was decreed that all sexual relations began with a bath. Hilde nearly giggled to mitigate the effect of his formal delivery. A moment later, though, she felt the familiar weight of shame. She looked down at her shoes, determined to hide her glazing eyes from Herr Ziegler. *Does he think I'm dirty?*

When Hilde saw the private bathroom, however, she scoffed at her resistance to bathing. The obergruppenführer simply wanted her to enjoy the luxurious setting. A mammoth tub rested on brass claws, fluffy white towels draped over the side. Submerged in the warm water, Hilde picked up one of the small, pink, rose-shaped figurines set in a porcelain dish. Placing it close to her nose, she smelled it. Smiling at the revelation that it was soap, Hilde submerged the rose underwater, then rubbed it between her palms. As bubbles formed, Hilde lathered her shoulders and arms, then extended a leg from the water like a film star. She was Marlene Dietrich in *The Blue Angel.*

She emerged from her bath baptized, ready for whatever awaited her on the other side of the door. After drying herself, Hilde put on the coral silk robe that hung on a brass hook. She swatted away a flash of embarrassment when she realized that Obergruppenführer Ziegler must have arranged to have it waiting for her. Hilde smiled as she squeezed her arms into the tight sleeves and tugged to close the front, flattered that Herr Ziegler assumed she was smaller than her actual size.

Hilde needed him to understand that she wasn't looking for a one-time dalliance. She wanted to be his mistress and

everything that came with it—fancy dinners, lingering conversation, expensive gifts.

Realizing that she had a bit of power in her ability to with-
hold sex, Hilde made her way to the chair at the small wooden
desk where Herr Ziegler was penciling some notes on a slip of
paper. "The event was a great success, don't you think?"

He did not respond. *Perhaps he didn't hear me?*

Hilde raised her voice a touch. "I was very proud to be your
guest at the event. The mothers seemed pleased."

Obergruppenführer Ziegler was lost in his thoughts, which
was understandable. His distraction was a small price to pay. He
was an important man, after all. Still, she wanted her first time
to feel special, so she tried again.

Herr Ziegler walked toward the window and closed the
curtains. As his hands let loose the curtain ties, Hilde bit her
lip, pushing back her complaint that the curtains were receiving
a more thorough seduction than she was.

"What are you thinking about?"

Herr Ziegler walked toward Hilde and placed his wristwatch
onto the desk. Leaning down, he kissed her forehead. "My sweet
Hilde, I have been talking all day long." He placed another peck
on her nose. "From you, I desperately need the quiet refuge of
your body." He kissed her again, this time on the mouth.

Hilde felt a sense of urgency, understanding that she would
need more than sex to maintain her connection with Herr
Ziegler. Lots of women could give him that. She would need
to produce something special to create an unbreakable bond
between them. Hilde needed to please him physically—and
have his baby.

— · —

Before he entered Hilde, Herr Ziegler licked his fingers and used his saliva to lubricate her. He slipped a finger into her and moved it around for a few seconds. "That's more like it," he said, sliding his fingers out, then grasping himself. Jutta had not prepared Hilde for that. She also hadn't warned her about the absurd noises Herr Ziegler made when he submerged himself fully in her body.

Was it odd that Hilde thought about Jutta the entire time Herr Ziegler—*call me Werner*—was inside her? She wasn't having sexual feelings but vivid flashbacks to their discussions about physical intimacy. *Thrust your hips and move as he does*, Jutta had once advised her. *A man likes to feel that you desire him almost as much as he wants you.* The first few thrusts did sting, as Jutta had warned, but Hilde got used to it quickly.

She lifted her head from the pillow, concerned when Werner sounded as though he was straining to lift a heavy object—or constipated. "Are you all right?"

"*Shh*," Werner returned, not unkindly. "That's it," he said before another series of grunts. "You're a good girl, Hilde." She looked up at his face, tight like a fist, and decided she wouldn't thank him just then. He needed to focus. She raised her hips to meet Werner's thrusts. He responded by telling her that she was a naughty girl. "You like me inside you, don't you?"

"Very much," Hilde said, silently chiding herself for such a formal response. Jutta had done a far better job preparing her for dinner with Werner than sex with him. *Does he want me to talk or be quiet? Does he want a good girl or a naughty one?* And most perplexing of all, *Didn't Jutta say sex would bring me a wave of pleasure?*

Hilde decided she would follow Werner's lead and grunted, though a bit more softly than her lover. It was one thing for a man to sound like an animal but an entirely different one for a lady. She wasn't quite sure about the etiquette of coital conversation but decided to take a chance and continued Werner's thread. Cautiously, she whispered, "Do you like being inside me?"

He shushed her again, then began pushing into her faster and more aggressively. The pounding was so hard, it moved her body up the length of the bed until she hit the wooden headboard. If she cocked her head to the side a bit, she found that her neck served as a shock absorber. Soon, though, her muscles balled with tension, a painful but merciful distraction from the bruising her *Muschi* was taking.

Werner then let out a low howl that sounded more painful than pleasurable. His body began to convulse in tempo with his voice, now a soft, rhythmic growl. Soon, he collapsed his full weight onto Hilde, his moist skin dampening hers. Minutes later, Hilde was alone in bed, listening to Werner hum under a rush of water. She wondered if he was using the rose soap, if he would think her childish for taking it as a memento when they left in the morning.

———

Hilde could not believe how quickly Werner fell asleep when he returned to their bed. She considered placing a call to her mother to let her know she wouldn't be coming home before realizing it wasn't necessary. Johanna was hardly the type to stay up late worrying about Hilde. A tangle of white sheets lay between them, and Hilde reached to touch Werner's shoulder as he slept. Her stomach growled with hunger as her eyes darted around the room for something to satisfy her till morning. Would Werner feel insulted if he woke up and found that Hilde had tiptoed downstairs to the dining room? Would he consider the move indiscreet in light of his marital status? Hilde decided she could stave off hunger for the promise of something more fulfilling, a brighter future.

Watching Werner's hairy chest rise and fall as he breathed, Hilde decided she would not share with Jutta how a man of nearly forty had distinctly spongier skin than people her age. But if the price of being with a powerful man was sinking one's fingers into loose skin, then so be it. She was a woman of substance who understood that the most important thing about a man was the kind of life he could provide for her. Remembering how he commanded the attention and respect of everyone at the Mutterkreuz ceremony made Hilde's heartbeat quicken. Here was a man changing the face of Germany. Thanks to Werner and a handful of others, Germany's next generation would know nothing but health and prosperity for a thousand years. He could have any girl he wanted, and he chose her. Now she just had to hold on to him. Rolling onto her back, Hilde lifted her knees toward the ceiling and prayed for a child.

# 14

## *Hilde*

I T HAD ONLY BEEN TWO MONTHS SINCE HILDE HAD FIRST met Werner, but he had changed her life entirely. Working at the reichsfrauenführerin's office, she was more than just a girl who believed in the Nazi cause; like Scholtz-Klink, she was a woman with a clear and important purpose in the world.

Hilde was invigorated by her work at one of the vibrant centers of the Reich, with its headquarters in a villa across the street from the Tiergarten. Her walnut desk faced an enormous window with a perfect view of the lush, green park. Women with smart floral dresses and straw hats, their children armed with ice cream cones and cloth dolls, passed Hilde's office on their way from the zoo. Party officers strode past her window, eyes forward with admirable focus.

The sounds from Lotte's typewriter were musical: the tap of the keys, the ring of the bell at the line break, the buzz of paper pulled from the spool. As Hilde answered the office telephone, the small staff of women chirped about an upcoming event to honor female guards who had just completed their training at

Ravensbrück, the new prison camp for women. Hilde held the heavy black phone receiver as the operator connected the commandant's secretary, confirming his arrival time at the celebration. She closed her eyes for a moment, enjoying the symphony of it all.

Her coworker Wilma placed a thin stack of papers on Hilde's desk. "Can you give this a fresh read?" she asked. "It's the reichsfrauenführerin's article for *Frauen Warte*. I've read it so many times, I wouldn't notice if her name was misspelled at this point."

"Of course." Hilde tried to sound casual, but she was elated to be privy to the words of the leader of the Women's League before everyone else in Germany could read them. She took great care with the onionskin pages, setting them on her desk and switching on her lamp.

The article was about volunteering for the party's charity projects while maintaining commitments at home. The piece awkwardly mentioned a billion-reichsmark fine imposed on the Jews to cover property damage on Kristallnacht. "Even after we collect from the Jews, there is much work to be done building a new Germany. That work needs dedicated volunteers like you!"

Hilde looked up from the paper and furrowed her brows. "Lotte?" she whispered across the room. "The Jews were *charged* for Kristallnacht?"

Lotte peered over her black glasses and rested her chin on her clasped hands. "I keep telling Wilma that part doesn't belong in the article, but the reichsfrauenführerin insists that we keep it. She says we need to discuss the fine as often as possible." Noticing the reichsfrauenführerin was behind her closed door, Lotte walked over to Hilde's desk and sat on the edge. She whispered, "Some people feel like the riots and arrests were punishment enough for the Jews. So we need to repeat our rationale until people get it. Kristallnacht cost Germany a great deal of money to clean up. And there's no price tag on the life of Ernst vom Rath."

Hilde knew she shouldn't think about that awful night. Every time she did, she couldn't help but feel pity for Herr Baum and his family. She knew that the Jews had instigated the violence with the assassination of vom Rath. Still, she would never forget the image of the little girl's bare feet covered in her grandfather's blood.

Hilde cleared her throat. "One billion reichsmarks?" she said, rolling her eyes. "They should be lucky that's all it cost them."

"Ha!" Lotte said. "I knew you would fit in here." She checked her reflection in her compact and touched the neat flaxen roll atop her head. "How would you like to have dinner at my home on Saturday night? I'd love to introduce you to Oskar and my boys."

Hilde felt triumphant. She was making new and important friends. And while her mother was back in Munich listening to radio reports about exciting events like the military parade for the Condor Legion weeks ago, Hilde had been in Berlin witnessing it all firsthand.

~·~

Lotte and Oskar had four sons under the age of eight, and each was clean, well fed, and well mannered. At dinner, Oskar wagged his finger at their youngest, who shuffled his last cubes of beef from one side of the plate to the other. Lotte's face became stonily serious. "There are children starving in Poland who would be grateful for this meal," she told her four-year-old.

When Johanna used to tell her three children the same thing, Hilde replied that she, Kurt, and Lisa would package the leftovers and send them east. Lotte's children, however, wouldn't dare make light of their mother's scolding. Little Josef looked up from his plate with wide eyes, then apologized and hurriedly speared the last pieces of meat.

After dinner, Lotte rewarded her brood with a reading of the new picture book *Der Giftpilz*, the poisonous mushroom. The cover was the murky green color of a stagnant lake, with an illustration of a hook-nosed mushroom with four little fungal offspring sprouting beside it. If the Semitic looks of the mushroom's face didn't make it clear enough, the illustrator included a *Judenstern* on its chest.

As much as Hilde admired Lotte, she couldn't help but think that she would have done a better job with the character impressions. Lotte did fine with the voice of the little boy, Franz. But the mother's voice was too lighthearted and singsongy. There was nothing ominous in Lotte's delivery. She read the part of the mother as if there were nothing at stake:

*"However they disguise themselves, or however friendly they try to be, affirming a thousand times their good intentions to us, one must not believe them. Jews they are and Jews they remain. For our Volk they are poison."*

Lotte made it sound like a happy story instead of the warning for children that it was meant to be. Didn't she realize that the publisher of the book was the same man who ran *Der Stürmer*?

Every week, Julius Streicher alerted German readers about the threat Jews posed. *Our health, our economy, and our lives are at stake! This story isn't supposed to be fun!*

Hilde quieted her internal judgment of her friend's performance and helped tuck the little boys into bed. Who was she to criticize this married mother of four who had been so welcoming to her? Oskar clearly adored her, and their sons were unfailingly obedient. She knew how to properly instill respect in her own children.

Oskar joined Lotte and Hilde for a nightcap in the backyard, where the family had created a cozy circle with wicker chairs. He leaned back in his seat and stretched his legs, polished black shoes catching the reflection of the moon. "Do you ladies have any idea how fortunate we are to live in Germany right now, as we help write this chapter in history?"

Hilde thought he was being a bit melodramatic, but it may have been the schnapps emboldening him. Either way, she wasn't about to spoil the mood. She sipped and smiled at her hosts. "Our children and grandchildren will thank us someday."

Oskar straightened up. "Speaking of our future grandchildren, Hilde. My friend Wilhelm is unmarried, and I think you two might really hit it off."

Looking down to keep herself from blushing, Hilde declined. "I'm flattered. It's just that my *Schatz* and I are pretty serious." She drifted into sweet memory of Werner's most recent visit to Berlin, the second since she had relocated. He told her it was for party business, but she knew he had made a special trip from Munich to see her.

Last week, they'd been together for the third time, and

Werner couldn't wait to get her to his hotel room. He began to trust her with his secrets about what excited him in bed, like placing her on all fours and penetrating her from behind. She intoxicated him with such pleasure that he was in a world of his own, unable to hear her soft whimpers of pain. When he finished, Werner always told Hilde that he enjoyed sex with her far more than with his wife.

It was unattractive to appear smug, so Hilde fought the impulse to smile too broadly at the memory. "I'm sure your friend is a fine man, but I am very much in love."

Berlin continued to enchant Hilde, with its wide, immaculate boulevards flanked with full linden trees. Walking home from work in the June evening, Hilde kept her eyes on the sidewalk to watch as flickers of sunlight passed through leaves fluttering in the breeze. She took in the smell of sausage from the Koschwitz *Würstchen* cart.

Reichsfrauenführerin Scholtz-Klink traveled often and was rarely in the office, but that didn't stop Hilde from adopting her style. She wrapped her two side braids around the top of her head and spiced up her outfits with ties in lively patterns like polka dots or colored stripes. With her first paycheck, Hilde purchased a beaded art deco–patterned purse that she had seen a fashionable-looking woman carrying while walking down Kurfürstendamm—or Kudamm as she now called it.

On workdays, Hilde and Lotte took walks together in the

afternoons, always along the same path. One day, they passed Tiergartenstrasse No. 4, and Lotte reached for Hilde's hand, stopping her at the regal-looking granite villa.

"Hilde, this will be the site of a new program the party is introducing." Lotte's tone grew serious, her voice lowered, and her eyes locked on Hilde's. "Your discretion on this is nonnegotiable, so if you feel you are unable to contain sensitive information, you must let me know now."

Hilde's agreement was immediate and absolute, so Lotte went on.

"In the fall, families with defective children will be given the chance to end their suffering," she explained.

Was this the streamlining of medical services that Werner mentioned at that first dinner at her parents' house? The way Lotte phrased it, the hospital sounded less rehabilitative and more euthanasic. Hilde pushed her hands into her skirt pockets and dug into her right thumbnail with her index fingernail. She wanted to give up this nervous habit, but the idea of having no place to transfer her discomfort was unimaginable. A little sting under her fingernail was nothing compared to the relief it offered.

"Lotte," Hilde began with forced hope in her voice. "Has the Reich developed therapies to cure defects?" Hilde was grateful that she and Lotte stood staring straight forward at the building, not having to face one another. Hilde envisioned her little neighbor, Ursula, squealing with delight as she ran into Hilde's arms.

"Someday," Lotte replied. "But even our doctors can't do that right now."

Silence hung between them as moments ticked by. Finally, Hilde turned to Lotte and scrunched her face with discomfort. "Are you saying we will...*kill* them?"

"That's a terrible way to put it, Hilde!" Lotte's voice felt like a slap. Collecting herself, Lotte paused before continuing. "There's a father in Leipzig begging Herr Hitler to put his son out of his misery. Poor thing was born blind with no legs. This is a mercy."

Hilde was about to suggest that sterilization might be a kinder solution. Yes, Germany would sacrifice short-term economic loss for the care and feeding of cripples. But surely that was a more humane choice than killing them.

As Hilde opened her mouth to suggest this, Lotte interrupted with a lifted finger. "We need someone who understands that great things happen only when strong people make difficult choices."

Hilde looked at Lotte in her starched white blouse with an oversize collar and wondered if women like Jutta and her were born with internal fortitude and self-assurance or if it was something they cultivated. Hilde remembered that Jutta had been right about Kristallnacht; Lotte was probably right about this.

Hilde nodded solemnly, conceding that kindness might sometimes arrive in unlikely forms. The disabled *were* suffering. Their caretakers were certainly burdened. And all this misery was at great cost to the state. Perhaps it was best for everyone if the Reich selectively removed these accidents of nature. Their families could be recognized for their sacrifice to the Reich. Perhaps they could receive a medal too, like the Mutterkreuz.

Then Hilde remembered that Lotte had said the program was top secret, so public recognition was out of the question. She kept her foolish idea to herself.

～•～

When she missed her monthly cycle, Hilde was surprised at her initial feeling of ambivalence. Of course she wanted to become a mother, and goodness knew there was no better blood than Werner's. Getting pregnant with his baby had been her plan all along. Yet the month she had spent working with the Women's League office had been the best in her life. She had attended important events with the highest echelons of the Reich. Hilde knew before the rest of the *Volk* that the last remaining Jewish businesses would be required to close in July.

One day, General Burgdorf's office called, saying that his secretary was out ill and they needed a stand-in for an important meeting. Hilde was the first to volunteer. She ran the four blocks to his office and took notes at a meeting outlining terms for a nonaggression treaty with Russia. Hilde Kramer was in the midst of everything exciting happening in the world.

There was nothing Hilde could do about being pregnant, though. She would have plenty of time to work for the Reich after she became a mother. The chance to bear Werner's child was a blessing that would secure her future. Look at Lotte. She managed to raise children and return to work. The reichsfrauenführerin had six children, and what a career she had!

Hilde felt a rush of excitement as she placed a call to

Werner's office. She sat at her desk chair and crossed her legs as if she were the heroine in a film. As she left a message with Werner's secretary, Hilde smiled coyly at Lotte and Wilma, who were listening to her with raised brows.

*Yes, you heard right. I did say Obergruppenführer Ziegler.* "Please tell him it's urgent," she said, placing down the receiver. *That's right, ladies. Werner Ziegler is my lover, and we are at the center of a very romantic entanglement.*

The following day, Werner stopped by the office unannounced and asked to speak with Hilde. Knowing that the reichsfrauenführerin was out of town, Hilde led Werner into the spacious, private office of her boss. As she closed the doors, she winked at Lotte, who crossed her fingers to wish Hilde luck. She didn't need luck, though. Hilde had something better— Werner's baby. Tapping into her inner film star, she closed the curtained glass doors. Gesturing for Werner to sit in the cushioned chair at Scholtz-Klink's expansive black desk, she told him she had very important news to share.

As Werner sat, the leather seat sighed with his weight. He folded his hands onto his lap and smiled, amused. "You seem quite serious today, Hilde."

"I'm with child," she blurted. With Werner's silence, Hilde's heart began to race. She stayed standing, her hands clasped behind her back fidgeting.

"*My* child?"

"Yes, your child, Werner!" Hilde snapped. "How could you ask me that? I've never been with anyone but you."

"All right, Hilde. There's no need for hysterics. It was a reasonable question. A simple yes will do," Werner said before placing his fingertips on the bridge of his nose. He remained quiet for a few more moments, an unbearable wait for Hilde.

"Aren't you happy?" Hilde said, trying to steady the quiver in her voice.

Werner looked up at her and gave a quick smile. "Yes," he said, pulling himself from his thoughts. "Yes, of course I'm happy. Reichsführer Himmler wants his men fathering as many children as possible. This is good news indeed. It's just…" His voice trailed off.

"Your wife," Hilde said, crossing her arms over her chest.

"Yes," he returned. "And my three boys. Hermann is still a child. He wouldn't understand, but there are ways to ensure everyone is taken care of." Werner picked up the phone and arranged for a doctor's exam. After letting out a series of sounds of agreement, he thanked the person on the other end of the phone and began jotting an address on a sheet of paper. Handing it to Hilde, Werner told her to go to a Dr. Gregor Ebner's office a few blocks away. "He is expecting you shortly."

Hilde remained standing in front of the reichsfrauen-führerin's desk, waiting—for what, she didn't know. Did she really expect him to lift her off her feet and spin her around the room? Did she think he would lay his hand on the miracle growing inside her belly? Werner was a pragmatist who showed his love through action. She had a doctor's appointment within minutes. He spoke about taking care of her. This was far more important than frivolous sentimentalities.

Werner picked up the phone again and looked at Hilde, who was still planted before him. "I'll need a minute, please."

"Of course," Hilde said, finally sitting in the guest chair at the reichsfrauenführerin's desk. "Take all the time you need."

"Hilde, I'd like to make a private call," he said impatiently. "And Dr. Ebner is waiting for you."

Hilde sprang from her seat. "Oh, yes," she said, pivoting toward the door. As she stepped out of the room, she heard Werner ask the operator to connect him with Reichsführer Heinrich Himmler's office.

Closing the door not quite all the way, Hilde listened for a moment longer. Lotte and Wilma had already left the office, so Hilde was able to eavesdrop with no inquiring eyes on her.

"Reichsführer!" she heard Werner say. "I need a special favor."

# 15

## Gundi

*Steinhöring*

S TANDING AT THE LARGE WINDOW OF THE COMMON ROOM, Gundi was enjoying the feeling of her baby moving in her belly. She knew that both she and her child might be in danger but couldn't suppress her delight in seeing the distinct six-month bump that was Leo's child. Like his father, the baby moved constantly, though Gundi couldn't tell if she was feeling an arm or a leg writhing inside.

Two black cars pulled up to the driveway, so Gundi assumed they were together. When the doors of the first car opened, Gundi saw a couple of young soldiers who had visited before—the future husbands of Edith and Agnes, who lived on Gundi's corridor. The other car, however, was filled with four officers, the youngest among them about forty years old. *What business could they have at Heim Hochland?*

When she saw Sister Dorothea escort the men to Sister Marianne's office, Gundi trailed behind, pretending she was on her way to the nursery. As the men waited for Sister Marianne, the officers stood at the hallway window, watching rows of girls outside doing calisthenics. A dozen young women, dressed in sleeveless white tops with the twin bolt insignia, reached their arms toward the sky before stretching to the left, then the right side.

"I'll take her," one of the officers said, pointing at a young brunette, as if he were ordering a *Springerle* cookie from the bakery display case.

The others laughed as another officer pointed at Ingrid, jumping over a gymnastics horse, her legs snapping open wide like a pair of scissors. "That's my girl, right there." More laughter.

Gundi felt sick. *Were these officers here to have sex with the girls upstairs?*

After dinner, Gundi headed to the second floor to do some sleuthing. Maybe there was something less distasteful than what she had assumed.

⌇

Renate was the first to notice Gundi peek her head into a large room upstairs, the hub for all eight bedrooms on the second floor. This didn't surprise Gundi; the few times she chatted with Renate, the lithe blond had shared observations about staff that suggested her antenna was always up. A few days earlier, Renate had nodded her chin toward Sister Irma passing by and whispered, "Wounded." Gundi sensed that Renate saw her as an ally since they were both older residents at Heim Hochland. Renate was all of twenty-one, making her the most senior girl upstairs.

Renate waved Gundi over to a spot on the rug where she was sitting with Marie and Ingrid. "It's about time you came up to say hello," she said. "We were beginning to think you were a snob."

The décor in the upstairs common room was quite different from the dainty figurines, tea sets, and paintings downstairs. The second-floor walls were covered with framed color posters extolling the values of the Reich. There was a series of German teenagers, girls with braids, boys with hair cropped close on the sides. Each of the teens held Nazi flags with various slogans about the promise of German youth:

*We take the fate of the nation in our hands!*

*Germany awake!*

*Youth for Hitler!*

Gundi joined the three girls sitting in a circle on the floor, Marie braiding Ingrid's spun-gold hair as Renate tossed almonds into the air and caught them with her mouth.

"I think Sister Marianne is immortal," Renate said with a laugh. "Has anyone ever seen the woman sleep? I got up for a bite to eat in the middle of the night, and there she was with the lights on in her office."

Marie's laughter made her brown ringlets bounce. Pursing her lips, she changed topics. "Did you hear Irene and her baby are going home next week? Little Gerhard is the cutest thing I've ever seen."

"How would I know that?" Renate clipped, scrunching her mouth to the side. "The married women never deign to even speak to us, much less tell us their comings and goings."

With that, Gundi jumped in. "Why is that?"

"They're top of the food chain here. We're just Hitler's whores," Renate said blithely as she threw another almond up and caught it in her mouth. "But really, the joke's on them. We're the ones who were handpicked by the Reich, not them," Renate bragged before catching her gaffe and holding her hand over her mouth. "No offense, Gundi. I mean, look at you. If you weren't already pregnant, the Reich would surely snatch you right up, and you'd be upstairs with us, lazing around and eating sweets all day."

"And having sex with strangers," Gundi slipped in, hoping her tone was light and teasing, not judgmental. She needed to stay in Renate's good graces.

Renate responded by sticking out her tongue playfully. "You mean enjoying variety before we settle down," she said. "And they're not strangers for long. The officers are very nice, good conversationalists and generous with gifts. You just have to accept the relationship for what it is—a very short-term love affair."

Gundi hoped the smile she forced looked genuine to the girls. "How were you... How did you find out about this...this opportunity?"

"My BDM leader recommended me," Marie boasted.

"One of my teachers suggested it," Ingrid said softly.

Marie continued. "It's a good arrangement for everyone." She pointed to her stomach. "I think of it as leasing space to the Reich."

Leaning forward, Renate moved Marie's hand down so her finger was now aimed at her *lap*. "That's more like it," she said with a laugh.

"I can't wait to get this part over with and get pregnant already," Ingrid said, barely audible.

Renate jumped in again. "She's just sore because she had to *rumsen* with some old guy with bad breath and skin tags all over his body."

"Renate! He *farted* after he ejaculated and didn't even excuse himself!" Ingrid couldn't help but laugh at the vile memory.

Gundi thought her stomach had settled down after her second trimester of pregnancy, but the talk of the old man's bodily functions sent a wave of bile into her throat. She grabbed a handkerchief and spit into it discreetly.

Patting her friend's knee, Renate assured Ingrid that everyone got a dud now and then. "You'll see. At next week's party," she said, "there will be plenty of young, handsome soldiers." Turning back to Gundi, Renate explained. "Sometimes one of us even marries a soldier we meet here, but if not, we still get a great education in every way." She winked. "Even the boring classes on household management will come in handy when we go on to be wives someday."

Gundi quickly removed the hand she had inadvertently placed over her belly; she felt nauseated by the indignity with which they were treated. These girls were being used as sexual playthings and breeders. Worse, their political indoctrination was so deep it seemed that they accepted their role. Still, selfishly, Gundi couldn't show her discomfort, or the girls would no longer confide in her. In her half-hour visit, she had already gained more understanding about Heim Hochland than she'd learned from Sister Marianne in the months she'd been there. *Keep your enemies close*, she heard Leo's voice advise her. The more Gundi knew, the better her chances of finally doing something truly meaningful for the resistance. When she left

Heim Hochland, she could tell the world about this secret breeding program. Surely, they would be disgusted and would intervene on behalf of these sexually exploited young women.

—···—

When she returned to her room, Gundi found that a letter from her mother had been delivered. Sinking into her bed, she took the paper from its already-opened envelope and smiled at the sight of Elsbeth's elegant script. She tried to imagine her mother sitting at her desk before remembering that it had been destroyed by the Gestapo.

Elsbeth apologized for not writing sooner but explained that she had been busy with her new job at the Office of Race and Settlement. "Dr. Ebner was kind enough to secure a very good position for me," she wrote. "Our home has been fully restored, and I must say, it's lovelier than ever, with new furniture and paintings. Our replacement dishes are fancier than my wedding china, if you can believe!"

*Has Mutti lost her mind? Dr. Ebner helped her secure a higher-paying job? She is grateful to the Nazis for restoring a house they had ransacked?*

Didn't Elsbeth understand what had happened? Gundi read the letter a second time for hints that Elsbeth had accepted the promotion under duress, but she couldn't detect any. That didn't mean she was a willing participant, just that she wasn't adept at writing in code. At least, that was what Gundi hoped.

Her friend Erich, on the other hand, knew exactly how to communicate with Gundi. She reopened the letter she had received from him a week earlier and read it again to comfort herself.

My Dearest Gundi,

My mother tells me that we are expecting a child in October. What a blessed miracle indeed. I know you will make a wonderful mother, and I consider the news of my impending fatherhood a true gift for many reasons.

My service in Austria has been most rewarding. You know how devoted I have always been to our beloved führer.

The men in my platoon hail from all corners of the Fatherland, and it is fascinating to hear about life in the countryside and small villages. One rifleman is most admirable in his dedication to our cause. He reminds me of our favorite teacher from *Mittelschule*. I wish I could recall his name.

Be strong and keep our baby safe.

Heil Hitler.

Erich

Wrapping her fingers around the edges of the paper, Gundi pulled the letter toward her heart. *Please be careful, dear Erich*, she prayed in silence.

She knew that Erich hadn't forgotten the name of their teacher, Herr Fischer. Her friend had harbored an unwavering crush on their instructor for three years. Gundi was charmed by his irrepressible spirit. Who else but Erich could find a lover among the barbarians in the army? Still, she worried about his safety. Erich had a short memory when it came to the cruelty of young men. How many times had Gundi held cool rags over Erich's bloodied face when boys at school had beaten him over his feminine affect? The only person beside Gundi who had known about Erich was Leo, who received the news with a shrug of his shoulders. Gundi prayed Erich was being careful.

At the sound of three knocks on her door, Gundi wiped away her tears with her dress sleeve. She quickly folded the letter and placed it under her pillow.

Sister Marianne opened the door and told Gundi that she had good news to share. She walked in and planted her buttocks on the foot of Gundi's bed. "The men who burglarized your home have been arrested."

Gundi stared blankly, confused.

Sister Marianne waved a hand. "Two Jews. No surprise there."

"Why…why would Jews burglarize our home?"

Rolling her eyes, Sister Marianne huffed, "They're thieves, Gundi. It's their nature. Officers caught two men sniffing around outside your home last week, returning to the scene of the crime to pester your mother."

*None of this makes any sense. Jews didn't burglarize our home. Nothing was even stolen. And why didn't Mutti say anything about anyone, two men no less, coming to the house?*

Sister Marianne continued. "Rather than arresting them on the spot, the Gestapo followed the Jews to a hiding place. Led straight to a nest of them."

Gundi felt as though the bottom dropped from the floor, sweating as Sister Marianne went on.

"They've all been sent to Dachau."

"The labor camp?" Gundi asked, wrapping her arms around her knees.

"Yes," Sister Marianne replied. "The Jews can busy themselves contributing to Germany rather than destroying it." She made her way to the door, then lifted her finger and turned back to Gundi. "I thought you'd be pleased to know that justice has been served, and your mother is safe and protected by the party. We take care of our girls and their families."

Instinctively, Gundi placed a hand protectively over her belly. "Do you happen to know their names?" she asked before realizing she needed to clarify. "The Jews?"

"I do," Sister Marianne replied, pulling a telegram from the pocket of her sweater. Squinting her eyes, she read, "Yosef Solomon and his son Leo Solomon." Looking up at Gundi, she asked, "Why? Do you know them?"

Gundi felt a body blow worse than when the class bully, Elisabeth Mühlau, hurled a medicine ball at her in their first year at *Gymnasium*. At least now she was sitting, so she wouldn't lose her footing; her training kept her from gasping aloud. Still, she couldn't help clenching her toes in her woolen slippers. Sister Marianne hadn't noticed, her nose buried back in the telegram.

*The Solomons had been in hiding in Berlin this entire time? And they had been safe until…* Gundi could not bear to finish her thought. Leo could manage to remain safe at Dachau, but Yosef wasn't a young man capable of hard labor. And what kind

of work would they have little Schel perform? Gundi had heard
that these Nazi camps were stingy with meals and hoped that
Rivka could talk her way into kitchen duty and steal extra serv-
ings of food for the family.

Gundi steadied her nerves before she straightened her back
and unfolded her legs. "No, no, I don't know them. I was just
curious." Although she knew she had responded exactly as Leo
would have instructed and although their baby could not hear
a word of the conversation, Gundi still felt she had betrayed
them both.

# 16

## *Irma*

IRMA WENT TO THE MATERNITY WARD TO DISCOVER THAT Hannah was gone. She rushed to Marianne's office and knocked on the door urgently. Not waiting for an invitation, Irma walked in and, with a tight throat, asked, "Where's Hannah?"

"And *guten Morgen* to you, Sister Irma," Marianne replied with the raised brow of mild reprimand. She removed her eyeglasses and gestured for Irma to sit. "Hannah went home this morning, as I told you she would."

"I thought you would give us some advance notice," Irma said. "I would have liked to say goodbye."

Marianne stood and began walking toward the door, ushering Irma out with her words. "I've explained this to you before. We try to keep emotions steady and attachments uncomplicated. I've been with the Lebensborn Society since the beginning, and over the last four years, I've learned that prolonged farewells are like striking a match in a forest." When Irma scrunched her face with confusion, Marianne continued. "Girls can get hysterical after childbirth, and the last thing I need the others to see is a dramatic scene that might give them ideas about keeping a child another family has already legally adopted." Extending her arm toward the threshold of her office door, Marianne excused herself. "I was in the middle of a report and need to get back to it."

Irma stepped out, and the door closed.

The following morning was the baby-naming ceremony, and Marianne had made it clear that Irma was to arrive in the common room at noon wearing a perfectly pressed white uniform. "If there's as much as a drop of milk on your dress, you will be asked to leave." Marianne had relaxed her shoulders and explained, in a warmer tone, "Very few people get to see Heim Hochland, so when they do, I'd like them to be impressed."

After the breakfast dishes were cleared from the dining room and the kitchen was cleaned, Irma watched the common room transform. Plush chairs and chaise lounges were carried to the basement, tables were pushed to the periphery of the room, and the royal-blue and burgundy Persian rug was vacuum cleaned until it was spotless.

The long table that had been surrounded by pregnant girls eating hot cereal just an hour earlier was now covered with a crisp red cloth. Irma watched servants carefully carry the heavy wooden table in front of the mantle, the portrait of Hitler hanging above. Moving together smoothly, the workers fixed a taut white skirt with a black Hakenkreuz around the table, pulling it tightly so that each arm of the swastika was perfectly straight. When they finished, Sister Dorothea checked a piece of paper with specifications for the layout and told the crew that it was time for the final touches. She wrapped her knobby fingers around a tall candelabra and placed it at the center of the table, then wreathed the surface with dried flowers. She then placed a crib mattress covered in black velvet on the parquet floor in front of the table. Eight wooden chairs were then set out for the baby's new family and their guests.

All Heim Hochland's residents—both apprentice and expectant mothers—were sent to the recreation room in the cellar for a mandatory screening of *Olympia*, a film about the Berlin Olympics in 1936. "We want them completely out of sight for the full hour," Marianne explained to Sister Dorothea. Quickly turning to Irma with a pointed finger, she explained, "The adoptive mothers don't like to be reminded of the birth mothers, so no mention of Hannah."

Irma bristled. *If Sister Marianne wants our guests to be impressed, why not let them see what makes Heim Hochland special? Our girls should be spotlighted, not hidden in the basement.* Of course, Irma understood that adoptive mothers would be far more unsettled by the sight of young women who were obviously not pregnant. Heaven forbid they should start asking questions about the different practices of the Lebensborn Society.

Later that morning, two black cars pulled onto the gravel driveway of Heim Hochland. Emerging from the first were two smartly dressed couples. Both women were outfitted in tailored blue dresses. Each wore a cloche straw hat with bright red ribbon fashioned into a flower. The women shared the same equine facial features and long front teeth. Peeking out from their hats was honey-blond hair.

The two women linked arms as they made their way to the front steps of the house, where Marianne rushed to greet them; their husbands walked a few steps behind, wearing their black

SS uniforms. One of the men adjusted his *Totenkopf* hat as he gently touched his wife's back, guiding her up the walkway.

The second car was filled with four SS officers, one of whom was carrying a sword in a scabbard that was so heavily adorned with National Socialist Party symbols that Irma could see them clearly from the window. Marianne reverently led the group into the house.

———

Before the ceremony, Irma learned that the couple adopting Hannah's baby boy was Olga and Gerhardt Becker. Olga introduced her family with a giddiness that leaked through her staid formality. "My sister, Sonja, and her husband, Karl, will be the godparents, and Gruppenführer Fredrich Grunebaum will officiate." The other three officers were Olga's brother and Gerhardt's two childhood friends.

One of Irma's jobs was to dress the baby in his white gown and hold him until it was time for her to place him on the black mattress at the altar. The baby's quiet contentedness erupted into urgent squawking the moment Irma crossed the threshold into the common room. She remembered the way Hannah held the boy upright and bounced him gently. Irma mimicked the movement, rubbing the baby's back. After a moment, the baby spit up on her sleeve before settling down. Irma scrunched her nose in distaste and patted the wet spot with a handkerchief, hoping Marianne wouldn't notice. Luckily, the scent of shampoo was strong, and she took a long whiff, raising the baby's head to her nose. Settling into her arms, the baby made a fist around Irma's index finger and kneaded his tiny feet into her hips.

"Hush, little one."

It gave Irma some comfort to see Olga trying to catch the baby's attention by widening her eyes, puckering her lips, and shaking her head. *She will be a doting mother*, Irma told herself.

As Irma placed the baby on the mattress, she knelt next to him and brushed his head with her hand to soothe him as he squirmed about.

Olga caught Irma's eye and silently thanked her, though her attention was quickly drawn to Gruppenführer Grunebaum sliding his sword from its scabbard. The new mother's mouth opened with horror, and she reflexively stood before her husband placed a hand on her elbow, assuring her that their baby was safe. When Olga sat down, Gerhardt gave her a gentle stroke on the back.

Carefully placing the tip of the sword on the child's stomach, Gruppenführer Grunebaum named the boy Adolf, promising that he would enjoy the privileges of a German citizen and the full protection of the Reich. He signaled for Marianne to come forward and lift the child from the small mattress, then asked the parents and godparents to join him at the altar. When all were situated, Herr Grunebaum continued. "Do you swear to uphold the values of the National Socialist Party and pledge your allegiance to the führer, Adolf Hitler?" Everyone, including Marianne, concurred with a bark of affirmation.

The gruppenführer nodded to Marianne, then Olga Becker, signaling it was time to hand Adolf to his new mother. Olga carefully received her delicate new bundle, immediately locking eyes with him and smiling. She kissed one of little Adolf's hands, then held him close. Herr Grunebaum handed Gerhardt a Lebensborn keepsake, a small silver cup engraved with the baby's name, birth date, and Reichsführer Himmler's signature. The gruppenführer then declared two-week-old Adolf Becker a member of the National Socialist Party in good standing. At once, everyone in the room lifted their right arms in salute. *Heil* Hitler.

Baby Adolf was placed in a tiny wicker basket for the drive home later, where he would no doubt be met by extended family and friends. Irma imagined the Beckers would host a grand dinner that evening, perhaps serving roast goose. Afterward, they would fill themselves with chocolate Linzer cookies and thank God for their new miracle.

# 17

## *Hilde*

FROM THE BACK SEAT OF THE CAR, HILDE NOW REALIZED that as elegant as the reichsfrauenführerin's office on Tiergartenstrasse was, it was nothing compared to the grandeur of Heim Hochland. As her driver turned onto the road to the sprawling estate and passed the statue of a mother nursing her child at the front gate, Hilde felt the Lebensborn Society extend its arms.

The driver opened the door and held out his hand for Hilde. An older nurse with a helmet of gray hair topped by a stiff white hat introduced herself as Sister Marianne. Looking the girl over, Sister Marianne stopped at Hilde's flat belly and knit her brows. "Welcome to Heim Hochland," she said, nonetheless reorganizing her face into a smile.

Yes, it was early in her pregnancy, but hers was a very special case. Hilde wondered if anyone knew whose baby she was carrying, hoping it might gain her special privileges like a bigger room or a private nurse. Hilde would enjoy any leeway her status gave her. If she wanted supper in her room or grabbed a second dessert, who would dare stop her?

Once Sister Marianne showed Hilde inside the house, the two paused at the entryway with a checkerboard floor. Hilde peeked to the left and saw a common room so majestic that it looked plucked straight from Neuschwanstein Castle some two hundred kilometers away. The spacious area was filled with embroidered silk chaise lounges and fringed velvet chairs where pregnant girls shared snacks and listened to the radio. Hilde's eyes were drawn toward the oversize window that looked out to the front yard. Sunshine flooded the entire room, illuminating the intricate gold and azure tile work above the arches leading to the back of the house. Every inch of the walls was covered, layered with thick wallpaper, sconces, and artwork.

Above a large marble fireplace hung a portrait of the führer that Hilde had never seen before. He was dressed in his full uniform and sitting back, relaxed in a lawn chair, a black dog at his side. Hilde thought the painting was intended to have a calming effect on the residents, showing the führer's gentler side. But Hitler's gaze looked like accusation to Hilde, though that was silly. She had done everything the party expected of her. And she was hardly the first girl to carry the child of a married man.

As they entered the common room, Sister Marianne called for one of the pregnant girls, who placed down her book and came to greet Hilde. She immediately knew that this girl with the compact melon belly would soon be her best friend. The girl, who introduced herself as Gundi Schiller, had the same self-possessed demeanor that Hilde had been cultivating in Berlin, from her serene facial expression to her confident, unhurried stride. Hilde imagined the two would be house leaders, offering the less experienced girls advice on the ways of the world. She wondered if Gundi was also carrying the child of one of the Reich's top men. Hilde made a mental note to ask Gundi later if she planned to marry her baby's father or if, like her, she would live the more free-spirited life of a mistress, enjoying motherhood without the suffocation of a full-time husband around.

Hilde's eyes flicked back toward Sister Marianne, who was having a hard time catching the attention of a younger resident. "Gisela!" she called again, but the girl was in rapt conversation, her hands gesticulating with great animation as she spoke with a nurse. Finally, after Sister Marianne's third attempt, Gisela looked up, then squeezed the nurse's shoulders gratefully before lifting herself from her seat and waddling over to greet the others in the entryway.

"Girls, please show Hilde around the house and grounds, and make her feel welcome at Heim Hochland." Sister Marianne told Hilde that a servant would bring her suitcase to her room and apologized for needing to rush off so quickly.

"Let's start outside," Gundi offered with a resigned flatness to her voice. Hilde made a second mental note: Gundi didn't seem to care for Sister Marianne. Maybe on their tour, she would make a wisecrack about Sister Marianne's big bottom. She knew that a common enemy bonded people.

The three girls walked through the common room, then down a corridor where, Hilde was told, some of the pregnant residents lived. All the bedroom doors were on the left; to the right was an entrance to the kitchen, then farther toward the back was a small door leading to the cellar.

At the very end of the hallway, Gundi opened the back door leading to a brick patio furnished with wrought iron tables and a swinging bench hanging from a large pergola. Beyond the area was a lawn so perfectly trimmed, Hilde noticed the stripes from its recent mowing. Bursts of colorful, flowering rhododendron and wild rose bushes were planted in the soil. It created an atmosphere of abundance but wasn't overpowering.

Gisela pointed to a garden gnome sitting beside a rose bush. "We name them after all the babies born at Heim Hochland," she said. "That's Theo, and over near the marigolds is Magda. There are nearly three hundred altogether, and sometimes we girls rearrange them for fun."

Hilde tried to tune out Gisela's inane chatter that accompanied her pointing toward a lake and forest in the distance. "Sometimes the girls upstairs sneak through the woods and go into town at night, but Sister Marianne would murder them if she ever found out, so don't say a word," Gisela whispered, holding a finger over her lips. Though Gisela was far friendlier than Gundi, Hilde had little interest in her. Perhaps it was because Gisela seemed too eager to please. Hilde didn't want a friend who just anyone could be chummy with. She admired Gundi's aloofness; her friendship would be a hard-won trophy.

Gundi appeared lost in thought, studying the forest as if it were the most fascinating thing in the world. She squinted to watch a flock of geese flying above the lake, mouth pursed in concentration as though she were doing a tricky math problem. When she lowered her eyes from the sky, Gundi began waving to Sister Irma in the distance. She was returning to the house with an armful of wildflowers.

Hilde smiled victoriously. Heim Hochland provided fresh flowers for its residents. This place was paradise.

"That's Sister Irma," Gisela told Hilde. "She's the nicest nurse at Heim Hochland."

Hilde tried to catch Gundi's eye and exchange a look of derision. *Ow, nice. Isn't that the most fascinating description?* But Gundi's gaze remained locked on the approaching nurse. Hilde could understand why Gundi found Gisela boring with her talk of garden gnomes and house rule breakers. But Hilde was a rising star in the Reich who would someday serve alongside the reichsfrauenführerin and bear several children for Werner. She wasn't just some silly farm girl who got herself pregnant like Gisela.

Once Sister Irma reached the backyard, Gisela introduced her to Hilde. "Our newest resident," she said, sweeping her arms toward her.

"I just love fresh flowers," Hilde told Sister Irma. But before the nurse could thank her, Hilde requested that her arrangement have extra cornflowers. "I love a colorful bouquet." She noticed Gundi lower her eyebrows and thought this would be a perfect time to win points. "After you've made Gundi's floral arrangement, of course." Then turning to Gundi, Hilde offered a wide smile. "I didn't mean to step on your toes. I just find that nice bright flowers can really cheer up a room."

Gundi didn't respond; she didn't need to. The understanding between them was unspoken.

Hilde continued, "Gisela, let's see the inside of the house."

When the girls made their way back inside, the first place they stopped was the common room, where Gundi stopped in front of a painting of ballet dancers rehearsing in a studio. Hilde stood by her side, straightening her posture as if she were in an art gallery. Gisela tilted her head up to examine the canvas and let out a short, unimpressed huff.

The dancers wore matching white tulle dresses and buns in their hair. One bent to tie her pointe shoes. Another extended her arms, one above her head, the other to her side. A third ballerina stood by a large window, pointing her foot onto a wooden floor washed in muted pinks and blues from the setting sun.

"You're not a fan of Degas, Gisela?" Gundi asked.

"I prefer his darker paintings," she returned. "The ballerinas are a bit overdone."

Hilde rolled her eyes. *Oh, for goodness' sake. Now the two of them are going to drivel on like pretentious museum curators. Who is this flighty little nitwit pretending to be anyway?*

Hilde was quickly distracted by a servant who had just entered the room with a tray of fresh-baked apples, marzipan pastries, spice cookies, and plum rolls. "These look delicious," Hilde gasped with delight. "Let's take a break and have some treats, shall we?" Not waiting for a response from Gundi or Gisela, she grabbed two of each and placed them on a plate, quickly turning to nab the best seat by the window.

Hilde let herself drop into the royal-blue chaise lounge and swung her legs up onto it, reclining luxuriously. She set her plate down on the marble table beside her and set her arms on the cushioned rests.

# 18
## *Gundi*

*July*

G UNDI WALKED INTO THE COMMON ROOM AND IMMEDI-
ately saw Hilde sitting in the front row of chairs that
had been moved upstairs from the cellar. She avoided meeting the Nazi zealot's eyes, which were sweeping the area like
searchlights. It was movie night at Heim Hochland, or as Dr.
Ebner had characterized it, *university*. Hilde's eyes stopped on
Gundi, then she patted the chair next to her. Pretending not
to notice Hilde's invitation, Gundi found a stool in the very
back of the room.

Sister Marianne stood in front of the white screen and
announced that the evening documentary was *Triumph of the
Will*. The opening shot was filmed from the cockpit of an air-
plane, clouds parting in the descent. Soon, viewers would visit
various Nazi rallies in the new, gleaming Reich. *How ironic*,
Gundi thought. *We have all seen this film before, boasting the
power and the strength of Germany. We have a bird's-eye view,
from a thousand meters above, and still it shows us only what Hitler
wants us to see.*

Gundi had long since given up on any real educational

programming at Heim Hochland, but she appreciated the chance to sit in a darkened room and play her own film reel in her mind—the first time she met Leo.

She closed her eyes and imagined it was August 1938 once again, and Gundi was back home in Berlin.

⸻

A friend who had already taken Professor Hirsch's political economy class told Gundi that the reading list was available to students early and that she should pay the instructor a personal visit. Professor Hirsch liked that, the friend said. The class was notoriously difficult, but Professor Hirsch favored students who made an extra effort to ask questions and engage with him during his office hours.

Though it was clear from the dark interior that Professor Hirsch was no longer inside his office, Gundi rattled the door-knob several times. Why did her time at the library always take twice as long as she planned? Noticing her frustration, an elderly custodian stopped pushing his broom and pointed toward the back entrance. "He just left a few minutes ago, Fräulein." She thanked him, then walked as quickly as she could without running.

As Gundi reached the back exit to the building, she opened the door urgently but stopped short at the sight of Professor Hirsch standing under a leafy tree with a young man in a newsboy cap. The instructor was as gentlemanly looking as she had been told, with cropped white hair and an orange paisley necktie. What immobilized Gundi, however, was the sight of her future classmate. His rich brown curls bobbed around his ears as he nodded in earnest agreement with Professor Hirsch. Yes, he was handsome, but there was something far more compelling about him, an indefinable something that quickened Gundi's heart and made her think, *I know you*. Of course, she didn't, in fact, know him, but she wanted to, forgetting momentarily where she was or why she had even come. *Something about a reading list?*

Stepping to the side, Gundi hid behind the doorframe for a moment. She wanted to watch this boy for just a bit longer before she approached Professor Hirsch. *Who is he?* Before she could consider the question, Gundi saw both the men's heads turn toward the building as if sensing her presence.

Feigning confidence, Gundi strode toward the tree. As she was deliberating whether to say *good evening* or just *hello*, Professor Hirsch straightened his stance and lowered his eyebrows at the boy hawkishly. "Be certain the package is delivered tonight," Professor Hirsch clipped at the young man, who bowed his head and left abruptly. Turning to Gundi, the professor's face softened. "That was just a messenger."

Professor Hirsch may have been an excellent instructor, but he was a terrible liar. It seemed odd to state "That was *just* a messenger" when Gundi hadn't even asked. *Just a messenger? As opposed to what, a Soviet spy?* He quickly regained his footing when Gundi introduced herself and asked about the reading list, but Gundi couldn't focus on the theories of Hermann Dietrich and Paul Moldenhauer. Instead, she spent the rest of the conversation wondering who that young man was.

Gundi could barely suppress her smile on the first day of

class when she caught a glimpse of the boy in the dark projectionist booth in Professor Hirsch's lecture hall. She pondered why he wasn't sitting in the auditorium with the rest of her classmates. *Could he be farsighted? Crowd shy?* Then it hit her. He was Jewish and couldn't be seen attending classes.

Gundi's attraction to the boy wasn't simply a matter of thinking he was nice looking. She found herself inexplicably drawn to him, even when his handsome face was a mere silhouette. No images were being projected in the lecture hall, and no other student felt compelled to look up toward the booth, yet her body naturally turned toward him. The pull was one way, though. Despite multiple efforts, Gundi could not catch his eye.

Right before class ended, Gundi saw the boy make a swift exit, so she followed him out to introduce herself. Hearing nothing but the rapid clack of her saddle shoes against the polished floors of the empty hallway, Gundi realized he must have run toward the exit and followed suit. When she finally saw his hand reach for the doorknob, she called out to him. "Stop, messenger!"

The boy turned to face her, teeth clenched and lips tight, a look that was both angry and resigned.

Winded, Gundi caught up with him. "More deliveries to make?"

Gundi had been certain that her flirtation would be well received. She had always found that having inside jokes or secrets could create a sense of intimacy with a boy, as if they had a little world known only to them. But he looked at her blankly, then let go of the doorknob and sighed. He turned to face her, planting his feet firmly and squaring his shoulders.

"Report me if you're going to, but I'm not interested in a game of cat and mouse."

Of all the first words Gundi had expected to hear, she had never considered these. She'd received nothing but positive attention from boys and men since she turned twelve years old. They always seemed to be finding excuses to be near her, not running the other way, so it hadn't occurred to her that she might be viewed as a threat.

"I'm not like that," she replied, feeling a rush of anxiety to convince him that she wasn't anti-Semitic. "I despise what Hitler is doing to the Jews," Gundi explained, hoping she was speaking with more conviction than she felt. Gundi did, in fact, hate what was happening to Jewish people. At the same time, she silently confessed that it had been more than a decade since her school teacher humiliated Sammy in the classroom, and she had slowly gotten used to anti-Semitism as the new normal. Now she was face-to-face with the consequences of the Nazi laws.

"Is that so?" the boy asked Gundi with a trace of sarcasm. "So tell me, Fräulein. Since you have such a deep hatred for the persecution of Jews in Germany, what are you doing about it?"

A long silence hung between them. Finally, she spoke, her voice painfully soft. "*Do* about it?"

"That's what I thought," he replied with a smirk. He shot out the door quickly, checking both ways before bolting toward the service road.

Gundi became a statue of herself, motionless. *Do about it?* she repeated silently. It hadn't ever occurred to her that she could do something. She was one person. The Nazis were omnipotent.

On her walk home from class, Gundi began silently defending herself against the boy's charges. She quickened her pace with every rationale. All Gundi could do was treat people with kindness. *She* wasn't the one who had enacted the anti-Jewish laws. She hadn't forbidden them from attending German schools. Gundi was a good person. Yet even as she silently pleaded her case, a small voice inside chided her. It was true that she wasn't a frog-marching Hitler lover, but it was also true that she had never once considered whether there was something she could—or should—do to help defend the Jews.

Lying in her bed that night, Gundi looked through her window at the stars, imagining each was a tiny hole in the black sheet between heaven and earth. She wondered about this boy whose name she didn't even know yet. Drifting off into delicious thoughts of him, Gundi promised herself that she would find him at the next lecture and ask how she could help. *He will teach me to be a better person.*

The boy never returned to Professor Hirsch's class, though. He was nowhere to be seen at university, neither in the shade of trees nor cover of night. After two weeks of hoping to run into him, Gundi decided to start her own search. She began at Professor Hirsch's office, knocking timidly on the mottled glass window of his door. He waved her in and nodded his welcome.

"Herr Hirsch, can you tell me what happened to the boy you were talking to outside the lecture hall a few weeks ago?"

He stared blankly at her, though his right cheek twitched slightly.

"Professor, I saw him in your class, in the projection booth."

Shifting uncomfortably in his chair, Herr Hirsch turned

away from Gundi and began leafing through papers on his desk. "I don't know who you are referring to," he replied. "I speak with many students."

Gundi closed Professor Hirsch's door and walked toward him with a light step. Lowering her voice, she whispered, "The Jewish boy."

Professor Hirsch turned quickly and furrowed his brow. "No!" he barked. "You are mistaken, Fräulein. There are no Jewish students in my class. I would never allow it."

She took a moment to adjust to this new version of Professor Hirsch before her. "I don't mean him any harm. I only want to—"

"Fräulein, I cannot be any clearer. I was not associating with any Jews." The way his voice caught on the last word confirmed her suspicion. Too many young Germans were reporting adults—their own parents even—for Professor Hirsch to take any further chances.

The next logical place to look for the boy was Grenadierstrasse, since the street was the most densely populated with Jewish businesses in all Berlin. Gundi knew she would have to use discretion entering Jewish shops, lest the watchful eyes of the Gestapo accuse her of being a Jew lover. She pulled a scarf over her hair and hunched forward as she looked for a butcher shop. Mutti had always said if you wanted to know what was happening in any community, look no further than the local butcher. They saw everyone and heard everything.

The neighborhood looked different from when she and Elsbeth had shopped there for groceries many years earlier, before the party considered patronizing Jewish businesses an act of disloyalty. The same bakeries, chemists, and haberdasheries lined the street, but now each shop window was painted with the word JUDE in yellow, some with the six-pointed yellow *Judenstern* beneath it.

When she ducked into Weisz's butcher shop, Gundi saw an elderly woman with a kerchief covering her head standing frozen behind the glass counter of an otherwise empty store. Her husband emerged from the back, wearing a long white apron, carrying himself with the gravity of someone twice his weight. He inhaled through his nose, summoning his courage, at the sight of Gundi. "Please, Fräulein," he said. "We have nothing more."

Gundi didn't blame them for wondering what a blue-eyed gentile girl was doing in their neighborhood. She wasn't exactly their typical customer these days, so she offered her widest, most reassuring smile and explained that she wasn't at their market to purchase meat. "I'm looking for a young man I saw at university." She laughed with self-deprecation, adding, "I don't even know his name, but I really need to find him. He has dark curly hair and—"

Frau Weisz interrupted Gundi with a gasp. "Fine," she conceded, moving toward the cash register and emptying the contents onto the countertop. "Fräulein, please, this is all we have."

Gundi looked at the money, then back at the couple, holding up her hands and backing away. "I'm sorry. I…didn't mean to frighten you. I was looking for a friend from university."

Herr Weisz said nothing, just nodded his head slowly and cautiously. His wife clutched her chest, covering a small locket on a chain.

Gundi had grown accustomed to being seen as a pretty girl,

a harmless decoration, rather than a danger to anyone. Her lips began to quiver as though she might cry. Instead, she apologized as she stepped back out onto the street.

She lowered her head and continued walking in the shadows, maintaining a steady clip so she wouldn't draw attention. Peeking through the windows, Gundi passed a tailor, hat shop, and furrier before noticing a bookstore a few doors down. She instinctively knew that it would be where she'd find him. Somehow the shop fit the boy, the little she knew of him. Its faded forest-green wood framed a large window with gold letters of the shop name painted beneath Nazi vandalism. Despite the disturbing sight of the angry scrawling, Gundi couldn't contain her smile when she saw the boy through the window and realized that she could recognize him from behind, his pomegranate-colored shirt crisscrossed by suspenders as his arm reached the top bookshelf. His fingers were long and lean like a musician's.

When the bell of the front door jingled, the boy turned quickly. His eyes registered who was standing at the threshold of Solomon's Books, and he greeted Gundi coolly. "What are you doing here?"

Taking in the familiar smell of freshly polished wood and old books, Gundi focused on the comforting scents as she fought back tears. *Why does he have to be so mean?* Trying to lighten the mood, she nodded her chin toward a bust of Beethoven perched on a shelf. "Is he your favorite composer?" Gundi asked.

The boy's face puckered with bitterness as he placed his hands on his hips. "I have to say, Fräulein, it's been a while since I've gone to the Philharmonic."

"Oh, right," Gundi said, flushing with embarrassment. "No one can stop you from listening to the phonograph, and I—"

He looked as though he was summoning his last bit of patience. "What is it you want?"

"I want to learn," she blurted.

He knit his brows, making it clear to Gundi that their last conversation had not lingered with him as it had with her.

"How to *do* something," she pressed.

He returned a blank stare.

"I want you to teach me how to help the Jews," Gundi said with a burst of uncontained excitement.

"*Oy Gott!*" he exclaimed, rushing toward her and lowering the shade on the glass door. "Did anyone see you come in here?"

Gundi adjusted the sweater sleeve he had pulled. "I'm not afraid," she said proudly.

"Did it ever occur to you that I am?" He opened the door and extended his arm. "You should go home now."

＝･＝

When she returned to Solomon's Books the following day, she passed the butcher shop again. Herr Weisz stepped back from sweeping the sidewalk when he recognized Gundi despite her hat and turned-up coat collar. She tried to offer him a cheerful expression, but he quickly averted his eyes. Part of Gundi desperately wanted to turn around and run home, far from this place where she bubbled with anxiety, not knowing how to comport herself. She fought the urge to shout, "I'm one of the good ones!"

When she made her way to the bookshop, Gundi watched the boy through the window for a moment. He was standing at the glass front counter, engrossed in a book. She opened the door, the bell jingled, and he looked up. His face sported a shadow of stubble that accentuated the cleft of his chin.

"What is it you want today, Fräulein?" he said, his temples receding as he loosened his jaw.

Gundi relaxed her shoulders and walked to the counter. At least this was something. At least he would talk to her. "I've been thinking about what you said to me after class," Gundi continued, realizing she would need to refresh his memory. "About doing something about the Jewish…" Gundi struggled for a moment, realizing that she had only heard about the *Jewish question* and the *Jewish problem*. She had no vocabulary for what was happening in Germany from the point of view of the Jews.

"Persecution," he said, his voice seeming to downgrade his animosity to mere contempt.

Gundi continued. "Yes, the persecution of the Jews. I want to do something to help."

She watched the boy's Adam's apple rise and fall as he swallowed hard. For a flash, his brown eyes softened, then quickly narrowed into suspicious slits. "Maybe we don't need your help."

Gundi was barely able to hold back her tears. "I…I don't understand. You hate me because I'm not doing anything, but when I tell you that I want to, you act like you hate me for that too."

She watched him grope for the right words. After a few moments, he walked around the counter and stood facing Gundi. "Ach, please don't cry. I don't hate you. It's just…" He trailed off for a moment, running his hands through his hair. "I don't know whether I can trust you."

She longed for him to hug her, but his honesty would suffice. She thought she would be able to keep herself from crying, but a tear escaped. "What do I need to do? To prove myself to you?"

He let out a long sigh, led Gundi to a stool, and gestured for her to sit. "If you want to do something, it can't be because you want to *help* the Jews. It has to be because you understand, heart and soul, that we are all inextricably bound. We don't need a savior. We need allies." He wiped away Gundi's tear with his thumb and smiled in spite of himself. A long silence hung between them before he whispered, "Would you be willing to deliver an envelope to a print shop in Charlottenburg tomorrow?"

The vagueness of the mission gave her pause. *An envelope. A print shop. And why Charlottenburg?* A sense of danger set in like fog.

In Gundi's moment of hesitance, he stepped back. "It's all right. You don't have to do this. I know you're a decent person. I was wrong to suggest otherwise. You don't have to prove anything to me."

Gundi buoyed herself, taking a deep, determined breath. "I'll do it."

The boy pressed his lips together as if he were reconsidering. "You can trust me!"

He looked at the ground and nodded solemnly. "I understand. It's that…" He paused, then looked directly into Gundi's bright blue eyes. "This is not a game. What I'm asking you to do has risks. Do you understand that?"

"I understand perfectly…" Gundi began before remembering she didn't know his name. "We have never been introduced."

The boy nodded his head toward the front glass of the bookshop that bore his family name. "Solomon," he said with his first full smile, dimples sinking deep into his cheeks. "Leo Solomon."

"I'm Gundi Schiller," she said, extending a hand.

"I know who you are," Leo told her as his face flushed slightly.

The following day, Gundi returned to the bookstore, ready for her mission. Leo handed her a plain white envelope that was to be delivered to—and *only* to—a man called Willy at an address Gundi committed to memory.

"What's in the envelope?" Gundi asked.

"Now it's your turn to trust me," Leo said, holding on to Gundi's hands. "It's better if you don't know."

Gundi paused for a moment, wondering what she had gotten herself involved in. "Leo," she said, shifting her weight. "Am I doing something illegal?"

"Yes, Gundi. You're doing something against the law." Leo took the envelope back. "This is a big risk, so I understand if you want to change your mind."

For a long moment, Gundi considered leaving. What if she was arrested? What if Willy wasn't at the print shop but a Gestapo agent was there instead?

Then Gundi remembered the looks on the faces of the butcher and his wife. She thought about how the fruit seller turned away from her in fear. And how Leo had mistrusted her.

Mutti never seemed to have any personal gripes with Jewish

people. But when it came to the anonymous monolith *the Jews*, Elsbeth said that they must have done something to deserve the hatred of the German people. Now Gundi began to wonder if it wasn't the other way around. If Jewish people were so afraid of people who looked like her, perhaps it was her people who had done something to deserve such mistrust. It was time to choose a side.

Gundi reached for the envelope between them. "Will this help end the persecution of Jews?"

"No," Leo replied, his voice cracking. "This single envelope isn't going to fix everything, but it may do a little good."

# 19

## *Hilde*

*August*

**H**ILDE WOKE WITH A WIDE SMILE ALREADY SPREAD ACROSS her face. Despite Gundi's obvious snub at the screening, Hilde was in good spirits. After the film, she had overheard Sister Marianne telling one of the cooks to prepare a special menu because Reichsführer Himmler and Propaganda Minister Goebbels would be visiting Heim Hochland later that week. Sister Marianne also told the cook that Werner and several other officers would be joining them.

Scanning the walls of her room, sun pouring in through the window, Hilde congratulated herself on creating such a homey setting. Everyone who saw it commented on the magazine clipping of the führer bending down to kiss the head of a young girl. Hilde could understand why people were drawn to it. The two were standing in a field of flowers at the Berghof, the snowcapped mountains of the Bavarian Alps a placid backdrop. It appeared as if nothing—not even the Jews—could threaten this world the führer and the girl inhabited. Another picture featured a crowd of young people watching in awe as rows of soldiers marched through the wide boulevard. Each spectator's fresh face sparked with elation, their arms lifted and stiff before them. They were a hundred weather vanes showing which way the wind was blowing.

Walking toward the WC, Hilde began thinking about what she would wear when Werner visited, how she would style her hair. By the time she reached the toilet, she had decided on the perfect dress. It was green with red and white summer flowers and a square neckline with a slender rim of white ruffles. This same trim finished the short, puffy sleeves. At first glance, the frock appeared modest, even patriotic. It was cleverly, stealthily sexy and worth every reichsmark Hilde had paid for it during her first shopping outing with Lotte in Berlin.

As she imagined her life with Werner after the baby was born, Hilde realized she would have to replace the hideous flannel nightdresses, like the one she had on, with more alluring negligees. On his visits to their secret cottage, Werner and Hilde would sit in front of the fireplace and share a drink after supper as their baby slept peacefully. She would read him comedy sketches that she had written for radio programs. He'd laugh so heartily that he'd have to steady himself from toppling over. "Hilde," Werner would say, "I've never met a woman who was both beautiful and funny, but you continue to amaze me."

Werner's visit later that week would bring her one step closer to that perfect future. As Hilde lifted herself from the toilet, though, she felt a sharp, stabbing pain in her lower belly. She had missed two monthly periods, and now it felt as though the cramps from both of them were coming at once. Sister Marianne had told her that discomfort was normal as a woman's body expanded to make room for growing life. But this didn't feel like the pain she'd felt earlier in her pregnancy.

Pressing her hands onto her stomach, Hilde stood and walked toward the door as if she could escape her fate by leaving the room.

*I can't be miscarrying! I've done everything the nurses told me to.* She silently made her case for why she was not—could not be—losing her baby. Hilde drank three large glasses of milk every day. She ate the exact portions of fruits and vegetables Reichsführer Himmler required of the girls. Hilde had done everything right.

She made it exactly two steps before she wrapped her arms around her lower abdomen and bent over at the waist. She lowered herself onto the floor, where she was hit by a second wave of cramping, followed by a third, then a fourth. Willing her baby to stay inside her womb, Hilde silently begged, *Don't leave me. I have big plans for us.*

With the final wave of cramping, Hilde's undergarments were flooded with a hot rush of liquid—blood she assumed. She couldn't bear to look down to see the red bloom growing beneath her, though. As long as she didn't see it, maybe it wasn't really happening. She reached toward the toilet rim and pulled herself up to sit on it again. Hilde didn't realize she was already crying when it all ended minutes later with the release of what looked like a handful of prunes into the bowl.

Though Hilde didn't remember having called for help, Sister Irma was suddenly in the WC with her, holding her in her arms.

Maybe there was something genetically unfit about Hilde

if her child hadn't survived. She couldn't suppress the quiet voice inside that reminded her that her family had lost a child to smallpox. Other German children had survived it, but Lisa spent weeks burning up with fever and vomiting every spoonful of broth their mother fed her. Perhaps the Kramers were a weak line.

"You're all right," Sister Irma said, almost as if she could hear Hilde's thoughts. Of course that was impossible, but Hilde felt exposed nonetheless.

She heard the thud of Sister Marianne's thick shoes on the hallway floor, then the creak of the door as she strode in. Sister Marianne took in the puddle of blood on the floor and looked away. "My dear girl," she said, frowning sympathetically, "you must be so disappointed." Waving a hand, Sister Marianne ordered Sister Irma, "Let's get Hilde to the maternity ward right away." As she darted from the room, she added, "It's been a busy morning already."

"Sister Irma," Hilde said, burying her head in the nurse's shoulder. "What does she mean by a busy morning?"

"Oh, Hilde," Sister Irma sighed. "Gisela had her baby this morning."

When Hilde looked up, she took in the pouches beneath Sister Irma's eyes. Hilde hadn't even realized she would miss having Sister Irma with her in the delivery room, holding her hand, patting her brow, and announcing the baby's sex at the end. Now she felt cheated out of all of it.

Hilde held on to Sister Irma's arm as she made her way to the maternity ward. The first thing she noticed was how sunlight streamed in through the large windows. Outside, the leaves on the trees in the front yard all stood motionless in the summer heat, looking as though they yearned for a single breeze to relieve them. It struck Hilde as unbelievable that the world outside hadn't changed a bit while her entire life had been permanently altered.

Hilde quickly registered the more important elements of the room: Sister Dorothea holding a bundle wrapped in a white blanket as she bounced softly, placing a knobby finger over her lips, warning her to stay quiet. Gisela was sleeping soundly in the only occupied bed of the ward's six.

Sister Marianne strode in and saw Hilde eyeing the baby. "A boy. Little Amon," she said with a lilt. Turning her attention to Sister Irma, Sister Marianne said it was time for the baby's breakfast. "Wake up Gisela and help get Amon fed. Then report to my office to fill out the paperwork."

Hilde heard Sister Irma let out a yawn before asking if she needed help getting into bed. Her first instinct was to accept the assistance. Catching Sister Irma's look of sheer exhaustion, Hilde waved off the offer and hoisted herself in bed.

Once Gisela opened her eyes and noticed Hilde was in the bed next to her, she blinked in confusion. Sister Irma placed little Amon in Gisela's arms and left the girls alone. "Wait," the new mother said groggily. "Hilde, aren't you due in—"

"Never," Hilde interrupted. "I'm due in never. I lost the baby this morning."

"Hilde, no!" Gisela said with a voice that was scratchy from screaming all night. "I'm so sorry. They put you in the maternity ward after a miscarriage? That seems cruel."

"Not at all," Hilde replied quickly, straightening her back and jutting her chin. "Gisela, I'm happy for you. Amon is so big and healthy looking. And I want to hear all about your wedding plans. When is Otto coming to Heim Hochland to meet his son?" There was absolutely no way Hilde would allow anyone to pity her.

She could mourn for the loss of her baby later, but for now, Hilde had a mission, one that would take clear-eyed focus to accomplish. Werner would be at Heim Hochland in three days, so she had another chance to become pregnant with his child. Yes, her body needed to recover from the miscarriage, but comfort was a luxury she could not afford. She knew how to grit her teeth and endure pain.

〜·〜

Hilde desperately wanted to recline in her bed like Gisela, but she hadn't earned that right. Plus, she had a job ahead of her. She had to make sure her seduction went off without a hitch, because she had no idea when she'd see Werner after that. There was no room for mistakes.

Since becoming a new mother, Gisela had just three activities she did with equal enthusiasm: nurse, sleep, and sketch. "Stay like that at the window, Hilde," Gisela said, picking up her drawing pad. Pulling green and red pencils from a box, she smiled brightly. "You look interesting in that dress."

*Interesting?* At least it was better than how disgusting she felt; each time she went to the toilet, she wiped away blood and tiny black clots. She refused the sanitary napkin Sister Irma offered, opting for discreetly folded tissue paper she changed frequently. The last thing she needed was for Werner to see a bloody napkin pinned to her underwear.

She remained seated on a soft chair by the window so that when Werner came to see her, he would find a girl whole in body and spirit. During BDM meetings, Jutta had spoken about tests of fortitude, and this was surely one of them.

As she sketched Hilde sitting beside the window, Amon sleeping in his bassinet, Gisela asked what Hilde planned to do now that she was no longer pregnant.

"Can you keep a secret?"

Gisela nodded emphatically. "Please tell me! I'm about to become a boring old hausfrau. I need something exciting."

"My baby's father is…was Obergruppenführer Werner Ziegler."

"Really?" Gisela said, leaning forward.

"He's coming to Heim Hochland to see me today, so we're going to try again."

"Oh, Hilde, it's so soon! Have him come back in two weeks." Gisela sighed, reaching for a glass of water. "You can try then."

Hilde resisted the urge to clench her jaw. Had she asked for Gisela's advice? Did delivering a baby suddenly make her an expert on relationships? Who was Gisela to think she understood Hilde and Werner's lives?

"No!" Hilde said with a patronizing chuckle, as if to suggest that Gisela couldn't possibly understand Werner's dilemma.

"He's very important to the Reich, and who knows where he'll be in two weeks? It needs to be today."

⇌

The seat by the window had an unobstructed view of the front gate where the guard stood, giving Hilde the perfect spot to monitor Werner's arrival. Hilde's heart raced when she saw the three polished black cars, each round fender decked out with Hakenkreuz flags.

She knew Werner could not risk arousing suspicion by rushing to visit her. Nonetheless, she grabbed a magazine from the stack beside the chair. Looking like a portrait of a lady reading, she flipped pages, glancing toward the door every few minutes. Whenever her bottom started to numb, Hilde ran to the WC to refresh the folded tissue in her underwear. Two hours passed. Baby Amon had been brought to Gisela for feeding a second time, and still no sign of Werner.

Finally, she heard the clop of boots approaching, so Hilde sat up straight in her chair, rearranging her dress one last time. She had just finished when he entered the room, sweeping his eyes across the near-empty nursery. Werner congratulated Gisela on the birth of her son and offered formal condolences on Hilde's loss, bowing his head slightly in her direction.

Gisela made it through the requisite niceties with Werner, then excused herself to the other room to visit her baby, winking at Hilde. The two had planned for Gisela to visit the nursery so Hilde could spend some time alone with Werner. After Gisela shut the door softly behind her, locking it so the couple wouldn't be interrupted, Werner focused his gaze on Hilde.

"You're looking very well, considering."

Hilde returned the compliment, admiring how refined he looked in his black uniform—boots, jacket, and all—despite the August heat. "You look very handsome," she offered. He didn't answer, and a moment of silence filled the room, interrupted only by the quiet crying of Gisela's baby in the next room. "I've missed you," she tried again, moving toward the window to close the curtains. Then she lowered her chin and locked eyes with him, walking across the room and wrapping her arms around his sunburnt, moist neck.

"You know, the best time to try again is right after."

Taking a step back, Werner curled his upper lip. "Come now, Hilde. This is hardly the time for such talk."

Hilde swallowed a wave of nausea, not sure whether it was due to her miscarriage or just the familiar punch of rejection. She had known there was a chance that Werner would refuse her advance. Of course, he was concerned about her discomfort so soon after miscarrying. She just had to convince him she was ready.

Hands quivering, Hilde knew what she had to do next. "Werner, you know you don't mean that," she said, running her index and middle fingers firmly up the inside of his pant leg, stopping just short of the buttons. He sighed deeply and closed his eyes, looking as though he was struggling to resist. He bit his bottom lip but could not contain a smirk.

Hilde circled Werner's crotch, then brushed over it lightly with her fingertips as she waited for him to rise. When the first part of her mission was complete, Hilde swiftly dropped to her knees before Werner, unbuttoning and lowering his pants and boxer shorts in a single, fluid motion.

She had never seen a penis before, not even on her other nights with Werner. It had always been dark, and he had simply reached down and slipped himself inside her. Even now, at such close range, she couldn't get a good look at it, only noticing it had a slightly purple hue and a tip like an eel's head. On their other nights together, Hilde hadn't noticed Werner's saggy *Hoden* hanging down like two rotten figs.

Listening to him mutter something as she gripped his member, Hilde closed her eyes with steely resolve and slid Werner's shaft into her mouth. He reached down to cup her face, but his hands landed on the back of Hilde's head. He continued to thrust himself into Hilde's mouth with the full force of his hips, all while maintaining a tight grip on her head.

*His wife never does this for him.* Hilde congratulated herself on being the sexually adventurous mistress. First, though, she had to make it through this.

*Open your throat.*

*He'll think about this next time he's with her.*

*Do I hear Gundi's voice outside?*

*The birds are so noisy today.*

Hilde opened her eyes but was poked by his coarse pubic hair before she could lower her lids again. One coil shed off and attached itself to Hilde's eyelashes, where it remained for a half dozen thrusts before fluttering to the ground. She shuddered at the thought of all the hairs she would have to scrape from the back of her throat after this was all over.

Hilde wanted to grab a pillow from the chair to place it under her knees but couldn't risk ruining the mood. She was so close. Finally, after three of the longest minutes of Hilde's life, Werner's breathing started to become labored. She pulled her lips away.

"What are you doing?" Ziegler snapped harshly as she remained kneeling before him.

"Take me," she whispered with a seductive smile, nodding her head toward the hospital bed. Her subtext was clear: *There is only one way we are going to finish this.*

Ziegler sighed heavily and laughed as he picked her up and carried her toward the bed, his pants still around his ankles. "You are a devil," he said playfully, placing a finger on her nose.

Then he lifted her dress and pulled her underpants to the side. Hilde couldn't tell whether Werner was handling her more aggressively or if she was feeling residual pain from her miscarriage, but the stinging was unbearable. Almost unbearable. She closed her eyes tight and wrapped her arms around him and pulled him closer.

---

The following morning, Sister Irma came to the maternity ward to bring fresh flowers for the young women, but Hilde had what she wanted most: Werner's attention and, quite possibly, his baby.

Tucked under Sister Irma's arm was a red cardboard box that looked like the game of Fang den Hut that even her sister, Lisa, had outgrown by her last birthday. Hilde thought it surreal to see a mother with her newborn at the breast perk up at the sight of a child's game, clearly eager to play. Or perhaps Gisela was just glad to see Sister Irma; the two were inseparable these days. Hilde felt a twinge of longing for a time when her mother would play with Kurt, Lisa, and her, moving her red cone around the crossed-circle pattern on the board. Maybe she'd join them after all. Hilde had accomplished a lot this week; she could afford to waste a little time on a silly game.

Before they began, Sister Marianne appeared at the door with a grave expression, asking to speak privately with Gisela. "When you finish nursing the baby, please come to my office," she said with a tone that was more sympathetic than usual.

"I don't mind if Sister Irma and Hilde hear," Gisela offered, looking down at Amon.

Sister Marianne sighed heavily. "Very well," she said, folding her hands in front of her. "We received a telegram from Otto today." She paused. "He says he's not Amon's father, Gisela."

Gisela straightened her posture, mouth agape. "How can he say that? He *is* the father, Sister Marianne. I swear he is!" She climbed out of bed, balancing her baby in her left arm, as she grasped at the telegram in Sister Marianne's hand. "I have love letters from him! He's learning how to run his father's furniture store so he can provide for us. We've talked about this since the beginning."

Sister Marianne seemed somewhere else for a flash. "Sometimes men are cowards," she offered. "This happens more often than you might think. They start to realize what a responsibility it is to be a father."

"But he wants the baby!" she protested, cradling Amon close to her chest.

Sister Irma began nodding her head emphatically. "I've read his letters. Otto is in love with her, Marianne. Something is very wrong here. He writes to her nearly every day."

Stiffening her jaw, Hilde bristled. *That just means he has too much idle time.*

"Someone is pressuring him, Marianne," Sister Irma offered. "Let's call Otto and his parents to Heim Hochland for a meeting and get to the bottom of this."

Sister Marianne closed her eyes for just a moment. "Fine. Perhaps he'll change his mind." She turned toward Hilde's bed. "We need to discuss your plans. Now that you are no longer expecting, you'll want to return home soon."

Hilde would never want to return to her parents' home in Munich. Not soon. Not ever. Johanna and Franz thought she was still working at the Women's League in Berlin, and that was how she wanted to keep it. If she returned home, her parents would assume she had failed at her post in Berlin, and that was the furthest thing from the truth. Lotte and Wilma always told her what an asset she was to the party. In her month at the Women's League, she had already received more praise at work than she had ever gotten at home.

If she wasn't pregnant from Werner's visit, perhaps Hilde should see when she could return to her post in Berlin. Rumor was that September was going to be an exciting time for Germany, with the Reich likely reclaiming more of its rightful territory from Poland. The euthanasia program for the disabled was scheduled to start in October. She would be able to see Werner more often, and they would have their baby in due time. Hilde smiled at the thought.

In the privacy of her own mind, she admitted that working for the Women's League again was even more exciting than the thought of a baby. She was only eighteen years old. There was plenty of time to have a family. She longed to be part of this moment in world history.

⌇

The following morning, Hilde noticed a tray of cold cereal and fresh apple juice on her bedside table. On the other side, she saw Gisela's perfectly made, empty bed. Scanning the room, Hilde looked for Gisela's hairbrush and sketchpad, but all her belongings were missing. She rose gingerly from her bed, threw on her robe, and walked toward the nursery, where she saw Sister Dorothea holding a swaddled baby.

Rushing toward her, Hilde looked at the baby in her arms. Sister Dorothea held Amon with his lips wrapped around the rubber nipple of a small glass bottle. "Where is Gisela?" Hilde asked.

Sister Dorothea looked up to meet Hilde's eyes. "Gisela will be going home this morning. And before you ask, Sister Marianne has already extended our best wishes on behalf of Heim Hochland, so there will be no further goodbyes."

# 20

## *Irma*

Irma was in the kitchen watching Klara, the head cook, prepare breakfast when she heard car tires crackle past the driveway and toward the back of the house. "Who's here so early?" Irma asked. Klara tilted her chin toward a small window that was opened a sliver.

An older couple whispered at Gisela as the man held her upper arm and pushed her into the car. "Shame," Gisela's mother clucked. Irma could only hear bits of Gisela's mother's snipes: "Should have known better…"

Irma wanted to run outside and hug Gisela. She wanted to scold her parents for their harsh words and let Gisela know that she was loved. At the very least, she wanted to get her address so they could exchange letters. Instead, Irma stood motionless, as if she were bolted to the ground. Where was the old Irma who threw glasses across the room and demanded explanations? Where was the woman who could walk away from a relationship without a glance back?

The cook came to join her, watching the car drive off. "That girl caused a world of problems for Sister Marianne," she told Irma, placing a hand on her back. "Dr. Ebner himself approved the girl for the program, but I heard that the party higher-ups blame Sister Marianne for not asking questions when Gisela's *Schatz* never showed up to visit."

⚊ ⚬ ⚊

Irma knocked on Sister Marianne's office door. "Gisela's room is empty," she said, feigning ignorance in order to see how her old friend would frame Gisela's departure.

"She went home this morning with her parents," Sister Marianne said. "It's a pity that we were deceived about the baby's parentage, but she has good German blood, and the baby has all the markers of Aryan stock, so the child will be adopted very easily."

Irma remained standing in the doorway. "Was she able to speak with Otto?"

"Who?"

"The baby's father."

"I'm not going to discuss that with you, Irma. I'm afraid you're getting too attached to the girls. I know you want to help them, but our job ends with the adoption of healthy German babies. I was going to give this to you later, but it seems like you need a reminder." The envelope was filled with photographs of the babies that Irma had helped deliver during her time at Heim Hochland. "I'm hopeful that you will draw strength from these portraits," Marianne said, smiling tightly. "We are ushers of new life and a new Germany. Our babies may leave Heim Hochland, but they always remain in our hearts," she said, far too stiffly for the sentiment.

Irma slowly flipped through the photographs, absorbing the

images. *Baby Adolf is so chubby now. Is that a little bottom tooth in baby Helga's gummy mouth? Susannah looks like a porcelain doll in that velvet dress.* The last shot was one of Marianne and Irma two decades earlier in their nurses' uniforms at Potsdam. Irma swallowed a lump of nostalgia, not for the place but for who she was in the photograph. She and Marianne seemed so sure of themselves, standing between two rows of cots that were lined up as neatly as the soldiers they held. Irma hadn't even taken a pregnancy test yet, but she must have instinctively known she was expecting, as her hand rested protectively over her belly.

Marianne put down her pen, blinked her eyes, and tried again. "Remember how productive we were at the hospital in Potsdam? I need that same focus from you here at Heim Hochland, Irma. Any more chatter about Gisela is going to be an unhealthy distraction for the girls." Reaching for her pen and returning her gaze to the forms on her desk, Marianne let Irma know the conversation was over.

Irma had known that Marianne's loyalties were with the Reich. She understood that her old friend had justified her arranging for young women to have sex with officers. But now, she also knew that Marianne wouldn't hesitate to serve the party's needs at the expense of the young mothers.

Irma returned to her room and sank into her chair, smiling as she took in the images of the babies once again. She popped from her seat and went to the supply closet to find a handful of thumbtacks. When she came back, Irma stopped at the threshold of the door, surveyed her barren walls, and plotted where to hang each image.

# 21

## Gundi

ELSBETH'S LETTERS HAD BEEN ARRIVING WEEKLY WITH regular reports about her work at the Office of Race and Settlement. Gundi was grateful to learn that her mother wasn't a true believer and only wished she had known sooner. Rifling through the collection of letters she kept in her dresser drawer, Gundi searched for last week's update. Elsbeth repeatedly told Gundi how *pleasurable* she found her job. The use of the word made Gundi sigh with relief. She had finally learned to communicate with coded language.

Just months earlier, Elsbeth had rolled her eyes at a neighbor who was carrying on about how pleasurable his new job was. "Spare me the false enthusiasm," Elsbeth had told Gundi once the man was out of earshot. "A job is a job. It's never *pleasurable*, or it would be called recreation. Work is work. You do what you need to in order to get by."

In an earlier note, Elsbeth tried to tell Gundi that Leo and Yosef had paid her a visit. She knew her grandchild was fathered by Leo. "I saw your classmate Leona and her father in town, and they told me that they've been planting all sorts of seeds in their new garden. How happy they seemed!"

Gundi had smiled momentarily at her mother's cleverness

before remembering that this exchange must have been just hours before Leo's family had been arrested. She held the stationery close and recognized her mother's perfume, then carefully folded it and placed the letter back in its envelope. Though she was relieved that her mother now knew the truth, Gundi still wished that Leo and Yosef had never visited the house.

Settling onto her bed at Heim Hochland, Gundi took small comfort in the fact that Leo and his family were safe at a work camp. As long as they were doing essential work for the Nazis, they would be all right.

Elsbeth's latest letter had little new information, but Erich reported that he would be sent to Heim Hochland once their baby was born in October. According to his commander, Erich could marry at a local party office. A baby-naming ceremony would be performed the following day.

She rose and paced the length of her small room, ignoring the pinch in her lower back. All things considered, getting married would probably be the smartest move for both Gundi and Erich. After all, the longer he remained a bachelor, the more likely his preference for the company of men would be discovered. But it wasn't a perfect solution. What in God's name would she do if the baby was born looking like Leo? She thought of Anna Rath, the Aryan woman in Nuremberg whose head had been shaved before she was marched through the streets as a crowd jeered her for planning to marry a Jew. Would that happen to her? And would she be putting Erich in danger? Gundi couldn't imagine that the Nazis would be particularly sympathetic to a soldier who claimed paternity to a baby he knew wasn't his. There were simply too many unknowns. She wished she were back in Professor Hirsch's economics lecture, where the equations were solvable and the worst thing that could happen to her was a bad grade. Silently, she tried to convince herself that everything would work out. She and Erich had posed as lovers to escape Nazi attention before, she reminded herself. Perhaps they could pull this off.

---

Back in the winter, just after Erich joined Leo's resistance group, the childhood friends had been paired together for an action. Students were coupled and told to walk through residential neighborhoods in Berlin, slipping anti-Nazi leaflets in household letter boxes. If they had been caught, Gundi and Erich would have been tried for treason. Yet now, as Gundi strode from one end of her room to the other, their work in the Edelweiss Pirates seemed like child's play.

She wondered what the group was doing now. Had some fled Germany, or had they been arrested too? Did they have any idea where she was? Did they know about Leo's arrest? Or did they think the two of them had run off together and abandoned their work? Maybe they should have, for all the good they did. Who knew if the forged identity papers and travel passes Gundi had delivered had even been put to use? Had anyone seen their anti-Hitler graffiti in U-Bahn stations, or had civil servants simply washed it away in the early morning hours?

---

After Gundi had earned Leo's trust delivering notes to Charlottenburg back in autumn, she'd had to do it all over again with his friends in the Edelweiss Pirates in November. They instantly greeted her with suspicion, especially Kris, the oldest member of the group. Sporting week-old facial stubble, he had the build of a dockworker and thick hands to match. Kris was the first to speak as Leo led Gundi down to the cellar of Solomon's Books for her first meeting. Without pretense, he shot, "Who the hell is this?"

Gunther, a boy her age with a brown buzz cut, scrunched his face quizzically. "This cannot be who you were thinking would—" he started before Sarah, the only young woman in the group, interrupted.

"Let him speak," she demanded. Gundi was grateful to have an ally, though it only took a moment to realize that her generosity was directed at Leo, not her. Sarah pulled the ribbon from her hair, casually releasing long curls and shaking them in a gesture that Gundi recognized from her own preening. "Let's hear what Leo has to say," Sarah said with wide eyes.

Gundi's stomach tightened as they argued over her presence. She pretended to study the gray cellar walls and crates filled with books to be repaired. The bottom box contained blank paper, ink, and canvas bags rolled tight like cigars. In the very back of the room was a mimeograph machine.

"She can be trusted," Leo told the group. "Gundi's already delivered letters for me, and no one has asked her a single question."

Kris shook his head and huffed a laugh. "It's good to be a pretty girl." Noticing Sarah look down, Kris patted her back. "You know what I mean."

Sarah exhaled loudly before locking eyes with Gundi. "There are certain risks that come with being a woman in the resistance," she said, pressing her lips together. "We need to know you won't turn any of us in. No matter what they do to you."

Everyone froze at the sound of boots thundering down the stairs. Two *Mittelschule* boys, clearly twins by the looks of them, apologized for their lateness. "Mama was going on about Karl not drying the dishes and—" The boys stopped dead in their tracks at the sight of Gundi. The brothers exchanged a cautious look. "Who's she?"

Kris took over. "You want to be part of this group?"

Gundi nodded, hoping no one noticed her hands shaking.

"All right, I have a special assignment that could use someone with your…special skills." He dug into his knapsack and held up a large, sealed envelope. "These papers will help get fifty Jewish children on a boat to England next week. I need them delivered safely to a colleague's apartment."

"I thought Kindertransport didn't start until December," Leo said.

Sarah jumped in awkwardly. "Thank goodness they're a little early. Kris got my little brother's name on the list." Turning to Gundi, she continued. "This is extremely dangerous, do you understand? If you are caught, the only way you will get out with your life is by betraying us."

Gundi had to admit that this gave her pause. Before she had a chance to swallow her fear, Leo jumped in and offered to deliver the envelope instead.

Kris held out a hand in objection. "You know where these papers need to go. None of us are getting through without the Gestapo harassing us, but Blondie will walk in and out of Stefan's apartment building with no problem."

Shaking his head emphatically, Leo protested. "She's too new. She won't know what to do if—"

"I want to do this," Gundi said. "If this helps fifty Jewish children, I want to do it, especially since one of them is Sarah's brother." She looked at her female compatriot, but Sarah's eyes were cast onto the floor.

Then Sarah looked up and smiled stiffly at Gundi. "My family will be forever grateful to you."

Envelope tucked in her schoolbag, Gundi made her way across Berlin effortlessly the following day. While most of the other members of the Edelweiss Pirates typically walked along side streets, Gundi took Unter den Linden straight through the center of the Mitte district, then continued moving through Prenzlauer Berg until she reached her destination: a large white apartment building on Christburger Strasse. As she moved through the city, Gestapo agents had looked at her, not with suspicion but approval. She smiled internally; she had found her place in the resistance.

Gundi climbed the staircase two steps at a time until she reached the fifth floor. Making her way to the end of the hall, she saw the door with peeling orange paint and a straw mat on the floor. She tapped one finger lightly twice, as instructed, and the door opened quickly.

"Get inside," whispered a heavy older man with a toothbrush mustache. When she stepped inside, the man offered her a cup of tea. Gundi stood motionless. This wasn't how the delivery was supposed to happen. Kris and Sarah told Gundi that she would enter the apartment, retrieve the envelope from her bag, then turn around and leave.

Registering her confusion, the man told her it looked suspicious for people to come and go too quickly, so there was no harm in having a cup of tea. "Really, I insist," he said.

Gundi had never seen an apartment like this before. She stood in a large room, like a warehouse with dark blankets covering the windows. In the corner was a mattress with sheets and a quilt tossed on it carelessly. Stacked brown boxes dwarfed the duffel bag of clothing beside the makeshift bed. On top of one of the boxes was a stack of paper cramped with handwritten notes and a shortwave radio beside it.

As directed, Gundi stepped toward a kitchen table and sat, bunching up her feet inside her shoes. She readjusted herself in her seat, shifting her weight from side to side, as she watched the man pour water from the kettle into teacups. "Are you...are you Stefan?"

He smiled and sipped his tea. "Stefan is dead." Gundi's entire body shook as she stood to leave, but the man calmly pointed his finger and lowered it, indicating that she should sit down.

"*Dead?*"

The man didn't respond, though he clearly had heard Gundi's question. His expression remained unchanged, eyes still on Gundi, seeming to tell her that he wasn't one bit sorry about Stefan's death. It was likely that he was the one responsible for it. *When did this happen? My God, is his body still in the apartment?*

"I need to go," Gundi said, grabbing her schoolbag. "I'm not... I'm late getting home."

The man was eerily calm as he pulled a pistol he had tucked into his back beltline. "Sit."

She began to weep without even realizing it. Gundi wiped her nose with her sleeve, understanding that she was going to die.

The thought of Elsbeth receiving the news that her daughter had been killed—an auto accident, the Nazis would surely say—gutted her. *Why did I ever get involved with the Edelweiss Pirates anyway?* Then she breathed in deeply as a voice within her replied: children needed her help. Still, her body was damp with fear, rippling in terror.

"Let me have the package you brought for Stefan," the man demanded.

"I don't have a package for him," she replied. "Stefan owes my father money…for a gun he bought from Papa. He sells weapons, knives and guns and ammunition, so Stefan needed to pay him. I'll just… I'll just go before Papa comes looking for me."

When Gundi stood, the man laughed and waved his pistol at the seat. "Sit."

Gundi's body dropped back into the chair, seemingly of its own will.

He nodded his chin toward Gundi's bag. "Let's have a look." The man set down his gun on the table.

Her breath sounded like paper being torn slowly. "I have to get home for supper."

The man set Gundi's economics book on the table with a thud. He reached into the bag again, avoiding the envelope. Gundi's appointment book, house key, and lip balm were now laid out before her. He reached in once more and smiled as he retrieved the key to her home, a box of matches, and her university identification. Glancing at the card, he looked up. "Nice to meet you, Fräulein Schiller." Finally, he snatched the envelope from her book bag. "Look here," the man said, holding up the envelope. "Do you know what this is?"

"No idea," she managed.

"Why would you be carrying an envelope if you have no idea of its contents, Fräulein Schiller?" The man grabbed a long letter opener and made a careless incision. As he examined the papers, Gundi searched for any plausible reason she would have Kindertransport documents that she was unaware were in her bag.

*A man asked me to hold them. I had no idea what they were. And no, I don't know who he was.*

*Someone paid me to deliver this envelope to Stefan and not ask any questions, and I desperately needed the money.*

*Someone dropped this envelope on the street, so I picked it up and was going to the police station as soon as I collected my father's money from Stefan.*

The man narrowed his eyes and lowered his volume. "I'm going to ask nicely, just once more. Who gave you the envelope?"

"I found it on the street," she said, watching the man stand and move closer toward her.

"You tell me right now, or you'll end up like your friend Stefan!" he growled, all former politeness gone.

"I don't know anything," Gundi cried. "I found the envelope. I don't even know what's in it."

The man moved toward Gundi and positioned himself behind her. She heard the click of his revolver. "Listen, you're not really who I'm interested in, Fräulein Schiller. You're just an innocent girl who got caught up in something bigger than she realized. Probably for a boy, I'd guess. I'm not looking for small players like you. Do you understand what that means?"

Breathing unevenly, she shook her head. She had no idea.

"It means that you're only worth as much to me as the information you can provide. Tell me who gave you this envelope, and I let you go. Stay quiet, and I kill you."

Gundi's eyes darted around the room. Fear prickled every pore, and every sense was heightened. It was as though her body understood she was going to die and wanted to binge its last bits of life. She suddenly noticed the aroma of boiling cabbage from another apartment in the building, her ears tuned in to Wagner playing across the hall, and she spotted a bug crawling across the wall at the other end of the room. A lump formed in her throat, knowing that fifty Jewish children, including Sarah's brother, would never get on that boat to England.

"Fräulein Schiller," the man said. "This is the last time I will give you the choice. Tell me who gave you this envelope, or I will kill you right now."

Gundi closed her eyes, feeling tears stream down her cheeks. She would never get to tell Leo how she felt about him. She would never see her mother one last time and make sure she knew—*really knew*—how much she cherished their relationship. She gripped the sides of her chair to steady her hands.

"All right," Gundi said, opening her eyes.

He smiled. "All right then, let's have it. Who gave you the envelope?"

"I mean, all right, shoot me," she said. "I know nothing."

She closed her eyes, waiting for the shot that would end her life. Her voice was ragged as tears streamed down her face and her nose clogged.

The man patted her on the shoulder. "Gundi," he said.

"What?" she squeaked, her eyes still clenched shut.

"Gundi, open your eyes," he said. When she did, the man was kneeling before her, his gun set on the floor. "I'm very sorry to have frightened you. We just needed to be absolutely sure you wouldn't crack under pressure. My name is Stefan. Welcome to the Edelweiss Pirates."

# 22

## *Hilde*

THE DAY AFTER WERNER'S VISIT TO HEIM HOCHLAND, Sister Marianne called Hilde into her office to ask about her plans. "Will you return home to Munich or back to the reichsfrauenführerin's office in Berlin?"

Leaning forward in her plush velvet chair, Hilde bubbled with excitement. "I think I'm pregnant again," she whispered.

Sister Marianne flinched. "When did you have sexual relations?"

"Yesterday when Obergruppenführer Ziegler was here to visit. I've been his mistress for many months, and we have a very…well, he's a very passionate man."

Sister Marianne looked away, barely suppressing a cringe. "I'm aware of that, but you just miscarried on Wednesday morning."

Hilde clenched her teeth to remind herself to remain calm. "I understand that, but Werner—excuse me, Obergruppenführer Ziegler—wants to be sure his child receives the best care possible, which is why he arranged for my stay at Heim Hochland in the first place." She sat taller. "Shall I tell him you refused to allow me to stay on?"

Collecting herself, Sister Marianne shook her head slightly. "I suppose you should stay until we know for certain."

Now, a week later, Hilde was still spotting from her miscarriage. As she sat on the toilet looking at her bloodstained underwear, her heart raced and her toes felt cold as she realized that she was probably not pregnant after all. She had known she wasn't likely to conceive again so quickly, but seeing her chance slip away left her feeling more alone than ever. Who knew when she and Werner would see one another again? Werner loved her, of course, but he was a busy man and this was an important time for Germany.

⌒·⌒

When Hilde opened the door to her room, her mood lifted as her eyes were immediately drawn to the pink Deutsches Reich stamp at the corner of a gray envelope. She had already written to Lotte to ask about her old job and was overjoyed with the quick reply. Rushing toward her bed, she tore open the letter and unfolded the thin white paper.

Dearest Hilde,

How terribly heartbroken I was to hear about the loss of your baby. As a mother, I understand your pain, but you are young and will surely bear children in the future.

Berlin is bustling despite this treacherous heat. Replacing you was no easy feat, as you are one of the most devoted young women we have ever known. Serendipitously, I found the perfect person while visiting Munich. I was introduced to your former BDM leader, Jutta Klinger. When she mentioned how close you two are, I knew she would be someone I could rely on. Like you, Jutta works with purpose and zeal. I could not be more grateful. Of course, I had to disclose your situation to Jutta, as she would have certainly wondered why you were nowhere to be found at the office. She has proven to be very discreet, so your secret is safe.

I wish you all the best in your future endeavors.

Heil Hitler.

Lotte

*That was it? I wish you all the best in your future endeavors? It was difficult to replace me but not impossible, it seems.* There was no mention of Hilde's offer to return to Berlin. Nor did Lotte suggest finding Hilde another position in the Reich. There were new offices springing up around Germany every month, yet all Lotte could do was wish her well. How had she become unimportant so quickly? Had she just imagined that she had had a special place within the party?

And how long had Jutta been working in Berlin with the reichsfrauenführerin? Tightening her face, Hilde wondered why her friend hadn't written to her once in the two months she had been at Heim Hochland. Hilde couldn't figure out which cut deeper—Lotte's dismissal or Jutta's backstabbing. She folded the letter and stuffed it back in the envelope, then lay down on her bed and began running the corner of the envelope under her fingernails. As she hit the sore spot beneath her thumbnail, she felt a sting of relief. *Stop feeling sorry for yourself, and figure out what to do next.*

—

Hilde realized that she was the only person who knew she was not, in fact, carrying Werner's child. All she had to do was spend the next few weeks finding someone to impregnate her, and then she could pass off the resulting baby as Werner's.

Renate had once mentioned that the girls upstairs sometimes snuck into town at night for a beer at the pubs. It was a half-hour walk to the town center. The road was wooded and dark but manageable on a night when the moon was more than half-full. How would Hilde get more information without revealing her agenda, though? It wasn't as if she could just ask Renate where the nearest spot to find drunk men to *rumsen* was.

Hilde climbed the spiral staircase to talk to Renate. The entire group of apprentice mothers was sitting in a large circle, each holding a workbook. Renate spotted Hilde and waved her in, putting up a finger to indicate that they would be finished in a moment. A new girl named Heidi finished reading aloud, "Women must be the spiritual caregivers and the secret queens of our people, called upon by fate for this special task! The woman's is a smaller world, but what would become of the greater world if there were no one to tend and care for the smaller one? How could the greater world survive if there were no one to make the cares of the smaller world the content of their lives?"

Ingrid clapped her hands together. "Good work, girls.

Tomorrow we will read about keeping your flower boxes looking cheerful."

Behind the closed doors of Renate's room, Hilde asked how to get to the pubs in town. "You can come with us," Renate replied. "We're going tonight. It's a great time!"

Hilde had already lied to everyone, telling them that she was certain she was pregnant again; it would be unseemly for the girls to witness her slipping out of the pubs for a quick dalliance. "Another time," Hilde said. "I'm beat today."

⌒

Hilde spent six nights sneaking out to the common room at midnight and watching the late-shift guard through the window, trying to memorize his routine so she could slip past him unnoticed and head to town. On the sixth night, Hilde startled at the sound of a woman's whisper behind her. "Boo!"

Gundi either had the softest step or was a spy in her former life, because Hilde hadn't heard the slightest sound from the girl now standing less than a meter behind her. "What are you doing up?" Hilde whispered.

"I like to grab a bite to eat late at night sometimes," Gundi replied softly. Hilde stopped herself before reminding Gundi that she had passed the kitchen. At least she was being friendly to Hilde for once. "I see someone is sweet on Max."

"Max?" Hilde shot back.

"The guard. His name is Max. Not the smartest boy in the Reich, but duly employed and loyal to Hitler. That's all that matters, right?"

Hilde scrunched her face. How could Gundi think Hilde would be interested in someone like Max when she was involved with Werner? Of course, one of the costs of being with Werner was that it had to remain a secret. But still, couldn't Gundi tell that Hilde could do a little better than Max the guard? "No, I definitely don't like Max in that way."

"Whatever you say." Gundi smirked as she floated back toward the kitchen. "I'll leave you alone so you can continue not staring at him."

When Hilde's eyes landed back on Max, she realized that Gundi was right. She'd been focusing her effort in the wrong direction. Hilde didn't have to become an expert on Max's habits to sneak out of Heim Hochland. In fact, she didn't have to leave the estate at all.

All she had to do was seduce Max.

At dinner the following evening, Hilde stealthily slid a few desserts onto a small plate sitting on her lap and covered them with a napkin. She felt certain that when she slipped out at eleven, an hour into his shift, the house spice cookies and bread pudding would serve as the bait she needed.

Max wasn't quite Hilde's type, with his wide grin that made him look as if he was seeing everything for the first time. Though he was tall and broad shouldered, like a swimmer, Max's face was too boyish for her liking. He would be a handsome man one day, but now, at around age twenty, his round facial features made him look like a child. He seemed as though he needed to be taken care of, not someone who could protect a woman.

Just before Hilde tripped out to introduce herself, her

confidence began to wane. What if Max politely thanked her for the dessert and awkwardly mentioned a *Schatz* or even a wife? What excuse would she give for wandering down to the gate to offer him cookies?

Hilde walked across the pebble driveway, trying to focus on the sweet smell of viburnum permeating the night air. Anything to distract her from the hard truth that getting pregnant was her only path forward.

Dressed in a virginal white sundress, Hilde made her way down to the guard station. At first sight of the half-moon earlier that night, Hilde had been grateful for the dim lighting that would help her move toward the gate undetected. She reconsidered her decision to walk barefoot as she stepped on a sharp rock.

"Hallo," Hilde whispered as she finally made it close to the gate. Her soft greeting was returned by the young guard snapping toward her, his pistol aimed squarely at her face. Hilde dropped the plate, desserts scattering onto the grass.

Max lowered the gun. "*Scheisse*, Fräulein!" he snapped. "You shouldn't sneak up on people like that. I could've blown your head off."

Opening her mouth to speak, Hilde took several gasps of air until she was finally able to regain her breath. "I...I just thought you might enjoy some sweets," Hilde explained, hoping that in a week, they would laugh about how their romance had started at gunpoint but that thankfully the only thing that was injured was a plate of cookies.

He wiped his brow with his jacket sleeve. "Thank you, Fräulein. No one's brought me sweets since Mutti."

After three nights of sharing desserts and stories under the starry sky of Steinhöring, Max was developing a palpable attraction for Hilde. But the girl Max had fallen for was a work of Hilde's imagination. She had told him that her name was Anna and that she was taking a break from her life as an actress. It wasn't totally unreasonable. Hilde could have been in show business if only her parents had encouraged her.

She told Max that she wasn't part of the Lebensborn Society but being hidden by the party. "An American film producer is trying to hold me to a contract to star in a picture with a bunch of lies about Germany," Hilde said, her heart speeding with excitement at the notion. "Naturally, I would have never agreed to such a picture if I had known what it was about, so I'm staying here while my manager works it out."

Max never questioned why Hilde—or Anna—would need to hide from a film producer. He just stared at her with slack-jawed awe, amazed that he was lucky enough to be sitting on the grass with a famous actress, even if he had never heard of her before.

Hilde wondered why Max felt the need to share his hopes and dreams, but she endured his blathering every night. He could never shut up about his ridiculous inventions. "It's a little robot that does tasks around the house, like turning on the radio for you," Max told Hilde. He and his father, an engineer for the party, had built a prototype in their garage. "You hit one button, and next thing you know, your wireless turns on without you even touching it."

Why anyone would want something like this was beyond her, but Max lit up as he talked about his ideas, so Hilde nodded enthusiastically.

A telephone without wires. *Sure, great.*

A hands-free clothing washer. *Because he knows magic, I suppose.*

After being with a man as amorous as Werner, Hilde was growing impatient with Max's constant chatter. They had been meeting every night for the past week, and he hadn't even kissed her yet. It was time for her to turn up the heat and start bringing more than just cookies to these meetings.

---

Hilde borrowed a blanket from the cellar and went to swipe cognac from the liquor cabinet in the kitchen. "Come on now," she whispered, jiggling her hairpin in the lock. On the third try, she heard the click of the latch lifting and opened the doors with ease. Hilde steadied her hand so she could fill her flask to the top. This was a special occasion.

Before Hilde left the house, she checked herself in the mirror. She pushed her breasts together and boosted them up so they peeked out from the neckline. As she walked toward the guard booth, she silently repeated everything complimentary anyone had ever told her.

*That's so funny, Hilde!*

*You're a real Hitler Girl!*

*We've never seen someone work as hard as you.*

"No desserts tonight, Anna?" Max asked, sounding a bit more disappointed than she had hoped.

"I'm sorry if I'm not enough of a treat," Hilde said with a flirtatious pout. "Maybe this will help." She opened her sweater to reveal a small hip flask tucked into her skirt waist.

Max's eyebrows rose. "You're really full of surprises."

She set down her blanket and sat, leaning back on her elbows. "Take a swig, and I'll tell you about the time I was discovered for my first stage show." Max joined her eagerly and flashed a smile at Hilde.

# 23

## *Irma*

A<small>N HOUR AFTER GETTING INTO BED THAT NIGHT, I</small>RMA still hadn't fallen asleep, so she put on her slippers and walked to the kitchen. A warm cup of milk always helped her sort through her feelings. The kitchen had become her favorite spot at Heim Hochland, with its giant butcher block in the center, iron and copper pans, spoons, and ladles hanging overhead. During the day, when Irma stood against the wooden doorframe watching the cooks pull baked goods from the oven, she experienced a sense of peace she had never felt before. More than she enjoyed the hustle and bustle of the kitchen in use, though, she loved having the space all to herself during late-night visits.

As she turned away from the stovetop, Irma heard the kitchen door creak quietly. Gundi had opened the door halfway, looking tentative, waiting for an invitation. Placing her hand on the curve of her belly, Gundi asked, "Are you having trouble sleeping too, Sister Irma?"

Irma mustered a smile. "No, no trouble at all," she replied, swallowing down the lie. She knew Marianne's rules: no polluting the girls' minds with their own troubles. "Would you care to join me? I was just thirsty."

"Yes," Gundi said with sarcasm. "There's nothing quite like

warm milk to quench one's thirst." Nonetheless, she accepted
the offer to join Irma. She eased herself into the wooden chair
at the table.

Irma thought Gundi's stomach looked awfully big for a girl
seven months pregnant, but she held her tongue and stayed on
safer ground. "Why don't I warm some milk for you too?" Irma
offered. "It's good for the baby's bones."

Gundi shrugged, distracted, then looked down at the table
and traced a scar on the dark wood with her index finger.
Minutes later, Irma placed a mug of warm milk in front of
Gundi and took a swallow of her own drink. The two sat in
silence, their only movements the occasional sips they took.
Finally, Gundi raised her eyes in a way that made Irma feel
she was being evaluated. The girl scanned her, then stopped at
Irma's eyes for a moment too long.

"What's it like?" Gundi asked. "When the baby is born.
Mutti always said she just sneezed and I came out without
causing her any pain at all."

Irma laughed. "Lucky woman."

Gundi sniffed and dropped her gaze. "Mutti always wanted
me to feel like I was perfect."

"That had to be nice."

Tightening her lips, Gundi nodded. "Mostly it was."

Irma reached across the table for Gundi's hand, hoping the
physical connection would lead her to reveal more.

Gundi kept her face motionless, eyes locked on the imperfection etched into the table. "I found a few of Gisela's sketches
in the…in her room."

"You did? Why were you in her—"

Gundi interrupted. "I'll show them to you. They're really beautiful. Gisela has a real gift for capturing a person's essence. Most are of her baby, but there was one of Hilde looking out from a window that almost made me feel sorry for her. There's one of you too. Would you like it?"

"Me?" Irma said, surprised at how moved she was. As Irma was thinking about where she would hang the sketch in her bedroom, Hilde strode through the door in her long cotton sleeping gown.

"I thought I heard voices in here," she exclaimed, waddling with great exaggeration toward the table and planting herself in the seat beside Irma and Gundi. She held on to the table with one hand while supporting her back with the other, cringing with discomfort as her bottom hit the seat. She had miscarried at the beginning of August but had somehow found herself pregnant once again. Who knew how the girl managed that feat in a household filled with women?

"I'd like a glass of milk," Hilde told Irma.

Irma didn't know why she was surprised by Hilde's treatment anymore. Still, each demand stung, especially after she'd cared for her when she lost her baby. Most of the girls at Heim Hochland treated Irma like a beloved *Tante*, making her feel both useful and valued in a way she hadn't in years. Piercing that comfortable bubble on a regular basis was snitty Hilde, a constant reminder that Irma was just another staff member.

"Sister Irma is a nurse, not your servant," Gundi clipped.

Irma pushed back her chair and returned to the stove. "It's fine. I was going to warm up some more milk anyway."

In the few minutes it had taken Irma to heat and pour

Hilde's milk into a cup, she heard Hilde turn the conversation toward herself. Her morning sickness was even worse this time. She had such a hard time falling asleep. She missed the baby's father terribly, Hilde said with a pause that begged Gundi to ask who it was. When Hilde realized Gundi was not going to inquire further, she dropped another hint. "It's difficult for a man in his position to get away," she said, waiting hopefully. "He's very high up in the Reich. *Very* high up."

When she turned around, Irma nearly laughed at Gundi's expression: inner brows raised and chin tucked slightly, as if amused by her housemate's self-importance. Catching Irma's eye, Gundi shrugged fractionally. *I am not playing this game*, her expression seemed to say.

Irma set the cup down on the table in front of Hilde, who looked up and offered a generous smile. "Thank you very much, Sister Irma," she said, seeming to fight—and lose—against the urge to glance at Gundi for approval. "I know that it's not your job to serve me, and I really do appreciate it."

Irma knew this type of girl, emotionally starving, scraping for crumbs of acceptance. She reminded herself to keep that in mind and sat down to join them, giving Hilde a pat on the shoulder that was both forgiving and comforting.

Hilde wrapped her hands around the mug and lifted it to her smiling lips. "Did I tell you I worked for Reichsfrauenführerin Gertrud Scholtz-Klink in Berlin?" She had. Many times.

Irma was torn when Gundi rolled her eyes in her direction. She wanted to connect with Gundi, but Hilde was clearly in need of an uncompromised ally, so she refrained from smiling at Gundi's gesture.

Hilde lifted her mug to her lips, then turned to Irma. "This milk really is delicious. Thank you again. Did you add nutmeg?"

Before Irma could answer Hilde, the girl continued. "My time in Berlin was thrilling. I was basically the reichsfrauen-führerin's right-hand girl. She was devastated when I had to leave but understands that bearing children is a woman's most important job." Hilde rested her elbows on the table and leaned her chin on her fists. "Some people assume that my father helped me get the job at the Women's League, but if anyone deserves the credit, it's my baby's father," Hilde said, waiting.

Gundi turned the conversation away from Hilde, asking, "What about you, Sister Irma? Do you have children?"

Irma got up from the table and brought her empty mug to the sink. Anything to avoid looking at the girls. "No, I never had children." Keeping her back turned, Irma steadied her voice. In her effort to deflect, Irma offered fragments of truth, hoping to glue together a plausible reason why she had no children. "When I was a young woman, we were at war. After that was a depression. Life in Germany was quite different before Hitler came to power."

Irma laughed silently at the irony. After twenty-two years, she was finally ready to confront the pain of losing both her marriage before it really began and her child before he or she was even born. But now she was prohibited from doing so because Marianne believed that revisiting difficult memories only created more discomfort. In some ways, she was right. Unburdening herself on these young women wasn't fair, especially since they were expectant mothers. Irma almost wished she could lock up her heart again. Almost but not quite. She knew that she would be here when the residents at Heim Hochland mourned their own losses. And when that happened, Irma would be far better equipped to help them navigate their feelings if she was able to understand her own.

She yawned, hoping the gesture wouldn't seem too exaggerated. "Girls, please excuse me. I'm absolutely beat," she said before making a quick exit. As she made her way back to her bedroom, Irma stopped at the linen closet and reached for a fresh handkerchief. On second thought, she grabbed two. She knew it would be a long night.

# 24

## *Hilde*

WHEN THE LAST BEDROOM LIGHT DIMMED AT HEIM Hochland, Hilde reached under her bed and pulled out a picnic basket filled with Max's favorites: marzipan candies, *vanillekipferl* cookies, and fresh apples. She filled her flask with plum brandy and sniffed her left wrist, hoping the perfume she had borrowed from Renate hadn't worn off yet.

The time for flirtation was over. If Hilde wasn't able to consummate her relationship with Max soon, her chances of conceiving in time to present this baby as Werner's would start to decline. Even drunk, Max remained a perfect gentleman, though. They kissed briefly the last few nights, but his hands remained by his sides. She didn't care how forward she seemed; tonight, she would make the first move. Hilde reminded herself that she had never missed a deadline at the Women's League. She wasn't about to start now.

"Anna," Max began, his voice thick with desire. "I want to hear your life story, from the first thing you remember to right here tonight," he said, flashing a smile before grabbing a crisp apple. "Even the stuff from before you were famous. I want to hear it all."

*What is wrong with this* Bananenbieger?

As he chomped away, Max added, "And then I'll tell you mine."

Hilde looked down to hide her angry expression. Her knit brows and clenched jaw would not help her case. "Max, I have a better idea," she said before she returned her eyes to meet his. "Why don't we make some new memories tonight?" Hilde playfully hooked his shirt collar with her finger and pulled him toward her.

As Max and Hilde lay on a blanket in the moist grass, Max took his time kissing not only Hilde's mouth but her neck and shoulders. Then he moved down, unbuttoned her dress, and ran his tongue over her breasts. Hilde shuddered at the feeling of cool night air snapping against her nipples. Ten minutes later, Max was shimmying his pants down to his ankles. "I'll be gentle, Anna." He lifted his head when he felt her move beneath him. "Is this all right?"

"Yes," she said, surprised at the reedy sound of her voice.

He smiled. "I want to make sure you, umm, that you have a good time."

If she were being entirely honest, Hilde would have to admit that she *was*, umm, having a good time. But tonight was about making a baby.

After a few more minutes, Hilde got used to the feeling of Max inside her. He made soft noises of pleasure and repeated her name—well, Anna's name, but she knew that he meant her. She began to relax into the rolling of their bodies merging together and let herself enjoy the building sensation.

Hilde returned to earth with a face reddened by heat and a body that felt exhausted. Deliciously spent. She rolled onto her back and lifted her knees.

"What are you doing?" Max asked.

"Calisthenics."

"You're the funniest girl, Anna."

───··───

The following evening, Hilde grabbed her notebook filled with comedy sketch ideas and headed to the guard station again. She knew that pregnancy didn't always happen the first time a couple had sex, so she would have to try a few more nights. It was always better to put in too much effort than too little. Besides, Max had told Hilde that he'd love to hear some of her radio show ideas. It would be good for her to practice in front of an audience for feedback. He had an easy laugh, and his chipped tooth gave his face an openness. It seemed to say: *See, I'm not perfect either. You can be yourself.*

The third night Hilde had sex with Max, she opened her eyes and studied his face, scrunched with pleasure. He looked ridiculous, but his vulnerability was also kind of sweet.

Afterward, Hilde tiptoed to the nursery, careful that the wooden planks of the floor would not groan under her weight. Four newborns lay sleeping in white cribs lined against the wall near the windows, their faces as peaceful as angels. Hilde focused on a little boy whose lips were pulsing as though he were nursing, causing his fat cheeks to rise and fall. She lowered the gate of the crib and leaned in to smell the baby's head, remembering Jutta's advice on getting pregnant. *Let your body know you're ready for a baby by involving all your senses. Put talcum powder on a baby blanket and sleep with it. Eat mashed bananas. Listen to lullabies.*

Hilde walked to the next crib. It held a baby girl with an abundance of blond hair. The infant's top curl was pulled together with a thin pink ribbon, which Hilde reached down and stroked. *Touch.* Hilde pulled back her hand and scanned the dark room. In the corner of the nursery was a changing station with diapers, safety pins, and lotions. Hilde squeezed ointment onto a diaper, then sprinkled powder onto it, tying it to create a sachet for herself. *Scent.* She rustled about more and found a tiny set of scissors, which she brought to the blond girl's crib and leaned over the gate. Slipping the ribbon up, nearly to the end of the curl, Hilde snipped just below the pink grosgrain and took a souvenir for herself—a perfect blond lock of hair held together with a little bow.

Walking back to her room, Hilde's stride grew heavier, which she took as a good sign. Her body was finally ready for sleep. Hilde made a quick stop in the kitchen and opened the refrigerator, easily locating bottles of baby formula. She unscrewed the lid off a bottle and pressed her lips to the rim, taking a quick sip. Gagging at the taste of fishy, sweet cream, she realized it was a mixture of evaporated milk and cod liver oil.

<hr>

The next evening, the girls were asked to gather in the common room to prescreen select scenes of a film being developed by the Ministry for Public Enlightenment and Propaganda, and Hilde was excited to give her feedback. What an honor it was to be asked to support the Reich in this way. Soon, she felt a familiar rush of annoyance; no one else was taking this opportunity seriously. Before the film began, there was too much chatter and focus on who was sitting with whom. Renate was carrying on that she didn't get her fair share of chocolate candies, while Ingrid playfully whipped her with a cat-o'-nine-tails she made from black licorice.

Hilde straightened her posture, sitting erect at the foot of the chaise lounge and clearing her throat. Other girls noticed her unflinching attention at the blank, lit screen, one dismissing her with a wave, another whispering to a friend. Hilde paid them no mind as she kept her eyes trained ahead, hoping the elderly gentleman who showed up to Heim Hochland with film reels would report back that one special mother-to-be was so dedicated to the Reich that she was transfixed just by the dust particles floating in the spotlight shining from the projector to the screen.

She stood and asked the projectionist to share a few words about the film and what Herr Goebbels hoped the girls could offer in terms of feedback. The man was likely the grandfather of a high-ranking officer whom the party humored by permitting him to wear the formal uniform while performing simple tasks like running a film projector. He looked like a clean-shaven Father Christmas with rosy cheeks and an ample lap for bouncing great grandchildren.

Herr Christmas told the darkened room that *The Eternal Jew* would be a documentary released next year to help Germans understand why Jews were a danger to their health, safety— their very survival. Sister Marianne stood at the back of the room, nodding her head in agreement. Sister Dorothea parked beside her, expressionless as usual.

As the ticking of the film reel began, Hilde held her hands over her mouth, making a show of her repulsion at the sight of Jews scurrying about their filthy ghettos with dilapidated carts filled with rags and rotting fruit. She huffed with disgust watching young Jews haggle over prices, caring only about money.

Hilde noticed Renate and Ingrid flinch at the next segment, a scene set in the home of a Jewish family. Several girls gasped audibly and murmured, revulsed by the sight of bugs crawling on the kitchen walls. How were the Jews unbothered by such unsanitary conditions? The film narrator explained that Jews felt comfortable in squalor. The Jewish family onscreen didn't even notice the hundreds of bugs as they continued their strange rituals of lighting candles and bobbing their upper bodies.

After the initial shock wore off, Hilde had to admit that while the content was compelling, the delivery did not hold the audience's attention. People still needed a story. Hilde heard Renate whisper that *The Eternal Jew* was an eternal bore and saw her fidget with the seam of her upholstered chair, flicking the tiny fabric tube back and forth. Ingrid extended her feet in front of her and began pointing and flexing them, watching them move as though this were the most fascinating thing she'd ever seen. A new girl, whose name Hilde didn't know yet, got up and went to the kitchen for far too long.

Hilde felt a prickle of anxiety, competing forces of excitement and fear, as she realized what the Reich's next film really needed—someone who understood how to entertain, how a story was structured. They needed her. As other girls started knitting and even whispering to each other during what should have been key scenes in *The Eternal Jew*, Hilde imagined storylines that would convey the same message in a far more engaging way.

*A German maiden (played by me!) is working on her family's farm when she meets a young man who is new to town. The newcomer does his best to blend in with the others. But the audience has already seen him shave off his funny beard and dress normally so no one can tell that he's a Jew. He fools the girl into falling in love with him and, sneaky Jew that he is, gets the girl's family to trust him. Then he asks for her hand in marriage.*

Hilde's heart sped as she realized what a perfect metaphor this story was for the migration of Jews into Europe. So much better than the dull maps and migratory patterns illustrated in *The Eternal Jew*. She imagined the costumes—a sexy dirndl for her character and a simple brown dress for her mother. She thought filming at the Berghof, or one of the führer's other retreats, would be ideal. Perhaps she would get to meet Herr Hitler!

*Then soon, the Jewish boy brings bad fortune to the German family. They lose their farm because, unbeknownst to them, the Jew is cheating them. The maiden's youngest sister gets a disease and dies! Everything this good German family has worked for over the years erodes, infected by something they don't yet understand.*

Her film wouldn't need corny music piped in to tell the audience that something sinister was going on. They would feel it in Hilde's acting. They would see the emotion on her face. She shifted in her chair, trying to contain her excitement.

*The final act would be the German family fighting back against the Jew. Perhaps my character would save the day, though more likely it would be her father or brother or the townspeople marching with torches. With a happy ending worthy of a Hollywood movie, my film will close with a shot of the Jew leaving, his dirty sacks tied on to his wooden carts.*

The projectionist asked the girls if they were inspired by the final shot onscreen, orderly rows of soldiers, marching toward their future. "Yes, yes," they assured him, though their glazed expressions just moments earlier suggested otherwise. Hilde looked over her shoulder only to find that Sister Dorothea had left the room and Sister Marianne had nodded off in her chair.

*Germany needs me. They might not know it, but the party could very much use Hilde Kramer in their fight for the soul of Germany.*

# 25

## *Gundi*

IT WAS LONG AFTER SUNSET BY THE TIME GUNDI COULD make her way back to her room to light the birthday candle she had swiped from the kitchen at Heim Hochland. In the six months since she had last seen Leo, Gundi had been keeping Shabbat using imaginary candles and silent prayers. Tonight, not only was she late to light the candle but her candleholder was an old steel nut she had found in the supply closet. Still, something about the light bursting from the match felt hopeful.

Gundi sat on her bed and smiled at the candle on her windowsill, then placed her hands on her full belly. *Once Papa comes home, we will light candles every Friday night and have Shabbat dinners with your grandparents.* Recently, the baby had started stretching a hand or a foot, but tonight he was quiet. Her child was already observant. Leo's mother would be proud.

She remembered how Rivka regularly closed the blinds of the windows at the front of the house before lighting the Shabbat candles. "Someday, we'll live in a world where we don't have to worry about rocks thrown through the windows, but for now, we'll have to be a little clever as we pray."

When Gundi heard the knock on the door of her room at

Heim Hochland, she blew out the candle and tossed it under her bed for later.

"Gundi, open up. It's me, Hilde!"

Lighting a candle was a small thing, but having to extinguish it reminded Gundi that there was no real respite from the Lebensborn Society. She bit her lip and let the lump in her throat dissolve and neutralize her look of annoyance. "Come in," she managed to offer.

Hilde nodded her head toward the plate of cookies in her hands and leaned against Gundi's door. "I thought we could have a party of our own while the girls upstairs entertain officers tonight."

Gundi's first instinct was to hurl her alarm clock across the room at Hilde. Instead, she smiled and hoped that by inviting her inside, Gundi could glean some valuable information. "Good friends and cookies," Gundi said warmly. "I think the girls upstairs should envy *our* party."

The two girls sat cross-legged on top of Gundi's bed like they were on a lifeboat out at sea.

Gundi began to fish. "Why aren't we allowed to join the party tonight?"

Hilde laughed and pointed at Gundi's belly. "You're a pretty girl, but you're not exactly what the officers are looking for right now."

*Of course Hilde already knew this place was a state-sanctioned brothel. And of course she had no problem with it.*

"Listen," Hilde said, leaning in. "I know we're missing out tonight, but we'll have a bigger opportunity to talk to *higher* ranking officers tomorrow. Can you keep a secret?"

Gundi nodded, hating how Hilde always needed to prolong moments when she controlled information. Both girls' attention was diverted by the slow creaking of a bed upstairs and a man's voice grumbling. Gundi moved her hands, urging Hilde to go on with her big secret.

"Right," Hilde continued. "Guess who is coming to see us tomorrow? And by *us*, I mean just the expectant mothers."

At the most inopportune moment, the rhythmic pounding of a headboard against a wall above them began. Two voices were muffled, but Gundi knew it was Renate's room that was directly above hers. It sounded like she was whimpering as a man barked angrily.

Gundi balled her fists, remembering all the nights she helplessly listened to her father shout at her mother. When Gundi was about ten years old, she had tried to intervene on her mother's behalf during one of her father's drunken rages, but Elsbeth quickly dashed between her daughter and her husband. The following morning, Elsbeth instructed her daughter to stay away from her father when he was in such a state. "Gundilein," her mother had warned. "Next time, you must stay hidden. Put your fingertips in your ears, and hum to yourself to drown the noise, but stay out of sight." But there never was a next time. Walter died of heart failure three weeks later. Elsbeth assured Gundi that her father had died peacefully in his sleep. It was a blessing that he didn't suffer.

A wave of nausea washed over Gundi as she imagined what was happening. Even Hilde looked concerned, her face crumpled with disgust.

A singular thud drew their eyes toward the ceiling. "I'm

going to get Sister Marianne," Gundi said, standing and moving toward the door.

As if on cue, Renate let out a sloppy laugh.

Hilde looked relieved. "Sounds like she's having a good time. Some girls know how to drive a man wild, I suppose."

Gundi stood motionless for an uncomfortable moment before returning to her bed. *All right. Renate is all right.*

"So, Hilde, what's the big secret?"

"I overheard Sister Marianne tell Sister Dorothea that Reichsführer Himmler and Herr Goebbels are visiting Heim Hochland tomorrow morning to talk to us."

Gundi swallowed hard. *What do they want to talk to us about?* She was never more grateful for Hilde's eagerness to fill the silence.

"I'm going to corner Herr Goebbels and tell him about the film script I'm working on," Hilde bubbled before launching into a lengthy description of it. She then scurried across the hall to her room and returned moments later with her screenplay. "I'll read you a few scenes. Some of the monologues are really powerful," Hilde said before launching in.

Gundi tried to tune out Hilde's story about a German farm girl seduced by a Jewish interloper, but her volume was hard to ignore. And as much as Gundi hated to admit it, she did want to find out how the story ended.

A deep sadness settled over Gundi when Hilde described the final scene where the Jewish man was exiled from the village. "So the Jew is just driven out of town?"

Hilde tilted her head and knit her brows. "You're right! That passes the Jewish problem on to the next town. My audience is going to want real justice. They're going to want blood." She paused to consider another option. "What if the Jew is sent to Dachau?"

"The work camp?"

"Yes, but I'll make it clear that he's one of the Jews who is executed right away."

Gundi's body felt submerged underwater, panicked and unable to breathe. Still, she had to dig further. "What makes you think they're executing people at Dachau?"

Hilde shrugged and smiled. "I don't think it. I know it. I worked for the reichsfrauenführerin, remember?"

*No, this isn't true. Hilde likes to make herself important by saying she has special, inside knowledge. Leo is fine.*

Despite Gundi's assurance to herself, her pulse raced with fear. "It's a work camp, Hilde. No one's being executed at Dachau."

"Suit yourself," Hilde said with a shrug, her eyes returning to her script. "I saw the reports myself. Most prisoners are put to work, but the dangerous ones are executed. It's for everyone's safety."

Gundi knew it was a matter of moments before she broke into tears, but tried to respond with nonchalance to Hilde's account. "That makes sense," she forced herself to say. "Hilde, I'm exhausted. Do you mind?" She pointed toward the door. Gathering every scrap of strength she had left, Gundi told Hilde that her film sounded wonderful. "I'm sure Herr Goebbels will be very impressed with it."

When she heard the door close, Gundi fell back onto her bed and held a pillow over her face to muffle her tears.

# 26

## *Irma*

THE STARLIT SKY HUNG LIKE A CANOPY OVER THE BACK patio of Heim Hochland. Irma usually enjoyed the sounds of the girls' laughter but was always unsettled by it when they were entertaining SS officers. Their giggles weren't a natural expression of amusement; they were performative. Irma could also recognize the high notes of female calculation when the young women spoke. In her mind, she could already hear Marianne's voice scolding her for focusing on the girls. *Eyes and ears on how our guests are enjoying themselves, Irma!*

Irma watched the soft bubbling champagne as she emptied bottles into crystal glasses, careful that they should not spill over. As she began to place them onto a round silver tray, she noticed an engraved letter B at the center. Her hand froze at the sight of it; she had long suspected that the fine things at Heim Hochland were ill begotten, but the knowledge that this tray had once belonged to a real person—Frau Baum, or Bloch maybe—pierced through her indifference toward the plight of the Jews in Germany. The Nazis were stealing from the Jews; they were robbing German girls of their innocence. She wasn't even able to hide behind the word *they*; she was part of it. Irma felt pressure on her chest and a thickening in her throat. She would think about this more privately, but for now, she forced herself to cover the surface of the tray with glasses and begin approaching pockets of girls fawning over visiting officers.

In her typical fashion, Renate made her way across the patio, eyeing the officers. Wearing an ivory gossamer gown, she looked like a bride shopping for a groom. "Delighted to meet you, Gruppenführer Müller." She threw her head back and laughed at something he whispered in her ear. "Oh my, aren't you the most charming man?"

Irma looked down, embarrassed for the girl who believed she was in control.

Marie wore a dress that flowed like America's Statue of Liberty. Like the statue, she remained in one spot and let an officer come to her to start a conversation. "Yes, we are having lovely weather," she replied. She waited until the man addressed her again before answering, "Battenberg. And where are you from, Herr Heydrich?"

Shy Ingrid stood at the periphery of the patio, running her hands along a silk rose dress that was pleated like a fan. Irma rushed over to remind her that if she remained on the sidelines, she would be stuck with the worst of this lot of men. "Take a look at the group talking to Sister Marianne," Irma whispered with a slight nod of her chin. Three men in their sixties surrounded Marianne, forming a cloud of smoke with their cigars. One had a turkey wattle of loose flesh that flapped when he spoke. Another had short teeth rimmed with brown stains and more discoloration spots on his face than a map of the lake district. Another had a round red nose with oversize pores that suggested a lifetime of alcohol overconsumption. "You need to start flirting with the younger men, or one of those beasts is going to be your companion for the evening," Irma whispered.

Ingrid shuddered and thanked Irma before quickly striding toward a cluster of men closer to her own age.

By midnight, couples had paired off and headed upstairs. A half hour later, as Irma was clearing glasses from the common room, officers began returning downstairs for drinks and cigarettes.

"Yes, of course I'll write," Marie tittered from the landing. The officer held on to the handrail and descended the steps backward, his eyes fixed upward. Considering the nature of the relationship, the scene felt oddly romantic to Irma. Had they just met? Was this an ongoing relationship? "Thank you for the bracelet," she continued before Irma saw the officer's finger cover his lips.

"Hush," he whispered.

Irma joined the staff in the kitchen. She was drying glasses when she heard Sister Marianne call for her. "I need your assistance, dear. You've been such a help this evening, but I need you for a little longer."

Resigning herself to her lot, Irma did as she was instructed and carried a tray with a crystal decanter into the common room, where officers smoked and waited to be served. Quietly, she began refilling glasses and picking up dirty napkins and olive pits. Irma was invisible to the men, who relaxed into cushioned chairs with the sated look that only came from sex.

"How did you like your first visit to Heim Hochland, Hans?" the eldest officer asked a younger man with slicked-back hair and a pencil-thin mustache.

"No complaints," he said, reaching back to rub his neck. "I think they must give these girls lessons here, because I'd never even heard of some of the things my girl was doing."

"Perks of the job," another officer said. They all laughed knowingly.

Irma could scarcely believe that uniformed officers had once made her feel safe.

"Let's move on to more important matters," another officer said, holding his glass up for Irma to refill. He puffed his cigar, his bright blue eyes squinting when the smoke rose too close. "We've located sixty Jews hidden in Munich, whole families, even a couple of babies. Attics, basements, barns."

*Hidden in basements? Why would Jews hide in basements?*

As if reading Irma's mind, he continued. "They'd rather live like rats than do an honest day's work at the Milbertshofen camp."

Irma focused on slowing her breath, terrified of the questions she might blurt out to these men. Why were Jews hiding when Germany had been urging them to leave for years? Why were children being sent to a work camp? Who was helping them hide?

Eduard. She needed to get back to Frankfurt to let him know that she now realized the truth. He was helping Jews; of course he was. That woman running into his cellar *was* the mother of a former student, as Eduard had explained. She wasn't trying to steal Eduard's heart; she was trying to save herself from deportation. Her child was probably downstairs as well. *My God, maybe there were others!* Irma's mind raced in tight circles. Why had she always assumed the worst in people?

Eduard hadn't been duplicitous. He had always been a kind and generous person. Why couldn't she have simply trusted him? Why couldn't she have seen that his false confession was him sacrificing his happiness for other people's safety?

Irma reminded herself to hide her panicked expression. Then a deep sadness settled in as she realized that she probably didn't deserve a morally courageous man like Eduard. But as she emptied the ashtray from the Nazi officers in the sitting room, Irma vowed that, from this moment on, she would work to become someone worthy of her dear Eduard.

# 27

## *Hilde*

HOURS AFTER THE PARTY FOR THE OFFICERS HAD ENDED, Hilde pulled back the curtains of her bedroom window and saw that there were no more guests on the patio. Two servants loaded dirty plates and empty glasses into bins. She couldn't make it to the front door without passing the kitchen, but she could sneak out the back and make her way around the side of the house. She knew it was risky to visit Max so soon after the party guests left, but she was buzzing with excitement. After Gundi pooped out, Hilde needed to talk to someone about the visit from the reichsführer and propaganda minister the next day.

Hilde had overheard Sister Marianne say she was meeting with Herr Himmler immediately after the presentation to the girls. That was when she would corner Herr Goebbels with her film idea. Before she did, though, she wanted to practice her quick presentation. Hilde knew she would have less than a minute to make her case, so she needed to make every word count.

Sitting in their spot, Max wrapped his arms around his knees. Hilde turned the conversation toward the film, and Max took the bait. "Has the party finally come up with a title, Anna?"

Everyone looked better in moonlight, and Max was no exception. The light erased his acne and illuminated his eyes. Had she actually grown fond of him? Or was she simply grateful for his, well, contributions? Hilde shrugged, deciding that it didn't really matter. She was thankful for his pliability, and she was in a generous mood. The least she could do was entertain him with something he could one day tell his grandchildren about. "The film will be called *Das Bauernmädchen und der Jude*," she said, facing Max, leaning her elbows onto her crossed legs. "I still can't believe I get to star as the farm girl." Hilde flung her hair, now loose against the cotton frock she wore in the evenings, and told Max about her film.

He nodded his head intently.

"This is more than the story of one German family," she said, sweeping her hand across the sky. In her mind, Hilde Kramer was no longer sitting on a patch of grass outside the guard station at Heim Hochland. She was Anna, gliding into the premiere of her film, stopping to chat with news reporters as an explosion of camera flashes illuminated her sequined gown. "No, this film is about so much more. It's the story of the Reich and the resilience of the German people."

Max picked up a stick that was sitting on the ground and began to brush it across the grass. He looked like a little boy practicing his letters. "Anna," Max said softly, still looking at the ground. "A big star like you has all sorts of men after her, but..." He hesitated. "Am I crazy to think we've got something really good between us?"

*If only I could hear those words from Werner.* Hilde felt a bite of anger toward Max, as though he had used up the limited number of romantic lines she would hear in her lifetime. But that was silly. Werner would say plenty of sweet things to her, especially once he learned that she was pregnant with his child again. Or at least he believed he was.

"A girl like you would never marry me, would you?"

Hilde placed a hand on her heart and pressed her lips together. "Oh, Max," she said, imagining herself on the silver screen. She would be standing at the bottom of a circular stairwell, wearing a ballroom gown, her hand reaching to lift his chin. "In another time and another place, we might have a chance, but not now, not here."

Max furrowed his brow, looking confused by Hilde's rationale. He nodded his head and reluctantly agreed. "It's probably for the best," he whispered. "Mutti would have my hide if I didn't marry Brigette Kaltenbrunner."

Narrowing her eyes, Hilde wondered aloud, "Who the hell is Brigette Kaltenbrunner?"

Max explained that Brigette was practically family to him already. "Our mothers grew up together, and they've wanted us to marry since we were in the cradle." Max shrugged. "If I can't be with you, Brigette will make a nice life for us."

*That is the fastest recovery from a heartbreak I've ever seen!* Hilde was mostly relieved that Max easily accepted their fate. But a small part of her was stung that he had gotten over her so quickly.

Max moved in to kiss her, but Hilde held her hand between them. "I have a big day tomorrow. I need my sleep."

"Will I see you tomorrow night?" Max asked, standing and brushing off his slacks.

In Hilde's heart, she sensed she was pregnant so there was probably no need to visit him again. She smiled sweetly. "Yes, I'll be back tomorrow night with all your favorite treats," she sang, relishing the thought of him waiting for her in vain. Then again, it was probably better to keep him available just in case, so she promised herself she'd check in with Max in a week or so. *Let him squirm a bit until all his thoughts of Brigette Kaltenbrunner are crushed by fear of losing me.*

Hilde scanned the house for activity, then ran back, hoping she would make it inside unnoticed. She trotted back to the house, fueled by imagining the look on Werner's face when she told him that not only was she the mother of his child but that she was about to become the Reich's next propaganda film-maker. With a satisfied smirk, she silently declared, *Step aside, Leni Riefenstahl.* Triumph of the Will *and* Olympia *were fine films, but Hilde Kramer is about to raise the bar.* She forgot all about Brigette Kaltenbrunner, or even Max for that matter. In less than a week, Hilde's future was going to look a whole lot brighter.

# 28

## *Irma*

THE FOLLOWING MORNING, IRMA CAUGHT MARIANNE FLIT-
ting about her office like a hummingbird. She moved a
paperweight to the front of her desk, stood frozen for a moment,
then picked it up and moved it somewhere else.

Seeing her old friend at the doorway, Marianne waved her
in. "Last night's party was a success. I already received a telegram from Dr. Ebner congratulating us on a job well done," she
reported, relaxing her shoulders. "Now we just have to make
sure this morning's visit from Reichsführer Himmler and Herr
Goebbels goes equally well."

Irma looked down at her hands, calming her nerves, then
lifted her head with a smile for Marianne. "I am hoping to
take a few days off next week to tend to some affairs back in
Frankfurt."

"Of course, dear," Marianne replied, agreeing that a change
in scenery was good for the soul. "First, I need a favor, though."
Marianne neatened a stack of papers on her desk and explained
that September would be a busy month at Heim Hochland.
Irma would be needed for a special mission to Munich to assist
the Reich in a resettlement program for children. "I need my top
nurse by my side," Marianne said. Before Irma could ask why

children needed to be resettled—or where they were coming from—Marianne leaned forward and explained. "Hundreds of Polish children have been orphaned, so our men have rounded them up and will bring them to Germany for adoption. They'll live far better lives here than they would ever have in Poland."

"Yes," Irma replied, hoping she sounded convincing. "That sounds wonderful." Irma watched Marianne line up her pencils next to her papers. "I'd like to check in on the girls upstairs this morning, if that's all right with you."

Marianne let out an incredulous laugh. "You don't want to hear the big announcement that Heinrich Himmler and Joseph Goebbels have come to make?"

"Sure I do, but I'm exhausted from last night," Irma said with a smile. "I wouldn't want my tired appearance to reflect poorly on Heim Hochland."

Marianne narrowed her eyes. "Are you certain that's your reason?"

"Yes, yes. What else would it be?"

"I don't know, Irma. That's why I'm asking. You seem a little—I don't know—different lately. Like your head is somewhere else."

When the telephone on Marianne's desk rang, Irma stood to leave. "I'll give you some privacy," she said, stepping backward gingerly toward the door.

---

Gripping the handrail, Irma climbed the spiral staircase. When her eyes reached floor level, she noticed that the mood in the communal area upstairs had transformed from a theatrical back-stage dressing room to a graveyard of abandoned dresses strewn about the floor. Most girls were still in their bedrooms with the doors closed, likely due to the empty bottles of *Führerwein* lying like fallen soldiers on the battlefield of their Persian rug.

The door to Renate's room was slightly ajar, so Irma walked toward it and peeked in. She saw Ingrid's back, long blond hair draped against her nightgown as she sat facing Renate, still in her bed. The girls noticed Irma immediately and waved her into their room. Irma startled at the sight of Renate's swollen cheek and the cold compress she held against her forehead. Before Irma could ask, Ingrid shrugged. "She overdoes it on the champagne sometimes."

"Is this true?" Irma's gaze focused on Renate, who was still wearing the overpowering cameo necklace and now-tousled celebrity waves.

Renate looked down as though she felt ashamed but smiled slightly, as if she also enjoyed her role as house vixen. Looking up at Irma and Ingrid, she tucked a loose strand of hair behind her ear and explained that she felt more comfortable when she had a few drinks. "It helps me relax when I get an ugly one, but I may have had a bit too much last night and fell off the bed," Renate confessed. "It seemed really funny at the time." She scrunched her face to suggest that it was no longer as amusing. Renate switched gears and asked Irma if she saw anything suspicious the previous night. "We had another theft up here, and I'm really upset. This time, they took my diamond earrings."

"They'll turn up, I'm sure." Irma patted Renate's blanketed

legs and gave an affectionate squeeze. "You should be careful of how much you drink."

Renate instinctively touched her necklace and bit her bottom lip. "Do you think it will hurt my chances of getting pregnant?"

"No, I…" Irma said, leaning closer to get a better look at the girl's swollen cheek. This would bruise and stay purple for at least a week. For all Renate's posturing, Irma couldn't help but see her as a little girl who had just fallen off the monkey bars at the playground. "No, *Mädel*. I think it will hurt *you*."

# 29

## *Gundi*

SOMEWHERE DEEP INSIDE, GUNDI SUSPECTED THAT HILDE was right. Dachau was more than just a work camp. After hours of crying in her bed, Gundi padded to the maternity ward and rifled through the medicine cabinet. Finally, in the very back, she found a small bottle of morphine. Weighed down by both grief and a near-term pregnancy, every step was a battle, and it was time to concede defeat. She was not going to be able to stop crying, much less fall asleep.

The small brown bottle offered no instructions on dosage, so Gundi did her best to guess how much she should take. A spoonful, the whole bottle. Honestly, she didn't care. She just needed to ease the pain that felt like a boot crushing her chest.

Discovering that Leo and his family were in a place where their lives were in danger was bad enough. Knowing that she was partly responsible deepened the pain. Gundi and Rivka had been so sure that it was safe to remain in Germany, even when Leo and Yosef insisted otherwise. "Let's go to Paris, Gundi," Leo had urged her privately. "We could get a little apartment in the Marais." He whispered his plea, trying to tempt her with a picture of their life together. "A bottle of wine near the Eiffel Tower, walking home along the Seine without seeing a single

Nazi. Or maybe we could go to America. One of Stefan's connections might be able to find us a sponsor in New York."

But Gundi had refused, all but dismissing his concerns. "If
everyone flees, who will stand up to the Nazis?" she had asked.
Now she cringed at the memory. Then came the realization that
was so shameful she had never admitted it to a soul, not even to
herself until very recently. Before Gundi had spent the better part
of a year unlearning the anti-Semitism woven into the cultural
fabric of Germany, on a deeply unconscious level, she had accepted
wholly the idea of Aryan supremacy. The day she spotted Leo
talking to Professor Hirsch at school, she had fully expected him
to greet her with warmth, gratitude even. It wasn't simply because
she was beautiful; it was because he was Jewish. She had assumed
that he would be flattered by her interest.

Gundi felt a solid kick as though her baby was reminding
her of his presence. *Maybe taking morphine could affect the baby.*
She placed a hand on her belly and returned the bottle to its
place. Perhaps she would warm a glass of milk instead.

Back in her bedroom, she tried counting sheep, as Sister
Irma had once suggested. Soon, the boot lifted from her body
and her pillow became a cloud. Gundi wiped tears from her
eyes, swollen from hours of mourning. *Hilde said* some *people
were executed, not all.* Hundreds of Jewish men had been
released from Dachau after their arrest on Kristallnacht and
had said nothing more than that they had been put to work at
an abandoned munitions factory.

Maybe Hilde was wrong after all. The world became gauzy,
and Gundi was transported to another time. It was February
again, the last time she saw Leo and his family.

"Easy on the clutch," Leo said, leaning toward Gundi in the driver's seat of a borrowed Coca-Cola delivery truck. Freshly fallen snow dusted the barren branches of the elm trees on Kurfürstendamm. The wet road reflected the afternoon sunlight. Their friend Stefan let the Edelweiss Pirates practice their driving whenever a vehicle was at his father's auto shop for repairs. To support his son's work, Herr Schulze always lied and told the automobile owners that parts were delayed or work took longer than it actually did so the resistance could put the vehicles to good use. Like many gentiles, Stefan's father wanted to do more but was terrified of the consequences. He told his son that this was his small contribution and said he was proud that at least a dozen young people had learned to drive on his borrowed cars.

Though Gundi had initially refused the driving lessons, Leo had insisted, saying every resistance fighter needed to know how to hot-wire and operate a vehicle. She'd eventually relented after Leo had convinced her that someday, she might have to save his life by shuttling him to safety. He was better at doling out guilt than he was teaching her to drive, she realized as the truck jerked forward whenever she lifted her foot off the clutch to switch gears.

"You're too eager," Leo said patiently. "You have to release the clutch slowly and listen for when it's ready to change speeds."

"I don't know what that means!" she shouted.

Leo demonstrated how a transmission works by making two fists, facing them toward one another, and rolling his knuckles together. "You see how they catch together?"

She did. But how that related to what was going on with the pedal and the stick up in the cab was another story. Gundi gritted her teeth, hating the feeling of incompetence, especially in front of Leo. She didn't want to be too eager. Too anything.

Seeming to sense her frustration, Leo guided Gundi's hand back on the stick and held his hand over it. "This takes practice," he said. "Let's try this again together." Gundi couldn't imagine ever feeling truly comfortable behind the wheel of an automobile, but Leo soon declared her ready for the road. "By the authority of the Edelweiss Pirates, I hereby declare Gundi Schiller a fully licensed driver. Autobahn beware."

As she and Leo walked up the front steps of the Solomons' house, Gundi had never felt more at home. They stepped in from the cold, and before they could inhale the first whiff of brisket, they heard Rivka hollering from the kitchen. "At long last, my two favorite icicles are home."

Gundi smiled, rubbing her still-mittened hands over Leo's wet coat.

"We'll be there in a minute, Mama," Leo called back before leaning forward to kiss Gundi, closing his eyes.

She pulled off her mittens, held her warm hands against Leo's cheeks, and whispered, "I love you." She couldn't tell whether Leo's eyes were glassy with emotion or still teary from the wind, but she didn't have time to ask.

"Yuck!" cried Leo's little brother, Schel, in mock disgust as he and Yosef made their way out of the study together.

Both the Solomon boys seemed to adopt their father's style—soft flannel shirts with black suspenders holding up corduroy slacks. Only on Shabbat did they replace their newsboy caps with yarmulkes.

In his typical booming jocularity, Yosef declared, "We were coming to stoke the fire, but it looks like the *Liebespaar* beat us to it."

Rivka swooped only as far as the kitchen threshold, wearing a long apron accented with splatters of beef gravy. "If my two funnymen could set the table…" She pointed to the kitchen by way of finishing her sentence. "Gundi, Leo, *Shabbat shalom.* Throw another log on the fire for us, won't you?"

Gundi obediently made her way toward the fireplace to follow Rivka's order but was quickly stopped by Leo's hand on hers. Turning toward him, Gundi saw his dimples sink into his cheeks as he smiled.

"Gundi," Leo whispered. "I love you too."

At dinner, Rivka smiled warmly as Gundi joined her in reciting the Hebrew prayers perfectly. Gundi could hardly wait to surprise her again when she joined in the blessing of the challah.

After the meal, Rivka washed dishes while Gundi dried and put them away, as naturally as if this had been their routine for years, though it had been only five months. Rivka leaned closer to Gundi, their arms now touching. "You love him, my Leo, don't you?"

Gundi blushed. She looked down and softly responded, "I do."

Rivka turned to Gundi and used her finger to touch the

girl's chin. "I've been meaning to ask you something," Rivka began, nodding her head toward the small table. "Let's sit."

Though Rivka's demeanor was pleasant, Gundi felt a rush of anxiety. In her experience, it was never a good sign when someone asked you to sit for a conversation they've been putting off for some time. Gundi felt the vinyl cushion give way beneath her as she dropped into the chair. She waited for Rivka to speak, which took uncharacteristically long as she had several false starts.

"We see how Leo looks at you, Gundi. And you know me, I'm a modern woman. You love who you love," Rivka began, hesitating again. "I already cherish you like the daughter I was never blessed with, proving yet again that God has a sense of humor." She pressed her lips to the side and shrugged her shoulders. "I prayed for a daughter, and what I got was the most beautiful shiksa that God ever spun together out of milk and honey and possibly a little fairy dust."

Gundi smiled, flattered, but also knew there was more to follow.

"*Shayna Madela*, can you promise me that if you and Leo marry, you'll convert to Judaism?" Rivka placed her soft hand over Gundi's and explained. "A child isn't considered a Jew unless the mother is Jewish, so—"

Just then, Leo walked in. "Mama, are you out of your mind?"

Turning to face Gundi, he recoiled at the earnestness on her face. She had been about to tell Rivka that she wouldn't mind at all, that she had actually felt a growing affinity for the warm candlelit Shabbat dinners and musical Hebrew prayers. Gundi felt connected to the Jewish faith and culture that encouraged questioning, debate, and dialogue. Gundi was about to tell Rivka that, in her heart, she had already converted and would be happy to formalize it through the synagogue when Leo had interrupted.

He lifted his hands, slapping his temples. "Nobody is converting, nobody. Do you both understand me?"

Rivka snapped, "We were having a *conversation*. Do you see a rabbi here? Do you see a Torah rolled out on the kitchen table? I'm asking a simple question here. I'm a mother. I'm curious. Is that a crime?"

Gundi looked up to speak, but before she could, Leo's voice cracked, and he quickly wiped tears from his eyes with his shirtsleeve. "I'm sorry, Mama. I'm so sorry, Gundi, but I'm afraid for us all. Papa and I both think it's time to go. It's no longer safe for us in Berlin. Stefan can get us papers, and we'll leave together."

"This is our home, Leo!" Rivka said. "Things are bad, but they'll get worse if good Germans don't fight back."

Gundi nodded emphatically and grabbed Rivka's hand.

When this had happened in real life, the discussion ended in a Shabbat détente. Everyone was ready for baked apples and more of Yosef's stories by the fire. It was cold outside, and they didn't need to make any final decisions that February evening.

But in Gundi's dream, the scene took a different turn, one where everyone had heeded Leo and Yosef's warning. In Gundi's mind, they were all together, aboard the deck of a ship, watching a tiny green spot in the distant fog grow into the Statue of Liberty.

The passengers on the boat all began stomping their feet as

they disembarked at Ellis Island. Then they started shouting, "Gundi, you're going to be late!"

*How can I be late if I'm on the ship deck with everyone else?*

"Gundi, wake up!" said Hilde, knocking urgently. "Herr Himmler and Goebbels will be here soon."

Gundi opened her eyes.

⌐•═•⌐

Gundi made her way to the common room and caught a glimpse of herself in the reflection of the large window. To her satisfaction, she appeared calm and confident: shoulders back and face placid. It was the polar opposite of how she felt inside. When her body flushed, she couldn't tell if it was tumultuous hormones, abject fear, or August heat. Smoothing her buttermilk-colored shorts, Gundi took a seat, adjusting the matching top that was generously pleated to accommodate her bulging belly.

The other girls whispered among themselves, trying to guess who the special guests were. The arrival of a large black Mercedes hushed the speculation. As the doors opened and the men emerged from the car, Gundi shuddered at the realization that Hilde had been right. The guests to Heim Hochland were Reichsführer Heinrich Himmler and Propaganda Minister Joseph Goebbels. *That doesn't mean she's right about Dachau*, Gundi tried to convince herself.

Walking behind them was Max, the baby-faced guard whom Hilde had been watching through the window earlier that month. As eager as she seemed to watch Max back then, she seemed equally committed to avoiding his gaze today. The eyes of every girl were locked on the glass window except for Hilde, who turned her head and discreetly cupped her face.

The driver looked like an oversize puppy, eagerly peeking through the window to scan the girls. He was at least one hundred and ninety centimeters tall and had the body of an athlete, dwarfing his superiors, especially Joseph Goebbels, who was a full head shorter and walked with a slight limp. Nazi hypocrisy at its finest.

Gundi imagined Leo elbowing her playfully. *When the girls upstairs try to make a child for Hitler, do you think it is more important for the babies to have the führer's blond hair or his great height?* Leo was alive. He had to be alive.

Sister Marianne stood in front of the fireplace clearing her throat, barely able to suppress her smile. The portrait of Hitler remained centered above the mantle, but the Degas ballerinas that had hung above the bookcase had been replaced with a painting of a mother watchful over her baby's veiled cradle. But before Gundi could guess who the artist was, her eyes were drawn downward to a shelf of the bookcase. There was another new item—a brass candelabra with two elaborately designed spirals flanking a multitiered stick, strikingly similar to the one at Leo's home. Every pore in Gundi's body prickled with fear.

Shifting in her seat, Gundi watched Herr Goebbels walk to the front of the room to address the girls. Like Herr Himmler beside him, the propaganda minister slicked back his brown hair and wore a tailored SS uniform with colorful medals and a swastika armband. What distinguished him was his waxy, corpselike skin and oversized ears. The reichsführer was as plain as a sliced potato, with few remarkable characteristics other than a deep groove at the center of his upper lip and chin cleft. How these men considered themselves a master race was beyond her comprehension.

"You have all seen the inspiring posters, enlightening the German *Volk* about the glory of the Reich," Herr Goebbels began. "We are here today to select one very fortunate young lady to model for a new series that extolls the virtues of German motherhood. Herr Himmler and I have viewed your files but wanted to pay a visit to see how you present in person." He pointed at young Mila and ordered her to stand and state her name and where she was from. When she finished her fidgety introduction, he lowered a hand, signaling that she should sit. Herr Goebbels then moved his fingers slightly to the right, letting the next girl know that it was her turn.

Each young woman seemed eager to impress. They all stood tall and lifted their right arms in salute to Hitler, but after that, it was anyone's guess what Herr Goebbels and Reichsführer Himmler were looking for. The room was charged with tension from the questions no one would dare ask. *Who do you want me to be? Strong and proud? Sweet and demure?* It was an audition where no one was certain of the role being cast.

When it was Gundi's turn, she watched both men's eyes scan the length of her body. "Fräulein, tell us about your hobbies," Herr Goebbels said.

*Does overthrowing the Nazi Party count?*

"Well, I like...I like dancing," she replied. The truth was she hated dancing, never quite understanding why anyone would enjoy flailing their body about. But there was no way she was sharing any truth about herself, no matter how small.

Herr Goebbels jotted on a paper that was clipped to a wooden board. "And what is your favorite film, Fräulein Schiller?"

"Um, *Olympia*, I suppose."

"You suppose?" Reichsführer Himmler asked with a chuckle. "Turn for us, please." She complied. "Stop," he demanded as Gundi stood facing the back of the room, catching Sister Marianne's hopeful smile. *Maybe they'll choose you*, she seemed to say. "Now stand at profile, Fräulein," the reichsführer added. He and Herr Goebbels whispered for a moment, then told her she was free to sit down.

She lowered her body carefully into her chair, angry with herself for not thinking more quickly on her feet. Why hadn't she stuttered when she answered their questions? Why hadn't she slouched or faked a facial tic? Maybe they would have not only ruled her out as a model but released her from the Lebensborn Society altogether.

Reichsführer Himmler and Herr Goebbels looked at Gundi again. The propaganda minister moved his pencil across his notepad and nodded his chin toward her. "Fräulein, stand again."

The other girls turned their heads toward Gundi, their envy palpable. She overheard Hilde whisper, "…because she's so big."

Herr Goebbels murmured something to the reichsführer, who nodded in agreement as Gundi rose. "Thank you, Fräulein."

And with that, she—and everyone else in the room— understood that Gundi was about to become the Nazis' poster girl for German motherhood.

# 30

## *Hilde*

THE MOMENT HILDE SAW REICHSFÜHRER HIMMLER disappear into Sister Marianne's office, she made her way to Herr Goebbels. He stood with his hands clasped behind his back as he admired the new painting in the common room.

"Herr Goebbels?" Hilde said, clutching the pages of her handwritten script. He turned and regarded her curiously before saying that he hadn't made a final decision on the poster model. "Oh, no, I wanted to talk to you about an idea I have for a film."

"For a film?" Herr Goebbels asked, looking at Hilde's flat belly. "Are you expecting?"

She wondered if he was just curious about her role at Heim Hochland or if Herr Goebbels thought pregnant women were incapable of having film ideas. "Yes, Herr Goebbels," she said and nodded, trying to hide the anxiety the question stirred. Hilde had had sex with Max frequently, but who knew if a pregnancy had taken root. Every night before she went to sleep, she had run her fingers along the lock of baby hair she had clipped. She tucked a clean, powdered diaper under her pillow. She had done everything right but also knew that life could be unfair.

Time was short, so without waiting for an invitation, Hilde

launched into her description of *The Farm Girl and the Jew*. "There's a German family, living in the countryside," she began, rattling with nerves. "And their life is good. But then a Jew comes to town."

To her relief, Hilde saw Herr Goebbels purse his lips, listening intently.

"He looks normal, but he's still a Jew," she continued, watching him nod. The sound of Hilde's racing heartbeat was an internal soundtrack. Thankfully, she had practiced on Max so many times, she could recite her presentation without thinking. She barely remembered speaking but suddenly found herself finishing up.

Herr Goebbels remained so still that Hilde could practically see him absorbing the idea. Finally, he crossed his arms and smiled. "Fräulein, it's an excellent idea."

Hilde gripped the papers in her hands, reminding herself to stay grounded. Surely, Herr Goebbels would not be impressed if she jumped in the air and screeched with joy. She closed her eyes, trying to capture this moment. This would be the start of her new life as a Reich propagandist. She had considered the work she had done at Reichsfrauenführerin Scholtz-Klink's office to be very important. But really, it was nothing compared to the contributions and influence of the Ministry for Public Enlightenment and Propaganda. Hilde had ideas beyond new films. She also wanted to develop a series of posters promoting the new resorts Germans could visit through the Strength Through Joy program. *Recharge today for a more productive tomorrow.* Or radio interviews of factory managers who discussed the increase in worker output since the implementation of the Beauty of Labor program. *Ja, adding plants and inspiring posters makes us all feel good and work harder too.*

She was about to share some of her other ideas when Herr Goebbels nodded his head impatiently. Hilde closed her mouth, admonishing herself not to be too talkative.

"It's an excellent idea," he repeated. "One that we are already working on."

*They were already working on her film?* "But…how?" Hilde asked.

"You can't think you're the only one with good ideas, Fräulein…" He paused, waiting for her to offer her family name.

"Kramer," she said, forcing herself to maintain eye contact. Her connection to her father wouldn't impress Herr Goebbels, but perhaps Hilde's relationship with Werner would help. He couldn't simply dismiss her as just another silly girl. "I'm a special friend of Obergruppenführer Ziegler," Hilde said, placing a hand on her belly.

"I see," Herr Goebbels said, shifting his eyes back to the painting. Then, gesturing to Hilde's belly, he added, "In that case, the most important work you can do for the Reich is right here at Heim Hochland."

There was little Hilde loved more than an opening for a rebuttal. The fight charged her, but she reminded herself to speak softly. "I believe I can do both, Herr Goebbels. I was an assistant at the Women's League in Berlin, and they said I was one of the hardest-working girls they'd ever seen."

"Precisely why we want you resting at Heim Hochland." A grin spread across Herr Goebbels's face. "Why don't you give me that," he said and nodded toward her script. "I'll show it to our film producers and see if there's anything we haven't already considered. We might be able to use a line or two of your dialogue."

Hilde stopped herself from stepping back and holding tight to her work. Why were her instincts telling her to run? She had always known party officials to be honorable and trustworthy. Were pregnancy hormones making her hysterical? Why did every pore of her body tingle with cold sweat as she handed Herr Goebbels the script?

"After my baby is born, I can be very useful to your office," Hilde offered with a slight tremor in her voice.

"I'm sure, but let's not get ahead of ourselves. I'll call Obergruppenführer Ziegler and see what his plans are for you." At the sound of Sister Marianne's office door opening, Herr Goebbels turned and walked away from Hilde without another word.

She watched her script disappear in his clutches. Somehow she understood that she would never see it or hear from Herr Goebbels again.

# 31

## *Irma*

THE NIGHT BEFORE IRMA AND MARIANNE WERE SCHED-
uled to visit Munich, the two women met behind the
closed door of Marianne's office. Marianne explained that the
Lebensborn mission had expanded now that Germany was at
war. The nation was swiftly reclaiming territory stripped from
them by the Treaty of Versailles that brought the Great War
to an end. Now, as Germany marched east, the Lebensborn
Society would help displaced Polish orphans find new homes
with German families. Ideally, the program would place infants
with families immediately, but Heim Hochland would add
new cribs to its nursery and build a playroom for children who
needed to be temporarily housed with them. War required sacrifice, Marianne told Irma. "And who is more worthy of our
charity than the little ones?"

The collection of photographs on Marianne's wall was
expanding, sprawling to fill the entire space behind her. The
faces looked like those of any other children: innocent, blank
canvases that would be colored by the environments in which

they lived. A wide-eyed baby in a diaper leaned forward on a stiff couch, touching his foot. Marianne had also added a photograph of a mother and child sitting in tall grass together, the woman in a vertically striped sailor-style dress. The child beside her looked about a year old and had a thick cowlick of hair and a stuffed dog.

Irma pushed her foot under the rug to release her nervous energy. It took her a moment to register that the new picture underneath the portrait of the führer, the toddler with a black fringe of bangs, was actually young Hitler. She wasn't sure if the photographer had unsuccessfully attempted to create a Renaissance-style halo of light, but the effect was a cloud of darkness surrounding him.

Irma's eye caught another new image—a sketch of Gisela's baby. Noticing Irma's gaze linger on it, Marianne smiled and said, "She should feel very proud of her service to the country. Little Heinrich is thriving with his new family."

*His name is Amon*, Irma protested silently.

Marianne lifted a folder a few inches from her desktop and let go, the crack of sound signaling that it was time to move on to the business at hand: their trip to Nazi headquarters in Munich, where they would prepare Polish orphans for adoption by SS officers' wives. "We will leave by nine to arrive at Braunes Haus by ten and make sure the children have been properly outfitted. As you know, the Reich is encouraging families to adopt, especially if they have fewer than four children of their own, but that doesn't mean these ladies are desperate. The children need to look adorable." Leaning forward on her elbows and lowering her voice, Marianne told Irma, "We have to bring the leftovers back to Heim Hochland, so let's try our best to find good homes for all of them." She handed Irma the folder filled with information on each of the twenty infants and toddlers they would be showing the following day. "There will be thousands of children who need our help in the coming months," Marianne said. She pointed to the folder to draw Irma's attention to it. "Familiarize yourself with each child so you can discuss their backgrounds with prospective mothers. The children were identified by our men on the ground in the east, so they've all been screened for racial fitness, but we need to discuss each child's special genetic predispositions." Marianne puffed like a bird before she showed Irma what she had already committed to memory. "Child Number One, three months, was born to *two* professional musicians. Number Two, eleven months, son of an Olympic bronze medal rower. Number Three, one month, mother was an opera singer."

Forcing a tight smile, Irma replied, "Oh, how—"

Irma was relieved when Marianne interrupted. Feigning excitement over the special talents of dead parents would have been too much. Marianne sounded more like she was selling appliances than talking about orphans who needed new homes.

Then there was the nagging question Irma was afraid to ask. She leaned back in Marianne's office chair and pressed her hands into the cushioned armrests to summon her courage. Adjusting herself in the seat, she began tentatively. "Why are there so many displaced orphans?"

Marianne waved a dismissive hand. "They're a poor country. Many of these parents put themselves in danger and pay a price for it. It's very selfish of them, if you ask me." Marianne straightened her back and gave a nod of self-satisfaction. "These children are fortunate that the Reich is giving them a chance for a new life."

Irma searched for the right words as the photographs behind Marianne peered out at her. She let her eyes drift toward the sketch of Gisela's baby, wondering where the girl was now. Irma was unable to shake the memory of watching Gisela hurried into her parents' car. Her blond hair was loose, undone, curtaining part of her face. Irma recognized the expression of a young woman who'd lost the future she had assumed was hers.

Marianne hardly noticed Irma drift off into the memory. She simply lifted an index finger toward the file in Irma's hands. "Study the children's attributes tonight. I'll quiz you on the drive to Munich tomorrow morning."

◦─•·─◦

"Our guests are the Reich's most important women, so I expect you to treat them as such," Marianne told Irma, lifting an eyebrow as they finished preparing the babies, straightening hair ribbons and cleaning little mouths.

Irma scanned the ballroom of the Braunes Haus, making sure everything was just right. She had been quizzed during the entire drive to the city. Not only did Irma know the background of all twenty of the children they would be showing, she knew about the women who would be there to adopt. Each was defined by her husband's rank and how many children she already had.

The most powerful woman in the room would be Margarete

Baer, wife of Rudolph Baer, one of the top men in the Reich Central Security Office. At forty years old, she already had six children of her own, half of whom were grown. Word was that she was gunning for a gold Mutterkreuz award next year, so she wanted to adopt two more children. Her best friend, Vera Gruber, only had three of her own children and was looking for a baby to fill out her family. The youngest mother, Alice Richter, had one small child and many years to bear more. Still, it was important for SS wives to set a good example for German women by adopting children.

Before Irma could respond to Marianne's reminder, she heard the titter of women's voices and the clack of heels ascending the wooden stairs. Her head turned urgently toward her boss. It was time.

The two stationed themselves outside the ballroom they had spent the last several hours transforming into a temporary nursery. In their white uniforms, Irma and Marianne stood erect with their shoulders back. Inside the cavernous room were rows of white eyelet-trimmed bassinets filled with infants and oversize playpens bustling with toddlers. One little boy had spent the morning pretending to be a dog, barking at and even biting the other children. Mercifully, he had managed to calm down. A baby who had been inconsolable a short while ago was sleeping soundly. It seemed slightly surreal to house a nursery in such a formal room—a three-tier chandelier, oversize portraits, and a waxed parquet floor. This was a room where the führer himself, along with the top men in the party, entertained foreign dignitaries and heads of state. But today the second floor was packed with children, stuffed animals, dolls, and baby supplies. Irma and Marianne had tied pink and blue satin ribbons around the ballroom's Doric columns to help soften the feel of the space.

Despite her reservations about the mission, Irma couldn't help but feel a certain sense of pride at a job well done. The children were all fed, bathed, and clothed to perfection. The daughter of the musicians, whom Marianne had told Irma about the evening before, was dolled up in a burgundy velvet dress with a white lace Peter Pan collar. Girl babies would surely charm the women in their mini dirndls; the baby boys looked adorable in their tiny lederhosen. The biter looked downright dignified in his black wool blazer and red clip-on necktie. When Irma tilted her head with wonder at the transformation, Marianne winked and gestured toward her hand tucked in her dress pocket. She smiled coyly, uncurling her fist to offer a peek of a small brown vial that Irma recognized from Heim Hochland. It was Veronal, the sleep medication they sometimes gave new mothers after delivery to help calm their nerves.

"Just a pinch to settle him down," Marianne whispered. "We'll make sure he goes to a family with a few big brothers. They'll Germanize that animal behavior right out of him."

"*Germanize?*" Irma whispered.

Marianne smiled. "Biology made them Aryan, but family will make them German."

Echoes of the women's heels grew louder, and one woman's voice was a touch stronger than the others. Irma couldn't make out her words, but the tone was both flitty and dominant.

Marianne turned her head to greet the eight women ascending the staircase. "Good afternoon, ladies," she greeted them warmly before snapping her arm to salute Hitler, a gesture they all returned.

Irma did so as well, then recited the line Marianne had scripted for her, though it nearly caught in her throat. "Shall we take a look at the future of Germany?" Yes, yes, they all agreed, wearing autumn's new fashions, making their way into the room. Margarete was at the tip of the flock in a pumpkin-colored wool skirt and matching short-waisted jacket with a brown gingham collar. Vera, Margarete's second-in-command, sported an identical look, though her cranberry-colored suit bore brass buttons, forgoing the whimsy of her friend's collar. A tall woman named Eva was in the back of the group, decked out in a zebra-pattern skirt and jacket with a black silk blouse and black T-strap leather shoes. Five others joined them.

As the women entered the ballroom, they let out a chorus of sighs and quickly dispersed to different sections. "Look at that darling," a young woman in an onion-dome cap said, pointing to a little boy in a playpen.

Her friend replied, "Oh, Alice, he's sweet, but I want a baby, not a toddler." She headed off to the row of bassinets.

Irma braced herself as she saw Margarete's arms pumping confidently as she strode toward her. Marianne spoke softly without moving her lips. "Let me handle this."

Margarete placed a gloved hand on Irma's shoulder, widened her eyes, and pouted as if to forewarn that she was about to say something charming. "I need your help. My husband wants another boy, but I'm desperate for a little girl. Do you have any boy-girl twins today?" Margarete's eyes scanned the other women as they considered children.

Marianne lifted her chin with pride. "We have a precious boy and girl born just weeks apart, and they are strikingly similar in looks."

Unsure of how to react, Irma nodded her head in agreement. She knew the babies, and yes, they did look a lot alike.

Marianne continued. "Both had highly educated, very talented parents. The boy comes from athletic stock and a father who was two hundred centimeters."

Margarete gently placed the tips of her glove onto her chest. "Two hundred? My goodness. What about the girl? We don't want a giant," she said with a laugh that Marianne matched. A moment later, Irma pressed out a reluctant giggle.

Marianne tapped the folder in her hands as if to let Margarete know she could review the file herself. "Frau Baer, the girl's mother was a perfect one hundred and seventy-five centimeters. She's strong and is already showing signs of a sweet disposition."

Nodding toward the folder, Margarete asked if there was a photograph of the girl's parents. She leaned in and whispered, "My friend adopted a girl through a Lebensborn home when the program started a few years ago and…" She held up a hand to stop herself. "All the program's children are beautiful, but some are more pleasant to look at than others."

Marianne smiled. "How very true," she said, opening the file and passing it to Margarete for a look.

Irma didn't need to see it again. The baby girl, Number Fourteen, whose birth name was Jadzia, was born to Bernice and Daniel Zajac, who lived in Katowice. The file included the wedding photograph of Jadzia's parents, marked 1936. The couple stood in front of a curtain with deep, shadowed folds and baskets of flowers set on the ground. Bernice wore a simple high-neck dress and held a modest bouquet; Daniel wore a traditional black suit with wide satin lapels. Irma couldn't help think about their wedding day, how when they posed for their portrait, they had no idea that, just three years later, it would be used to help a Nazi wife decide whether their orphaned baby girl was pretty enough to adopt.

⌐•⌐

Baby Aleksy was an easy sell. As promised, he was larger than most ten-month-old boys and could not only walk but run. Irma was surprised to see Margarete kneel to the floor and hold her arms open for Aleksy to speed into.

"Oh look," she heard a woman squeal. Irma, along with everyone else in the area, turned to see Dawid, the biter, in his long red tie, fast asleep in the woman's arms. She ran her fingers tenderly through the boy's shock of blond hair and welled with emotion. "He knows I'm his Mutti."

As Irma walked toward the kitchen to retrieve a formula bottle, she looked at the women tenderly holding the children. Vera cradled a sweet little boy who was placing his fingers into her mouth as she pretended to nibble the baby's chubby hand. He immediately reached down and began toying with the shiny buttons on his new mother's jacket.

By the time Irma returned to Margarete, Marianne was by her side, rolling a ball toward the boy. "There you are, Sister Irma," she huffed impatiently. "Frau Baer will take the boy. Please let her have a closer look at the girl."

Irma held baby Jadzia and led Margarete to the diaper changing table, looking away as the child flashed a gummy smile. She soon reconsidered, forcing herself to meet the gaze of this sweet baby. *I know what it's like to lose somebody you love, little one. I'm sorry about your parents, Jadzia.*

Her thought was interrupted by Margarete's horrified gasp, alarming everyone around them. Turning to Irma accusingly, she snapped, "What's wrong with her foot?"

Looking down at the diapered child, Irma noticed that Jadzia's foot was fisted as if she were tense. Irma cupped the baby's left foot in her hands, warming it with human touch. When it relaxed, Irma pressed gently on the sole of the baby's foot until it remained flat. Moments later, her foot curled again.

"I'm sure it's nothing," Marianne said, rushing over. "She's had a long journey from Katowice. A little loving care from her Mutti, and she'll be good as new. Her family's medical records are perfect."

Irma looked toward the floor, grateful the child couldn't understand.

"Even if your daughter has a small problem, you know the Reich will help you. Look at Herr Goebbels," Marianne continued.

Margarete moved her purse strap from her hand to the crook of her elbow and shook her head. "Not today."

"She's a good girl," Marianne whispered with a tight throat. "Herr Baer is going to be so overjoyed with his new son, he probably won't be ready for another baby for several months. Look at her. She's practically identical to the boy. You'll raise them as twins, and no one will be the wiser." Lowering her voice even more, she reminded Margarete that if the girl had serious problems, she could always return her.

Margarete was still for a moment as she considered. "All right," she said, turning her head to smile at the baby. "She does have an awfully cute little face."

On the drive back to Steinhöring, Irma watched Munich pass by through the window of their automobile. The sun was setting earlier now that autumn had arrived. Silhouettes of linden trees looked stark against the bright light of the streetlamps. As their automobile rolled down the street, Irma felt chilled by the endless row of Hakenkreuz banners fluttering from flagpoles hanging from every window, rooftop, and lamppost.

"Did you enjoy our outing?" Marianne asked.

Irma nodded. "It was enlightening," she replied, managing to sound sincere.

"Good. I wanted you to see all the charitable work the Reich, and the Lebensborn Society in particular, is doing. Do you have any questions about today, dear?"

Irma shook her head and continued to look out the window so Marianne wouldn't see her glassy eyes. Of course she had questions. The one that was most pressing, the one she could never ask, weighed on her heavily. *If Jadzia's family is so healthy and strong, what happened to her parents?*

# 32

## *Hilde*

H ILDE WANTED TO BE THE SORT OF GIRL WHO COULD WAIT until she got to the toilet to check for blood. But the moment she woke to stomach cramping, she pushed aside her blankets and reached down to slide her underpants down to her thighs.

*No blood!* She fisted her hands victoriously but reminded herself that the day was young and her cycle had certainly been thrown off by her miscarriage in August. It was too early to confirm a pregnancy, but not too soon for her to feel it. A woman had intuition about these things. Plus, her swollen breasts and uterine cramps felt exactly as they did when she was pregnant before. Feeling buoyed, Hilde pulled up her underpants and swung her bare feet to the ground to start her morning routine: scrubbing her face, braiding her hair, and brushing her teeth.

Hilde put on her floral frock over her head and pulled the ties into a loose bow in the back. She smoothed her hand over her belly, thankful for the promise of growing life.

At breakfast, Hilde poured a generous serving of milk into her cold cereal and added a few extra almonds and berries.

She closed her eyes for a moment a4nd made a wish. *I am eating for two.*

Nothing could bother Hilde today, not even watching all the girls fuss over Gundi's big photo shoot that afternoon. Sister Irma would escort Gundi to a studio in Munich where she would pose for the Reich's new poster series.

"Remember every last detail," Marie urged.

Even Renate echoed the sentiment. "We want to hear everything!"

Gundi smiled primly as she brought her spoon to her mouth. Honestly, she was so stuck up, acting like she was royalty, too good for the rest of them. It was unfathomable that Gundi had zero appreciation of how fortunate she was. She said and did all the right things, but Gundi acted as though being chosen as a model for the Reich was a burden instead of an honor. Hilde was grateful she wasn't born perfect looking like Princess Gundi; apparently, beauty bred laziness. Hilde had to work for everything she had. Would she have cultivated her sense of humor if she instantly won people's affections? Would she have written a movie? At the thought of her script in Herr Goebbels's hands, Hilde deflated in her seat but quickly shook away the unpleasant thought.

Today was a day of celebration. She was definitely, probably pregnant. And she heard Sister Marianne tell the kitchen staff that Heim Hochland was expecting guests today. Now that Germany was at war, several soldiers would come to Heim Hochland to marry their *Schätze* before heading off for duty in the east.

Gundi wasn't even smart enough to realize how lucky she was to be at a Lebensborn home. Regular German citizens had to manage on rations, but the girls at Heim Hochland had the best of everything—meat, dairy, even sweets! What more did snooty Gundi want?

Gundi might have been disappointed that soldiers who were already stationed in Austria weren't allowed to visit the house. Poor Gundi would have to wait until Christmas to marry her baby's father. Boo-hoo for her.

<hr />

Six days later, Hilde's period still had not arrived. If she thought she had been elated the week earlier, it was nothing compared to how high she was flying now as her cramping continued with no sign of blood. Werner hadn't been able to visit, but Hilde had expected as much. He had a nation to defend.

Hilde sank into her favorite chaise lounge by the window. She kicked her feet up on the chair, clutching a copy of *The Womanly Art of German Motherhood* as she watched the sky transform from watercolor streaks of lavender to a spill of blue ink.

She was halfway through the tome, reading a chapter on nurturing a child's sense of self.

*The German mother has a duty to instill in her children the knowledge that they are the rightful keepers of civilization. At the same time, mothers must ensure that the heads of their children don't swell with ideas of grandiosity or turn*

*to fulfillment of individual desires. Praise children infre-*
*quently and focus not on their accomplishment, talent, or*
*skill but rather how these assets benefit the Reich.*

She was soon distracted by the sound of Sister Marianne's footsteps. "Hilde! I was just on my way to your room. I have some important business to discuss with you."

*Business? Did Herr Goebbels tell Sister Marianne that there were, in fact, elements of my script that weren't in the ministry's version?*

Hilde followed Sister Marianne to her office. "Close the door, dear," Sister Marianne instructed with an unusual softness in her voice. She opened the drawer of her desk and pulled out a telegram. "I received word from Obergruppenführer Ziegler today," she said with a tone far more serious than Hilde was comfortable with.

"Is he all right? Has he been injured?" Hilde suddenly felt dizzy with panic and gripped the armrests of her chair.

"He's fine, dear." Sister Marianne paused, then looked at the telegram again. "He's very angry with you, and I must say, you've given him good reason."

Without thinking, Hilde lunged forward and tried to grab the telegram from Sister Marianne's hands.

Pulling it back like a matador being rushed by a bull, Sister Marianne demanded that Hilde sit. "It is exactly this type of impulsiveness and indiscretion that Obergruppenführer Ziegler is upset by."

*Angry? Upset? What have I done wrong?*

"Apparently, when he was at the house for poster model

selection, you told Herr Goebbels that you were carrying his child."

"Herr *Goebbels's* child?"

Sister Marianne's mouth was agape. "No, not Herr Goebbels's child. Obergruppenführer Ziegler's, of course!" She sighed loudly and looked down. "Hilde, I hate that I have to ask you this, but have you had relations with Herr Goebbels as well?"

Hilde wanted to snap back that of course she hadn't had a relationship with Herr Goebbels. The mistake was because of Sister Marianne's sloppy phrasing. But there was no time to score petty points. Hilde just shook her head and insisted that Sister Marianne tell her what she had done wrong.

"Hilde, you don't just tell people that you're carrying the child of a married man, especially one of the obergruppen-führer's stature."

Before Hilde could argue that she wasn't telling just anyone, Sister Marianne held up her hand.

"Now, the obergruppenführer cannot be sure who else you've shared this information with," Sister Marianne said, nodding her head with sympathy. "So he regrets that he has no choice but to cut off all ties with you."

When she tried to stand, Hilde's knees buckled beneath her, and she was suddenly back in her chair. She worked to keep her voice steady. "Sister Marianne," she said with forced levity, as though this had all been just one giant misunderstanding. "I only mentioned this to Herr Goebbels."

"And me," Sister Marianne clipped.

"But you already knew."

"But you didn't know that I knew when you told me," Sister Marianne said, seeming not to enjoy winning this debate. "Hilde, the point is that you have proven to be indiscreet, and associating further with you is not a risk a man in his position can take."

Then Sister Marianne lowered the boom. Obergruppenführer Ziegler's name would not be on Hilde's baby's birth certificate, nor would he claim paternity of the child. Of course, the Reich would stand by Hilde and allow her to remain at Heim Hochland until she delivered. The child would be adopted by a suitable German family two weeks later.

"For one mistake?" Hilde shouted. "Let me talk to Werner. He'll understand how sorry I am and that it will never happen again!"

Sister Marianne's expression shifted slightly. Every part of her dropped a few centimeters: her cheeks, chin, shoulders. Her compassion for Hilde had been on a ten-minute timer, and it had just expired. "Listen to me, young lady. Germany is at war, and Obergruppenführer Ziegler has far more important things to think about than you."

Hilde willed herself not to cry. She was pregnant with Werner's baby—well, as far as *they* knew, at least. That had to count for something. Surely, Werner wasn't willing to cut ties with his child so easily. Hilde sat straight as a rod, stared into Sister Marianne's eyes, and bluffed. "Fine then, but I'm not giving up my child for adoption. I'll return home to Munich, and my parents can help me raise my baby."

Sister Marianne sat back in her chair and frowned. She folded her hands on the desk and looked at Hilde with renewed kindness. Sighing loudly, she looked at Hilde. "Dear, you don't have a baby. The child belongs to the Reich. Shall I show you the papers you signed when you arrived at Heim Hochland?"

Hilde opened her mouth to speak, but no words came out. She could only cry, so Sister Marianne continued.

"If you want to keep the baby, find yourself a husband in a hurry. Or place the baby for adoption, knowing you did your patriotic duty for the Fatherland. The child will live a splendid life, I assure you." The nurse stood and made her way to Hilde and hugged her. "Men are cowards, dear. Dry your eyes, get a good night's sleep, and consider your options. Giving a child the chance to live in the new Germany is a gift in and of itself."

That night, Hilde lay on her bed and checked herself again for blood but knew it was in vain. She was pregnant. Of course she was. She had a few hours before Max started the night shift at the guard station, and Hilde had a decision to make.

She could go to the maternity ward, look for a sterile object, and try to terminate the pregnancy on her own. She quickly dismissed that idea; she'd heard of too many girls who slipped up and injured themselves. There was a rumor that a girl back home in Munich had died that way. Even if Hilde was successful with her abortion, the timing would be suspect. Sister Marianne had been compassionate earlier, but she might not be as understanding if she learned that Hilde had broken the law banning abortions for Aryans.

Hilde had been so good about resisting the urge to cut

under her fingernail, but she needed her crutch as she deliberated. She could give up the baby for adoption and return home to Munich. Her parents would never know she had a child, and she was confident that the Women's League would help her cover her tracks by typing up a phony letter of commendation for her year of service. Her baby would be raised among the party elite and live a grand life. The only downside was that she would be right back where she started—living in her parents' home with no career and no prospects for marriage.

Which left Hilde with a third option. She could confess to Max that she was pregnant with his child and marry him. For once in her life, she wouldn't have to lie to get what she needed. Max was nice enough company and actually seemed to like her. There were challenges, like his thinking her name was Anna and believing she was an actress. She had also disappeared for a week, leaving Max waiting and wondering what had happened to their relationship. Days ago, she ducked behind the staircase when she saw Max approaching the house with a handful of wildflowers. She'd heard Max ask Sister Marianne for Anna and felt a punch of remorse when she watched his face crumple with confusion upon hearing that no one by that name lived at Heim Hochland.

---

If ever there was a time that Hilde Kramer would need sharp acting skills, it was now.

"Anna?" Max whispered as Hilde walked in the darkness toward the guard station. As her figure grew closer, his shoulders dropped with relief. "Anna, where have you been? Are you all right?"

Hilde ran into his arms and fell into Max's embrace. "I've been terribly sick, and…"

"Sick?" Max interrupted, gripping her shoulders and holding her back for a look. "Is it serious? Are you…are you going to be all right?"

This was the right decision. Hilde would bask in this feeling of someone genuinely caring about her for the rest of her life. Max would be a fine husband. "Yes, Max, I'm better now. I'm…" She looked down shyly. "I'm carrying our baby."

He stepped back and crossed his arms over his chest. "*Scheisse*, Anna, this is a surprise."

She readied herself to bark back that it could hardly be *that* big of a surprise. They had been intimate many times.

"Anna," he said, shaking his head in disbelief. "I never thought…" Max trailed off and looked down.

"Aren't you happy?" Hilde cried.

"Sure, I'm happy, Anna. It's just…well, when you said no…" He sighed. "Mutti really wants me to marry Brigette."

Hilde was free-falling into the familiar abyss of rejection. This was an all-time low for her; Max's mother didn't even know about her, and she already preferred someone else for her son. More concerning to Hilde was why a grown man cared so much about what his mother wanted.

It took every bit of Hilde's strength to remain standing and not fall to the ground in tears. She would not let Max have that satisfaction. She snapped, "You should have thought about that before you decided you wanted to *rumsen*!"

"You're right," Max returned. "You're right, Anna. I need to take responsibility for this baby. Let's get married on my day off this Friday."

*Let's get married this Friday?* She wanted to scream that this was the worst marriage proposal ever. No proclamation of his undying love. No painting a picture of their idyllic future together. This was more of a marriage suggestion than a proposal. Yet it was her only option.

She surrendered to her fate and replied, matching his lack of enthusiasm. "Fine, Max, let's get married, but there's just one thing," she said. "Anna is my stage name. My real name is Hilde, and if we're going to be married, I want to leave my past fame behind and never speak of it again. Ever."

The two sat on the grass in their usual place, looking up at the orange sliver of a moon. Max mapped out a plan. He had just been called to serve in Warsaw, so Hilde would stay at Heim Hochland until she delivered their baby, then move in with Max's parents in Bamberg.

"Mutti will get used to this," he said, kissing Hilde's forehead. "She usually doesn't stay angry at me too long. I guess she's just protective because I'm her only son. You just keep being your sweet self, Anna... I  mean Hilde. You're going to win her over in no time at all."

Hilde's regret was like quicksand.

As Max continued, Hilde realized that his was the voice she would hear for the rest of her life. First thing when she woke up, last thing when he went to sleep. Max and his many, many thoughts.

"Oh, and, Hilde, I think it's great that you don't want to

talk about your acting career anymore, because Mutti has very strong feelings about girls in show business. She thinks they're whores, which I know isn't true, but—"

"She thinks what?" Hilde asked, not bothering to mask her outrage.

"I don't feel that way, Hilde. I'm only telling you this because I want you to be prepared. Mutti's pretty set in her ways, so I can't expect her to change. She's just old-fashioned and thinks women who crave attention have loose morals. But we won't tell her about your past. It will be our secret." Max kissed Hilde's nose reassuringly. "I bet she's going to love you."

# 33
## Gundi

*Munich*

AT THE PHOTOGRAPHY STUDIO OF GUSTAV SCHENK, GUNDI stood in front of a white screen next to a little boy who couldn't have been more than three years old. He wore a brown cap with blond stubble peeking from the bottom. The photographer's assistant, Wilhelm, had helped the child change into a tiny Deutsches Jungvolk uniform that had been created especially for the photo shoot, since the child was many years from joining the league.

"Hold Mutti's hand!" Herr Schenk commanded, pointing at Gundi.

The boy's tiny head zigzagged the room, searching for his real mother. He sprinted off the set and into her arms, burying his head into her skirt and sobbing.

*Poor boy*, Gundi thought. *Does Herr Schenk really think telling a child that his Mutti has been replaced by a stranger wouldn't be upsetting?*

After that, the photographer suggested they take a break and move on to another pose. Herr Schenk shouted to his assistant, "Bring the baby so we can create a pose with a mother of two children expecting her third!"

As commanded, Wilhelm scurried behind the white background and returned with a tiny baby doll he carelessly held
by the foot.

"The *large* doll, you nincompoop! The baby has to be at
least nine months old," the photographer snapped, gesturing to
Gundi's full-term swell.

A chisel-faced man then joined Gundi on the set. Posing
as her husband, he stood over Gundi protectively as she sat in
a rocking chair, holding their baby. After the once-frightened
little boy saw that this was all just a game of make-believe, he
joined in and happily played his role as big brother.

Herr Schenk coaxed Gundi. "Place your hand on little
Martin's shoulder, and look up toward your beloved Arthur. Let
me see the love."

Most unsettling for Gundi was that she had no idea
what imagery the propaganda ministry would use as background for these posters. Today, she stood in front of a plain
screen, but the party would transform it to whatever scene it
wanted. Herr Schenk mentioned that the motherhood series
would likely use wildflower fields and mountain ranges, but
he didn't have any real information. For all he knew, Herr
Goebbels would place an army of soldiers marching behind
Gundi.

By the end of the day, Gundi stood alone in front of the
blank screen. The room was uncomfortably warm, and she
wiped the sweat from her forehead with her dress sleeve as
Herr Schenk stood back and appraised her, strumming his fingers against his chin. He moved toward Gundi and placed her
hands on her full belly, instructing her to look into the distance.

She flinched at his touch, then forced a smile to distract Herr Schenk from her show of revulsion.

"Beautiful, beautiful," the photographer said, lifting Gundi's chin. "The German *Mutter*. So strong and hopeful."

She felt quite the opposite. Nine months pregnant, Gundi's lower back pinched every time she took a step. Standing still on her swollen feet wasn't any better. Her mind volleyed between thinking about how badly she needed to urinate and how selfish she was to care. Leo could be dead. Her child would be ostracized from German life if his features were visibly Jewish.

Herr Schenk's tone was encouraging, but his words taunted Gundi. "Think about your baby's future in the beautiful new world Germany is creating. He will have the best of everything, Gundi!"

She struggled to maintain her composure, barely able to contain her tears, much less conjure a smile.

The photographer lifted his head from the camera and looked at Gundi. "Goodness, I've made you emotional. Hold that expression and look into the distance. That's beautiful, Gundi. The German mother is deeply moved by her patriotism." Herr Schenk craned his neck, likely in search of his missing assistant, before returning his gaze to Gundi. "All this hard work will be worth it when you see how beautiful you look on the posters."

She closed her eyes for a moment and took a breath, trying to chase away the thought of the world seeing the images of her. Stefan and Sarah and the rest of the Edelweiss Pirates. What would Professor Hirsch think?

"Wilhelm! Bring the model a glass of water," Herr Schenk shouted to the back room where costumes and props were kept. When Wilhelm never appeared, he waved a hand dismissively. "We have everything we need from you today, Fräulein Schiller." He folded his camera and lifted a black veil over the tripod. "In no time, everyone will know that you, Gundi Schiller, are the face of the new Germany."

# 34

## *Irma*

*Frankfurt*

IRMA REMOVED A KIDSKIN GLOVE BEFORE KNOCKING ON Eduard's door. A proper knocker had still not been installed, which she considered a good sign that there wasn't a new lady of the house. But soon Irma's gut twisted as she heard the tapping of high heels against the wooden floor inside. She looked down at her own feet in their functional work shoes and fingered the string tie of the pastry box she had brought as a peace offering.

The door swung open to Eduard's daughter, Gerda, whose expression froze as soon as she saw who it was. "Irma, I wasn't expecting—" She interrupted herself before stepping outside to continue. Gerda closed the door behind her and glanced each way down the street, explaining that she was looking after her father's house while he was out of town for the week. Crossing her arms over her chest, Gerda shook her head. "He won't be back until Sunday night."

Irma swallowed hard, disappointed not only by the news but by Gerda's cold reception. She looked down and put her glove back on just to occupy herself. "May I come back Sunday night? I'd like to talk to him."

Gerda shifted her weight and sighed, sympathy thawing her just a bit. But not enough. "No, Irma. That wouldn't be a good idea." She looked as though she was deliberating whether to say more, then continued. "You really hurt him, Irma. Let him be."

Peeking into the house, Irma longed to go inside to sit down for dinner and hear about Eduard's students and the silly things they said in class, to tease Eduard about the bite marks he left in his pencils.

Sighing again, Gerda placed her hand protectively on the doorknob. "Irma, you could have killed him hurling that glass across the room."

Irma thought that was a bit dramatic, but she couldn't defend her actions.

"You destroyed my parents' wedding crystal. I'm sorry, Irma, but we don't have room in our lives for this kind of instability."

"May I come in and explain? I understand now—"

"No," Gerda said, straightening her back again, turning her head slightly to each side, tracking the happenings on the street. "You need to go now." Backing up into her father's house, Gerda paused for just a moment.

"I brought his favorite cookies," Irma said, her throat closing with the pain of rejection. "May I leave them for when he returns? You don't even have to tell him they're from me."

With a sheepish half smile, Gerda reached for the box. "Thank you, Irma," she said with a wave. "God be with you."

Irma had expected the world outside Heim Hochland to look different now that Germany was at war, but the only real change she noticed was the row of soldiers bolstering security at Frankfurt's Hauptbahnhof and the dearth of young men on the streets. The abundance of swastika flags was nothing new. Conspicuous displays of patriotism had been a part of the German landscape for several years now. She was grateful that bombers weren't flying overhead as they were across Poland. Still, there was something unsettling about this quiet normalcy when the country was at war.

Resting her head against the window of the train, Irma hid her tear-stained face. The last thing she wanted was someone trying to strike up a conversation on the long ride back to Munich. The autumn days were growing shorter, but in the amber light of early evening, Irma took small comfort in the familiar sight of the rolling hills of farmland, grass neatly grazed by cows and sheep. Church steeples dotted the scrolling landscape of small villages and open fields.

Irma suspected it would be a long time before she saw Eduard again, so she closed her eyes and revisited the night they met, back when everything was possible. No accusations had been hurled; not a glass had been thrown. It was a crisp winter night two years earlier, and Irma would have skipped the Christmas market if she hadn't remembered that her bosses, the Rheinhold brothers, were bringing their children to the office the following day. No one expressly told the staff to give the six Rheinhold children small gifts, but they all knew it was expected. Irma resented the tradition but wasn't about to make waves over it. Her plan was to go to a toy seller's stall, purchase a few toy soldiers and Steiff bears, and head home. The errand was to take half an hour at most.

As much as Irma hated to admit it, she was enchanted by the sight of falling snow glittering in the sky. Illuminated by thousands of colorful, electric lights, Römerberg Square was a magical place. A large golden tree was placed at the center of the square where actors costumed as angels and fairies flitted about and entertained the children. Dozens of stalls were filled with wooden stars, glass ornaments, and Christmas tree candleholders for sale. An old man with leathery hands and a thick wool coat sat at a worktable, making wreaths for customers as they waited, using the greenery, berries, and ribbon of their choosing. Irma took in the fresh pine scent of the season.

Irma had been to Christmas markets before, and they always made her nostalgic for something she had never had. She double-wrapped her scarf around her neck and rubbed her gloves together before deciding to treat herself to a warm mug of mulled wine.

Checking the price on a toy blimp strung from a stall beam along with tiny accordions and bugles, Irma heard the bells at Old Saint Nicholas Church. According to the woman standing beside her, this meant it was time for the choir to begin. Irma decided to walk to the stage at the golden tree and listen to some seasonal music before she made her purchases and called it a night. She stood with the crowd, misty clouds of cold air coming from each of their mouths as they waited for school children to take the stage. The *Mittelschule* students came on first and placed themselves on the back three rows of stepped benches. They were followed by the primary school children, who stood in front of them at the stage level. Finally, three little ones, who looked as though they were barely in kindergarten, were escorted onto the stage by a gentle-looking man. He instructed them to sit on their bottoms before he scurried offstage.

A woman with a white bun stood, facing the children, and raised her index fingers to conduct the music. With a whisper, she reminded them that they would begin their concert with "O Tannenbaum." Before the choir could release its opening note, though, a little boy sitting in the front looked out into the audience, wide eyed and forehead wrinkled, and wailed "No!" before bursting into tears. The choir members directly behind him patted the young child on the back, and the audience called out words of encouragement. One of the fairies ran over and tried to comfort him with a twirl of her magic wand, but the sobbing child was having none of it. The poor dear.

The boy was inconsolable, his face crumpled and red, until his teacher—Eduard, as it turned out—joined the children onstage. It took some effort for Eduard to lower himself into a seated position on the stage floor, but when he did, the little boy stopped his tears and hopped onto his teacher's lap. The audience laughed and offered a hearty round of applause as the music began. Looking back, Irma realized that this was the moment she fell in love with Eduard, before they had even met. She felt a tender pang of loss.

By the time the train reached Nuremberg, the sky had blackened, so the remainder of Irma's journey was spent watching house lights and storefronts whiz by like fireflies, all the while chiding herself for not having faith in Eduard when he assured her the woman in his basement was a friend in need. She bit her lip with regret, recalling her own callous response when her housemate at Frau Haarmacher's had asked for her help. Would it have been so hard to join Charlotte at the hospital when she'd needed her?

She would give anything to go back to the Römerberg Christmas market again, to introduce herself to Eduard after the children's performance and congratulate him for saving the show. This time when he told her that his consolation of the young boy was nothing, she would take note that this was a man who cared about children more than his ego. This time, when Eduard showed her over and over again that he was a decent man, she wouldn't be foolish enough to doubt it.

# 35

## *Gundi*

*Steinhöring*

G UNDI'S FINGERS CURLED TIGHTLY AROUND THE EDGES OF
the bed, the cool metal frame and crisp white sheets a
relief, a sharp contrast to the thickening heat of the delivery
room. "Open the window," she begged Sister Marianne, working the words through gritted teeth as Sister Dorothea stood
beside the bed, grimacing with apology.

Gundi's heart hammered in her chest as she wept, but the
fear of childbirth was the least of her problems. Her true terror
was over the fact that she was about to deliver a baby who might
well bear a strong resemblance to his Jewish father.

What if her baby inherited the Solomons' strong Sephardic
features: Rivka's dark skin, Leo's and Schel's close-set brown
eyes, and the chunky dark curls they all shared? If her baby
favored his father, Dr. Ebner would be furious when he learned
Gundi had used precious resources on a baby the Reich considered racially inferior. She could be fined, or even jailed, for
having relations with a Jew.

Gripping the rails of the bed even harder than before,
Gundi released a series of staccato huffs as she struggled to ask,

"Is this…is this normal? The baby's crushing my spine!" Finally, "Something's wrong!" she shouted.

"Hush," Sister Marianne called back to her. "Everything is perfectly fine, dear. Try to breathe through the pain. I've delivered hundreds of babies in my day, and I assure you, this one is going perfectly."

Gundi's heart raced even faster as she wondered if she would be arrested for violating the Nuremberg Laws. Would she be shaved bald and publicly humiliated like poor Anna Rath? Would she be sent to Dachau? And what would become of her baby?

Gundi began bargaining with God. *Give me a baby with my light skin and blond hair, and I will do whatever you want. Please let this baby look more like me than Leo.* She silently offered a deal: *I'll take more pain in childbirth for less in my baby's life.*

She alternated between wounded whimpers and jagged breaths, unable to speak as her body was torn from the inside. Gundi knew the tears wouldn't stop until either Sister Marianne or Sister Dorothea said the words she desperately needed to hear: *What a perfect baby you have, Gundi.* Until then, she was a million tiny flecks of herself floating in disarray.

Sister Marianne peeked up from between Gundi's bent knees and gave her right foot an affectionate squeeze before lowering her head back to the job at hand. All Gundi could see was the stiff tip of Sister Marianne's white hat looking like a sailboat anchored between the cliffs of Gundi's thighs.

"You're stronger than you know, Gundi," Sister Dorothea said softly.

Gundi sighed at the platitude, bristling that Sister Irma

picked now of all times to take her holiday. Sister Marianne told the girls that Sister Irma had gone to a National Socialist mountain retreat, part of the Strength Through Joy program, but Irma had confessed privately to Gundi that she was heading back to Frankfurt to try to reconcile with her former *Schatz*. Apparently, she had treated him unkindly and hoped to win him back. It had all sounded incredibly romantic to Gundi until she realized that it meant the nurse she most trusted would not be by her side for her baby's delivery. Now she was stuck with Sister Dorothea, the nurse all the girls nicknamed Metropolis Maria after the robot in the film. She did have a perpetually expressionless face and total lack of emotion, but at least she seemed kind, Gundi silently consoled herself. *But will she remain so if my baby doesn't look like the photo of Erich placed in my file?*

Trying to slow the adrenaline coursing through her veins, Gundi focused on the metal rolling cart with surgical scissors, forceps, disinfectants, and sutures. She eyed a small white basin sitting beside the sink with a glass bottle of clear liquid set on its edge. The lone spot of color Gundi registered was outside the window: a golden oriole perched on a branch of a beech tree.

Finally, the sunset cooled the temperature of the room, but seven hours of labor had left Gundi overheated, even as Sister Dorothea patted her brow with a cool washcloth every few minutes.

Sister Dorothea remained by Gundi's bedside, absorbing the pressure from her patient's firm grip. "Squeeze tight and think about holding your baby," she whispered.

Gundi allowed herself to imagine the unthinkable. What if Leo had been executed? She inhaled deeply to sweep away her thoughts and focused on Sister Dorothea's soothing words. *Think of holding my baby. Soon, all this will be over, and I can return to Berlin, where Mutti will be waiting for us. Leo and his family will surely be back home by now.*

Her reverie lasted just a moment as the baby continued its entry into the world, apparently using claws and jackboots. Was every birth like this, or was her child coming into the world armed and ready to fight?

Gundi saw Sister Marianne's bright cheeks slacken before she heard her baby's first precious, needy squawk. Bobbing her head on the pillow, Gundi tried to catch a glimpse of her newborn but could only see Sister Dorothea's stony face as she cut and tied the umbilical cord. Sister Dorothea's eyes darted between Gundi and the baby as she pressed her lips together with concern. "A girl," Sister Dorothea announced with barely a whisper, then wrapped the baby, still slick with fluid, in her arms and took her to the basin. In a flash, Gundi saw the abundance of dark brown hair, bouncy wisps that promised to soon curl. Her tiny fingers splayed as if they were reaching for Gundi while Sister Dorothea gently rinsed her off.

Lumbering toward the basin, Sister Marianne's eyebrows knit together, and she grabbed a small flashlight to shine on the baby's face. "Brown eyes," Marianne said, looking over her shoulder before returning to inspect the child's body. "This baby's skin is nearly black."

Gundi held back the bile that rose in her throat when she heard Sister Marianne's unspoken accusation. She rushed to defend herself. "I was very dark as a newborn too," she said, her words strung together on a taut wire. "Everyone thought I was a little Gypsy baby when I was born."

Neck craning toward the sink, Gundi tried for a better look at her baby, avoiding Sister Marianne's eye. She caught a glimpse of her daughter's chubby little arm covered in delicate white bubbles, which only highlighted the child's dark skin.

Sister Dorothea chimed in from the sink. "I've seen this many times before," she said, her eyes never leaving Gundi's baby. "Infants can have very different coloring at birth."

"Not *this* different," Sister Marianne returned quickly with a chilly tone.

Sister Dorothea, struggling to maintain an atmosphere of normalcy, placed the freshly diapered bundle in Gundi's arms and told her it was time for the baby's first feeding.

Mesmerized by the sight of her baby's tiny toes, Gundi hardly noticed Sister Marianne's lips pucker like a drawstring pouch.

"Feed that child, and we will talk in the morning," Sister Marianne instructed. "Sister Dorothea, help Gundi get the baby latched on properly." Casting another icy gaze on Gundi, Sister Marianne continued. "If there's anything you need to tell me, do so now before Dr. Ebner arrives for his visit. Heim Hochland is a model Lebensborn home, and I will not have you involving us in a scandal."

"No," Gundi said, feigning calm. "There's nothing." Her eyes locked on her daughter's delicate layer of silk skin and rheumy eyes, Gundi whispered, "Welcome to the world, my beautiful girl." Even in this awful moment, Gundi could not contain the joy of holding her baby. Leo's baby. Their little dumpling. "Your name is Nadja, after your Papa's grandmother. She has a sister named Talia you'll meet someday very soon." Nadja let out the softest sigh Gundi had ever heard, as if to say, *Ahhh, there you are, Mutti.* The two merged like a pat of butter melting into a fresh muffin.

———

Gundi woke to the blurry sight of Sister Dorothea holding Nadja by her bedside. It must be time to nurse her again. In her five months at Heim Hochland, Gundi had watched more than twenty Nazi propaganda films as part of the Lebensborn educational programming, yet no one had bothered to give her practical information, like the fact that newborns needed to be fed every two hours. As the fog in Gundi's mind cleared, she noticed that Nadja wasn't squawking for her breast as she had been earlier that night. The baby was fast asleep.

The moon shining through the window illuminated Sister Dorothea, who held a finger over her lips and handed Nadja to Gundi. She looked like she was holding a lantern under her face, about to tell a ghost story around the campfire. "Listen to me very carefully, Gundi," she whispered. "You must tell me now. This child is a *Mischling*, isn't she?"

Pulling her bundled baby close, Gundi shook her head. "No, no, she isn't. I'm German, and so is her father."

Sister Dorothea's eyes shot toward the door, double-checking that they were alone. Lowering her voice further, she said urgently, "Gundi, listen to me. I have very good reason to believe that Nadja's father is Jewish, and I need you to be honest with me."

"No," Gundi whispered, pulling herself back so far, she felt the metal bars of the headboard press through her pillow. "Erich Meyer is one hundred percent German," Gundi said emphatically, feeling a jab of guilt. But she needed to focus on protecting her child, so she scrunched her face with disgust. "I don't even know any Jews."

Sister Dorothea lowered her eyes in a rare show of feeling, frowned, and shook her head. "That's good news for you," she returned. "Because Dr. Ebner will be here on Friday, and Sister Marianne wants him to screen Nadja. She believes your baby is a *Mischling.*"

Gundi's head snapped up, meeting Sister Dorothea's intense stare. Their standoff ended when Sister Dorothea offered a tight smile and went along with the lie.

"Not that it matters to you," she said, watching Gundi's face closely, as if trying to confirm her suspicion. "But it's a good thing Nadja doesn't have any Jewish blood. It would be heartbreaking for you to lose her."

*Lose her?*

"Thankfully, that's not the case," Gundi said, hoping her voice wouldn't catch. "But why would the Lebensborn take a Jewish baby from a mother? No good German families want to adopt an *Untermensch.*"

The expression on Sister Dorothea's face shifted slightly. Leaning closer to Gundi, she whispered, "If Dr. Ebner found that Nadja was Jewish, even a *Mischling*, she wouldn't be adopted. She would be given a lethal injection."

Unable to contain her gasp, Gundi clutched Nadja, turning her away from Sister Dorothea.

"I knew it!" Sister Dorothea continued. "Your baby *is* a Jew."

"No! No, she's not. It's just so…it seems so cruel. To murder innocent babies. They wouldn't."

Sister Dorothea's feet moved like a windup toy as she made her way to the door. She grabbed the knob and opened it to check if there was anyone on the other side before returning. The nurse sat in the chair beside Gundi's bed. "I know your baby is Jewish. If you were a true Nazi, you wouldn't call it *murder*. You'd call it cleansing, purifying, euthanizing, liquidating, but never *murder*."

If Sister Irma were the one delivering this news, Gundi would trust her without hesitation. In all her time at Heim Hochland, Gundi hadn't had any sort of meaningful interaction with Sister Dorothea. No one had. Gundi's arms were shaking. What did Sister Dorothea want? She couldn't take any chances, especially with Sister Marianne already suspicious about Nadja's parentage. Perhaps Sister Marianne had sent Sister Dorothea to extract a confession.

Gundi shook her head. "All right, poor choice of words, but that doesn't mean my baby—"

"Gundi, if your baby is Jewish, I can help get you and her out of here. Tell me right now if my friends and I should risk our lives for your Jewish baby or if I'm gravely mistaken and have put myself in danger by confiding in you."

The room was silent. Was this a trap? Perhaps Sister Dorothea was trying to alarm her by telling her there was a greater danger to Nadja than there actually was. Then Gundi remembered the November pogroms, the shattered glass and burning buildings. Anna Rath dragged through the streets of Nuremberg after her head had been shaved for the crime of loving a Jew. She recalled Hilde's report of executions at Dachau. Gundi realized she couldn't be sure how far the limits of Nazi cruelty went. Perhaps they would murder a child. Could anyone possibly be that evil?

Gundi looked at the child in her arms and knew what she had to do. She had no choice but to trust Sister Dorothea. She whispered, "I...I need your help."

# 36

## *Gundi*

SITTING AT GUNDI'S BEDSIDE, SISTER DOROTHEA explained the plan. "Tomorrow night at eleven, bring Nadja down to the cellar," she whispered. "You must be very careful, because Sister Marianne will still be in her office. Behind the board games on the bottom bookshelf will be a change of clothes for you and a rucksack I made to carry Nadja in." She glanced toward the door and lowered her voice. "There's a fallen tree about fifty meters from the pond that marks a safe entry point into the forest. The path in the woods is mostly clear, but keep your eyes on the ground. I've tripped over tangles of vine on the trail many times." In a rare moment of tenderness, Sister Dorothea brushed her fingers across Nadja's head. "No falls with this little one in your arms." Back to business, Sister Dorothea continued, quickening her pace and glancing at the door. "Stay on the main path, and about halfway through the forest, you'll see a fork in the road. Go right."

Every muscle in Gundi's body bunched. "How will I know… How do I know that I'm halfway through a forest I've never been through?"

"I usually carry about five kilos of supplies, and it takes me ten minutes to get to the midpoint and another ten to the main road. You'll arrive at the bottom of a shallow ravine that leads up to Sankt Christoph Road. There will be a brown blanket rolled like a log for you at the exact spot where you should stop and wait at the side of the road. Stay hidden until you see a black Opel Blitz military truck pull to the inlet. A man dressed as an SS officer will get out and say, 'What a bright moon tonight.' When you hear that, run from your hiding spot, and he will help you into the back of the truck."

Gundi held her hand against her chest and whispered. "It's a long way to the pond, Sister Dorothea." Her face furrowed as she envisioned the open field with only a handful of birch trees to provide cover. "What if someone sees us? What if..." She drifted off, her drumming heart interrupting her thoughts.

"The girls upstairs take this route to sneak off into town all the time," Sister Dorothea responded.

Mind buzzing, Gundi wondered if Sister Marianne was truly oblivious to girls popping out to the pubs in Steinhöring or if she just looked the other way. The difference could mean life or death for Nadja. Gundi shook away her questions, remembering what Sister Dorothea had told her about the fate of Jewish babies.

"I understand," Gundi managed, feeling acutely aware of every pore on her skin pebbling up into gooseflesh. "Where are we going?"

"Geneva," Sister Dorothea replied.

"Switzerland? No, no, I need to go back to Berlin. I can't... no," Gundi sputtered, shaking her head frantically. "Nadja's father, he's probably back home now, and Mutti, she's... I can't go to Switzerland."

Sister Dorothea closed her eyes tightly, summoning her patience. "Don't you think Berlin is the first place the Nazis will look for you?"

Gundi realized Sister Dorothea was right. If the Nazis were able to track her down in Hamburg when she and Elsbeth tried to flee months ago, they would have no problem finding her in Berlin.

Sister Dorothea reached for Gundi's shoulders and clenched her jaw. "Listen to me. You're going to Geneva where you and your baby will be safe, and that is the end of the discussion."

Unaware that she was now shaking her head, Gundi offered a new plan. "Your friends can take me to the countryside. Nadja and I will change our names and live in hiding until the war ends."

Sister Dorothea stiffened as she placed her hands in her uniform pockets. She leaned toward Gundi and said, "This is not a taxi service, and this mission is not for you. We are trying to save Nadja's life by making room for the two of you on the truck. Do you understand?"

*Not for me? Who is the mission for? And why do we have to leave Germany?*

Sister Dorothea seemed to read Gundi's mind and held out a hand to stop her from asking questions. "The less you know, the better."

～•┌

After their late-night discussion, Gundi lay awake even as the sky turned purple, promising to lighten to lavender, then blue.

She knew she should sleep while she could, but every time her lids began to droop, they quickly popped open again.

Later Thursday morning, Sister Irma opened the door and peeked in. At the sight of the bundle in Gundi's arms, her eyebrows arched, and she bit her bottom lip, as if to contain her smile. "I heard there was a special delivery to Heim Hochland!"

Gundi waved her in, smothering a yawn, just as Nadja stirred and began to fuss. Gundi pressed her cheek to Nadja's and began to hum, something she had discovered soothed her baby. As if she had nothing else on her mind, she asked, "How was your reunion with Eduard?"

"Never mind that," Sister Irma said, her smile stiffening. "Let me have a look at your sweet baby." She raised her brows. "She *is* dark, isn't she?"

Gundi steadied her breathing, feigning nonchalance. "Who mentioned Nadja's dark?"

Sister Irma pulled a wooden chair beside Gundi's bed. "May I hold her?" Gundi agreed and watched Sister Irma cradle baby Nadja in her arms and give her a gentle kiss on the forehead.

Gundi pressed. "Who told you about Nadja being dark?"

Her eyes never leaving Nadja sleeping in her arms, Sister Irma made a dismissive huff. "Oh, Sister Marianne, but pay her no mind. Dr. Ebner will be here tomorrow, and he'll put her mind at ease." She placed a fingertip on Nadja's little nose and spoke in a soft voice. "Good morning, *Schnuckiputzi*," she said before returning her gaze to Gundi and letting her know the baby needed to be fed.

Gundi stroked Nadja's cheek to get the rooting reflex, as Sister Dorothea had taught her. Nadja's lips snapped shut like a mousetrap as she latched onto Gundi's nipple.

Sister Irma didn't seem to have a clue about Nadja's father being Jewish, but she lowered her voice and leaned toward Gundi. "Marianne is feeling anxious because the party is losing confidence in her after the…situation with Gisela. It's a poor reflection on the household management when a named father denies parentage," Sister Irma said, looking down. "And then an officer's wife returned a Polish baby girl she adopted from us at the Braunes Haus last week. She said Marianne pressured her into taking the girl. So now she's being overly cautious, but you have nothing to worry about. Tomorrow morning, this will all be sorted out."

Gundi regretted that she couldn't share the truth with Sister Irma or, at the very least, say goodbye and thank her for her kindness. But Sister Dorothea and her friends were risking their lives for her safety, and there was no way she could jeopardize that. Perhaps there was something Gundi could leave behind as a signal that only Sister Irma would understand. If Gundi dropped her marcasite hair comb outside Sister Irma's door as she left, would the nurse remember admiring it? Would Sister Irma recall Gundi telling her it was a gift from her *Tante* Ulla, her mother's sister whom she adored? Would she understand that it was Gundi's way of saying goodbye?

<hr />

Nadja had been fed, her diaper changed, her clothes put on. At ten in the morning, Gundi decided to bring Nadja to the nursery where three Polish orphans had been brought to Heim Hochland just days earlier. Sister Marianne let the residents know that there would be more children arriving. Soon, Heim Hochland would be brimming with new orphans, and it was their privilege to help.

Sister Irma bounced a baby girl with bright blond curls and a metal brace on her left foot. Standing by the large window, her back shielding the baby from the direct sunlight, she scrunched her face and buried it in the baby's belly, cooing, "Who's a little *Knuddelmaus?*"

The child's giggles reminded Gundi of soap bubbles floating toward the sky.

Sister Irma kept her voice high as she landed her index finger on the baby's doughy belly again. "You're a little *Knuddelmaus*, Jadzia." Suddenly aware of Gundi's gaze, Sister Irma turned toward the door. "Come on in," she said.

Eyeing Heim Hochland's three newly recruited nurses, each holding a baby wrapped in a white infant blanket, Gundi smiled politely.

"It's time for morning baths," Sister Irma said, reminding Gundi of the National Socialist practice of bathing babies twice daily and taking them outside for sunshine. Gundi would miss Sister Irma but not the strange Nazi rituals at Heim Hochland.

Throughout the day, she did her best to behave no differently from the other new mothers at Heim Hochland, but she drew the line whenever a nurse suggested she take Nadja off to the nursery. After the first few refusals, Sister Karla, one of the new nurses, warned Gundi that children who were not taught independence young were bound to become weak. "It is Nadja who will suffer if you're a nervous mother," she offered, not unkindly.

Gundi looked out the window and reminded herself that by the next day, she would be far away from Heim Hochland. "You're right, Sister Karla," Gundi said. "I will bring this up with Dr. Ebner during his visit tomorrow."

After lunch, Gundi decided to plant herself in the common room with Nadja in her arms. Silently, she said goodbye to girls, both expectant and apprentice mothers, as they passed by her. Those who stopped to admire Nadja or ask Gundi about childbirth had no idea that this would be their last time together. When Gundi saw Hilde, she clutched Nadja and braced herself for a callous remark about her baby's coloring. Instead, Hilde made her way over to Gundi with a look of exhaustion and contrition. While her chest was once puffed out, now it was her eyes that were swollen.

"Your baby," Hilde said, bending down to have a closer look. "She's beautiful, Gundi. Good for you."

Gundi liked some of the residents just fine—Renate was always good for a diversion—but only when she thought about never seeing Sister Irma again did a lump form in her throat.

Her sentimentality was derailed when she noticed a new painting hanging beside the gauzy impressionist canvas of a mother watching her child in his bassinet. This one, bold in its coloring, had the simple subject of a chubby-cheeked toddler wearing a bright red top. The child was seated on a mustard-colored chair, his head resting on a yellow table as the boy slept peacefully. How perfect the scene appeared. But Gundi recognized the coiled signature of the Polish artist Stanislaw Wysianski and knew the painting of the child had been stolen like so many others at Heim Hochland.

When the grandfather clock struck ten, Gundi had hoped she would relax a bit, knowing that it was now just one hour until her escape. Instead, her stomach writhed with anxiety, pregnant with terror. Still, she put on her nightgown and brought a cup of milk with her to the maternity ward, wishing everyone sweet dreams.

***

At ten thirty, Gundi snatched Nadja from her bassinet beside her bed in the maternity ward and tiptoed back to her room to change her clothes, praying Nadja would stay quiet as they passed Sister Marianne's closed office door.

She made it to her room to put on her travel clothes and grab a few items. Gundi was pleased that the trembling of her hands was barely noticeable. Her jitters did not betray her, even when she put Nadja down for a moment to secure her mother's diamond dragonfly brooch to the center of her brassiere.

At two days old, Nadja slept most of the time anyway, but Sister Dorothea said they'd need to err on the side of caution and give the baby a mild sedative right before they left so she would slumber through their journey. Gundi was reluctant but planned on dipping her finger in the vial just after she made it to the basement, a few minutes before their departure. The last thing she needed was Nadja fussing as they fled Heim Hochland; the sound would certainly be heard in the still of night.

Nadja's closed eyelids looked like walnuts in their shells. After slipping into the canvas skirt Sister Dorothea had sewn,

Gundi smiled gratefully, realizing that Sister Dorothea had made the waistband from elastic. *Is Sister Dorothea a mother herself? This thoughtful touch has to have come from a woman who has given birth.* Gundi fingered the wide hem filled with jewelry the nurse had stolen from upstairs. Earlier that day, Sister Dorothea had handed her a set of art deco black onyx earrings Marie had been given by a young soldier, a grasshopper brooch made from emerald and yellow diamonds gifted to Ingrid, and a ring of small diamonds shaped like a daisy that Renate had carelessly left on her bedside table. "Give these to Rolf, the truck driver," Sister Dorothea had instructed.

Gundi had stuffed pillows under the blankets of her bed in the maternity ward so it would appear as if she were sleeping soundly. Now, back in her room, she wore a night robe over her clothing and slippers over her wool socks. She placed Nadja in her favorite position, her little chin resting on Gundi's shoulder. As Gundi began the short walk down the hallway toward the back of the house where the cellar door was located, she could see that the kitchen light was on. Someone in the house was awake and, from the sound of it, distressed. A woman was weeping softly, desperately trying to muffle herself. There was a quick, crackling sniffle followed by a delicate whimper. But Gundi could afford neither curiosity nor compassion right now. Her face tightened when she realized the voice was Sister Irma's. How she wished she could step inside and console her, but it was impossible.

Nadja opened her eyes and made the slightest squeal, bringing Sister Irma's sobs to an abrupt halt. Gundi chided herself for not giving Nadja the Veronal earlier, but she had been sleeping so soundly already. She quickly turned and scurried back toward her room, grateful that she was still dressed in her robe.

"Gundi?" Sister Irma called a moment before she reached the open door. "Gundi, why aren't you in the maternity ward?"

"I...I forgot my...my brush." She began rummaging through the drawer of her nightstand, hoping the charade was convincing. Gundi knew she had to leave quickly, but Irma's tears moved her. "Are you all right, Sister Irma?"

Sister Irma held out a yielding hand. She averted her eyes and nodded. "Yes, I'm fine." Looking down, she was unable to contain her tears any longer. "No, I'm not."

"I'm terribly sorry, Sister Irma. Why don't you warm some milk for us, and I'll meet you in the kitchen in a few minutes to talk?" She hated the deception, but it was nothing compared to the pain Gundi would face if Dr. Ebner... She couldn't even finish the thought. "I need an extra blanket from downstairs. I'll just be a few minutes."

Sister Irma's eyes shot toward the cellar door. "I'll come with you. We'll have more privacy downstairs anyway."

"No, that's all right. I don't need a blanket after all. I'm fine."

Sister Irma smiled and sniffed away her sadness. "Don't be silly, Gundi. Let's get you a blanket."

Eleven gongs rang out from the clock.

As the two descended the stairs into the darkness, Gundi decided the best course of action was to alert Sister Dorothea that she and Nadja weren't alone. If Sister Dorothea heard her warning, at least she could hide and protect herself. "Thank you for coming to the cellar with me, Sister Irma," Gundi said stiffly. She could only hope that Sister Dorothea would forgive her for the slipup and work to readjust the plan. Gundi stopped at the fourth step and turned back to Sister Irma trailing slightly behind. "I just remembered that blankets are stored on the main floor now, on the east wing near the nursery," Gundi suggested. "Why don't you grab one, and I'll get a game for us to play?" Considering the absurdity of her idea, she tried to explain herself. "Whenever I'm feeling sad, a good game always takes my mind off my problems." She felt herself sliding further into an abyss.

"Blankets are right downstairs," Sister Irma said, sidling past Gundi until she reached the bottom of the stairs.

Gundi gripped the rail with one hand and followed Sister Irma down quickly, hoping she had given Sister Dorothea enough time to hide in a dark corner of the room.

Instead, she was bent over looking at the selection of board games, something that might have been more plausible if there were even a single light on. Sister Dorothea glanced at Gundi and shook her head, disappointed.

"Good evening, Sister Irma," Sister Dorothea said. "Gundi. Are you two looking to play a game of Juden Raus at this late hour?"

"No, I just... I came down for a blanket," Gundi explained, looking sheepish.

Sister Dorothea lifted herself and walked to a linen closet across the room. She pulled out a brown wool blanket and walked back to the women quickly. Handing Sister Irma the blanket, she said, "There you are. Now, if you'll excuse me."

Gundi placed a protective hand on the back of Nadja's

head. "Sister Irma was heading back upstairs, but I'd like to talk to you for just a moment."

"I'm sorry, Gundi, but we'll have to talk tomorrow. I'm afraid I've had some disappointing news and need some time to myself."

*Did the plan fall through? Had her contact been caught?*

"Sister Dorothea, forgive me, but I *am* leaving with Nadja tonight, one way or another," Gundi said, giving her baby a tiny bounce. Before Sister Dorothea could respond, Gundi turned to Sister Irma and decided to trust her instincts. "Nadja's father is Jewish. I need to leave tonight before Dr. Ebner gets here tomorrow and finds out. He'll... He won't... Nadja won't make it."

Sister Irma lifted her hands over her mouth in surprise, looked at Nadja, and shook her head. "He wouldn't. He couldn't be so—"

Sister Dorothea interrupted with a whisper that hissed through clenched teeth. She lowered her shoulders, struggling to remain calm. "He would, he has, and he will again. Gundi, I am furious with you for your mishandling of this, but we have to act quickly. You need to leave right now if you're going to make it to the meeting spot in time." She thought aloud, "And you, Sister Irma, what do I do about you?"

Gundi jumped in. "She can be trusted."

Sister Irma remained quiet for a moment, appearing lost in thought. She quickly snapped back to the present. "You're certain of all this, Sister Dorothea?"

"I've seen it with my own eyes."

Sister Irma blinked quickly, taking in what she had heard.

"I'm more than willing to stay here and remain silent, but also, I'm a terrible liar. If I leave with Gundi, the party will assume that I was the one who assisted her, not you. Shall I go with her?"

Sister Dorothea scanned Irma from head to toe as if something about her appearance might reveal her trustworthiness. She narrowed her eyes. "If you turn us in, even to save yourself, dozens of good people will be killed."

Sister Irma nodded solemnly. "Which is why I will never do such a thing. I swear to you."

"I need you to promise that afterward, you'll never return to Heim Hochland and never speak of anything you see tonight. Do you understand?"

"Yes, yes, I do."

"Good, because I want to be perfectly clear, Irma Binz," Sister Dorothea said, stepping closer to highlight their height difference. "If you put any of my friends or our work in jeopardy, I will personally hunt you down and kill you in the most unpleasant manner you could possibly imagine."

Sister Irma shook her head, then pulled in Dorothea for a hug. "Thank you," she said. "Thank you for what you're doing."

Surprised by the embrace, Sister Dorothea's body stiffened until, after a few moments, she lifted an arm and awkwardly patted Sister Irma's back. Stepping away, Sister Dorothea removed her sweater and handed it to Sister Irma. "You'll need this." Then she gave each of the women a flashlight and a quick nod. "There's no time to waste. You two need to leave, now."

# 37

## *Gundi*

*Bavaria*

G UNDI AND SISTER IRMA WALKED THROUGH THE THICK
spruce forest without exchanging a word. Flashlights
scanning the ground, they alerted each other to slippery
patches of moss through gestures or an occasional chirp that
mimicked the natural world around them. Sister Irma offered a
soft owl hoot when she found herself ankle deep in fern fronds,
to which Gundi replied with a light trill of thanks. She needed
these bits of sweetness to distract her from fears too unbearable
to imagine.

By the time they arrived at the bottom of the ravine, Gundi's
and Sister Irma's undershirts were almost as damp from perspi-
ration as their boots were from foliage. Thankfully, the Veronal
was doing its job, and Nadja slept soundly in the rucksack
Sister Dorothea had made her for the journey. It looked like an
ordinary canvas sack but had extra room added at the bottom
to hide Nadja's dangling legs and a top flap of mesh fabric that
covered the baby's head. If Gundi ever saw Sister Dorothea
again, she would praise her for her masterful engineering.

Gundi felt a flash of hope when she spotted the blanket

rolled to look like a log, just as Sister Dorothea had promised. Nearby, it appeared as if someone had placed six large stones on the side of the ravine to purposely serve as steps, but Gundi couldn't be certain that was the case. She wrapped her left arm around Nadja and leaned forward and kicked her boot against the stones to see if they were loose. The first three were secure, not slipping even the slightest bit, so Gundi reached and grabbed the fourth stone and shook it before carefully climbing up. Once they made it to the road, Gundi felt a momentary sense of relief before taking in the vast darkness before her. She could make out the trees lining the path, but as she glanced left, she realized there was a bend about twenty meters before them. Was that where the truck would come from, or was that the direction they were heading? When she looked to her right, it was only slightly better. She could see a straight ribbon of asphalt that soon disappeared into blackness.

Gundi and Sister Irma found their way behind a blackberry bush on the shoulder and sat to wait for the truck. Gundi ran her hand across Nadja's back, taking a moment to feel the fluttering breath of her baby. She then unstrapped Nadja from her sack and placed her on her lap to look at her more carefully. Nadja's tiny head flopped to the side, and her little legs instinctively lifted and crossed over one another like a pretzel. She folded her spindly arms close to her body like an old woman clutching her purse. "Does she seem all right?" Gundi whispered to Sister Irma.

"She should be just fine," Sister Irma whispered. Seeing Gundi's mouth round with concern, she corrected herself. "She *is* fine. Nadja looks like every other healthy infant I've ever seen."

Gundi glanced at the wristwatch that Sister Dorothea had given her, a dainty stretch band of platinum, and saw that the meeting time had passed and there was no sign of a truck.

*Did we miss it? What if the truck never comes? Is this the right spot? Was the driver caught? Did he tell the Gestapo that we're here?*

"We're good. We're safe," Gundi whispered, continuing to run her fingers through Nadja's thick fuzz of brown hair. She finally spotted two glowing lights turning from the bend in the road. "That's him!" Handing Nadja to Sister Irma, Gundi leapt to her feet and sprang from behind the bush in the recess in the road.

"No!" Sister Irma called, louder than she should have. "Wait until he pulls over!"

But before she absorbed Sister Irma's warning, Gundi was standing by the side of the road, making a visor with her fingers, nearly blinded by the oncoming headlamps.

When the lights dimmed, Gundi realized that what had stopped before her was not a truck. It was a car. Its doors opened after the engine stopped. Two men slammed their doors and made their way toward Gundi. *Two* young men— not one as Sister Dorothea had told her. As they came closer, Gundi shuddered at the sight of pistol holsters strapped over their brown leather jackets bearing the flying eagle insignia of the Luftwaffe.

*Maybe this is a disguise. Perhaps there was a change of plans*, Gundi thought, her heart now lodged firmly in her throat. "*Guten Abend, die Herren*," Gundi said, suddenly realizing she had made a grave error.

The men's black boots crackled as they hit the gravel with every step they took toward her.

Nervously, she tried again. "Such a bright moon tonight, isn't it?"

"*Heil* Hitler!" they returned.

She had made a dangerous mistake. Gundi was grateful that Sister Irma hadn't followed her toward the road. *Don't look at the blackberry bush. Do not even glance in that direction.*

The soldiers were younger than Gundi. She could imagine their mothers helping them tie the red neckerchiefs of their Hitlerjugend uniforms not long ago. It was easy to envision the boys hiking the Black Forest, slicing the air with machetes they'd fashioned from tree branches. One of them still had acne.

"What are you doing out so late at night, Fräulein?" the boy with the pimples asked, more an accusation than a question. The other soldier carried extra padding but had the confidence of someone who was in the best shape of his life. The way his lips curled at the sight of Gundi told her that this freshly armed Nazi had spent most of his short life being overlooked by pretty girls, and now felt he deserved more from them.

The soldier's teeth looked like a picket fence when he smiled at his friend. "I'll search the girl." The burly soldier grabbed Gundi's arm, pushed her against the front of their car, and bent her over the hood. She considered fighting back, scratching and biting her way out of his grip. But there were two of them, and they had pistols. Who knew if Veronal slumber could be pierced by the sound of gunfire? She couldn't risk finding out if her baby would awaken and cry at the noise.

Her left cheek pressed against the cool metal of the black Mercedes. Gundi felt an angry hand gripping the back of her thigh. She couldn't tell which boy was resting his chin on her shoulder and whispering into her ear, "Don't you know it's not safe to be out alone at night, Fräulein?"

Closing her eyes tight, Gundi decided that if the soldiers raped her, she would remain silent and endure the torture to give Sister Irma time to run back into the woods with Nadja.

Before she could beg for mercy, Gundi saw a new set of headlamps turn the bend and slow at the scene. The boys froze in the spotlight, waiting for the canvas-covered truck to stop.

A tall SS officer with an angular face jumped down from his truck seat and strode furiously to the car without pausing to turn off his lights or motor. "What are you doing to my daughter?" he snapped.

"*Heil* Hitler!" the boys said, this time their voices high and meek.

"We thought—" the pimpled soldier stammered.

"You thought? Get the hell out of here before I decide to get your name and report you," the officer barked. Turning to Gundi, he softened his body and opened his arms.

Gundi fell into the stranger's embrace, crying "Papa" loud enough for the fleeing soldiers to hear. "Thank goodness you're here."

The airmen hurried to their car and peeled away.

"Where's the baby?" the officer replied.

Gundi remained frozen. If this man knew she had a baby, he had to be Sister Dorothea's connection, didn't he? Or had the plan gone awry and a real Nazi had been tipped off about a Heim Hochland escape? If that were the case, though, he wouldn't have needed to say he was her father and scare off the boys, Gundi reassured herself.

"Fräulein, it's a lovely, bright moon tonight, wouldn't you say?"

When Gundi exhaled with relief, she felt like a balloon she had once accidentally let go of before tying its knot. In releasing all its air, the balloon took flight, a dizzying, aimless whiz around the room before dropping to the floor. She was relieved but exhausted nonetheless.

"Gundi?" he asked.

Once Gundi confirmed, Sister Irma emerged from behind the bush, a protective hand on Nadja's head.

Rolf introduced himself, then nodded his chin at Sister Irma. "Who's she?"

Gundi and Sister Irma's rushed explanation must have sufficed, because Rolf waved a hand, seeming to remind himself that plans needed to be flexible in this line of work. Her hand-off of the small sack of jewels brought Rolf's shoulders down as a smile appeared on his face. He reached his hand into the bag and quickly pulled out a handful of glittering necklaces, pins, and rings. Dropping them back into the satchel, he shook his head in admiration. "Dorothea has the stickiest fingers of any of us." Pivoting abruptly, Rolf pointed at Sister Irma. "She's in uniform. She can sit up front with me."

He opened the back doors of his truck and stepped in to push aside four large cargo boxes marked with medical red crosses with swastikas painted in the center. He then lifted three wide wooden floor planks that revealed a hidden compartment where Gundi and Nadja were to ride. Sister Irma held the baby, and Rolf offered a hand to assist Gundi as she climbed into the truck. Stepping inside the compartment and then struggling to sit on the uneven bottom, Gundi sighed, feeling as though she were lowering herself into her own grave. She reached out her arms to Sister Irma, who gave an encouraging smile before placing Nadja into her hands. She lay down flat against the floor, placed Nadja on her chest, and wrapped her arms around her baby. As Rolf dropped each board, Gundi flinched as though she were hearing gunfire. Watching the last wooden board placed over her, she was enveloped in darkness.

Soon they were all on the road, Sister Irma in the passenger seat, Gundi and Nadja in a shallow underbelly with a floor made of corrugated metal that someone had tried to soften with hay. It was a nice gesture but didn't provide much relief when the truck made its way over rough terrain. Gundi used her palms to create a helmet for Nadja, which was more successful than her attempt to anchor herself by pressing her feet against each side of the compartment. Her legs weren't long enough, so every time the truck made a sharp turn, Gundi felt like her entire body was a cloth being scrubbed against a washboard.

The truck ride was physically uncomfortable for Gundi, but she took solace in the fact that a small hole had been cut between the back and the cab so she could hear the conversation between Rolf and Sister Irma. Rolf was a German soldier who had abandoned his post in the Protectorate of Bohemia and Moravia and joined the resistance. He decided he could truly serve Germany by fleeing Bohemia and returning home and undermining Hitler's efforts. There were a lot of resistors, Rolf told Sister Irma. "Not enough doctors and nurses to keep up with the need, but a lot of brave people doing good work."

"Work like…" Sister Irma trailed off, though Rolf seemed

to understand the question. Gundi assumed she had pointed toward the back of the truck. "What do the nurses do?"

"Mostly tend to sprains, broken bones, scrapes, but I'm afraid we're going to see more as our work gets...bolder."

"Bolder?"

After a long pause, Rolf simply returned, "Yes, bolder." This apparently reminded Rolf that Sister Irma would now need identification papers as well. "Lift your foot mat. Pull the metal tab. There you go. Now open the box, and look for papers for Nurse Kathe Klees."

Gundi could hear the crinkling of papers and Sister Irma reviewing the details of a woman Rolf said had been killed just months earlier.

"How did she...?"

Rolf cleared his throat. "A hero. Kathe died a hero. I should have returned her papers weeks ago. I just—" He didn't finish explaining.

The truck moved onto an unpaved road, and Gundi held Nadja tighter, running her fingers against the silky skin of her baby's legs. She swallowed hard at the realization that neither Leo nor her mother would get to meet Nadja until after the war. How long would this war last anyway? The Great War went on for more than four years, but this one had to end more quickly. Practically every home in Europe and America had a radio, so people would soon learn what was happening in Germany. The world couldn't sit by idly when they discovered how evil the Reich was.

Their route so far had been mostly on dirt roads, and Gundi clutched tight to Nadja as the angry drumming of cargo boxes and wooden boards rumbled above. She had two persistent fears. *What if the planks above us give out and we are crushed by the boxes? And what if this flimsy bottom drops while the truck is moving?* Gundi couldn't tell if her throbbing headache was from these troubling questions or the steady banging of metal against the back of her skull.

Inside the cab, Rolf explained to Sister Irma that she and Gundi would soon transfer to another truck that would make a quick stop to pick up four more passengers—a Jewish family—then drive to the border crossing at Basel before heading to Geneva. "One of our men is a guard at the checkpoint, but his shift ends at nine tomorrow morning, so..." He trailed off. Rolf's voice perked up again, optimistic. "These things go seventy kilometers an hour, so you'll make it in time."

Gundi silently willed Sister Irma to push for answers. *Why do we need to board a new truck? Who are these new passengers?*

"You're not coming to Switzerland with us, Rolf?" Sister Irma asked instead, heavily. After a long silence, Sister Irma pressed. "Rolf, I'm asking you a question."

"This truck is filled with medical supplies stolen from the Nazis so we can use them for our people. When we get to the farmhouse, I've got a new mission, and you two will transfer to a different truck."

"You won't be driving the new truck, Rolf?" Sister Irma asked, her voice thready with disappointment.

"No, Klaus will take you the rest of the way. You'll be in the lower compartment of that one with Gundi and the Jewish family," Rolf explained. "That will be filled with gold bullion the Nazis believe your driver will be delivering to the Union Bank of Switzerland. Border guards are more than happy to let dark money make its way quietly out of the Reich and into safe harbor at UBS. And the Swiss are fine letting it in as long as it keeps them on Hitler's good side."

"The resistance has gold?"

"We have bricks that bear a striking resemblance to gold. Our real cargo is people."

---

Gundi felt the truck slow, then halt, and heard the engine stop. Rolf's boots clopped to the back of the truck, where he quickly opened the canvas covering and pulled up the planks of wood. Gundi squinted her eyes as moonlight sliced into her hiding space. Gripping Nadja with her left arm, Gundi accepted Rolf's extended hand with her right one and worked herself into a sitting position. Sister Irma reached for Nadja so Gundi could gain her footing as she climbed out of the truck and brushed loose strands of hay from Nadja's blanket, then her own hair.

"We have twenty minutes before you need to be back on the road again," Rolf told Gundi. "Change the baby, take a squat in the woods, do whatever you need to." As Gundi's eyes readjusted, she took in the thickets of trees, their trunks straight as soldiers, with the exception of a handful of beech trees stooped like old men. Laying across a carpet of foliage was a fallen spruce tree that two men were using as a bench outside an abandoned farmhouse. They were the first to greet Rolf, standing, then walking toward him.

"Who's this?" one asked, nodding his chin toward Sister Irma.

"Change of plans," Rolf replied. Once again, this response must have been enough, because the men shrugged and led the crew inside to an open room where wooden planks lifted from the walls in places where nails once secured them. A sagging ceiling was hastily patched with dried leaves wrapped in twine. In the corner was a makeshift infirmary where a nurse stitched the arm of a comrade by the light of a lantern. A young man sat on the ground with a cigarette dangling from his lips and held a radio close to his ear. He listened to a BBC update on the Battle of the Bzura, where Poland's Poznań Army had just retreated after German forces had overwhelmed them in just ten days. Gundi listened carefully to the English broadcaster's report, delivered through static that sounded like rain hitting pavement.

*"Initial successes by General Kutrzeba's Poznań Army in push-ing back German armies in their attack on Warsaw have been quashed. German superiority in numbers caused Polish forces to retreat to their original starting point. Twenty thousand Polish sol-diers were lost."*

The man pulled from his cigarette and exhaled a blue plume of smoke, then dropped his head into his hand and shook it. Beside him on a crate were maps of Germany, its backroads, forests, and mountain ranges. A woman Gundi's mother's age, in an apparently stolen SS uniform, stood behind an emaci-ated man sitting on the floor, gently combing through his hair stubble and inspecting his scalp. The bony man had open sores on his feet and flinched as the woman placed a hand on his shoulder. "You're safe now, Louis," she assured him.

"Excuse me," Gundi whispered, pointing to the medical supplies. "May I borrow...um, have a bandage to make a diaper, please?"

The woman dressed as an SS guard handed Gundi a long gauze strip and gestured toward a damp bath towel hanging from a nail. Gundi was grateful not only for the kindness but the chance to eavesdrop on their conversation. Dozens of questions swirled through her mind: *Had the man been a prisoner at Dachau? Had he been released? Had he escaped? Had he seen Leo?*

She would listen as she changed Nadja's diaper. As she wiped her baby clean, she wondered where to rinse the diaper. Surely it would be offensive to offer a poop-stained cloth to the resistance. Yet how could she waste precious resources? Gundi lifted Nadja's legs and laid the bandage under her waist, then proceeded to crisscross each long strip over Nadja's front.

"...amazed you got out," Gundi heard the guard say.

She could only hear bits of Louis's raspy response: "Brutal... barely...back to St. Gallen."

Gundi wrapped each strip of gauze under one of Nadja's legs and then pulled them back up and around until she could belt the two ends in front. As she fastened the diaper pin, Gundi lifted Nadja to place her back in her rucksack. She felt the warmth of flesh. Turning Nadja around, Gundi sighed, exasperated. Her makeshift diaper had left Nadja's entire backside exposed, a little triangle peekaboo opening. She unwrapped the bandage and tried again.

Finally, as she lifted the groggy child back into her arms, Gundi could no longer hold her tongue. She turned to the woman disguised as a Nazi and the escaped prisoner. "Did you...were you at Dachau?" she asked Louis, who responded with a nod. "Did you by any chance meet Leo Solomon? Or Yosef, Rivka, or Schel Solomon?"

Louis lifted his gaze to meet Gundi's and tried his best to smile. "I'm sorry. I didn't meet anyone there by that name." He returned his glassy eyes to his lap.

Gundi noticed Nadja stir and lift her arm as if she were a student raising her hand to answer a teacher's question. The baby's small mouth began to pulse, reminding Gundi that it had been a little more than two hours since she and Sister Irma had fled from Heim Hochland. It was time to nurse her baby. She went outside and sat on a large stone, her back toward the house, and placed Nadja on her lap as she opened her blouse and slid her breast from its brassiere cup. Gundi held her hand over her grandmother's brooch so it wouldn't scratch Nadja's face, but she dared not unpin it, as it was the only thing of value she owned. This was their future.

When tickling Nadja's cheek failed to trigger the rooting instinct, Gundi manually expressed a trickle of milk and coated her nipple with it. She then slid it across Nadja's lips, inserting it into her baby's mouth. To Gundi's great relief, she felt a warm suckle accompanied by the prickling of the milk flow from her breast.

Gundi already eyed the bush she would squat behind afterward for a quick *Pipi*. When she returned to the driveway, she noticed a second truck had pulled in. Their time was almost up. Standing in front of it was a man in a belted trench coat with a Red Cross armband. This was Klaus, Rolf explained. He would be driving Gundi and four others to Geneva in the white medic truck. At the border, Klaus would say they were on a humanitarian mission, and it would be understood that they were smuggling goods out of the Reich. Since they had a friend at the border, the inspection of the truck would be less than thorough.

"Hurry back and get settled into the truck," Klaus told Gundi before quickly turning his head.

"Louis, you're in my truck now," Rolf called before rushing to help him slip on a pair of shoes and walk to the truck.

Stepping outside, Sister Irma had replaced her mud-stained Lebensborn uniform with a gray wool frock. Her hair was neatly combed now, unlike the bird's nest resting on Gundi's head. Rubbing her puffy eyes and holding back a yawn, Gundi asked why she wasn't wearing her nurse's uniform.

Sister Irma looked far too serious for Gundi's comfort. "I need to stay behind," she said.

"Here?" Gundi shook her head emphatically. "In the woods?"

"Good Germans are fighting back," Sister Irma said. "But they get injured, so this is where I need to be."

Part of Gundi wanted to hug Sister Irma with gratitude. At the same time, she felt a stab of terror that Sister Irma couldn't join them in Geneva. "Irma," she whispered solemnly. "Nadja's father. His name is Leo. Leo Solomon. And he was arrested in June. If you see him, please tell him where Nadja and I are. Tell him he has a beautiful daughter who looks just like him."

"Of course," Sister Irma said, looking at Klaus, already in the driver's seat of the truck, flapping his hand to hurry Gundi along.

Quickly, Gundi turned back to Sister Irma. "Are you sure you'll be all right? Where will you stay?"

Gundi could tell Sister Irma was mustering a smile for her benefit. "I'll be just fine, Gundi. Don't you worry. The Reich is looking for Irma Binz, the Lebensborn nurse who left her assignment without authorization." She stood a bit taller. "But that person no longer exists. I'm Kathe Klees now."

Gundi closed her eyes and squeezed Sister Irma's hands, trying to memorize the pads of her palms, the smooth shells of her fingernails. "What you're doing, Sister Irma," Gundi said, shaking her head. "It's remarkable."

"That's part of the problem, Gundi." Sister Irma wiped away a tear. "I don't want to be in a world where helping one another survive is remarkable." Sister Irma waved and dabbed her eyes with a handkerchief. "We'll see each other again," called the nurse. "This war can't go on much longer."

# 38

## *Gundi*

*Germany*

GUNDI FELT THE TRUCK SLOW AND HOPED IT MEANT KLAUS was picking up the Jewish family rather than running into trouble. Her best guess was that it had been an hour since they'd left the farmhouse where Klaus had anxiously announced that it was one thirty.

She placed her lips on Nadja's cheek, inhaling the comforting scent of her baby. As they came to a stop, Gundi bumped her head and flinched, careful not to make a sound. She realized that there was nothing quite like lying on her back in complete darkness to remind a person of her vulnerability.

She heard the slam of Klaus's cab door and trot of boots making their way across rocky soil. There was a brief murmured exchange amid heavy breath as the voice of an unfamiliar woman grew louder as she and Klaus approached the truck. "Where are the others?" Klaus asked.

"Our parents didn't... The Gestapo found our spot."

"*Scheisse!*" Klaus huffed. "What about your hosts?"

"They were arrested too."

When the back door opened, Klaus removed the boards,

the same type of makeshift hatch Rolf had created for Gundi in his truck. The moon had brightened the sky to a cobalt shade, but the figures looming above were mere silhouettes. Gundi could tell by their slender bodies and long hair that they were two young women standing beside Klaus, but little else distinguished them from shadows. Behind them, she heard leaves quivering in the wind as Klaus gestured for the two young women to climb inside.

Gripping the entry frame for balance, the taller woman pulled herself up into the opening of the truck and looked down into the compartment. Turning back to her sister, she said with forced cheer, "Look, Louise, a baby!" Then to Gundi, "Louise loves babies."

Louise did not respond, nor did she move closer to peek at Nadja. Instead, she lifted her sleeve and wiped her forehead. Trying again, the older sister asked if Louise wanted to be next to the baby for their ride. And again, Louise said nothing.

"Helene!" Klaus barked. "There's no time for conversation. Set yourself down." He touched Louise's back, moving her toward the entry.

Once she was inside, Helene was visible to Gundi. She looked to be about Gundi's age, maybe a year or two younger. Her lips were chapped, as were those of Louise, who was making her way into the truck, eyes downcast and focused on nothing in particular. Gundi could now tell that Louise was no more than a *Mittelschule*-aged girl, whose wide-set eyes and pointy chin were identical to her sister's.

Klaus suppressed a yawn, dug into his knapsack, and handed Helene and Louise a small *Brötchen* and a block of cheese with a smoky aroma. "We'll get you a proper meal soon." He wrestled the planks back over their hiding place, flinching before he placed his right index finger into his mouth. Gundi watched Klaus hold on to the last plank with his left hand as he used his teeth to coax out a splinter. Quickly, he turned away and spat into the dirt before slamming the door shut and rushing back to the cab.

The truck began to roll forward, and Gundi could hear Helene chewing her roll feverishly. After swallowing her first bite, the girl offered to share with Gundi.

"No, thank you. I'm…I'm…" Gundi tapered off. What was she supposed to tell her—that she had eaten bratwurst and cabbage for supper just seven hours earlier?

Plus, as much as Gundi was loath to admit this, the sisters' pungent odor was overwhelming. She hated herself for noticing, her stomach for roiling, but the stink of aged sweat was almost unbearable. She slapped herself mentally for the thought. It wasn't their fault that they hadn't been able to bathe.

The ride smoothed, which likely meant they were on a main road now, though Gundi had no idea which one, since the only places she had seen in Bavaria were Heim Hochland and a portrait studio in Munich. Gundi heard Klaus curse and felt an increase in their speed. The rhythmic thudding of the tires sounded like a racing pulse.

As the ride progressed, Gundi learned that Helene and Louise were Jewish sisters from Ulm. They had spent the last two months with their parents, hiding in the barn of family friends, gentiles who were working to get them travel visas from Switzerland to America. Their parents had been deemed enemies of the state because they were active in their labor union back when they were eligible to work at German factories. "They fought for fair wages for the very people who later accused them of being Communists," Helene said, her voice thick with grief. More recently, they had been organizing in other ways the Nazis objected to, though Helene didn't offer any more information.

Not only had the family's travel papers not shown up earlier that night, but the Gestapo did. The sisters weren't sure who had turned them in. Helene said that Louise confessed that an elderly neighbor had spotted her closing the barn door the day before. "But Frau Schnell is two hundred years old, so I don't think she could see that far," Helene whispered. "I say it was the *Schweinehund* who was supposed to deliver the transit papers who betrayed us."

The sisters had been in the woods behind the barn collecting wood when two black Gestapo cars pulled up to the house. Helene's voice cracked when she told Gundi that she hadn't heard the cars arrive; the sound of her mother's wailing was her alarm. They peeked from behind a fallen tree and saw four Gestapo shoving their parents into the back seat of one car, their friends into the other. The last words Helene heard from her mother were insistent pleas that her daughters were off visiting their grandparents in Mittenwald. Helene laughed bitterly. "We have no grandparents nor do we know a soul in Mittenwald."

The sisters had remained in the woods for an hour, Louise rooting herself in place, convinced that their parents and friends would be released the next day. But if they waited, the sisters would miss their ride with Klaus. Helene had grabbed Louise by the hand and practically dragged her the entire way to their meeting spot with Klaus, assuring her younger sister that their parents would want them to go on without them. They would catch up later, Helene promised.

Turning to Helene, Gundi asked, "Is Louise going to be all right?"

"I don't know what that even means anymore," she returned. After a long pause, Helene asked, "I did the right thing, didn't I? We had no other choice than to run, don't you think?"

Gundi fumbled around until she found Helene's hand and squeezed it. "Yes, you made the best choice under terrible circumstances," she said, grateful that Helene could not see her pained expression. She knew how it felt to question her decisions, to wonder if she had cost loved ones their lives.

Gundi's and Helene's fingers remained laced together, one hand softened by lavender lotion, the other hardened by months of life in hiding. Gundi felt Helene's bulbous knuckles wrapped in skin dry as autumn leaves. Helene must have noticed the difference as well, because she pulled Gundi's hand up close to her face and inhaled deeply. "I haven't smelled lavender in ages."

Without warning, the truck began to swerve and veer left, far too fast to be safe. Louise let out a shriek as Gundi's and Helene's bodies pressed into hers on the right side. Gundi's skin moistened the same way it did whenever she awakened from a falling dream. What sounded like a giant claw scraped against the side of the truck. Gundi's pores opened and tingled with terror as she wrapped herself around Nadja to protect her from whatever impact awaited them. *Are we going to hit another*

*automobile? Will we plummet down a hillside?* The crackle of
the truck tires against the gravel sounded like a firing squad
unloading its rounds. Gundi closed her eyes tight and tried to
remember the Hebrew prayer to say before dying. *Shema Yisrael
Adonai Eloheinu…something else…* She tried to remember, but
at twenty years old, Gundi had figured she would have a long
life to learn that prayer.

As the truck slowed and limped practically to a halt, Gundi
squeezed Helene's hand. A loud bang rang out, followed by
breaking glass. Louise whimpered, and the ammonia scent of
urine filled the hidden compartment. Gundi strained to hear
the inevitable sound of footsteps outside the car, soldiers' gruff
voices demanding to search the vehicle. But after a moment of
silence, it was only Klaus who called out. "Sorry 'bout that."

Gundi flushed with relief and pressed her foot against a
wooden board above her, sliding it off to the side. "Hold Nadja
for me?" Gundi asked Helene, pushing away the second board.
She sat up, and Klaus was already there standing over them.

"Everyone all right back here?" His hands shook as he
removed the third plank.

"What happened?" Gundi demanded.

"I dozed off," Klaus conceded sheepishly, shrugging and
scrunching his mouth to the side as he inspected the side of the
truck. "Just a few scratches and a busted headlamp."

*Dozed off?*

Climbing out of the truck, Gundi discovered that their
vehicle had slid across the two-lane road and was now facing
oncoming traffic, which, thankfully, was nonexistent at the
moment. But that could not last very long. Someone would

drive this road sooner or later, and all they would see was the single light of a truck that was halfway tucked into the roadside bushes.

She ran back to retrieve Nadja, then held her baby firmly with one hand and began to unstrap her rucksack with the other. Tossing the jumble of canvas and straps at Klaus, Gundi snapped at him to put it on.

Klaus stared, confused. "Why am I—"

Gundi interrupted with an exasperated sigh. "Klaus, put the…" She waved her free hand, giving up and reaching for the waist strap. "Pretend it's a belt," she clipped.

Klaus managed to buckle the bottom of the rucksack. She then smoothed the main compartment over his belly and chest and tossed two leather straps over his shoulders.

"Why are you—"

"Klaus, listen to me. I'm taking the wheel and driving the rest of the way. You need to sleep."

"I'm all right now," Klaus argued. "Believe me, I couldn't fall asleep now if I tried."

Gundi raised her eyes to meet his and stared at him for a moment. "Klaus, I am so grateful for your help, but I will be driving us to the border."

Her voice had the sobering effect of a cold splash of water. She looked at him again and handed Nadja to him, knowing the faster she secured the rucksack and got Nadja inside it, the faster they could get back on the right side of the road. When Gundi finished, she slipped Nadja into the pouch strapped onto Klaus, then fought her way into the driver's side through cracked branches.

Only when they were sitting side by side did Klaus fully absorb what was happening. He turned to Gundi, his face bunched with tension. "You know how to drive a truck?"

"Every resistance fighter knows how to drive one of these." Her confidence was short-lived as she looked at the panel of glass-encircled instruments to gauge speed, kilometers, and petrol. Then, of course, there was that blasted stick shift she had never quite mastered.

Gundi took a deep breath and heard Leo's voice as clearly as if he were sitting beside her. "Don't be too eager," he admonished.

She pressed the clutch, then moved the stick to the left and up to first gear. The Red Cross truck jerked forward, as had the Coca-Cola truck during her practice sessions in Berlin.

Klaus moved the stick back into neutral and turned to Gundi. "You sure you know how to drive?"

Before Gundi could reply that it was *his* driving that landed them halfway off the road, she saw a set of bright headlamps appear in the distance. The lights looked about the size of pfennigs, but she wasn't able to guess how far off they were. It wasn't until Klaus gasped and shouted, "*Fick nein!*" that Gundi knew the approaching auto was coming at them dangerously fast, especially considering that half of their truck was off the road and obstructed by foliage. Would the other truck see them in time to at least slow down and lessen their impact?

"Klaus, let's switch!" Gundi cried, waves of terror rushing through every part of her.

"No time," he returned. "Get into gear and drive!"

Gundi pushed the stick shift into first gear and released the clutch. The truck jerked forward and stalled. She tried again.

Gundi tried to ignore Klaus's voice shouting brilliant ideas like "Put it into gear!" and "Drive the fucking truck!" Instead, she imagined Leo beside her, gently coaching her to listen to the transmission and find what he called the "sweet spot." She tried again, then once more. She looked up at the vehicle coming at them, seemingly unaware of their presence. On Gundi's fifth try, the truck moved forward just as the other car began honking. The truck crossed the road, scarcely missing the oncoming car. As it passed them, the car continued honking in staccato fury.

Gundi's heart finally slowed once they moved past danger and she shifted into second, then third gear.

With every passing kilometer, Klaus shared new possible scenarios of how their mission could fail. "It's three already. We're never going to make it to Basel by nine. If Fredrich isn't at the border crossing, we're doomed."

Placing a hand on Klaus's shoulder and biting the inside of her lip, Gundi hushed him. "Fredrich will be there."

Klaus laughed, though he was clearly terrified. "Do you think he can simply tell his commanding officer that he wants to stand around after his shift ends? You don't think that will arouse any suspicion?"

Gundi was determined not to let Klaus's anxiety become contagious. She began to hum the melody of a lullaby Elsbeth sang to her throughout her childhood. Even when Gundi was a teen and snuggled in her mother's bed, reading novels side by side with their toes touching under the blankets, Elsbeth would teasingly let her daughter know it was time for sleep by singing "Schlaf, Kindlein, Schlaf." Now, Gundi hummed the tune, choking back sadness. She hadn't seen her mother in five months and didn't know when she would be able to return home. The song also served as a stark reminder of something that hadn't really sunk in as she spent her last couple of days focused on survival: she was now a Mutti herself. The lullaby soothed Gundi somewhat but had a greater effect on Klaus, whose head dropped to his chest as he nodded off to sleep.

Gundi fumbled with Klaus's road map, folding it into smaller pieces so she could hold it close to read. She sighed with relief when she found the route they were on and saw that navigating would be fairly straightforward. Other than the sound of Gundi's racing heart accompanied by Klaus's snoring, the next ninety minutes were relatively silent. Trying to make up for the time they had lost with their accident, Gundi sped ahead, feeling the road rumble beneath her. She knew it must be rattling like a roller coaster for Helene and Louise in the back, so she gripped the steering wheel to steady the ride as much as she could. They might arrive with a few bruises, but Gundi was determined to make it by nine. They had already passed Tübingen, and a sign alerted them that they were approaching Stuttgart in just over forty kilometers. If they could get there by five, it was still another 270 kilometers to Basel. They could make it. Just barely.

"Klaus!" Gundi called, rustling him from his slumber. "Grab the bottle in the side pocket of Nadja's pouch, will you?"

Still groggy from sleep, Klaus looked at Gundi as though he'd never seen her but complied nonetheless.

"Shake the bottle and coax the nipple into Nadja's mouth." Gundi wondered if Klaus was a father himself as he helped Nadja with ease. Feeling her bra begin to moisten, Gundi asked if Klaus had a handkerchief to lend her. "Actually, I'm going to need two."

The sun began to rise as a yellow sign alerted Gundi that they would pass Baden-Baden in another half hour. Mutti had always wanted to visit the spa and take the cure there. Gundi promised herself that when this was all over, she would never let Elsbeth utter the word *someday* again. When they were reunited, they would travel to Florence and see Michelangelo's David. The whole family would visit the Leaning Tower of Pisa and listen to Leo and Yosef explain why it didn't fall over. She felt easier at thoughts of her future with Leo. Like Sister Irma said, all wars must end.

Gundi continued south with the Rhine River until her eyes began to blur. She struggled to stay alert, suddenly feeling a bit more forgiving for Klaus's earlier transgression. Trying to distract herself, Gundi called back to Helene and Louise. "You need to be absolutely still. We're almost at the checkpoint." Silence. She hoped they were just being cautious. *They're all right*, she assured herself, remembering that she and Nadja had been able to breathe just fine back there.

Gundi looked at the clock. Eight fifty. There was no time to pull over and switch drivers. "Is that...is that the border crossing, Klaus?"

He nodded his head quickly, brows raised with fear as he unstrapped Nadja's rucksack from his chest and placed it gently between his feet.

"Careful with her! Tell me what to do," Gundi shot rapid-fire. "What's the plan?"

The border crossing station came into closer view and left Gundi as perplexed as she was panicked. She had imagined that a nation at war would have a grand complex crawling with armed soldiers. The crossing at Basel was no more than a single gray booth with a long wooden rod that lifted and dropped to let vehicles pass. A sign warned approaching automobiles to stop with a bold *Achtung!* There were two strands of barbed wire extending the barrier on each side of the gate, far less than Gundi had expected. And almost surreal to her was the small café and fuel station, both open for business, just meters away. They had made it before nine, though, even if it was with just minutes to spare.

"Klaus!" she snapped, trying to mask her look of worry. If she could see the facial expressions of the German soldier standing at the gate, surely, he could see hers too. "Klaus, what is the plan when we get to the checkpoint?" Gundi downshifted and slowed the truck, stopping behind a camouflage-green convertible Mercedes Benz with four officers on board. They were third in line.

"Remember? You tell them *we're on a humanitarian mission.* He'll know what that means," Klaus replied, reaching for their forged travel papers under the passenger floor mat.

On the German side of the border, a guard wore a long black trench coat with a Mauser rifle strapped onto his back. He let the car in the front of the line pass, then clomped toward the second as it pulled forward. The guard seemed weighed down by his thick leather boots and a helmet that looked like a cannonball. Gundi watched the driver of the car in front of her, how he handed over his papers as though he had nothing to hide. She would mimic the Nazi driver's casual reach for the papers and the way he nodded his head, unbothered by whatever questions the guard was asking. The guard said something that caused the four officers to step out of the car, boots swinging from their respective doors onto the ground. As the young guard aimed his flashlight into the front seat and rooted around, he leaned into the back, checking behind seats. After groping the bottom of the car, the guard opened the trunk, moving the contents from one side to the other.

An older guard sat by the booth with one boot resting on the thigh of his other leg. Holding a clipboard in his lap, he tapped a pencil across a sheet of paper, pursing his lips with consternation at whatever he was reading. On the opposite side of the border were two Swiss agents, one who was smoking a cigarette and leaning his elbow against the border gate. The other was unusually tall and thin, almost like a piece of stretched rubber. He was in the midst of regaling his coworker with what seemed to be a humorous story.

Gundi then noticed two guards heading toward the German station, one checking his watch. Gundi looked at the clock. Two minutes until nine.

As the younger guard approached the truck, Klaus pulled the rucksack hood over Nadja, who was mercifully still asleep. "Young man, brown hair, stubby legs. That should be Fredrich," Klaus whispered, squinting through the windshield.

"Haven't you met?" Gundi couldn't imagine this man with a hawkish scowl was a friend of the resistance.

"Only once," Klaus replied. "It was dark."

Gundi rolled down her window and smiled. "*Heil* Hitler," she said. "I…we are just—"

The guard interrupted and barked, "*Heil* Hitler. Papers."

There was no way this was Fredrich. Fear ricocheted through Gundi's body as she realized they would likely be apprehended. She would be arrested and never get to see Nadja grow up. Neither Leo nor her mother would ever meet their little girl. Her heart beat faster. Rivka and Yosef would never hold Nadja in their arms or call her their little matzo ball. A chill ran through her, knowing her daughter's fate. Helene's and Louise's. Even Klaus's.

But to her relief, the young guard winked and nodded at Klaus. Lowering his voice, he asked, "What the hell happened to your headlamp?" He waved his hand, reconsidering. *Let's just get you through quickly*, he seemed to say with the gesture, his eyes darting toward the guards waiting for the shift change. He leaned in and whispered, "Just hand me your papers so I can *check* them. Hurry."

As Klaus reached for the papers on his lap, a voice called out from the booth. "What's the matter with your light?" the older man shouted, putting down his clipboard and waddling toward the truck. He leaned forward and squinted his eyes to check out the broken headlamp, then looked at Gundi. "We have girls driving for the Red Cross now?" His eyes shot to Klaus in the passenger seat, then back to Fredrich.

"We're on a *humanitarian mission*," Klaus replied.

"Fine, but why are you driving with a broken headlamp?" the guard asked Klaus through the open window.

"We had a little accident," Gundi replied, hoping the guard's eyes would move from Klaus to her. The rucksack was designed well enough to hide Nadja, but the baby was starting to wriggle about. She needed to divert his attention from the passenger seat.

"Ha!" said the guard. "Lady drivers."

"Tell me about it," Klaus replied with a chuckle. "I've been up for days, and my girl said she knew how to handle one of these things."

The older guard gave a nod, the gesture seeming to say he understood: *the pretty ones aren't always the smartest.* He then began telling Klaus where the nearest service station in Basel was located. "They'll switch out that bulb in no time and buff out some of these scratches. Sounds like your engine's running a little rough too. Have 'em check to see if your spark plugs are gummed up."

"Good idea," Klaus replied.

*Good God, are these* Bananenbiegers *going to talk automobiles?*

Suddenly, there was a loud thud from the back. It sounded as though Helene or Louise had accidently let one of their boots hit the flooring.

The older guard lowered his eyebrows quizzically. "What have you got back there?" he asked as Gundi reminded herself not to tap her foot or fist her hands to relieve her nerves.

"Our cargo has been clanking around back there all morning," she said with a bit of a pout. "Don't be too angry with me for banging up the truck," she begged Klaus. Gundi returned her gaze to the officer and smiled sweetly, hoping her expression made the older guard want to protect her from Klaus's ire.

The guard pulled his mouth to the side skeptically before a flash of recognition crossed his face. "You look awfully familiar. Have we met before?"

"I'm certain I would remember if we did," she replied. "Though maybe you've seen me on the new Reich posters."

"That's it!" He shook his head vigorously. "You are the new German mother! *Mein Gott*, my daughter has all your posters in her bedroom."

*Get through this. You can do this.* "That makes me so happy. What is your daughter's name?"

"Ilse. She's our youngest," the guard said. "She says the pure love you show for your little boy in the picture is an inspiration to her." Seeming to remember that his subordinate was watching, the older guard straightened his belt and looked to the side. "Has Fredrich given you any trouble this morning?"

"Trouble? Goodness, no. He checked our papers with great care. A nation at war can never be too cautious."

"Yes, yes, I agree," the guard said and chortled. "Next time, leave the driving to your friend over there. We need you focused on inspiring the next generation of German mothers." He patted the side of the truck and waved his hand to the Swiss guards, signaling that they should let the truck through as Gundi rolled up the window. "Take care of that light. Safe travels. *Heil* Hitler."

She smiled and caught a glance of Fredrich standing behind his commanding officer, the slightest grin assuring Gundi and Klaus they had made it. Exhaling more air than she realized her lungs had been holding, Gundi shifted into gear, then released the clutch. This time, she moved forward with only a slight jolt and drove ahead.

This was it. They were safe. Yet Gundi's heart pounded in her chest, terrified that the guard would get word of her escape from Heim Hochland and chase them down. Damp with anxiety, she gripped the steering wheel until her hands cramped. After they were out of sight of the guard booth—no sirens following, no green trucks with swastikas painted on the sides— her eyes began to well with relief. She was free. As free as she could ever be, knowing that her country was now a dictatorship and Leo's family was in danger. She hoped that Sister Dorothea would spin a plausible story that would keep Elsbeth out of trouble over her daughter's disappearance. But for now, she would focus on the fact that her daughter, perfect and beautiful Nadja, was safe.

Klaus reached for Nadja's rucksack, placed it on his lap again, and uncovered her head. Nadja was still sleeping, though her lips were starting to pulse as though she would soon want to be fed again.

Gundi turned back toward Helene and Louise. "Are you all right back there?"

"Yes!" Helene shouted over the sound of Louise's soft weeping.

As the adrenaline from their exodus wore off, Gundi settled into a peaceful exhaustion. She reminded herself that she had made it this far and would do whatever she needed to in order to protect her daughter. She would sell Oma's dragonfly brooch, she thought, touching the piece pinned to her brassiere. Elsbeth told her it was worth more than she earned in three months. Gazing at Nadja's sleeping figure, she formulated a plan for their future. She knew that she could stay at the refugee center in Geneva with Helene and Louise for a while, but she would need to find a job. With as many refugees as there would surely be pouring into Switzerland, Gundi felt guilty using their resources. She had learned how to type in school and could likely get hired at an office. They would survive until they could be reunited with their family once the war ended.

The road stretched before them, weaving its way through hilly farmland. As it straightened, the Alps came into view, their peaks piercing a layer of fog in the distance. Nadja began to rustle. The baby blinked her eyes and blew tiny bubbles of saliva. Then came the soft squawk of her baby waking up.

"*Guten Morgen,* little one," Gundi said. "We're safe now."

Securing the wheel in her right hand, she unrolled the window with her left and inhaled deeply. The sweet, earthy scent of autumn. Gundi and her daughter had a long road ahead. But at least they would travel it together.

# Author's Note

Although my father grew up in Brooklyn, his family had a plan to survive the anticipated Nazi invasion of the United States during World War II. His Polish-Jewish father had seen enough violence against his people to never feel completely safe, even in his new homeland. My father was a toddler, and the plan included his adoption by the Kihl family, German neighbors in their two-family house.

My father told me of this many times as I was growing up in New York City in the 1970s. This was more than family history; it was a warning: we are Jewish and must always have an escape plan.

A few years ago, I watched an Amazon series called *The Man in the High Castle*, based on the Philip K. Dick novel, which brought to the small screen my worst nightmare. An alternative history, the show is set in the 1960s after the Germans have won the war and most of the United States is part of the Reich. In one episode, a beautiful German woman explains that she was bred through the Lebensborn Society, where SS officers impregnated "racially valuable" young women. I was nearly certain this was a fictional element of the show, like the episode where the Nazis blew up the Statue of Liberty. If the Germans had really created a breeding program, wouldn't everyone know about it?

That night, I sat down at my computer and began to search for the Lebensborn Society. I found that it was a secret Nazi program that began in 1935 as a maternity home for single mothers with Aryan pedigree as well as a breeding program for German young women. I came across a faded black-and-white image of four Lebensborn nurses, each gazing adoringly at the newborn cradled in her arms. Then there was a photo of a group of young women wearing swastika-embroidered tank tops and black athletic shorts, lined up for inspection by a Nazi matron who seemed to be admiring one of the girls' voluptuous forms. Another photo featured a baby-naming ceremony where infants were welcomed to the Nazi Party by soldiers who laid swords on the babies' bellies.

The Lebensborn Society, which translates to "Spring of Life" in English, existed in the same world as Nazi death camps. In its ten years, approximately thirty homes were in operation by the end of the war and had produced nearly twenty thousand children. I couldn't help digging deeper, watching Nazi propaganda films and more recent documentaries about adult children of the Lebensborn Society.

I soon found that the Lebensborn Society took an even darker twist once the war began in 1939. Lebensborn architect Reichsführer Heinrich Himmler added a new, more efficient way to create "child-rich" German families where every mother earned her Mutterkreuz medal for raising four or more healthy children. German soldiers were ordered to kidnap Aryan-looking infants and toddlers from countries they occupied, mainly Poland. Often the children were orphans, their parents killed by the very Nazi soldiers who snatched them. Other times, babies were torn from their mothers' arms and loaded into military vehicles headed for Germany. Once the children were brought to their new homeland, the party sought to "Germanize" these approximately two hundred thousand children before placing them for adoption. With infants, the process was often as simple as a name change, but toddlers had to be taught basic German language and customs before being placed with their new families. Some children, especially older boys, refused to adapt and were sent to concentration camps and murdered.

I wanted to learn more about the young women who volunteered for the breeding program. Why did they agree to have sex with SS officers they had never met before? Why were they willing to give up their babies to high-ranking Nazi officials and other German families in good standing with the National Socialist Party? How had they become so indoctrinated that they viewed having a child for Hitler as their patriotic duty?

In writing the novel *Cradles of the Reich*, I created three female characters who land at a Lebensborn home: two expectant mothers and a nurse, each representing one of the faces of German citizens during the Third Reich. Ordinary Germans could have chosen university student Gundi Schiller's path and joined the resistance. Like Hilde Kramer, an aimless high school student, they might have embraced Adolf Hitler's movement. Or, like nurse Irma Binz, Germans could have decided to keep their heads down, focus on their lives, and assume that reports of persecution of Jews and other minorities were exaggerations from the *Lügenpresse*, the so-called lying press. In *Cradles of the Reich*, I bring together these three strangers at the bucolic Heim Hochland (High Home Country) Lebensborn home in Bavaria, where each woman has an agenda at odds with the others'.

Though *Cradles of the Reich* is a work of fiction, Heim Hochland was one of the actual maternity homes, and I featured historical figures, including Nazi Party officials such as Lebensborn physician SS-Oberführer Gregor Ebner and Women's League leader Reichsfrauenführerin Gertrud Scholtz-Klink. The story of Anna Rath, the gentile woman who was marched through Nuremberg after her head was shaved by townspeople upset that Rath intended to marry a Jewish man, is real. The Edelweiss Pirates, the Nazi resistance group that Gundi and Leo belonged to, was also an actual student-led group working to undermine Hitler's efforts in Germany. The new member of the group, Sophie, is an homage to Sophie Scholl, a brave young University of Munich student with the White Rose resistance group who, along with her brother Hans, was executed by the Nazis in 1943.

Gundi, Hilde, and Irma are fictional characters, but Hilde was inspired by a real Lebensborn volunteer, Hildegard Trutz. A true "Hitler Girl," Trutz claimed that her time in the Lebensborn Society was the best in her life. Like all Lebensborn homes, the palatial Bavarian castle where Trutz lived was furnished with artwork and antiques looted from Jewish homes. In an interview after the war, Trutz fondly recalled that at this luxurious estate, the food was excellent, and there were plenty of servants. She proudly delivered a baby that was the product of a Lebensborn-arranged liaison with an officer she described as handsome though dull-witted. She was happy to see her baby adopted by a good German family. Hilde was the most challenging character for me to develop, because it meant trying to embody someone who would have viewed my family as *Untermenschen*, subhumans. I hoped to understand how she became a participant in the November 1938 pogroms the Nazis dubbed Kristallnacht, the Night of Broken Glass. I wanted to examine a young woman's path to becoming a true believer without making excuses for her heinous acts.

In writing nurse Irma's character, I consulted written accounts of Germans who were initially indifferent to the plight of Jews but eventually had their consciences resuscitated. What would that take?

And with Gundi, I found it enlightening not only to read about the Nazi resistance movement but to study the work to dismantle white supremacy in the United States today. One of my favorite exchanges to write was when well-intentioned but naïve Gundi asks her Jewish love interest to teach her about the plight of the Jews so she can help. He lets her know that it is neither his job to educate her nor is it hers to be his savior.

To further help me understand the ethos of the German Reich, I formed an unlikely friendship with eighty-nine-year-old Rolf Schultze, a neighbor who shared his childhood memories in Berlin. He was part of the Deutsches Jungvolk, the junior arm of the Hitler Youth, and his honest account of his early love for Hitler was enlightening. Rolf and his elementary school friends were told they were special, the great hope for the future of their nation. As an old man on his front porch in

San Diego, Rolf's voice quivered as he recalled walking with his father on Müllerstrasse the morning after Kristallnacht. The seven-year-old boy asked his father why the windows of a haberdashery were broken, why some stores had been vandalized. Rolf's father shook his head, signaling that his son should not ask such questions.

In my effort to ensure the novel's cultural and linguistic authenticity, I reached out to Bernhard Schlink, bestselling author of *The Reader*, who graciously supported my effort to shed light on this little-known but important part of German history. Among his many insights was letting me know that Gundi's search for her Jewish classmate should end after her first visit to a kosher butcher shop. (I would have had her try every store on the block, which would have been dangerous for an Aryan in 1939, lest she be suspected of being a "Jew lover.") On a lighter note, Bernhard also introduced me to many German colloquialisms, including the dated slang *rumsen*, meaning sex, which is used throughout this novel.

Meetings with older members of the German American Societies of San Diego also helped me glean insight into German life during the 1930s. Most of the members were more than willing to share their childhood memories and answer my questions about German customs. They confirmed that a teenager might indeed roll her eyes at her mother. They also told me that Germans did not eat popcorn at the movie theater. A white-haired woman in her nineties quipped, "Who had food?" Understandably, a handful of members were suspicious when I told them about the subject of my novel. At a luncheon, a woman snapped "We're not all Nazis" before leaving the table.

On the whole, the group was gracious and welcoming, especially board member Monika Parme, who extended herself
generously to help with this project.

I tried to provide the novel with historical accuracy by
reading textbooks and documents and taking courses through
the Museum of Jewish Heritage and Tel Aviv University. I
consulted with experts like Randall Bytwerk, a professor of
communication who specializes in Nazi propaganda, who was
a wealth of information on numerous practices and events,
including Adolf Hitler's fiftieth birthday celebration. These
details were especially helpful when writing the scene where
Hilde desperately tries to impress a high-ranking SS officer by
speaking knowledgeably about the event. Architectural historian Charles Belfoure helped me identify building styles so I
could design accurate cityscapes. German food historian Ursula
Heinzelmann and her wonderful book *Beyond Bratwurst* helped
me set the table with meals people in that era favored and clear
it of "trivial" foods like cubed cheese.

There were some questions that could not be answered,
though. In the final days of the war, the Nazis burned records
from the Lebensborn Society, so I could not confirm the exact
number of Lebensborn homes, babies born, and children kidnapped. There are several conflicting accounts, some claiming
that sex parties and liaisons did not occur at all. Others say they
participated in such breeding efforts and clearly recall their
sexual encounters that were for the express purpose of breeding
"a child for Hitler."

Sadly, many anti-Semitic elements in *Cradles of the Reich*
are real, such as *Der Giftpilz*, the picture book likening Jews

to poisonous mushrooms that Hilde's coworker reads to her young children. The board game Juden Raus (Jews Out!), tucked away in the recreation room at Heim Hochland, is something many German families had in their homes. Also real are the racial screening tools described in the opening chapter where Gundi is examined by Dr. Ebner. The eye-color buttons, the skin-matching swatches, and the skull-measuring calipers all can be found today at the Museum of Jewish Heritage: A Living Memorial to the Holocaust.

As infrequently as possible, I took creative license to better serve the narrative. For example, young women in the Lebensborn Society were given pseudonyms for their stay. However, juggling two names for each resident became clunky and confusing, so I chose to have characters address each other by their real names. The *Neues Volk* article on people with disabilities that Hilde cites actually ran in May 1939, not April 1939 when the scene takes place. The inaugural Mutterkreuz award ceremony took place in late May, not early May as written. Also, Reichsfrauenführerin Gertrud Scholtz-Klink or the Women's League likely did not have any involvement in the infamous Aktion T4, the murder of people with physical and developmental disabilities. It's not that the Women's League had any moral objection to such a program; it simply wasn't the type of work it did. Nonetheless, I felt it was important to spotlight this horrific program since it was part of the Nazi plan to create a so-called master race.

Certain elements, such as the layout of Heim Hochland and the naming of the garden gnomes, are products of my imagination.

Although my initial interest came from a small detail of a television show, once I learned it was a real Nazi program, the Lebensborn Society grabbed hold of me and did not let go until I had researched and written this novel. I love reading historical fiction because it allows me to learn about history through the more intimate lens of personal relationships. It is my hope that this novel about three German women provides fodder for discussions about the social environments that allow women's bodies to be politicized and commoditized.

*Cradles of the Reich* covers a dark period of history, but I hope readers will be heartened by how the connections women forge can carry us through the most harrowing of times and sometimes even drive us to act with heroism we hadn't realized we were capable of.

# Reading Group Guide

1. Gundi, Hilde, and Irma have starkly different attitudes toward the Nazi regime and their places at Heim Hochland. Whom did you most identify with? Whom did you find most compelling as a character?

2. Compare Hilde's and Gundi's experiences during the November pogroms the Nazis called Kristallnacht. Did either of them really understand the broader context of this event?

3. As Hilde tries to impress Nazi officials, she represses her conscience to say the right things. What motivates her to seek status within the Reich? What does Hilde want out of life?

4. How did the Reich's propaganda about self-sacrifice smooth the way for Lebensborn homes to function?

5. There are many examples of the Reich's coordinated effort to dehumanize Jews, from the picture book about poisonous mushrooms to the documentary *The Eternal Jew*. How do these materials relate to Lotte's insistence that "great things only happen when strong people make difficult choices"?

6.  Put yourself in Gundi's shoes when she learns that the father of her child has been framed for a crime and sent to a labor camp. Would you be able to keep your secret? Would you look for a way to help Leo?

7.  While the book focuses primarily on birth mothers, adoptive parents are an enormous part of the machinery of the Lebensborn Society. What circumstances led Germans to become adoptive parents? How, as in the case of the "displaced" Polish orphans, does adoption contribute to genocide?

8.  How does Gundi's self-image get in the way of her first attempts to find Leo and get to know him?

9.  Gundi's escape from Heim Hochland almost fails several times. Which close call made you the most nervous?

10. Irma says she doesn't want to live in a world where helping people survive is remarkable. How can we make that more ordinary in the modern day?

# Dear Reader,

Thank you for reading *Cradles of the Reich*.

After spending three years alone in my writing cave learning about the Lebensborn Society, it has been a joy to travel the country meeting readers at libraries, bookstores, temples, social clubs, and zooming into living room book groups.

I'd like to take this space to answer questions I'm asked frequently. If there's something I don't cover, I welcome your comments and questions on Goodreads, social media, and email.

## ***IMPORTANT NOTE: SPOILERS AHEAD***

If you haven't yet read *Cradles of the Reich*, don't go any further! The questions I address were asked by readers after they finished the novel.

## Why weren't the stories of the protagonists wrapped up?

When *Cradles of the Reich* concludes, each character is headed in the direction of her future. Gundi has safely crossed the Swiss border with her baby, and I imagine them settling in Switzerland and desperately searching for news of Leo and his family; Irma has joined the resistance, where she will use her nursing skills to care for wounded partisans; Hilde is going to marry Max and live in his rural family home with a prickly mother-in-law. But she won't be held back for long. In fact, Hilde will be a central character in my next novel.

## Will there be a sequel?

I am currently working on a new novel about Hannah Kaufman, a Jewish student who is deported to the Theresienstadt ghetto with her grandfather Oskar. Theresienstadt was a Czech "show camp," used for a Nazi propaganda film, ironically titled *Hitler Gives a City to the Jews.*

When the propaganda film crew arrives at Theresienstadt, Hannah recognizes a familiar face—her childhood friend Hilde Kramer from Munich, now working for the Ministry of Enlightenment and Propaganda.

As in *Cradles of the Reich*, the setting is bleak, but the story focuses on women's friendships and how these can help us rise to heroism we didn't know we were capable of.

## What happened to Leo?

I made the choice to leave Leo's fate unknown because many Holocaust survivors returned to their homes without knowing what had become of their loved ones. I wanted readers to experience that sense of wondering what happened to a person they had grown to care about, even if it was just a character in a novel.

In writing *Cradles of the Reich*, I also grew very attached to Leo and looked for a way to save him. But the more research I did, the clearer it became that Leo would likely not have survived more than a week at Dachau. The Nazis would have questioned him about his resistance network, and knowing Leo, he wouldn't have given up a single comrade before the Nazis shot him.

**Was it depressing writing about Nazi cruelty?**

Writing about man's inhumanity toward man was sobering, and there were some dark nights at my keyboard, especially when writing from pro-Reich Hilde's point of view. It was emotionally taxing to crawl into the skin of characters that believed the world would be better off without Jewish people, including my family. But once I learned about this horrific program, I felt compelled to write about it because the most effective way to prevent the rise of fascism is to recognize its early warning signs. A key move in every dictator's playbook is to control women's reproductivity either by mandatory abortion or forced childbirth. Writing about the Lebensborn Society became a mission, so I felt more charged by a sense of purpose than depressed by the content.

**Did you get to meet any grown Lebensborn children?**

After *Cradles of the Reich* was published, I received an email from seventy-seven-year-old John Gundersen. He told me he was one of the last of the Lebensborn children conceived, that his birth mother was a sixteen-year-old Norwegian girl who "signed up and lined up to have sex with Nazis to have a baby for Hitler." His birth father was a German pilot. He was adopted by a Norwegian family but has lived in the United States for most of his life and now runs a surf shop in California. He discovered he was a product of the Lebensborn program after seeing a documentary about it on the History Channel. He traced the names on his birth certificate and was able to confirm that his birth parents were participants in the Nazi breeding program. He found the information "interesting" and does not seem bothered by it. Other Lebensborn children, now in their late seventies to early nineties, suffered greatly as children and adults. Many were physically abused by their adoptive parents and ostracized after the war. Thankfully, some who were kidnapped as children were able to joyfully reconnect with their birth families.

The most famous person born from the Lebensborn Society is Anni-Frid Lyngstad (Frida) from the music group ABBA. In interviews about meeting her father, German sergeant Alfred Haas, when she was an adult, Lyngstad says it was difficult to connect with him.

### Are you available for book club visits?

Yes! I love chatting with book clubs, so please visit Novel Network at novelnetwork.com to schedule a time for me to Zoom in.

Let's stay in touch! My Instagram and Facebook handles are both @JenniferCoburnBooks, and you can email me and learn about upcoming events through my website, jennifercoburn.com.

—Jen

# Acknowledgments

Writing *Cradles of the Reich* was a dream project for me because it was fascinating to explore how a civilized society fell under the spell of a fascist dictator. But even more gratifying was experiencing the generosity and kindness of so many people who shared their time, expertise, and stories about the Lebensborn Society and the Third Reich.

My daughter, Katie O'Nell, who tirelessly worked through social and political issues, developed characters and plotlines, and read every page multiple times. I'm grateful for her insight and wisdom, which has always belied her age.

San Diego has one of the most supportive writing communities an author could hope for. My friend Denise Davidson at the *San Diego Union-Tribune* was the first person to make me seriously consider writing this novel when she listened with rapt attention as I told her about the Lebensborn Society. When I asked authors Susan Meissner, Michelle Gable, Liz Fenton, and Jill Hall for advice, they were quick to offer support and encouragement. Writing Women of San Diego, a professional networking group, was also a great source of inspiration and a wellspring of knowledge about book publishing. Susan McBeth, the founder of

Adventures by the Book, is the best friend an author could have. Her events and book club network are truly top-notch, and I'm thrilled to work with this consummate professional and excellent lunch buddy.

My agent, Marly Rusoff, changed my life the morning she called and said she loved *Cradles of the Reich* and was certain she would find the right home for it. After two years at my keyboard wondering if this project would ever see the light of day, I am so fortunate to have found a tireless and passionate advocate like Marly. She introduced me to publicist Kathie Bennett, who has been nothing short of a wonder to work with.

I am thrilled to work with Sourcebooks and their incredible editorial and marketing teams. Shana Drehs shared a love of this project from the start and made good on her promise to help me make *Cradles of the Reich* the best novel it could be. I greatly appreciate her incisive notes and marginalia that always made me smile, even when it meant rearranging timelines I'd flubbed. I am so grateful that the Sourcebooks marketing team includes Molly Waxman, Cristina Arreola, and Anna Venckus, who created a plan to help ensure historical fiction readers hear about *Cradles of the Reich*. They are insanely smart, creative, and dedicated to helping readers connect with this story. My thanks to the sales team, who worked to make sure there was room on every bookstore shelf for *Cradles of the Reich*. I greatly appreciate Kelly Lawler and Heather VenHuizen, who designed this gorgeous cover, and Heather Hall, who managed the editorial production of this novel. Sabrina Baskey also combed through the manuscript numerous times, adding comments that made the narrative more engaging (and grammatically correct). And, of course, I appreciate Sourcebooks publisher Dominique Raccah for believing the story of the Lebensborn Society needed to be told.

I did much of my research from reading textbooks, historical documents, and watching propaganda films, but I learn best by talking to people, so I am very grateful to the subject matter experts and Germans who shared their knowledge. Bernhard Schlink, author of *The Reader*, was kind enough to read *Cradles of the Reich* and offer notes on cultural and linguistic authenticity. I must have driven Professor Randall Bytwerk nuts with my dozens of emails about rules on displaying propaganda posters, protocols of Nazi ceremonies, and functions of the Ministry of Public Enlightenment and Propaganda. Nonetheless, he always answered graciously and with a wealth of information. Ursula Heinzelmann helped me set the table with authentic German foods, and Charles Belfoure guided me through creating German cityscapes.

Rolf Schultze was a young boy when he joined the Deutsches Jungvolk in Berlin and tearfully shared how he had once idolized Hitler. I cannot sufficiently express my gratitude for this now-eighty-nine-year-old man's unfiltered honesty about his early childhood fear of Jewish people. I also visited the German American Societies of San Diego and spoke with several of their older members. Monika Parme was welcoming and very open to having difficult conversations about Germany's past.

I am lucky to call writing coach and San Diego Writers Festival cofounder Marni Freedman a friend. Her late-night calls, especially as she juggled dozens of projects, meant the world to me. She's the Jewish mother every writer should have. I also had the good fortune to work with Alexandra Shelley, a brilliant developmental editor who asked the right questions and offered three different ways to solve every problem I'd created for myself. I shudder when I think of the utterly awful scenes she suggested slashing and am grateful for her gentle guidance in filling the gaping holes in my early drafts.

My friends and family were wonderfully helpful in the writing of *Cradles of the Reich*. Offering early feedback and support were Eilene Zimmerman, Rachel Biermann, Edit Zelkind, Irina Swedback, Rachel Schindler, Richard and Lora Ellenson, Debbie Breen, Bill Monaghan, Laurie Black, Audrey Jacobs, Marcia Wollner, Rabbi Laurie Coskey, Kathy Krickett, William O'Nell, Carol Coburn, and Brienne Hayes. My good friend and former work husband Jonathan Dale was a crack research assistant, who put so much heart into finding answers to the toughest questions. It was a real treat to be able to work together again.

Finally, I am a volunteer at Reality Changers, a nonprofit that supports low-income students in becoming the first in their families to attend college. Every young person I've worked with has inspired me to challenge myself to reach beyond my comfort zone, but one student's perfectly timed text gave me the final push to write this novel. Though I had wonderful support from my writer friends, I was nervous about whether I could write in a genre so different from what I'd done before. Then Martha Montoya, a Reality Changers alumna and new student at UC San Diego, texted for advice on a class. Here was a young woman with the moxie to be a first-generation college student, reaching out for support and figuring things out as she went. When we ended our exchange, I knew I would follow Martha's lead and take on writing my first historical novel. I have deep love and admiration for every student at Reality Changers I've had the privilege of collaborating with and learning from. The organization has changed thousands of realities, including my own.

# *About the Author*

Jennifer Coburn is the author of a mother-daughter travel memoir, *We'll Always Have Paris*, as well as several contemporary women's novels. Additionally, Jennifer has contributed to five literary anthologies, including *A Paris All Your Own*.

When Jennifer is not going down historical research rabbit holes, she volunteers with So Say We All, a live storytelling organization in San Diego, where she is a performer, producer, and performance coach. She is also a volunteer with Reality Changers, a nonprofit organization that supports low-income high school students in becoming the first in their families to attend college.